FIERCE OBSESSION

S. MASSERY

To those who can't keep a secret to save their lives
& those who love them anyway

—

And to Kalia,
my favorite insult coordinator (thanks for the chirps) and hockey
encyclopedia

Special thanks to Kristy, Brittany, Natalie, Maria, Alaina, Beth, Lindsey, and Maddy for your support!

———

patreon.com/smassery

INTRODUCTION

Hello dear reader!

If you've read me before (or any book in the Hockey Gods series), you know they run quite dark.

This book contains themes common to dark romance, including dubious consent, manipulation, use of restraints, and blood and breath play.

Knox would like me to inform you that he absolutely has done nothing wrong, he's the innocent party, anything said or done against him is pure conjecture, and he'll plead the fifth if necessary.

Thank you and happy reading!

xoxo,
    Sara

AURORA

I still remember the first time I met him.

A dazzled child starstruck by the older boy next door. The one with blond hair that flopped in his face, that his mother was always fondly brushing back from his forehead. The blue eyes that were brighter than the sky.

But as older boys went, he didn't want a shadow.

The first time I met him, in the sloping backyards that weren't bound by fence lines—no one in the neighborhood bothered with that, not at that time—he pushed me in the mud for touching his hockey stick.

They had a goal positioned in the middle of the yard and one of those boards that's supposed to feel like ice. I was fascinated, sure, because I'd never met anyone who needed to practice outside of the rink. Or maybe I just hadn't met anyone my age who cared enough to do so.

But I wanted to try. The scuff of the puck against that white, dingy board drew me across the lawn like a magnet. I just remember reaching, my fingers skimming the taped handle, and his hands on my shoulders. The bark of possessiveness, of ten-year-old anger.

I was knocked flat. My fingers curled into the grass as wetness from last night's rain seeped through my jeans.

Never mind that my dad was the coach for the ten and under, and I was probably a better player than him and his younger brother combined. I'd been on skates since before I could walk, after all. Chasing after my dad on the ice, a tiny stick in my hand and pigtails sticking out from under my pink helmet.

We were at the rink almost every day. Mom shooed me off with him gladly. Anything to keep me out of her hair, to burn off my never-ending, restless energy.

At that age, professional hockey was a far-off dream that I pictured every time I closed my eyes. Playing for the women's league, getting to play for the US in the Olympics. The roar of a crowd after a goal, the rush of cool air on my cheeks, and the collision of teammates celebrating. A gold medal.

It was everything I ever thought I could be, bottled up in a pair of skates, a helmet, and a stick.

Then I got sick.

And as it turns out, my father didn't really care much for chasing dreams with me if it meant putting my health in jeopardy.

What a disappointing, crash-to-earth moment.

But the boy who'd pushed me in the mud... well, I suppose we were on a collision course from the moment we moved into the house beside his. That was the beginning of the end. I thought getting sick was hitting rock bottom, but I had no idea how hard I would eventually land.

1

AURORA

The alcohol has made me silly. I don't enjoy rowdy clubs, and I don't like big crowds. The last time I was properly drunk, I was nineteen and under the supervision of one of my cousins. It was the after-party of a funeral, and I had every right to be blinded by liquor.

Who has an after-party for a funeral?

My mother, that's who.

Anyway, it's different now. I'm twenty-three. I'm celebrating the successful launch of my book, which took off way faster and better than I ever could have anticipated. Like, it blew *up*. And although it came out four months ago, it's still selling extremely well.

The book is everywhere, and yet, I remain relatively unknown.

Pictures of me are scarce. I haven't posted any on my author accounts anyway, and I've never done a signing or met a reader. I think I prefer that to the fame—or infamy—that success might bring. You know, celebrities.

"Cheers." Beth pushes another shot in my hand and taps hers against it. "To new starts."

Just because I coast by unknown doesn't mean my best friend will let me stay in the shadows. And tonight is worth celebrating, because we're finally living in the same city since we left our hometown for college.

We're at a club of her choosing, just outside the VIP section. We've got stools at the bar in front of rows of booths, and the atmosphere is decidedly... rich. The men wear starched white dress shirts with the sleeves rolled to their elbows, ties forgotten, suit jackets shed, and hair slightly, purposefully disheveled.

It's an aesthetic that Beth seems very much into.

"Cheers," I reply, happy and warm. I toss back the shot, which tastes more like water than anything else, and close my eyes for a moment. Then they pop open at another urge. "I need to pee."

"Toilets are over there." Her gesture is vague, in the direction of the far back corner.

There's a guy on her other side who's been glancing at her since she joined me. She pivots slightly toward him, smiling, and immediately he dives into conversation.

Beth has been my best friend since ninth grade. We survived going to different colleges in different states, then another two years while Beth got her master's degree. She moved out to Denver four months ago. And now I've joined her.

New York was depressing. Cloying. I used to love the city, but instead of finding inspiration, I just found it small.

People think New York City is this huge place until they live there for a few years.

I slip off the stool. My legs are a little unsteady, and the floor tilts.

Okay, maybe I've had too much to drink.

I head the way Beth pointed, skirting the VIP section and going down a long, dimly lit hallway. None of the doors are marked, but two of the three are locked.

The third one swings open under my hand easily, admitting me into another hall. This one is brighter, which probably means I'm going in the right direction. I run my fingers along the wall. My cheeks are hot, my body in that weird sort of numb stage of drinking.

I press the backs of my hands to my face. I just need to quit while I'm ahead, or else I'll forget everything that happened tonight. I've wondered how I got home before, and the thought of doing that again kind of makes me sick.

Voices drift toward me.

"...against the Colorado Titans."

I stop, recognizing the name. The Colorado Titans is the NHL team here in Denver.

The door to my left is ajar, and the rest of the hall is empty.

"They're a top team," a man says. "You can't guarantee a loss."

"That's the beauty of it." The second voice is also male. "You wanted a sure thing, and you're getting a sure thing. Against the Guardians, they're the favorite to win by three."

My brow furrows.

"Reading between the lines here, you've got someone...?"

The second guy scoffs. "Don't worry about the how. In fact, the less you know, the fucking better. I just expect you to hold up your end of the deal."

"I never said I wouldn't," the first murmurs. "I'll get the money together."

I touch the door. Just to steady myself, and because I'm

desperately curious to know what the hell they're talking about.

The thing is, I've done everything in my power to not think about hockey for the last six years. I gave up watching it, although Dad still sends me highlight reels that I watch late at night, racked with guilt.

I turned something that was ours and made it ugly.

My touching the door, however, was maybe slightly worse than I thought. Because I'm drunk, and my balance is shit in these heels, and suddenly I'm falling through the doorway and stumbling right between the two men.

They both look at me.

Then at each other.

"This isn't the bathroom," I manage sheepishly, running my hands down my shirt. "My bad."

"No," one says slowly. The gruffer first one, who seemed to be questioning the other. "It isn't. Back the way you came, girl."

I step back and bump into the second one. He grips my upper arm.

"Steady," he murmurs. "Did you hear us talking?"

The first guy stiffens.

I glance over my shoulder at the one holding me. He's younger than I originally imagined. Maybe in his thirties, with a reddish beard and hair. His eyes are brown. His jaw is square. He would be cute if he wasn't looking at me like I might be a problem.

"Um..."

"Tell us the truth," the first guy urges. "What did you hear?"

I shake my head. I should lie. I should just come up with something on the spot, but drunk brain doesn't really work in time with my mouth. So by the time I consider making anything up, I'm already talking.

"Just something about getting money together. I don't know what it was about. I'm sorry—"

"She's wasted," one sneers.

I don't know who. I'm focused on my shoes and the sudden urge to puke.

"Have another drink. On us." The red beard guy slips a twenty in the front pocket of my jeans, and he spins me toward the door.

I stumble on my way out, but I definitely don't stop.

At least I didn't say I overheard all of their conversation. Getting the money together, not knowing what—that's reasonable.

My shoulder hits the wall, and I let out a grunt of frustration. I stop in the hall and try to yank off my heel. I fumble with the clasp when they resume their conversation. Albeit a little quieter.

"It's not a problem."

"It might be a fucking problem."

My heart is beating faster. They're talking about me, aren't they?

"We'll discuss this on Friday. Do your part. Or else."

I get my shoe off, then the other one. As soon as my heels touch the floor, I take off. And maybe I will have that next drink, if only to forget this conversation.

I swear, it's like a scene right out of my book. Danger, a relatively hot, grumpy guy. But I didn't fall over drooling, and I didn't want to be there. And I'm definitely no heroine.

For a second, it kind of sounded like they were talking about rigging the Colorado Titans games for their gain. However that would work. I'd imagine if they fixed a game and bet against the Titans, they could rake in a good amount of cash. Maybe even more if they're running their own gambling ring.

But that's not possible. There are too many moving pieces in a hockey game, too many variables. It couldn't be possible... right?

2

KNOX

I'm really fucking good at my job.

But not when I'm staring down the barrel of a gun.

It's a metaphorical one, but a gun nonetheless. But I feel it aimed in my direction, ready to mow me down in a spray of bullets.

"Is that who I think it is?" Jacob Rhodes, my best friend, stops beside me. He follows my gaze up to the second level of the arena. "I've only seen her photo before."

I nod slowly.

Aurora McGovern is at a fucking Colorado Titans game. We're wrapping up our warm-ups, with half of our team already off the ice. We're playing the New York Guardians, of all the teams. Before I was traded to the Titans, I played for the Guardians. I know, and am friends with, most of the Guardians. Except it's all business now.

No hard feelings, but it would've been nice to get a few games under my belt with the Titans before facing my former team.

And now she is at the game.

A woman I swore I'd never lay eyes on again.

I grit my teeth and turn away. She's in one of the suites, her royal-blue dress alluring and seductive and totally aggravating.

I haven't seen her in six years, and she looks better than ever.

"Head in the game," Jacob advises. "You told me something similar, didn't you?"

I grunt. "She came here to piss me off."

"Or..."

"There's no or. She came here to make me angry."

Because six years ago, on my last day home for winter break of my freshman year at Crown Point University, I stood outside her house and told her I never wanted to see her again. And then, when she asked me for a divorce, I laughed in her face.

Under no circumstances is Aurora McGovern to get anything she wants.

She's not even paying attention to us. She's sitting in front of the glass of the suite—and I'm going to find out who she suckered to get into it—with a glass of champagne in her hand. Not only that, she's talking and laughing to someone I can't see.

I tighten my grip on my stick and step off the ice before I do something stupid. I let Jacob herd me toward the locker room, while I spend the next fifteen minutes trying not to lose my shit. It doesn't really work, and I play less time than I want. But every time I get on the ice, I'm not in the right headspace.

Coach knows it. Before the third period, he screams his head off at me.

And I totally fucking deserve it.

I sit on the bench with my helmet in my lap, resigned to not playing. My attention swings between Aurora and the game. Back and forth and back and forth. The game is going poorly, and I can't seem to pin it on anyone in particular. We're all just sucking, and my old teammates are playing like a well oiled machine.

They slip around our d-men, draw our goalie forward, and slip the puck in behind him. Or they hinder his sight by packing bodies in front of the crease. It's fucking slaughter, and the weight of shame hangs on my shoulders.

With Aurora here to witness it all.

She's laughing. Smiling. Not even *watching*. Although she probably doesn't even have to watch to know how sloppy we're playing. She's just a distraction. A silent, judging distraction who wants me to mess up.

The horn blows, our loss echoed in the defeated quiet of the crowded arena. We get up from the bench and skate out to bump fists with my old teammates, to congratulate them for the easy kill. They offer me quick pats on the back, sympathetic smiles.

Yeah, yeah.

"Well, that could've gone better," Church groans once we're in the locker room.

Camden Church. Captain. Right wing. Objectively handsome, I guess. I'm not really one to judge either way. But he's a good captain, a solid team leader, and he comes up with fun chirps. Listening to him talk to opponents usually brings out our smiles.

He doesn't have much more to say right now, though.

All of us feel disjointed. Coach orders an extra practice tomorrow, which is guaranteed to be painful. And then we're released to get out of our sweaty gear and shower, to put on brave faces. I, for one, am going to get drunk.

It doesn't help me forget about Aurora, though, because

it isn't until later, sitting at a bar surrounded by my teammates commiserating our loss, that I accept my anger.

She can't be here.

Denver is mine. I didn't inform her that I was claiming
it, but she couldn't have missed the news that I was being
traded to the Colorado Titans. It was everywhere. There
was even an article about it.

And even if she missed it, her parents definitely
would've heard about it. So why didn't they pass it along?

Stupid.

As if by magic, as soon as I allow myself to sink into it—
Aurora fucking McGovern walks into the bar. In the blue
dress. With her auburn hair shiny and in loose waves
around her shoulders. She looks more like a movie star than
the girl I used to know.

Before I can stop myself, I'm striding across the room to
her without hesitation. I catch her arm, ignoring the
shocked expression, and drag her toward the door.

Out we go, around the corner into the alley. It's chilly,
the temperature dropping, and the wind has been picking
up steadily in the last few weeks. As soon as the sun sets,
the cold really sets in. It's only October, at the top of our
season, but we're hurtling fast toward winter. And in
Denver, that's no joke—or so I've heard.

Everyone keeps telling me about these infamous
winters, and we haven't even had snow yet. I want snow.
I want the bite of frozen wind when I first walk outside,
the crunch of frosted grass under my feet. Eventually,
maybe, it'll happen. I love winter, because winter means
hockey.

But right now, I focus on *her*.

She stumbles a bit when I release her, whirling around
to face me. She brushes her hair back, tucking it behind her

ears. Instead of scowling, she smiles. She doesn't seem off put by me, and it only sets my blood on fire.

"Knox," she greets me. "What a surprise."

"What the fuck are you doing here?" The vitriol in my voice can't be missed.

Her smile gets faker. "Well, I was planning on having a drink. It's what people do at bars."

"I meant Denver in general. And more specifically, a suite at the Titans game."

"Oh, of course. Good of you to be *specific*."

She takes her time smoothing out that royal-blue dress. It's a shimmery fabric that clings to her breasts and waist, flaring gently out at the hips. If she did a spin, I'm positive the skirt would fan out around her legs. How she's not shivering in that, I have no idea. The long sleeves are doing nothing to keep her warm, especially because the outlines of her nipples are visible through the fabric.

Do not think about her nipples.

Finally, she says, "I was invited."

Obviously.

"And thanks, by the way." She meets my eyes and gives me another smile.

It's so plastic, it hurts to look at. It calls to mind all the times she gave me real smiles. Warm ones. Her laughter was a thing of beauty. Now, I can barely remember what it sounds like.

"Thanks for what?" I scowl.

Just talking to her hurts, but I don't know how to make her go away without resorting to drastic measures.

"For losing the game. You won me a lot of money."

I stare at her.

Un-fucking-believable.

"You bet against me?"

"I bet against the Titans," she corrects. "Don't worry, Knox—it was a one-time thing. Just to prove a point."

I step closer. "Don't you fucking say my name."

"Okay, babe. Whatever you want."

She presses up on her toes. I freeze when her chest brushes mine and her lips touch my ear. My heart is going out of control, and I'm sure she can feel it. While she's calm, cool, collected, I'm quickly spiraling.

Which isn't *fair*.

I dragged her out here to tell her to get lost. To leave my city, to stay away from the Titans. And here she is, having easily sidestepped the conversation and gone right into fight mode.

The Aurora I used to know would've run away scared if I used my height to intimidate her.

This one seems to welcome it.

"I have a feeling you'll be seeing a lot more of me," she whispers. She backs away before I can do anything else, slipping around me and heading back for the bar.

Her breath against my skin sends delayed chills down my spine. It's all I can do to remain still and not chase after her. I want to throttle her, though. I want to make her bleed and beg for forgiveness, and then I want her to apologize for ruining everything.

Maybe I do need to resort to drastic measures. Maybe I should let out all this anger on the one target who actually deserves it.

Betrayal cuts deep, and the wound she created hasn't stopped burning since the day I left home for good.

3
AURORA

H oly shit.

"You didn't tell me you owned the bar the Titans go to," I hiss at Beth, closing the door to her office a little harder than I should've.

She rolls her eyes, closing her laptop. "I didn't think about it."

Right. Of course not.

"Besides, I'm hardly ever out there."

Beth came out to Denver once her dad couldn't keep up with the bar anymore. He divorced her mom when Beth was a kid and moved out here. He owned this place for ten years, co-running it with her uncle. Eventually, they turned it over to her. But before that, it was his dad's. And probably his dad's dad's. Who knows how far back the history of this place really goes.

Her master's degree in architecture went to shit, but we don't talk about that. We don't talk about a lot of things, actually. But a year after Beth took over, she managed to convince me to join her.

I drop into the open chair. "It wouldn't be a problem under normal circumstances, except I just ran into Knox."

Her eyes widen. "*Oh*."

"And that was after watching him play," I add. "Which was a bit torturous."

She snickers. "Did he play well for you?"

Not in the slightest. I spin the ring on my finger, contemplating telling Beth the full story. As far as she knows, he signed the divorce papers the first time I asked. That was the last time we talked about Knox. Although, unfortunately, it's not the last time I've thought about him. Usually, I do all I can to divert that line of thinking.

I don't seek him out, I don't search his name on the internet. I didn't even realize he had been traded to the Titans until the announcer called his name at the start of tonight's game.

"Anyway." I clear my throat. "A heads-up about this being their hangout spot would've been nice."

She sighs. "I'm sorry. I didn't think about it. Knox is new to Denver, too, isn't he? You know I don't follow hockey. If they don't come in here with their jerseys on, I wouldn't recognize them." She rises. "Come on, we can sneak into the kitchen and have Heath make us something. It's no use sulking in here all night."

I consider that. I mean, I was just on my way in after the game when Knox accosted me—I had barely made it ten steps into the bar. And Beth's explanation makes sense. She's never been a big hockey fan, only coming along to the games in high school with me when I made her.

My stomach growls. And as much as his anger rattled me in hindsight, I don't tend to run from a fight. I never have. And the thought of pissing him off by not doing what he says brings me an inexplicable dose of joy.

So I smile and say, "Something like burgers?"

"He can probably whip that up." She leads the way down the hall and into the kitchen, weaving amongst her employees.

There are a few waitresses collecting dishes from under a warming lamp, more rolling napkins and silverware at a desk in the corner. She catches the attention of one of the guys behind the line, orders food for us, then takes my hand and practically drags me out of the kitchen.

"*Elizabeth*," I whisper-yell.

Forget what I said about not running from a fight.

"You can't be afraid of your ex forever," she calls over her shoulder, still pulling mercilessly on my wrist.

I'm not *afraid*. I just don't want to deal with him. Our encounter outside was enough to remind me of why all our communication has been through lawyers.

The last time I sent the divorce papers—another try to see if he'd finally give up—he sent a handwritten note to my lawyer, who then texted me a photo.

No, thank you. His scratchy handwriting was as familiar as my own, and I hated the way it got to me. My eyes burned. I didn't cry, though. I haven't cried since... well, since I was nineteen. Four years seems like a lifetime ago, even if it passed with a snap of my fingers.

We take seats at the end of the bar, and Beth's bartender immediately serves up two green martinis.

Appletinis.

I eye the glass. "You trying to get me drunk?"

She rolls her eyes. "I'm trying to get you to relax. And this is our drink."

Was our drink.

I pick mine up and carefully cheers her. After a tiny sip, I set it back down and scan the crowd. It's not as crazy here as the club was the other night, and Beth has transformed the space from the pictures she used to show me from visiting her dad.

It's darker, sexier. The vibe is dark reds and golds, velvets and low lighting. Oh, and it's right across from the arena. Which is honestly why I thought it would be safe. Why would the Titans come *here*? Except for the vibe.

"I like what you've done to the place," I murmur.

She smiles. "It needed a facelift. Before, it was just..."

"A sports bar," the bartender finishes, setting down the burgers in front of us. "And now it's luxury, thanks to our talented Liz. Enjoy, ladies."

I snort. "They call you Liz?"

She shrugs, and I glance around again. The far back corner is the busiest. I catch a glimpse of Knox with other guys, all surrounded by women.

"Ignore him," Beth advises. "It's not like you'd ever go back to him."

Well, that's the truth.

But...

As I told him: I *will* be seeing more of him.

I heave a sigh and pick my drink back up. I try not to look over again, but he's like a magnet—or a train wreck. Either way, I find myself twisting to eye their corner again. I recognize some of the guys. Camden Church, the Titans' captain. Scofield, Lawson, Haverhill.

The last, the goalie for the Titans, spots me across the room and smiles.

It would've been fine if Knox was never traded to the Colorado Titans.

I lift my left hand in a small wave. The ring on my fourth finger catches the light, and I smile at Joel Haverhill.

Knox's teammate, sure. But more importantly—my fiancé.

Before I met Joel, I hadn't gone to a hockey game in *years*. I was still riding the pity bus that I was forced to quit playing in high school. That all my dreams of the Olympics were crushed with a diagnosis, ground into a fine powder and scattered on the wind.

We actually had a nice meet-cute. One for the story books, ironically.

Beth was visiting me in Boston, and we had decided to go skating on the Frog Pond in the Common. It was practically a rite of passage for tourists, and Beth was definitely a tourist. Even though I hadn't gone to a hockey game in years, I still liked to skate. Still craved the ice.

And who was there, showing off?

None other than the Colorado Titans' infamous goalie, Joel Haverhill. While doing some fancy trick, he crashed into me. Took us both down, although he was very apologetic. So sorry for his actions, in fact, that he took me *and* Beth out to dinner that night.

My best friend left the next day, and he took me out for our second date. Never mind that he had played an afternoon game in Boston and was supposed to be flying back to Denver. He blew it off just to see me again.

After that, we stayed in contact. Through the season, all the way up to their Stanley Cup playoffs run. I visited him in Denver, he came to Boston. The romance was a whirlwind, and he proposed six months after we'd first collided.

Which I accepted.

Joel comes up and drapes his arm over the back of my chair.

"Hey, sugar." He kisses my cheek. "Come to commiserate?"

"I came to get a burger." I take a bite, winking at Beth.

She snorts, and Joel snags a fry off my plate.

"You remember Beth?"

"Elizabeth," he greets her. "Always a pleasure."

"Likewise," she murmurs.

"Come on." His lips press to my ear. "The guys have been asking about you."

Oh, goodie.

Beth snickers into her appletini. I snag mine and finish it off. Liquid courage, or whatever. Joel's hand winds firmly around mine, tugging me off the stool and after him. Such a difference from the way Beth forced me out of her office—in an exasperated sort of way—and from how Knox dragged me out of the bar—in an angry way.

His grip is confident but not mean. Not hurried. He looks me up and down, taking his time so I see him checking me out.

"You're so fucking hot," he murmurs.

I smile. "I picked the blue dress with you in mind."

He grins.

We arrive at the back corner.

"Guys," Joel calls, drawing attention to us.

The attention isn't bad. Church, Scofield, Lawson. Hockey players I got familiar with fast once I started watching hockey again. It's Knox's glare that kicks up my heart rate. I stare back at him, my grip tightening just a little on Joel's hand. Knox's focus flicks down to our joined hands, and the absolute utter shock on his face is enough to smooth out the crescendo of panic arcing through me.

He didn't notice the ring. He doesn't talk to his goalie, I guess, either.

I look up at Joel, then back at his teammates.

"This is my fiancée, Aurora."

4

KNOX

Un. Fucking. Believable.

Aurora sits next to Joel, and all I want to do is strangle her. Then remind her cold, dead corpse that she can't marry him, because *we're still fucking married*. I have a very intense vision of climbing across the low table and wrapping my hands around her throat, drinks going everywhere, mayhem breaking out. Her wide, witch eyes boring into mine until she can't hold on any longer.

But I manage to bite my tongue. The waitress returns with another whiskey for me, and a freaking green martini for Aurora. I gulp mine down eagerly, spinning this moment in my brain. Trying to make it make sense.

She got with a goalie. *My* goalie.

It smarts a little too much to be sober, so I make it my mission to get as drunk as possible. Did she do this on purpose? Did she pick him to torment me?

I mean, *come on*, Aurora.

At one point, she stands and heads for the restrooms. I don't know how long we've been sitting here. I've tried not to look at her, but she draws my gaze back repeatedly. Even when Lawson tells some wild story that should've had me cackling.

I'm kind of fuzzy at this point. The waitress has made sure my glass was never empty for long, smiling at me like she wouldn't mind taking *me* to the restrooms. Or the back office.

I've seen that expression before. Not on Aurora's face, of course, but other women. The ones who want me for whatever reasons they fathom in their pretty little heads. Not because of me, obviously. No one knows the real me.

Well, no *woman* knows the real me.

Minus Melody Cameron—I think she'd get close. She's one of my best friends nowadays and in love with my other best friend. Jacob Rhodes. They make a cute couple. And I wish like hell Rhodes had decided to join us tonight, but he went home to his woman.

I sigh and stand. The girl on my lap—*not sure when she got there*—lets out an irritated huff, forced to her feet, and moves out of my way. I pat her ass, grumble something about needing to piss, and follow slowly in Aurora's wake.

She's a fucking magnet.

It's not even a surprise when I push open the door to the women's bathroom instead of the men's. She's at the sink, her head down, the water running. Her hair is pulled over one shoulder, exposing the curve of her pale skin and her pretty, fragile neck.

She doesn't look up until I'm right behind her.

I wrap one hand around her throat, the other across her mouth. Her back bumps into my chest, and my palm catches her swallow.

And her rapid heartbeat.

Having her this close is almost too much. She smells like lilacs. I can't remember if that's how she used to smell.

Or if her hair was ever this shiny. Or if her eyes were ever this hateful.

She's got a splotch of blue in one of her green eyes. Sectoral heterochromia. It was a big deal when we were kids. Some of them tried to make fun of her for it—but that ended rather quickly. If there was one thing my brother and I agreed on, it was that Aurora shouldn't be fucking taunted by bullies.

Now it's just another thing to separate her eyes from all the rest.

"Hello, sunshine," I say in her ear.

She shivers.

Delicious.

"I thought I told you to get lost."

Her lips move against my palm. My traitorous dick twitches. I squeeze her mouth harder, putting my face right next to hers.

"Whatever you were about to say, I suggest you rethink." It's a rush being this close to her. A rush that I have to fucking ignore, because this isn't just some random beautiful girl. "No amount of excuses are going to work on me. You're engaged to the goalie of the Colorado Titans? What do you think he's going to do when he realizes you can't marry him?"

She lets out a noise.

Finally.

She grips my wrists, tugging, but I've got more strength. I push her forward, going with her, until her hips are pinned between mine and the sink.

The restroom door opens.

Aurora makes another noise, something between a groan and a plea for help.

I look over my shoulder at the waitress, and I thrust

forward. Like I'm fucking Aurora, never mind the long skirt between us. It's the show that matters.

"Almost done, babe," I tell the waitress, winking. "You're next."

She blushes and backtracks.

As soon as the door closes between us, Aurora elbows me in the gut.

Hard.

I release her, stepping out of range, and smirk.

Her hair is messed up, her lipstick smeared. I make a show of righting myself and let my gaze go from her black boots to the top of her head.

"How long do you think it'll take for rumors of us to spread to your fiancé?"

She shakes her head at me. "I don't know, Knox. Not all rumors are true."

My name on her lips is like razor blades slicing into me. Death by a thousand cuts. I step forward, and she lifts her chin in response.

"Crazy girl," I murmur. "You want to go against me?"

"We've been against each other since you left for college, *Knox*," she replies. "What are you going to do? Divorce me?"

I laugh. "No."

I touch her hair again, twisting it around my fingers. Tugging her head back. She's fucking putty in my hands, and she doesn't even realize it. Her hair is soft, her eyes are accusing. It's why I lean in and trail my lips down her throat. Categorizing her scent, remembering it for later.

Goosebumps rise on her skin. I'm close enough to see it, to taste her if I just opened my mouth a little...

"It's too late," she whispers. "I've already filed abandonment charges. You *abandoned* me in the eyes of the court—so you don't get a say in whether we divorce. It's up to a judge."

I bite her.

It's really just an impulse, but the way she immediately reacts, I relish it. I don't break her skin—I'm not a fucking animal. I bite until it hurts, until I know it'll bruise, and then I release her. There are teeth marks in her skin, at the slope between her neck and shoulder.

"You're an ass," she snarls, covering the bite mark with her palm.

It's like pissing on a tree. Marking her as mine. I hope when Joel peels her dress off later, he questions her about it. And I hope she comes up blank with excuses.

She turns back around, meeting my gaze in the mirror and slowly lowering her hand. She pulls at her dress's collar, seemingly *satisfied* with how it covers the now-red bite. She picks her purse up from the ledge just under the mirror. She fixes her hair, runs her hands down the sides of her dress. She reapplies her damn lipstick.

And then she's gone, slipping out the door, and leaving me standing here like a fucking fool.

Abandonment. I never thought of it that way. Never assumed that was a loophole she'd actually use. But the longer I stay in the restroom and look into it, and how to prove it, the angrier I get.

And then... a plan forms.

"Knox?" The waitress slips back into the restroom.

I stash my phone, the wheels still turning. Even as she locks the door and shimmies out of her skirt, giving me a *fuck me* expression, and my dick responds accordingly.

Because at the end of the day, I've got a reputation to keep.

And my wife is not going to derail it.

5

AURORA

The typewriter is new and shiny and absolutely *not* perfect.

I broke my last one, my perfect old one, in the move. I'm not sure how it happened—I packed it poorly maybe, or it got jostled too much—but when it arrived the frame was bent and it seemed like it had barely survived a hurricane.

But this is no time to mourn. I've got readers clamoring for another book, begging for a side character to be written, and the story ideas have run dry.

I haven't written a word in six months. The book came out right when my break was ending, and then... I think I froze.

How can I top the last?

I was in a dark place when I wrote it. Like, angry at myself and everyone else, and I took it out on characters who were cruel and vile, and later... a little bit soft for the heroine.

I scrub at my face.

When I met Joel, I had just finished the first draft of the

book. It wasn't really a topic of conversation until it came out and then my name was everywhere. Then we talked about it, sure, but it wasn't a *thing*. It was just my job.

A weird one, at that.

We did talk about my love of writing on typewriters. About how the clicking of the keys, the run of ribbon ink against the individual letters, was the sort of atmosphere I enjoyed most about writing. I didn't just write—it's the *experience*. Like diving into a still lake on a perfect, sunny day.

I tried to explain it to Joel, and he nodded like he understood. Not that he did. Beth doesn't really get it either.

But now I'm in a new city, with a fiancé—and a big rock on my finger—and I've got nothing. No character ideas, no storyline, *nothing*.

Maybe if I bang my head on the desk, something will come out?

My phone lights up, ringing on silent, and I heave a sigh at the name scrolling across the top of the screen.

Alaina Logan, my divorce lawyer. She's been a godsend these last few months, working diligently to track down Knox. When she texted me that he had replied with a stupid, handwritten *no, thank you* to our latest attempt, I went into the office and had a drink with her.

Because *fuck* him.

So hearing from her out of the blue could either be good or bad, and I'm not sure I'm in the right frame of mind to deal with either option.

Still, I answer.

"Aurora, glad I caught you." Alaina is almost always business first, pleasantries second. "You know how we were proceeding with the abandonment?"

I get up from my desk and cross to the window. "Yeah..."

"Well, there's been a little development. Knox has retained a lawyer who's arguing that you haven't been abandoned due to..."

A lump forms in my throat. "Due to what?"

"He's saying that although you resided in different states, it was only because of his hockey career. He maintains other aspects of the relationship. Financial. Sexual." She clears her throat. "And now that you're living in the same building, it can be viewed as you two reconciling—"

"Right," I interrupt. Because all I can think about now is Knox's lips on my ear. And his hands wrapped around my mouth and throat.

It was three days ago, and I still wake up with my heart pounding, dreaming of his hands on me in other places.

They're traitorous thoughts.

"He hasn't, though."

She's silent, and my stomach swoops.

"Aurora..." She pauses. "Are you sure? His lawyer is saying there's a witness of your affections. They've offered evidence of financial maintenance, as well. I'm sorry, but I don't think this is the best course to pursue."

Fuck.

I flex my fingers, trying to get rid of the nervousness coursing through me. Of *course* Knox would do something to jeopardize my wedding. I never got to do the big affair— the expensive white dress, picking out flowers and colors and bridesmaids, walking down the aisle. Arranging seating charts, caterers, venues, cake. Doing everything with my mother at my side, offering her expert opinion.

In actuality, the list is enormous and never-ending. Not quite how I pictured it as a kid, flipping through bridal magazines.

Not how I pictured it when I married Knox either.

"What can I do?" I force the words to come out evenly, refusing to admit—except to myself—how much Knox continues to mess with me. I haven't seen him in years, and yet it seems like he's around every corner.

Outside, the world moves on. Denver is beautiful. I like my condo, the bustle of the city below me. I like my doorman. I like that there's a pool and a gym in the building. Beth's apartment is only a few blocks away, with a million coffee shops and restaurants between us.

It makes me feel a little less lonely to know I'm always surrounded by people.

"I hate to say it, but—"

I blow out a breath. "You think I should talk to him."

"I do," she presses. "We've tried every route but that one. The one where you try to have an honest conversation—"

"Honesty is not always the best policy," I interrupt. "And I did try to talk to him."

"When?"

I open and close my mouth. She knows about Joel. She knows meeting him reinvigorated my efforts to get Knox to sign the divorce papers. And they're fair papers. I don't need money from him. I don't want any more contact. There's nothing to split, no combined assets. Just two people parting ways.

Not that he sees it that way. He sees me as the villain of his story. Some monster he's got to keep locked away so no one else can get hurt by me.

Maybe that's a noble way of looking at it.

He could just be doing it out of spite.

"I'll try again," I mumble.

"Great. The Titans will probably be at their practice rink

this morning." She chuckles. "You could always ask your fiancé."

I groan.

For all appearances, Joel and my relationship is hot and heavy. A fast-moving freight train that cannot be stopped. And it is… sort of. Minus the fact that when he asked me to move in with him, I declined. Said I wanted to live apart until the wedding made things official. And that I'm keeping him a bit at arm's distance in other ways, too.

It's not that I don't love him, because I do. Joel and I clicked. But my space is sacred. I've got books to write, and I cannot be distracted by handsome hockey players who just want to get in my pants all day.

That could be an exaggeration. I don't know.

But I'm not finding out, because Joel lives in another building, precisely three blocks in the opposite direction from Beth. He comes over to visit. He occasionally spends the night. But not for very long. He doesn't even keep a toothbrush here.

Weddings are supposed to be that pivotal change, right?

I write—and read—about heroines who are swept off their feet, madly in love, and the wedding just kind of makes things official.

I'd just prefer Joel and my wedding to be the start of our story. Not the end of it. Not like with…

"I'm hanging up," Alaina says. "Let me know how it goes."

"Yeah." I hit the *end* button and toss my phone onto the desk, once more focusing on the abandoned typewriter. *Why did I buy a pink one?*

For the hundredth time, I resist the urge to pick it up and chuck it out the window.

Instead, I sit. I place my hands on the keys and take a breath.

If I'm going to confront—no, sorry, *converse*—with Knox, I better get out my aggravation on the page. Even if it's not for a story, I can crumple it up and toss it out later.

But what I end up writing instead... is the story of how we ended up married in the first place.

6

MANUSCRIPT

CHAPTER 1

I spend my sixteenth birthday in the hospital.

We were on our way to Dad's summer hockey intensive—he took a job as the assistant coach for the ten and ups—when this weight pressed down on my chest. I couldn't breathe. My heart raced, but no matter how hard I gasped, nothing brought air into my lungs.

The last thing I remember is my dad's shout.

And then I wake up in the hospital bed, a monitor attached by cords to my chest, another clip on my finger reading my blood oxygen. It's quiet before I open my eyes.

I remember the near-silence, the hum of the equipment around me, and it dissipates faster than snapped fingers as soon as I open my eyes.

My parents are on either side of me. Mom is always worried—Dad's the calm one. But he's anything but calm now, his brows pinching in, his lips in a tight little line. His normally tan face is pale, and his palms are sweaty. He's holding on to my hand with both of his in a death grip.

"Aurora," Mom whispers. "You're okay, baby. You're in the hospital."

I nod slowly. It isn't the first time I've been here, although it is the first time my chest has ached quite so bad. Like I went toe to toe with an elephant, and instead of fighting, it decided to sit on me.

"You had surgery," she adds.

My mouth is dry, and it takes a minute to swallow those words. Surgery. The doctors said there was a slim chance I would need a repair. But—

"Don't worry," Dad interrupts my thoughts. "We've got this covered. We've talked about this."

The money. The insurance. Late nights sitting on the stairs in the shadows, eavesdropping on my parents' conversations about medical bills, prescriptions, deductibles, copays. Things that shouldn't have hurt us but just seemed to keep stacking higher and higher.

Tears fill my eyes, and no amount of comforting makes it any better.

"I'm sorry." My voice comes out low.

Mom pours me a cup of water and puts the straw between my lips. She strokes my hair, exchanging a glance with Dad. But they don't say anything. They don't say it's not my fault, but they don't blame me either.

It just is what it is.

One of the nurses shoos them out an hour after visiting hours end, but still I fight sleep. I kept checking the heart monitor, watching the steady bumps. Trying to pick out if they were coming unevenly, too fast or too slow. If there might be something else wrong with my heart.

I've got a weird thing about sleeping in hospitals. There's so much death here. And life, too, if I think about it enough. It's cyclical. Around and around life and death skate. But closing my eyes seems, in my opinion, too much of a temptation for death.

"Hey, sunshine," a voice comes from the doorway.

Knox Whiteshaw. Next-door neighbor since we moved in almost a decade ago. Once he realized I could kick his ass on the ice, he got a lot nicer to me. Especially when my dad became the coach of his league.

"What are you doing here?" I rasp.

He slips in and closes the door. He manages to keep one hand behind his back until he's right up next to me, then he reveals his little surprise.

A single flower. A yellow rose.

"Yellow for friendship?" I raise my eyebrow.

He snickers. "Yellow for you. For sunshine."

"People usually associate Aurora with blues and greens. The Northern Lights, you know?"

"Nah." He taps my leg.

The feel of it zaps through me, going straight to the butterflies in my chest, and I shift to the side. Making room for him to sit on the bed.

"Are you okay?"

I shrug.

"Sunny."

"I'm fine," I mumble. "I had surgery. All's well that ends well."

He frowns. "My parents said it came on suddenly—"

"It did. But it's fine. *I'm* fine." I've got to believe that.

He grunts. "Well, we missed you kicking the kids' asses at camp."

"I do not kick their asses." I roll my eyes. I *help*. But I have a feeling it's all about to go down the drain. A lump forms in my throat, and the humor falls away. Quietly, I admit, "Dad had that look that said all my dreams were going to disappear."

The Olympics. Playing on the greatest US women's team, winning gold. Being a champion. Sometimes I want it so bad, I dream about it. I can taste it.

And now...

Knox pulls his phone from his pocket, showing me a video from the summer intensive. Little kids wobbling around on skates, following the puck with single-mindedness. I feel his gaze on my face as I stare at the screen. I refuse to look at him and see something I don't want to acknowledge.

"Did they have fun?"

"No one kicked their ass, so yeah." He puts it away just as the door opens.

The nurse makes a noise in the back of her throat, caught between surprise and frustration. "Visiting hours are *over*, Aurora McGovern. Young man, you need to leave."

"Right." Knox stands, setting the yellow rose in the pitcher of water on the rolling stand next to my bed. Just drops it in like it belongs there. "Goodnight, Sunny."

He strolls out without a backward glance.

The nurse shares a secret, quiet smile with me.

And I smile back.

I've always had a thing for the bad boy. How could I not? I was practically guaranteed to fall for the wrong guy —I've got a defective heart, after all. It's only fair to assume it would lead me astray in love when it can't even beat properly.

7
KNOX

I slam my hand on the red *stop* button, and the treadmill rapidly slows to a halt. I use the bottom of my shirt to dry my face, and when I drop it, Camden Church is standing next to my machine.

"What's up?"

He raises an eyebrow. "I can't check in on my new rookie?"

I shrug and hop off the treadmill. "I suppose you can. I thought I was the only one here."

"I had a meeting with Coach. He mentioned you were down here." He watches me for a moment. "You okay?"

"I'm fine."

"You played like shit the other night."

Ah. He trails me to the weights, and I stack plates on one of the bench press bars.

"Spot me?"

He moves into position, and I lie on the bench. I grip the cool metal, lifting the heavy bar off the rack. We're silent for a few reps. He seems to be pretty chill like that. I only moved here once the season started, and I haven't really got to know them as a team yet. Not the full-on bonding that the Guardians put me through after I signed on with them.

Which is fine.

"You went hard against Joel at practice yesterday," he comments.

I grunt.

The way I want to tell him all my problems is actually irritating. I sometimes feel like I can just keep talking forever—but when it comes to Aurora and my predicament with her, I'm all clammed up.

His hands hover under the bar as soon as my movements slow, but I push through. I breathe out hard on the lift, then take it down for another rep. My muscles burn. I manage three more before Church steps in, guiding the bar back on the rack.

I sit up, and he comes around.

"This isn't a you problem," I say.

"It's a team problem if you have issues with my goalie."

It's always about the fucking goalie. I shake my head and scowl, wiping at my face again. But I'm done—I don't need a lecture from the captain about how to treat a teammate. I can be cordial. After all, I've been *cordial* for years. I grab my water bottle and head for the door. We don't have practice today, although getting on the ice is appealing. Just shooting some pucks, working on my trick shots.

We've got an away game tomorrow in California, which means an early practice before we get on the plane. And my *issue* isn't the fact that he's another goalie fucking up my life. It's that when I see his face, I picture him fucking Aurora. And it pisses me off more than I can possibly describe.

"Hey," Church calls. "I'm here if you want to talk."

I wave him off without looking back.

On the ice are a bunch of kids chasing after a puck. I suppress my groan and head to the locker room, my hopes of getting out there dashed.

After a shower and change of clothes, I head back to my condo. I bought it in the same building as Jacob because I didn't like the idea of being alone in a new city. Call me a whiny baby or whatever, but I like being social. I like knowing I've got friends close by.

Which should mean I'd want to do the teammate bonding shit, right?

Negative.

The doorman smiles at me on approach. "Mr. White-shaw. Good day."

"Nice to see you, Jerry," I greet him on my way through. "Excellent Denver morning, isn't it?" It's brisk, a little rainy. I'm hoping for snow, *still*, but no one else seems on board with that.

He murmurs his polite agreement.

I chuckle. He's full of shit. It's a terrible morning to be stuck opening the door for people. He's wearing a long coat that goes down to his knees, black gloves, a hat. He's more prepared for the weather than I am, I'll give him that.

I jog up the steps into the lobby and past the reception desk, to the wide hall of elevators around the corner. I silently thank Jacob every time Jerry runs interception with the puck bunnies who try to overstay their welcome.

I hit the *up* button once, twice. Four times, just for the hell of it.

When the elevator chimes, I make a beeline for the opening door—and nearly crash into someone.

"Sor—"

It's Aurora. The apology freezes on my lips as soon as I register her. First the hair, then her eyes. I stop myself from getting out of her way. Instead, I step forward and block the elevator doors.

She narrows her eyes at me. "Move."

"Nah." I crowd her backward until the doors close, then hit the button for my floor. Then I focus all my attention back on her.

Her auburn hair, that deep russet color, is pulled up in a bun on top of her head. Do you know how much trauma that color hair gives me? Every time I caught a flash of it in the stands. Hell, even on campus in college. Or out walking the streets of New York. I'd see it and *boom*, be transported back to our hometown.

She's wearing an oversized white Titans sweatshirt, the T logo with the dark-blue capital T over mint-green waves drawing my eyes to her tits. Black leggings, white sneakers. I understand why she's wearing my hockey team's logo, but I fucking hate it.

Her hand is planted on her hip. Her nails are mint green. The ring on her finger is ostentatious. I hate it immediately.

"Were you visiting someone?" I question.

I want to reach out and wrap my hand around her neck again, feel her pulse flutter against my fingers. She tips her head back as I come closer. Her brows furrow when I actually make contact, holding her throat lightly. She swallows against my palm.

The elevator stops, the doors opening. I can't move away, can't let go of her. It would be so easy to squeeze. She's pressed to the wall. Her hand isn't on her hip anymore—she's gripping the railing at her back with both hands.

"Answer the question," I whisper. I tug at the sweatshirt, revealing the bite mark. It's a nice bruise now, but definitely a bite. How did she explain that to her fiancé?

"I—" She wets her lips. "I live here, you jackass."

Oh, sweet agony.

"You and Joel?"

She shakes her head. Her breathing isn't coming easily. "Just me."

I hum.

The elevator doors close again. We zoom downward, responding to someone else's call on another floor. We stare at each other, and precious seconds go by. Her heartbeat drums against the pads of my fingers.

"You're not going to marry him," I finally say. "You can't."

She tilts her head to the side. "No? There isn't *anything* you want in exchange for my freedom?"

There's a warning chime again, right before the doors open, and I quickly step back. I drop my hand away from her, ignoring how hard we're both breathing. Jesus, I barely touched her and her chest is heaving.

Is there anything I want in exchange for her freedom?

"No, sunshine. Knowing you're chained to me is the sweetest joy I know."

Her gaze hardens.

I don't even care what floor I'm on—I'll take the stairs up to my condo. I leave her alone in the elevator, glaring at me like she wants to kill me.

Maybe she does.

But now I know that she lives here. *Alone.*

And that's another gift in and of itself.

A couple of steps off the elevator with Aurora, I turn and watch the doors slide closed. But suddenly she stops it, sticking her hand out, and joins me on the sixth floor. She cocks her head again, eyeing me up and down.

"I hope you have a plan for when you get yourself

kicked out of the NHL." She brushes past me toward the stairwell.

Oh, no she doesn't.

I chase after her. "Excuse me?"

"You're going to fuck up your career, Knox. It's only a matter of time." Aurora shrugs, pushing out and heading down the stairs.

I laugh and follow. "I don't see your meaning."

"You get traded to the Titans, can't focus because you're so intent on hating me and Joel, play the worst season of your very short rookie career... and then what? Do you think they'll keep you? Do you think any other team will want you?"

My stomach cramps.

She keeps moving, trotting down the steps faster than I anticipated. She's leaving me behind—and I don't like it. I skip steps and hit the landing of the second floor only a moment after her. I grab her shoulder and spin her around, backing her against the wall.

"Ooh," she goads. "Are you hoping someone else will walk in and interpret this as a sexual situation?"

"It worked, didn't it?"

"It worked," she agrees. She presses her hand to my chest.

Her palm fucking burns through my shirt, although she doesn't react to my miniscule flinch.

"You're not going to sign the papers," she says.

"Obviously."

She smiles. "Okay."

I don't love that look. Like I walked into a trap. Her hand moves higher, her fingers brushing my Adam's apple and sweeping to the back of my neck. They dig in, little pinpricks of pain that do nothing but turn me the fuck on.

The last thing I want is an erection for Aurora fucking McGovern.

She pulls my head down. I don't know why I fucking go with it, but call me a curious masochistic. She rises on her toes and brushes her lips across my ear. Goosebumps break out down the backs of my arms.

Her warm breath coasts along my skin, and her throaty whisper follows. "Good luck at your game tomorrow."

Fuck.

She slips out from between me and the wall, continuing down like I didn't just—like we didn't just—

The door bangs shut behind her, and my brain catches up to my dick. Which is rock-hard and throbbing.

Not good.

In fact, very, *very* bad.

8

AURORA

"I missed you," Joel croons in my ear. His hand is under my shirt, and his erection is digging into my side. Not that I particularly mind. I invited him over because I needed some form of distraction.

Knox lives in my building.

It's not something Joel would've thought to tell me. But upon interrogation, he also revealed that a few other guys live here, too. Jacob Rhodes. Royal Lawson.

Camden Church, captain, lives a few blocks away. The other guys are scattered throughout the city, although some have houses. The veterans who put down roots in the area, like Dawes. Although Dawes is out for a few weeks, at least.

Or so the rumors say.

"I missed you, too," I reply. Belatedly.

The distraction isn't working.

I tug his hand away and roll on my back. "Sorry," I breathe, covering my face. "I just—"

"No need to apologize, sugar." Joel shifts, hopping off the bed. "I'll be right back."

I peek as he crosses the room, disappearing into the bathroom.

As soon as he's gone, I jump up and make a mad dash to the kitchen. I left my phone plugged into the charger, and I quickly scroll through my texts from Beth. I told her I was keeping a little secret from him, and we debated the pros and cons of telling him. Although I wouldn't admit to her what it was. The shame of revealing my prior lie—about Knox signing the papers ages ago—was too heavy.

I move to my office, sitting at the desk and glowering at the pink typewriter. The first chapter of the story I started, which was nothing more than an outlet for my jumbled emotions, sits in the drawer.

Once I finished, I pulled the last page free and tucked it out of sight.

Out of sight, out of mind, right?

Except now, as I feed another piece of paper into the typewriter, I feel the urge to keep going. To travel back to when I was sixteen, to relive those feelings.

It's a sort of penance, in a way.

I type *Chapter Two* and pause. Hovering. The keys are too slick, too plastic. The click of levers isn't as satisfying, and once again I mourn the loss of my original. I also realize that it's fully pretentious of me to do it this way, but it's just the process. Otherwise I'd delete, delete, delete... at least if I crumple up a page in anger, I can go retrieve it from the bin and smooth it out.

Then, later, I redraft it into my computer. Those are long, late nights spent squinting at my scribbled notes to myself, the words crunched into the margins or the back of the paper.

Hands touch my shoulders. I almost jump a foot.

"Inspiration strike you?" Joel asks, kissing my neck.

I tip my head to the side and close my eyes. "Something like that."

"I'll leave you to it, then." His lips linger. "I'll see you tomorrow."

I turn and grab the front of his shirt before he can pull away. Our lips meet, and his hand cups my cheek. The kiss deepens, his tongue tasting my mouth, until we're both breathless. He presses one last, much more chaste kiss, to the corner of my lips and withdraws.

He lets himself out, and I linger in my chair.

But only for a moment.

I get up and change, tugging on shorts and a snug sports bra, my running shoes, and the key fob that'll let me into the gym. Because I'm overwhelmingly restless, and no amount of sitting still or creative output is going to fix it.

Except when I get down there, I find a Titan.

Not Knox, thankfully.

Jacob Rhodes.

He glances at me, then does a double take. He's Knox's best friend. I have a zero percent chance of him not saying something to me. But he actually stays silent as I move to another treadmill and step on, powering it up to a quick walk at a decent incline.

Every so often, his gaze bores into the side of my face.

I forgot my headphones, of course. I've got nothing to tune out the dull sounds of his feet slapping the tread and mine at a more crawling pace.

What feels like eons later, he slows to a walk.

"Aurora?"

I frown, but I don't otherwise acknowledge him.

"You're messing with him," he says. "Being here. Living here."

"Oh, come on." I scoff, putting my feet on the sides and

facing Knox's teammate. "I didn't know he was going to be traded. I certainly had no plans of living in the same building as him. Or you, for that matter. Trust me, I would've picked anywhere else."

He shakes his head.

"If you want *me* to stop messing with *him*, tell him to sign the freaking divorce papers." I hit the *end* button, my mood officially ruined.

I'll go run outside. It's raining and cold, but the foul weather will serve me good. It matches my mood.

He doesn't follow me out, thank goodness.

But Knox is waiting for me.

I automatically scowl but otherwise ignore him. It doesn't help that I catch his smile out of the corner of my eye.

"I saw Joel leaving," he comments, following me down the hall. "Why don't you live with him?"

"Because I want some independence." I shoot him a pointed look. "What are you doing? Stalking me?"

"Right time, right place."

God.

I hit the button for the elevator and face him, planting my hands on my hips. He's dressed to exercise, too. Shorts and a t-shirt, a black ball cap hiding his dark-blond hair. He leans against the wall beside the elevator button and crosses his arms.

He has no right to be so goddamn hot.

"Tell me something, sunshine."

"I'd rather not."

"Are you in love with him?"

I scoff. Of all the questions to ask. "Of course I love him. You're reaching."

"And he loves you, I presume." He's looking at me weird. There's a lot of anger, but also this twisted curiosity. It makes me want to crack open my chest and tell him shit.

Which is stupid, because I am *over* Knox Whiteshaw. In fact, I've never cared less about someone. He could step in front of a bus and I wouldn't even gasp.

Quit lying, Aurora.

The elevator opens, but neither of us move to step in. I don't know why I don't go. I should. But he's skeptical of my relationship with Joel. Questioning it.

The doors close again.

"He loves me. I love him. End of story, Knox."

He bristles when I say his name—it just makes me want to say his name more. I don't even know why he's acting like such an asshole. It's not like I purposely tried to ruin his life. I have no recollection of actually doing any such thing.

One day, we were fine. The next, he was yelling at me in front of my house. Telling me that he's never coming home, that he doesn't want to see my face ever again.

That's history. That's *our* history.

And it should stay in the past where it belongs.

I jam my finger on the button again, and the doors open. I enter, my legs unfreezing, and Knox follows. He's like a dog with a bone, refusing to let me go in peace. He leans against the wall, arms crossed, and looks me up and down.

"I don't think he actually loves you," he muses.

His blue eyes end up on my face, and so hot with loathing I imagine I might burst into flames if he stares any longer.

"I think this was just a Joel Haverhill thing to do. Goalies are known to have a screw loose, you know? One thing led to another, and you roped him into an engagement." His gaze flicks to my stomach. "Are you pregnant? Is that why you want to marry him? You're ashamed to have a baby out of wedlock?"

Jesus.

"That is such an antiquated way of thinking," I snap. "And if I was pregnant, I'd sure as hell not tell you."

We arrive on the first floor, and I hurry outside. I pick up a jog, ignoring the cool morning mist. I should've stayed in the gym, but I somehow ended up in Titan land. Who knew Jacob and Knox would prefer their building's fitness center opposed to the arena's?

The one thing I will not contemplate is Knox's sudden... *interest* in me. It's weird. Of all the things I thought he'd do, ignoring me would've been at the top of the list.

It takes me two blocks to realize I have an unwanted shadow. The little hairs on the back of my neck rise, and I glance over my shoulder. Knox's expression doesn't change when he sees that I see him.

He stays half a block behind me. No matter how fast I go, or how slow, he matches my pace. He's breathing down my neck from a distance, and my pace is all off. I'm stiff and sore by the time I reach the coffee shop a mile away, my predetermined stopping point.

I hate running. Jogging. Whatever you call the mess I just did—it was an impulse to get away from Knox. Not that it worked very well, seeing as how he's not only a nuisance but a stalker, too.

The café is busy at this time of day, but I love the atmosphere. All dark academic vibes. Most of the walls are covered in deep-blue bookcases. The floors are warm wood. And they don't just have tables, they have comfortable armchairs with side tables scattered around, too. Some have blankets folded over the back. Lamps and wall sconces instead of overhead lighting.

I keep meaning to come here to work. Not with the typewriter, that would be a little obscene. But when I'm editing, maybe. Or I could suck it up and take my laptop—not that the writing thing is really going so well at the moment.

My heart is beating steadily, my watch confirming it. I stare at the face for a minute as it rechecks, but my jog only raised my pulse a little.

The forced cardio is paying off, then. Which should feel satisfying. But instead, it just makes me yearn for *more*. Things that are probably still out of reach.

My phone buzzes. I answer the incoming call from Joel. "Hey."

"Hey, yourself. Sorry to interrupt your work—"

"I went for a run, actually. Now I'm grabbing a coffee before heading back."

"Oh, cool. Well, I just got the okay for you to travel with us tomorrow. If you want."

I pause. The door behind me chimes, and Knox strolls in. The fucker isn't even red in the face, unlike me. Just because my pulse didn't speed up doesn't mean my flush decided to stay home. No, I can *look* at an exercise machine and my face will flame.

He stops behind me, in line for the cash register, and ignores me. I keep one eye on him, although he pulls his phone out and starts typing.

"Aurora?" Joel asks.

"I suppose I could travel with you," I reply. "I've never been on a private jet before."

Knox's attention flicks to me, his brows lowering in a classic scowl.

Joel chuckles. "You'll enjoy it. If you don't mind some of the guys acting like heathens. But it'll be more comfortable than flying separately, and we're flying back the same day."

Oh. "I kind of assumed you'd be staying over."

"We've got press this week. Anyway, I've got a meeting with PT. See you tonight?"

"Yeah, of course. Love you."

"Love you, sugar," Joel answers.

"Love you," Knox mocks under his breath as soon as I hang up. "I'd love to put that to the test."

"Oh, yeah?"

He smiles.

Bait taken. *Shit.* This is familiar, too. A weird, awful sense of déjà vu, except it used to be harmless bets. Now... not so much.

"Yeah, *sugar.*"

Great, he heard that.

His smile turns into a sneer. "You tell him that you're married to me. See what he says. And if he leaves you high and dry, well... I guess you'll have deserved it for lying in the first place."

The barista at the register calls for the next person.

"That's you," Knox prods.

I step up and order my usual. I've barely finished my sentence when Knox orders for himself.

"You've got this, right, *babe*?"

I wrinkle my nose. He moves past me to the pick-up spot. He ordered a cold brew with an extra shot of espresso and cold foam, which kind of sounds good but also... what the fuck? The barista eyes him, then me, and I roll my eyes and pay.

But I definitely don't stand next to him to wait. In fact, I stand about as far away as possible.

"Rory," a barista calls.

I move faster than Knox, maybe on the fact that he wasn't expecting the newish nickname out of her mouth, and pick up both cups. I hurry to the exit, gripping both. Because he's a psychopath, he follows.

"That's mine," Knox calls.

"Then you should've paid for it," I yell over my shoulder.

He catches up too damn easily. "You're more like a grumpy cloud lately."

"Because I keep having to deal with you on top of everything else going on," I huff.

The speed we're walking is wearing on me. Even though Knox is at least six inches taller than me, and not struggling in the slightest, I don't want to give him the decency of a nice amble back to our building. So my breathing comes harder as I push myself faster, and I do my best to ignore *him*.

I cross the streets when I shouldn't, darting between oncoming cars, and all the while his chuckle follows me. We almost get hit a time or two. I mean, I wish they would take Knox out.

That would solve all of my problems.

I'm sweating by the time I get to my building. The doorman hefts open the glass-and-metal door upon my arrival.

"Ms. McGovern. Mr. Whiteshaw," he greets.

Make that *our* arrival.

"Jerry," Knox calls cheerfully. "Did Aurora here ever mention that we're married?"

I stop and whirl around. Without thinking, I chuck his fancy, expensive *cold brew* at him. The cup hits him dead center of his chest, opening and exploding across his shirt. It goes everywhere. The floor, the doorway.

"Sorry, Jerry," I choke out.

Knox just gapes at me.

So I do the rational thing—I turn and flee.

9

AURORA

I sit at my typewriter and flex my fingers.

Load in the paper.

The pink is too shiny, too new. I scratch at it, but the lacquer it's covered in is too strong. My nails are no match for it, and it remains unblemished.

What I need to do is write something besides that chapter about Knox. I mean, it wasn't even really about him —it was about me. Me being sick. Me losing my dreams. And him, what, picking up the pieces? Being *nice*?

No.

No, no, no.

We're not going to remember Knox as nice. We're not going to remember him as anything but an asshole who's getting in the way of me marrying Joel.

One of my side characters is mentioned quite frequently on social media. Readers are clamoring for his story, but I've got nothing. I've *had* nothing since... well, six months ago? Since I met Joel?

That's a coincidence.

It's not like being happy sucked away my creativity.

I type the character's name, moving a little too fast. Two of the letters come down at once and get jammed.

"Stupid fucking piece of shit," I growl.

I fix it and lean back, covering my eyes.

Joel's going to be here soon. In fact, just as I'm thinking that, there's a knock at the door. I push back from the desk, absolutely grateful for the distraction. Before I make it out of the room, I realize I took the ring off.

He knocks again, but I spare a moment to find it next to the typewriter and slip it on. Then I go answer, pulling open the door with a broad smile.

The smile drops when I see, instead of my adoring fiancé—my loathsome husband.

"What do you want?" I snap.

He steps forward. "Is that any way to greet your husband?"

I shake my head. "Maybe if you acted like one—"

He forces his way in, kicking the door shut behind him. My stomach flips, especially when he grabs my upper arms and walks me backward. Because this is new and... *interesting*.

I hate that it's interesting. Hate that I'm actually intrigued by what he's doing. I mean, I know him. *Knew* him. He's good at his core. But did I somehow damage it? His core. His soul. Blacken it, twist it.

"What were those abandonment conditions you threw at me?" he muses, still walking me backward until I hit the wall just beside the window. "Financial... well, we both know you still benefit from me in that regard."

His gaze drops to my chest.

I push at him, but he just shakes his head.

"Let's see it, shall we?"

"You better not—"

He grips the collar of my shirt and rips it.

He fucking rips my shirt open like a heathen, revealing my dark-grey sports bra. "This explains the uniboob," he mutters. "But it's got to go, too."

I laugh. "You're going to come in here and assault me?"

"Are you going to tell me you don't secretly like it?" He tilts his head, his blue eyes lasering in on me. "Don't you write about this in your book, sunshine? The villain does despicable things to the girl, but she's okay with it. She's Stockholm Syndromed into giving a shit about him. And they live happily ever fucked-up after."

"That's fiction." I lift my chin. "It's different."

"You're just as depraved as me, I think. Shall we find out?" He leaves me standing against the wall. He goes to my kitchen like he owns it, opening and slamming drawers until he finds what he's looking for. "Hold still. Wouldn't want to cut you."

He returns with a box cutter.

"You've got to be kidding me."

"Do you think Joel will get the picture when my name is carved across your breasts?"

He flicks the shoulder of my shirt off, revealing the bite that I fucking *bandaged* to hide it from Joel. I said something about burning myself with my hair curler a mumbled lie that doused me with guilt.

"I think he'd believe me if I said you did it against my will," I counter.

"Do you think he'd still feel that way if he knew we were married? Do you want to bet on that?" He smiles. Wicked, fierce thing.

"Get out."

He laughs. "Now, now. You're not running this show."

I try to move past him, but he rushes me. He slams me

into the wall, his shoulder digging into mine. My breath leaves me in a whoosh, and I grab on to his arm automatically. He pulls at the front of my sports bra and slices downward. The strain on the fabric eases the blade's path, and I close my eyes when it falls open.

"You asshole." I cover myself, turning half away from him.

He leans back. Staring down at my breasts, even as I try to cover them up.

"There it is," he breathes. He traces the scar that goes straight down my chest. "My *financial contribution*. The gift that keeps on giving, isn't that right?"

"It's not like you gave me your heart," I choke out.

He goes still, his finger at the bottom of the scar. He tips his finger, digging his nail into my skin. Pushing me back with just that slight pressure and the cut of his nail.

"You don't think so?" he asks.

I blink.

Is he serious?

No, he can't be. He's absolutely lying. And I didn't mean it like that anyway. I meant—

He knows how you meant it.

"Nicked you," he adds, running his finger up to where he must've accidentally cut me. Or on purpose cut me— who knows. He smears the little droplets of blood that have welled up. "And that's my physical contribution for the day."

He steps back, leaving me standing there like an idiot. I pull the pieces of my shirt together and try to gather some of my dignity back.

"And emotional?" I force out when he's almost at the door.

Maybe I'm still an idiot.

He spins around, still moving backward. "Emotional... hmm... how about this? You fucking devastated me six years ago, Sunny. And now that we're in the same city, I plan on repaying the favor."

The door closes behind him, leaving me alone to contemplate what the fuck I'm going to do about him.

And Joel.

10

KNOX

I'm seated behind Joel and Aurora because I like to torture myself. I've turned over our last interactions all night. And her breasts. Because *fuck*, those were perfect. Exactly the right shape and weight, and her nipples were dusky pink. They pebbled when I cut her sports bra. She didn't flinch away from the box cutter either.

Maybe she *does* like the shit she writes about. Which Melody only hinted at, and obviously teasing Aurora about it yesterday did the trick to rattle her. I took the book back from Mel and have it sitting on my nightstand, but I haven't cracked it open yet. Because I'm not a reader, for one. And I don't think I want to be in Aurora's head like that.

I was fine without her in my life. In fact, I was happy. But now she's crash-landed in Denver, and I can't seem to shake her. She's living in my fucking building. She's sleeping with my teammate.

Even breathing the same air irritates me.

So maybe I should just read the book and dive into her fully. Get a clearer picture of her.

Joel is sleeping. Or meditating. He's got noise-canceling

headphones on, and when I last walked past, his eyes were shut.

I know next to nothing about him. Jacob is across the aisle from me, texting with someone. Melody, I'd bet. I switch seats and drop down next to him, elbowing his side to get his attention.

"How's Mel?"

He eyes me. "Fine..."

"Is she staying home, or...?"

He stows his phone and faces me. "Yeah, she's working on a painting. What's wrong?"

It's daylight, and our goalie is fucking sleeping.

Or meditating.

I jerk my thumb over my shoulder in his direction. "What's his problem?"

Jacob squints at me, then his gaze moves to where I assume he can see Joel. The fucker took the window seat, leaving Aurora on the aisle. Not that she seemed particularly perturbed by that the last time I checked. She was typing rather furiously on her phone, her head bent.

Either tattling about me to her friend or writing her next big hit.

"I don't think Haverhill has a problem," Jacob says in a low voice. "You're the one with the problem. And you keep taking it out on us."

I roll my eyes. "I do not. I'm just—"

"You're fixating."

Well, *duh*. "We all fixated at one point or another," I mutter.

Jacob sighs. "Miles kept it together for a year while you fucked around with Willow. The least you can do is keep your shit together for a few games. She'll get bored and stop coming."

Maybe.

I fold my arms over my chest. He doesn't know her like I do. He doesn't know that, at one point, she lived and breathed hockey. Plus, she's still got a decent arm on her. After she chucked her drink on me—which was impressive, to say the least, and refreshing in the strangest way—I showered and went to her condo. Because Jerry the doorman gave me her unit number, and I wanted to make her squirm.

I'm used to girls folding. Give them a smoldering look and they fold.

But Aurora...

Hmm.

I haven't really tried a smoldering look on her. I haven't gone the sweet route at all.

Although as she unbuckles her seat belt and gets up, heading for the bathroom at the front of the plane, I find myself following. I never learn my lesson—or maybe just to see what she'll do if I *did* try to get in her pants.

How fast will she fold?

Jacob sighs loudly behind me, but I ignore him.

She doesn't notice me. The bathroom on our plane is bigger than the tiny closet ones on commercial airlines, and I catch the door before she can lock it. I force my way in and flip the lock, triggering the lights.

There's enough space for both of us, although it's tight. She's a hairsbreadth away. *Inches.* In black jeans and a blue form-fitting Titans long-sleeve shirt. Her hair is in loose curls around her shoulders. Makeup flawless, heavy. Her lips are blood red, and her tongue peeks out, flicking against her lower lip.

"What are you doing?" she asks.

I don't give her a hateful glare. This is a test, after all, so I ramp up the charm. I inch forward, reaching for her waist.

"I just wanted to touch you," I murmur. "Is that so bad?"

Memories of our past flicker in my head like movie stills, a rolodex of images against the back of my mind. Of sixteen-year-old Aurora. Seventeen. Eighteen.

Yelling at her in front of her house, the satisfaction of her tears almost overwhelming.

Pain makes me feel good.

Everything else makes me feel... comfortably numb.

I'm happiest when I'm numb.

Touching her yesterday wasn't enough.

She doesn't stop me right now. She didn't stop me then either. Not really. Not like I thought she would. I didn't really know what she would do then, and I still don't know now. Although when I pick her up and plant her ass on the narrow counter, her lips part.

"I know." I say it like I'm admitting a dirty secret. "I know you, sunshine."

I lean in so fucking slowly, waiting for her to push me away or laugh in my face. And when my lips brush her neck, her breathing fucking stops. I'm so tuned in to her, I can't help but notice every little thing.

My hands are on her waist, but they don't move. She's gripping the counter, allowing me to kiss her neck. Just above the bandaged bite mark. I suck, gently at first, then harder. Until my teeth score her skin again.

She jerks, finally shoving at my chest.

"Goddamn it, Knox," she whispers. "Why did you do that?"

"To see if you'd push me away." I smirk. "But you're not getting out of this so easily."

Her brow lowers. "What the hell does that mean?"

"It means I'm standing between you and the door, and my dick is hard." I step back and lean against the locked door, slowly undoing the button of my slacks. "You can bend over and let me use your cunt... or your mouth. I'll let you choose this time."

I can't read her expression. She seems to be considering my words, and she shifts her weight. Then, to my complete shock, she gets on her knees.

Holy shit.

To say I used to dream of Aurora's mouth would be the understatement of the century. She was the prettiest girl in high school. The fact that she lived next door to me was an added bonus.

She inches forward, tipping her head back. I shove my slacks down with my boxers, freeing my cock. It's getting harder by the second, all my blood flow leaving my brain and traveling to my groin.

Her breath... my God, her warm breath hits me, and a shiver sweeps up my spine.

"Suck it like you mean it, sunshine," I order.

She gets even closer, somehow without touching me. "Did you pay the girls you've fucked to lie about your dick size?"

I blink. "What?"

Aurora holds up her pinky. "I mean... I was expecting more. Based on the rumors about you. But it's okay, little guy." She's talking to my dick. Like it's a petulant toddler. "Not every guy can be hung like my fiancé."

"You're going to pay for that," I growl. Without thinking, I grab her face and jerk her forward, sliding the head of my cock into her mouth.

She doesn't even react. Her hypnotic green eyes are

stuck on my face, her tongue out. A bit of saliva drops from her lips, landing on the floor between her knees. She looks like a prim and proper girl on her knees for me.

I fuck her face, and she acts like she's at the fucking spa.

I hate her.

I've never hated anyone more.

So I push her until she *does* gag, choking around me. I grip her hair tighter, twisting the silky strands close to the roots until it's probably painful. She can't breathe. Her face is slowly getting redder, her eyes filling with tears.

"Not so small, now, hmm?"

When her eyes roll back, I pull out. She sucks in a breath through her nose, her nostrils flaring. Just the moment of reprieve before I do it again. Going farther and farther, just trying to get her to break.

Doesn't help that it's the best head of my life. Her throat feels like every other girl's—it's her cutting glare that's turning me on. I race toward my climax, grunting with every thrust. It's a hard, quick ride, and I don't bother to warn her when I come. I hit the back of her throat, the rings of muscle clenching around me with her swallows. Although she chokes on it again, and satisfaction blasts through me.

The post-orgasm bliss hits a second later.

I release her hair, and she sits back on her heels. She runs the back of her finger under her lip, then frowns. Her eye makeup is smudged, too, from tears that rolled down her cheeks.

Aurora climbs to her feet. "I hope you don't judge yourself against other guys' dicks in the locker room, Knox. If I didn't know better, I'd think that's where your complex comes from."

My mouth drops open. From an orgasm to insult?

"You didn't think I was small when you were choking on it."

"I sometimes gag when I take pills." Her expression is all disdain, and she holds up her fingers to show me how big those *pills* are. "Yeah, seems like it's a decent comparison."

She fixes her lipstick and hair in the mirror carefully, all while I stare at her like she's an alien. Because she is. She just choked on my dick, but she's acting like she didn't. When she's finished, she tilts her head and waits for me to move aside.

I shift out of her way. I can't believe her.

She thinks I'm *small?*

I just—

She just—

She unlocks the door, and the lights flicker out. Without a word, she leaves me alone in the dark bathroom. And I'm left replaying the moment, trying to discern what the fuck just happened.

11

AURORA

I round the corner toward what I *thought* were the locker rooms, and come to an abrupt halt. Because I clearly just interrupted a conversation I immediately wish I hadn't.

Two men whispering.

Which probably wouldn't normally be a problem, since it's a hallway outside an NHL locker room, and I've passed a dozen *official* people talking in low tones.

But they stop when they notice me, and shock flickers through me when I realize I recognize one.

Although it takes me a minute to place where I know him.

That night at the club.

Fuck.

The guy with the reddish hair and beard stares at me for a long moment, and I know he's realizing the same thing.

What're the odds we run into each other here? During the second intermission of a Titans game?

"Luke—"

The red-haired man waves off his colleague's words. He

motions for me to come closer, and my feet move of their own accord. It's only when I get within reach that a prickle of fear slides between my shoulder blades.

"I didn't catch your name last time," he says to me.

"Aurora." My voice is faint.

"Aurora..."

"McGovern."

He nods. "And thanks to my friend here, you know my name is Luke."

My mouth dries. "Yeah."

"What are you doing here?" His gaze lifts over my head, then focuses back on me. "There's security. Did you sneak past them? I think you have a bad habit of doing that."

I shake my head and raise the badge Joel had given me. It got me past the security guard easily. By that I mean, I'm allowed to be down here. I'm not actually doing anything wrong, except interrupting this conversation.

Luke takes it. He's dressed formally, in a charcoal-gray suit and blue tie. The guy next to him has a dark-blue polo and slacks on, and a badge similar to mine clipped to his belt. He's squinting at me, confused, but I don't really know what to say.

I still have no idea what's going on.

I was honest with Knox outside the bar last week. I *did* bet against the Titans because I wanted to see if my theory was right. And I won a good chunk of money. Even though the Guardians were a playoff team, apparently the odds were skewed in the Titans' favor.

Maybe that's it, then.

The odds didn't make sense.

And them losing didn't make sense either. They were playing fine.

Luke hands me back my badge. "Get out of here."

"Aurora?"

I try not to wince. But... damn it, I do. And Luke seems to laser in on that, even as his face transforms from vaguely threatening to... *charming*.

"Knox Whiteshaw," he calls. "Keep up the good work."

Good work? His head has only been partially in the game. I've been watching through my fingers, torn between wanting Knox to get checked into the boards every time he gets the puck and willing Joel's reactions to be fast, to catch or block any puck that comes his way.

And yet, the Titans are still down by one, with one period left to play.

Knox is in his full hockey gear, skates and all. His helmet is tucked under his arm, and his stick is in his other hand.

He was already six inches taller than me, but now it's more like ten. I have to crane my head back to see him.

"You know Ms. McGovern?" Luke questions.

Knox inclines his chin. "Yes, sir. And you know her...?"

Sir?

"We just met," Luke informs him. "You look like you just finished press. Your coach is probably waiting for you."

"Right." Knox dips his head, then eyes me. "Aurora, walk with me."

I don't feel the question in his phrasing, but I nod anyway. He doesn't touch me until we're around the corner. He glances around, then grabs my upper arm and hauls me through an unlocked door.

It clicks shut behind me, plunging us into darkness.

A split second later, Knox's phone flashlight illuminates the space. He finds the switch by the door and flicks it, stowing his phone again. He glowers at me.

"What the hell was that?" he demands.

"I was coming down to wish Joel good luck," I snap. "I don't know what you think you saw—"

"I think I saw you talking to the Titans' owner's son and the assistant coach."

Well, shit.

"Luke's dad owns the team?" I clarify.

Knox sniffs and turns away from me. "Obviously."

He can somehow be hot and off-put at the same time. His hair is pushed back off his face, damp with sweat or water. Hockey guys are always dumping water on their heads. His white jersey, with stripes of mint green and dark blue on the arms and sides, is caught on the pads in the back. It obscures the number nineteen.

I resist the urge to fix it.

Instead, I try to figure out the connection between the team, Luke, and the conversation I overheard at the club. I suspected that they were rigging the bets, but now it's more clear that he has the power to fix the games, too.

"What's your problem?" Knox asks, suddenly in my face.

I backpedal and bump into the door. "I don't have one, although you seem determined to make yourself my problem."

He laughs. "Yeah, well, I like searching for trouble."

I don't know what that means. And I'm not really keen to find out. But...

I make a point of checking my watch. "You're probably needed back in the locker room."

Knox grunts. "Yeah, probably."

"What was it you said to me? 'I'm between you and the door, and...'" I raise my eyebrow. "What should your toll be?"

His gaze darkens. "You want me to touch you, sunshine?"

I smile. "No. But maybe I can keep you here until you agree to sign the divorce papers?"

"I'll sign them when you break the news to Joel that you're still married." He raises his eyebrows. "If you're so confident..."

"Fine." Shit. I didn't really mean to agree, but he just makes me so *angry*.

His eyes flash. That's the only warning I get before he grips my upper arm and forcibly moves me away from the door. I stumble in his hold, and I automatically reach for something to steady me. My fingers graze his stick, and I seize it.

It's been too long since I've held a hockey stick. His is too tall for me, but still. I run my fingers up the shaft, to the tape at the top.

He's breathing hard, glaring at me, when my brows furrow.

"You don't tape your stick like this." I flip it around and examine the blade. "What is this?"

This is—that's—

He grabs the stick back and picks up his fallen helmet. "Don't," he warns.

"No." I follow him out into the hall, down toward the locker rooms. "No, we're going to talk about this. You don't tape your stick like that, Knox. I know you. But you know who does tape their stick like this?"

"Aurora, drop it—"

"I do." I push into the locker room right after him. "Did. Whatever."

He wheels around. "Go back to your seat."

I scowl. "We're not done talking about this. Especially since you gave me eternal shit for it when we were kids."

My dad kind of let me figure out how to tape my own stick. And as such, I went a little more tactile on the grip. And then it stuck. Although Knox had some *opinions* about it, every time he had to use my stick he complained.

And now he's doing the same thing?

It's almost insulting.

And definitely unusual.

"I want an explanation," I continue, planting my hands on my hips. "And then I'll go."

He sighs.

"Dude," someone calls. "No girls in the locker room."

Knox flips him off, then herds me out. Which is probably good, because I'm not sure how I'd explain this conversation to Joel. Although after a quick peek around, I don't spot my fiancé.

"There's no explanation," Knox says shortly, as soon as I'm out of the locker room. "Go away."

I laugh. The door swings shut in my face, but I know better than to try again. It's not my space.

"Rory?"

I turn toward Joel. He comes down the hall from the opposite direction Knox and I came from. Which means he missed our interaction.

My relief helps my smile.

"Just wanted to say hi," I murmur, stepping up and kissing him.

"Hi," he replies. "Meet you down here after?"

"Of course."

He touches my cheek.

I get out of his way, and he disappears into the locker room. I wait for a beat, then another.

The thing is, I'm not confident Joel won't freak out when I tell him about Knox and me. I love him, yes, but we're still learning each other. I met him six months ago, and I'm fully aware that this is what they call a whirlwind romance.

But Knox is giving me no choice. I want to marry Joel. I want to be divorced from Knox.

Which means being honest... as soon as the game is over.

I take my seat and lean forward when the Titans skate out. Joel's all focused when he comes onto the ice, heading to the net and scuffing up the crease. He drops into a stretch, the other players zooming around.

My gaze snags on another player. Knox easily finds me in the crowd. It's almost unerring how quickly he does it. His gaze burns, and I force myself to look away. I don't even know how he knows where I'm sitting.

The last game I went to, Joel got me into a suite with some of his friends. That was an interesting experience, meeting those guys. They're not exactly who I would've pegged Joel to be friends with. They all wore suits and drank expensive liquor. But it was a home game and all that, so maybe they were just taking advantage of the grandeur of the situation.

I glance up at the glass-walled suites. It's better to be up high, sure, but I grew up watching hockey from the glass. And the bench.

Suddenly, the people around me start cheering. It takes me a moment to realize that we're on the big screen, a group of us with me smack in the center. I wave, forcing a smile, and then look back to Joel.

Because he grounds me, unlike Knox. And this atmosphere.

And the run-in with the owner's son, who suddenly drops into the recently vacated seat beside me. He leans back, waving and smiling, and I make myself smile brighter.

"Aurora," he says, like he's chewing on my name. "McGovern."

"That's me."

We're drawing attention.

"Romance author. I didn't expect that." His attention stays on the ice and his players. "What brings you to the game? And the locker room?"

"Just... visiting a player."

"Knox Whiteshaw?"

"I know him, yes." It's not so much the truth as skirting the question. Mainly because I don't want to draw unnecessary attention to Joel, and—well, I guess that's it. Knox is new to the team, and life would be a whole lot easier if he just, you know, was traded again.

"Is the conversation you overheard the other night making more sense?" he asks. "Now that you know who I am."

I wince. *Now* would be the time to lie. To deny.

Before I can open my mouth, he continues. "It's actually a good thing we ran into each other again, Ms. McGovern. My operation is running into a few snags, and it could use your help." He glances at me. "Some people just need a little extra motivation."

The third period begins. Knox wins the face-off, shooting the puck over to Scofield. They're a swarm of white-jersey players around the darker home-jersey color of their opponents.

"Who needs motivating?" I frown. "I don't really know

anything. Or anyone else on the team. I'm not really involved in hockey at all."

"Somehow, Aurora, I think you might be the perfect candidate. Here's what you're going to do." He holds out a slim black phone. "You're going to carry this with you. And when I call, you're going to answer."

I shiver. This feels like something out of a book. Something I'd concoct in my head. If only I was a heroine destined for her true great love, instead of... me. A girl suffering from writer's block and delusion.

"I don't know how I can help," I mumble. I don't take the phone.

"Your connection to Whiteshaw." He pauses. "And Haverhill."

A chill sweeps down my spine.

"Fun mess you've gotten yourself into, don't you think? Married to one, engaged to the other." He chuckles. "It took my people less than fifteen minutes to discover that one. You flew on our jet at Haverhill's request. It's his ring on your finger, his bank statement confirmed it. So here's the thing. You help me, or I resort to more drastic measures to force your hand."

"Drastic," I repeat. I'm pretty sure I've gone pale. My hands are shaking, but I mask it by keeping my palms pressed to my thighs. "I don't suppose you'd elaborate?"

"Well, I'd start with Haverhill." He tips his head. "He's not the greatest goalie, is he? If he has an accident, if, say, his legs were to shatter... well, we would get the other Whiteshaw. Then you'd have to pick my next target—your husband or his brother."

He pushes the phone at me again.

This time, I take it.

I don't even know what he wants from me. I know nothing, although my imagination runs wild enough.

He stands and buttons his suit jacket, then slips down the row and disappears up the aisle. As soon as he's gone, I blow out a shaky breath. I'm screwed.

12

AURORA

I dream of blood. A high-pitched scream echoes around the room as blood pours from Joel's mouth and eyes. He's on the floor, gagging and choking. He scratches at his eyes, making everything worse.

There's no saving him.

I'm shaken violently, and I jerk upright in bed. I'm sweating, cold and hot at the same time, and my heart is going a thousand miles a minute.

Joel stares at me, the concern etched on his face almost painful.

Alive, whole, *not* covered in blood.

I burst into tears.

"Hey," he murmurs, drawing me close. "What's wrong?"

I latch on to him and bury my face in his neck. I can't voice the fear, the dream. He'll ask why my subconscious is focusing on his death, and I definitely can't tell him that it's because he's been threatened.

So I let him hold me as I sob, until eventually the

tremors subside and I can breathe without hiccupping again.

"Sorry," I whisper.

He doesn't stay over very often. We're practicing that whole separate-lives-until-marriage thing. It's just something I've always wanted to do. Maybe because my parents got married right out of high school and moved in together. My aunts used to gossip that I was out of wedlock. Another reason that Knox's comment about me marrying Joel because I was pregnant stung at the time. And why my parents would rush to get married.

I never asked my father about it, though. I didn't want to hurt him by believing the rumors—or even considering believing them.

Not that it would be the worst thing in the world...

I don't know.

Joel strokes my hair, then releases me. He gets me a glass of water from the kitchen, making his way back in the near-total darkness. My fingers wrap around the cool glass, and I take a sip.

Almost immediately, I cough. It burns on the way down.

"Joel!"

"Vodka," he says in a low voice. "Think of it as a balm to the nightmare."

I wrinkle my nose, but I drink the rest of it. Just another swallow or two, then I hand it back. I don't like the way it tastes, but the smoldering fire in my belly is nice.

"Okay," I breathe. "Kissing me would help, too."

He obliges. His hands wander, creeping up to palm my breast, pinching my nipple. An ache starts between my legs, and I squeeze my legs together. He smiles against my lips, and his fingers slip under my panties.

His fingers push me over the edge quickly, the climax crashing over me. I arch, gasping into his mouth. The vodka has made me feel warm, and the orgasm doubles it. I can barely keep my eyes open, and I don't fight when he wraps my hand around his erection.

It brings flashbacks to Knox.

Unwanted ones.

The look in his eye, the feel of his hand in my hair. The smell and taste of him as I choked—

Joel groans. I rise on my elbow and eye him. Then crawl lower, dipping my head and taking him in my mouth. I use my hand and my mouth, and he never touches my head. He groans and warns me when he's about to come. There's a split second when I consider swallowing, but I pull away and finish him with my saliva-slickened hand instead.

Ropes of cum shoot up onto his stomach, and he sighs. "I fucking love your mouth."

I hum. We clean up and drop back into bed, satiated. The nightmare all but forgotten.

He falls asleep quickly, while I stare at the ceiling. I *should* fall asleep fast, but I'm left struggling not to toss and turn. And to not think about the blood.

Or Knox.

A new ache—or the same one again, maybe—starts between my legs.

I shouldn't want what he did to me. I should be focused on the man in my bed, who is arrogant and sweet at the same time, who is confident and in love with me.

Instead, I am just a terrible person.

A terrible person who needs to tell Joel the truth. No matter the consequences.

In the morning, Joel finds me curled on my sofa. I've got a cup of coffee in my hands, a blanket over my lap. And I've been staring at the black screen of the television for the last twenty minutes.

"Good morning," he greets me, kissing the top of my head. He pours himself coffee and wanders back. "You're up early."

I shift. "I have to tell you something."

God, he's handsome. Crashing into him on the ice is a vivid memory. Feeling his weight press down on me, and then the easy strength in lifting me back to my feet. His quick smile. Dinner with Beth. And then dinner alone.

Things with Joel have always been easy. It was easy to decide to go on a second date with him, then a third. Easy to talk to him on the phone, to talk about things like my mom and my childhood. Although Knox was always left out of it. Joel is a warm bath that you can slip into at the end of a long day. He's the peace that awaits you when you're tired and miserable.

I didn't have any doubt about his commitment. Or his proposal. Or the decision to move to Denver. It was just... simple.

I liked it. I liked that things with him were uncomplicated, because the *other* relationship was too complicated to even unknot.

But now... well, now we're complicated, too.

"You seem worried," he comments.

"It's because I don't know how you're going to take it." I set aside my coffee. "I..."

"It's okay."

He sets his aside, too, and takes my hands. He's so sweet. Maybe some people wouldn't find that attractive, but I do. His sweetness, his caring. He has quirks, sure, but what hockey player doesn't? He has rituals and sometimes he goes quiet, usually leading up to a game or just following it.

Which makes this extra hard, because I know there's the part of him that's still processing the game. Still working through what he could've done differently.

I once asked him what he dreamed about, and he said hockey. No hesitation. Past games, made-up games, old tapes of playoff games where he self-inserts into the goaltender's position.

Such an easy answer, I almost questioned it as a lie. But I chose not to, at the time, because I didn't want to look deeper.

But now I'm wondering if he ever gets nightmares beyond losing the seventh game of the championship series. Probably. He's human.

A human who hasn't introduced me to any of his family, but still.

It's not like I brought him home to meet my father and his new girlfriend.

"I'm married," I blurt out.

He stops. His brow furrows.

"I'm working on getting a divorce, but it's... he's not cooperating." I wince. "I should've told you before. A while ago. But it's just been hard, and when you asked me to marry *you*—"

"Are you saying you don't want to marry me?" he interrupts.

"No! No, of course I want to marry you. I just can't until he signs the divorce papers." And I should definitely tell him who the *he* is, but I can't seem to say his name. "I'm sorry, Joel, I lied to you and I feel awful, but I didn't want to put off telling you any longer."

Another lie.

If Knox wasn't forcing my hand, I probably wouldn't have said anything. Ever.

Joel considers me carefully. The sleepiness has vanished, and he pinches the bridge of his nose. He's considering it. All sides of what I've told him.

"Do you want me to talk to him?" he asks.

I jerk. "Absolutely not."

"I just... Who did you marry? Who is this guy?" His voice is cautious. Like he's trying to work out a puzzle. "You're twenty-three, Aurora. When did you get married?"

"It happened years ago." I grip his hands tighter. "It's, um... Knox."

The realization crashes into him. I watch it morph his expression from slightly hurt to *furious* in a second, and he yanks his hands away from me.

"You're married to Knox Whiteshaw."

"Yes," I whisper. "I'm sorry."

"You didn't think that was something I should've known *months* ago?" He stands. "Jesus, Aurora, you're married to my teammate?"

"Your *new* teammate," I argue, rising to face him. "I didn't know he'd be traded to the Titans. I'm not a mind reader."

"And I'm a fool." He laughs. "Fuck. This explains his asinine behavior, at the very least. And I've been walking around clueless. Do you have any idea how that feels?"

I cringe, but he's completely right.

"This explains so fucking much," he says, more to himself than me. "Why, as soon as I brought you around to the guys, he started acting like an asshole toward me. Your little game with the two of us cost us *games*, Aurora. This is my career at stake."

I scoff.

The reason they lost their first game is because of Luke pulling the strings, not *me*. But I can't say that without giving away the rest of my lies, so I keep my mouth shut.

He takes my hand, squeezing it. "In case you need this spelled out for you—we're done."

He pulls the ring from my finger, staring at the diamond for a long moment. Then he tucks it in his pocket and disappears into the bedroom.

I stay still while he gathers the few things he has. Not that there's much. His Titans sweatshirt I wore to the last game, the toothbrush and change of clothes he brought over last night. He tosses everything into his hockey bag by the door and slings it over his shoulder, giving me one last cutting look.

It isn't until he slams my front door shut behind him that the reality crashes down on me, and the pain echoes through my body like a gunshot. I fall to my knees and cover my face with my hands, keeping the sob suppressed for as long as I can.

There's some part of me that acknowledges that, up until this month, I hadn't cried in years. And here I am, tears burning my eyes and refusing to fall, as my relationship crumbles before my eyes.

Knox was right. My relationship with Joel wasn't strong enough to withstand *him*.

If he had just signed the stupid papers, none of this would've happened.

After trying to practice slow breathing, the heels of my palms pressed to my eyes, I drop my hands and rise. I cross to my office and open the bottom drawer of my desk. There, in a small box, is the ring that Knox gave me when we were teenagers.

Sixteen and seventeen.

It's one of those silver Pandora rings, simple and clean and very clearly something a seventeen-year-old could afford with the help of his mother. Not something a professional hockey player would give his girl, like the big diamond that had sat on my finger declaring my engagement to Joel.

There are memories attached to this ring, though. Memories I don't want to resurface, but I can't fight it when they come flooding back.

I sit at my desk, the ring now out of its box and next to my typewriter.

The only way to get through this is to write about it. So I pick up where I left off and continue the story of Knox and me.

13
MANUSCRIPT

CHAPTER 2

Knox comes back the following night. He closes the door and tiptoes over. "You awake, Sunny?"

I smile. "Yeah."

"Good, because you know what tonight is?"

"Um..."

"Midnight," he prompts, taking a seat at the foot of the bed and revealing a small box. With a cupcake inside. "You'll officially be sixteen."

My smile falls. "Kind of sucks that I'm stuck in here."

"Well, we're making the most of it. So..." He fishes out a candle and lighter from his jacket pocket, setting all three aside. "For later," he promises. "But first, your present."

I sit up, wincing. My chest hurts, but my whole body feels bruised. My throat is raw from being intubated, my voice still a little raspy when I try to speak louder. And my hair has been up in a bun for the past twenty-four hours.

Why am I self-conscious?

Knox presents me with a tiny, wrapped package. I take it like it's fragile, carefully sliding my fingers under the taped edges and peeling it open with care.

It's a framed photo of me on the ice, locked arm in arm with my dad. He's smiling down at me, I'm cheesing at the camera.

It's from last year's season. Dad coaches squirts, and I help out. *Helped out*. Past tense.

We had a conversation today about my heart. About how, given the severity of the hole, intense exercise and impact could put my health at jeopardy. Hit in the right way, at the right time, and my heart could stop. The closure they inserted to close the hole in the wall of my heart, separating the chambers, could fail.

"Do you want to talk about it?"

"No." I cross my arms.

He nudges my leg. "But..."

Ugh. "Just because it's you," I whisper. "A few years ago, during my yearly checkup, my doctor heard a heart murmur. They did some testing and found I had a hole in my heart from birth. Minor. Until now, I guess."

I leave out that my parents are already stretched thin with finances.

"They put in something through my groin." My face heats when his gaze drops to my lap. "Um, like a catheter, it goes up the artery to my heart. I get to go home tomorrow."

He nods carefully. "So you have something in your heart."

"Yeah."

"Okay." He pauses. "I'm glad you're not dying."

I look away. "Jury's still out on the dying thing. My dad just banned me from playing hockey ever again."

He's suddenly a lot closer. His hand cups my cheek,

forcing me to face him again. "You can play vicariously through me, Sunny. Every time I'm on the ice, I'm skating for you."

A lump forms in my throat.

"I'm going to hold you to that."

14

KNOX

The bar is crowded. It's not really an excuse, but maybe an explanation for why I don't see her at first. That, and I'm distracted by the girl next to me. She's been flirting nonstop, although I have a feeling if I were to outright reject her, she'd just move on to one of my teammates.

We're celebrating a home game win. It was by the skin of our teeth; my goal tied us with two minutes to go, and then Jacob's goal in the last ten seconds of the game sealed the deal. It helped that I haven't seen Aurora in almost a week.

I'm well on my way to getting drunk. Celebrating the fact that she hasn't shown her face in a few games, too.

Haverhill's been particularly stoic. I spotted him talking to Lawson, one of the d-men, in hushed tones after practice. But besides that, he seems to be keeping to himself. He sure as shit didn't show up to drink with us.

Love life in peril, maybe?

But anyway. I sip my drink and lean back, smiling at the

girl, when Aurora appears. It's like the crowd just fucking parts for her.

She's in a tight, slinky black dress. It shimmers in the low lights. The top is tied behind her neck, and it plunges between her breasts, almost to her navel. She's showing way too much skin, and I can't take my eyes off her.

The dress stops mid-thigh. Her legs are toned and more tan than I expect, and she's strapped into daring heels that have to be five inches, at least.

She breezes past Royal Lawson, who checks out her ass on the way past. And Camden Church, who raises his eyebrows in surprise. Because they know her as Joel's fiancé, and he's not here.

Instead, her gaze is focused solely on me.

And when she drops into my lap, wrapping her arm around my neck and pressing her left hand to my chest, I think time stops.

There's a new ring on her finger. Or should I say, an *old* ring.

One that brings immediate flashbacks.

She smiles brightly. "Honey, I'm home," she sings. "Did you miss me?"

I narrow my eyes, ignoring the way my stomach twists. "What are you doing?"

"You're the one who wants to be married, Knox. I'm just being a good wife." She kisses my cheek with her blood-red lips before I can stop her.

The girl who was sitting next to me leaves without a word.

"Wife?" Church asks.

She drums her fingers on my chest. When she twists to face him, she makes sure to grind her ass against my groin.

She smiles at Church. I put my hand on her hip and squeeze. A warning, maybe?

My brain is still playing catch-up.

"It was our little secret," Aurora says in a fake whisper. "Knox is shy in that regard, although I bet you wouldn't know anything about that, right?"

"And Joel...?"

She sighs. Her whole face goes *crestfallen*.

I grip her hand and inspect the ring. She doesn't move as I twist it on her ring finger. But sure enough, I recognize it.

Why she kept it, though...

"She was trying to make me jealous," I find myself explaining to my teammates. The ones paying attention anyway. "And it worked."

She meets my gaze and smiles slightly.

Aurora McGovern *smiling* at me? Even though it's the barest hint of one, just a tic of the corners of her lips upward, I'll take it. I mean, I shouldn't want to take it. I should want to destroy her. And I'd think she would want to destroy me, too, now that she's showing up here without a fiancé.

But there will be time for mutual destruction later.

Right now, I just want to kiss her. And maybe push her limits, see how far she'll take this ruse. So I do, not caring that her lipstick is going to be all over my face in a matter of seconds. Not caring that we have an audience.

Actually, maybe boosted by that.

She leans into the kiss, relaxing against me. The rest of the room fades out, until it's just the feel of her lips on mine. I nip her, then coax my tongue into her mouth. She smells like lilacs but tastes like strawberries and tequila. I groan into her mouth, sliding my hand up her arm, to the back of her neck. Then into her hair, where I grip and pull and change the angle.

And she lets me.

Her nails dig into my arms, then my neck. Then my hair, tugging as sharply as I tug on hers. She shifts her dress up and swings her leg over, straddling me, never once breaking the kiss. The fucking glorious, epic kiss.

Until she breaks it off and whispers, "I told him just like you wanted."

"So?" I mumble, my word making our lips brush again. There's a haze of lust surrounding both of us. I've never been so turned on in my life, and from the look on her face... neither has she.

Interesting.

"So... the divorce papers are waiting," she says.

Ah.

"That's what this is about?" I pull her hair, tipping her head back. "You come here, tell my teammates we're married, then try to strong-arm me into a divorce?"

"I'm just waiting for you to follow through." Her eyes narrow. "Unless you always planned on going back on your word."

I laugh. I'm hard as a rock and *arguing* with her. Thank God she's straddling me, hiding my boner from the others sitting around us. Although we seem to be in our own little bubble.

"I'll follow through, all right," I murmur. "Wife, meet husband. It's foolish that we live in two different condos in the same building."

"Knox—"

"We'll compare, see who has the better one." It seems logical. "Although I've already seen yours. And, sunshine, I hate to tell you this..." I lean in. "But mine's bigger."

She rolls her eyes and ignores the innuendo. "I'm not moving in with you."

"Fine, I'll take the downgrade." I think on that, then shake my head. "Never mind. But right now, you need to skedaddle." I push her up, setting her on her feet, and rotate her away. My palm strikes her ass, making her jump. "Bye, *babe.*"

"Skedaddle?" She glares at me over her shoulder. But then she smiles. And when she sashays away, it isn't to the door.

It's to the bar.

"Dude." Jacob scowls at me. "What the hell?"

I shrug, wiping at my lip. There's lipstick there, sure enough. I stick my thumb in my mouth, tasting it. Imagining I'm tasting her again.

"Seems like my plan backfired."

And by that, I mean it seems Aurora's declaration scared away all the puck bunnies. Well, the ones who were interested in me. There are still some girls hanging around Lawson and Scofield.

Jacob seems ready to leave. Melody isn't with him, which was upsetting when he showed up without her. But he mentioned that she's been painting more at night. Then he said he wanted to fuck her against a canvas, and I tuned him out.

Sort of.

I mean, if he fucks her with paint everywhere, I think people might pay a lot of money for that shit. I would. Maybe not of them. They're my best friends. But... well, if Aurora covered herself in paint and rolled around on a canvas, I'd buy it just so no one else could get the impression of her tits or ass.

Ugh. I need to stop thinking about Aurora.

She's talking to someone at the bar. A guy.

And we're right back in the game.

"Hey—"

I ignore Jacob and stomp across the bar. Beth is there, too. She looks from Aurora to me, her eyes narrowing. I don't give a shit about her, just the asshole trying to talk to my girl.

Shit.

She's not my girl.

But she's not *not* my girl. She actually is mine. I changed my mind.

I married her, I get to keep her. I called dibs. That's basically what marriage is, after all.

"Walk away," I advise the man as soon as I'm up close. He's an ugly fucker. I'd assume he has some boring job in finance, maybe insurance. Nothing suited for Aurora.

He takes one look at me and scrams.

"Come with me." I hook my arm around Aurora's waist and practically drag her off the stool.

She stumbles into me, making some noise of protest, but she doesn't have much of a choice.

She ruined my buzz.

Outside. Back to the alley I first threatened... well, *questioned* her. I push her against the wall and stare at her a beat, then attack her mouth again.

I don't want to kiss her, but I'm pretty sure I'll stop breathing if I'm not inhaling her scent. If I'm not tasting her.

She arches into me. I grab at her waist, her hips. I squeeze her ass and lift her, and her dress rides up as she wraps her legs around me. She bites my lip hard enough to draw blood, and I tear my mouth away. I track bloody kisses down her jaw and neck, nipping until she's shifting against me.

"This is so wrong," she murmurs. "I don't want you."

"Yeah, right," I growl. "So hate fuck me, sunshine."

She stills. "I'm not going to fuck you, Knox."

"And I'm not going to fuck you either. It's a fucking saying."

"No, really." She shoves at my shoulder. "Not here. Not in a luxury bed. Not if you were the last guy on earth."

I slip my hand between our groins and shift her panties aside. She's fucking soaked. Her eyes flutter when I brush my finger over her clit.

"You don't want this, hmm?"

She's right, though. I'm not going to fuck her. I promised myself that six years ago, and I plan on sticking to it. Even if I come close to the line... even if I toe it. Even if I touch her with other parts of my body.

"No," she lies.

I think I like when she lies. I like that she convinces herself of something, even when the opposite is true. Because Aurora might say she hates me, might say she doesn't want to touch me, might say my dick is tiny, but we both know they're all lies. She doesn't hate me. She betrayed me, but she doesn't hate me. And she wants to touch me. That's why she's wearing my ring again.

Last and most important—my dick is *not* tiny.

I pull away, and her mouth drops open.

"How will I drive you crazy tomorrow?" I ask her. "The possibilities are limitless."

She shakes her head at me, and I shrug. What she did to me six years ago is far worse than anything I could do to her. Although I'm sure going to try to match it.

"You asked for this, sunshine. And payback is a bitch."

15
AURORA

"You know the best part about living in the same building?"

I groan and roll over.

Try to roll over.

Something catches me around the middle. A hand?

I blink in the darkness, trying to wrap my mind around what the fuck is happening. My arms are over my head, and my mattress is dipping to the side.

And there's Knox.

He sits even with my hip, holding my waist to keep me from going anywhere.

"I'll just tell you," he says. "The best part about living in the same building is that everyone has the same keys! Imagine that. So while *this* is my key..." He holds up one on an unfamiliar ring. It glints in the light that comes in through the windows behind him. "This is yours. They're the same shape, right?"

I lick my lips. "I assume you have a point?"

"Of course. It means, wife, that all I had to do to get into your apartment was get a bump key. It's like a master—"

"I know what a bump key is." I pull at my wrists, but they don't move. "Did you tie me up?"

"Handcuffs are coming in the mail next week," he says solemnly. "I figured my tie would do for now."

The funny part is that I don't even really care that he's tied me up. It doesn't feel *strange* or out of character. Not after he's put his hand on my throat, or made me choke on his dick in the plane bathroom, or kissed me until I saw stars at the bar.

Sneaking into my condo kind of sucks. It's definitely an invasion of privacy.

"I don't suppose telling you to get out would work?" I try.

He tilts his head, considering it. "Could you try begging? Maybe on your knees, with your mouth open..."

"Fuck off."

"What was that? You want to suck me off?"

I groan through my teeth. "Do you have a point, or..."

"Just fulfilling my husband duties and sexually satisfying my wife," he says. "According to my lawyer, that's required. So smile for the camera!"

I close my eyes just as he takes a fucking selfie of us, the screen going white to shed enough light on us. When I open them again, it takes a second for the white spots to recede.

"You are an asshole."

"Obviously."

All this time, and he hasn't touched me more than at my hip. Now, though, he pushes at the hem of my shirt. Lifting it higher, until it's up past my breasts.

"I was thinking about what you said," he says, more to my tits than my face. He leans down and licks my nipple, groaning a little.

It feels good. And bad.

And good.

He keeps lapping at it until it's stiff, and I can't help but try to squirm away. But his hand on my hip presses down, keeping me steady.

"Knox," I exhale.

He makes a noise in the back of his throat and finally moves down, kissing the scar. It tingles, the sensation never fully returning after the surgery. Lower, across my stomach and to my panties. Which he pulls down easily, past my knees and off my legs entirely.

"I was thinking about your toll." He shifts, moving my leg up. His breath hits my core. "I didn't pay it."

"That's okay—"

"I really want to pay it."

And then his mouth is on me.

His fingers dig into my thighs, my ass. Dragging me closer, until my arms are straight and I've got nothing to grab on to for purchase. The tie is tight around my wrists, and he's holding me hostage while his mouth—

I close my eyes. He licks and sucks with an expertise that makes me want to kick him. Because he learned how to do that somewhere, and I doubt it was a magazine. Or porn.

"You can stop now," I warn when my hips buck. "You should stop."

"I think I want to taste you come on my tongue." He looks up at me. "I think I want to hear it, too."

I blow out a breath. "Well, you're in for disappointment."

"Uh-huh."

"Yeah," I lie.

He goes back to my pussy. Which is really... I mean...

nope, words are failing me. My hips buck involuntarily again, and I try desperately to twist away from him. I'm going to have bruises from how tightly he grips my thighs and ass.

When his finger runs down my center, I groan. And it keeps going, until he pushes it against my asshole.

"Knox," I gasp. "Don't."

He sucks on my clit and thrusts his finger deeper, fucking my ass. Which, I'll be honest, is not something I was expecting to feel remotely good. But it does. He's doing something to me that I don't understand.

I hit a new dimension.

My vision and hearing go out, and who knows what I say. Or do. All I know is the extreme pleasure burning through me, and the way he brings me back down, the orgasm's aftershocks ringing through me.

He pulls away, and I go limp.

"You taste just as I imagined," he says, standing over me.

He leans down and kisses me. Open-mouthed, his tongue plunging into mine. I can't do anything but take it, and I taste myself on his lips. Everywhere. Until he's satisfied.

"Sleep well," he says on a laugh.

And he goes. He leaves the room, while I wait in silence. Even though my wrists are still tied, and I almost expect him to come back and undo the knots, I know he won't.

My front door closes.

I let out a groan. Because what the *fuck* was that?

Then I'm faced with getting free. I inch myself up the bed until I can get my mouth near the knot. I pull at random pieces until it loosens. And finally, I'm able to slip free.

I sit up quickly, yanking my panties up and my shirt down. I feel... raw. Exposed in a way I haven't in a long time.

And I don't like it.

16

AURORA

My phone buzzes.

I reach for it, sighing, but when I grab it... I realize it's not *this* phone that's going off. My heart skips, and I jump up and rush for the other one. It rattles on my desk, insistent, until I flip it open.

Yes, it's an old-school flip phone.

L: Knox can't play well tonight

My stomach is all but in my throat, and my fingers shake as I text back.

Me: What does that mean?

L: His coach is putting him on second line. If he pulls the shit like the last game, we'll be paying you a visit.

Uh-oh. Knox scored late in the game, with Jacob following it up. The visiting team barely had contact with the puck for the last three minutes of the game. Which was apparently a mistake.

I don't know what to do, and I've got no one to ask.

Knox wouldn't believe me. I mean, who would believe that the owner's son is rigging his own team to lose? How much money could he possibly be making from betting fraud?

I screw my eyes shut and try to think about that first conversation. I've done this so many times, recalling every little detail I can, but none of it is helpful. I was too drunk, and when I woke up my memory was hazy.

It's still hazy.

Me: Okay.

As far as I know, the team is leaving this morning for their away game. They're playing in North Carolina. Which means I have maybe an hour to intercept Knox.

Hmm.

I stare at the wall, my author brain kicking into gear.

Can I take him out of the game entirely? Or... I don't know. I putter around my kitchen, scroll my phone, but it's all hopeless.

Until I find the bottle of laxatives Beth gave me as a joke a few weeks ago. She said travel binds her up, which is completely too much information, but...

I laugh, then slap my hand over my mouth.

I can't poison Knox with laxatives, can I?

Would it kick in on time?

The fine print on the bottle says six to twelve hours, which would be perfect. So now I just need to figure out how to get them in Knox's system.

Think, Aurora, *think*.

Coffee. I know his coffee order.

It's probably not a good idea to combine with laxatives, but whatever. If it makes him play shittier—*pun intended*—then I'm all for it. And realistically, it's a lot less harmful than, say, admitting everything to him and hoping he goes along with it.

Fifteen minutes later, I'm walking back to the building

with my coffee in one hand and Knox's cold brew in the other. I don't have Knox's cell phone number, not that I would want it, but after pleading with the doorman for a minute, he tells me Knox's unit number.

And off I go. I make a pit stop at my apartment and mix in the laxatives, then take a nervous sip of my own drink. I leave it behind and head up two floors.

When I knock on his door, I'm hit with an unexpected flurry of nerves.

He cracks it open a minute later. He's wearing gray sweatpants—a girl's weakness, I'll be the first to admit—and nothing else. His chest is bare, his abs tightening and flexing under my gaze.

Six pack.

Pecs.

Damn.

I stare at him for a long moment, my mouth going dry.

Did he look like this in high school?

"Take a picture," he says. "It'll last longer."

"Funny." I make a face. "I'm not going to the game. And, um, I thought I'd just be nice for once and wish you good luck. Seeing as how I won't be there to distract you."

He squints at me, then the coffee. "Why?"

"Because..." I shrug. "I don't know. We're married. You won't divorce me. So isn't it better if we're civil?"

Knox seems to consider that. And for a second, hope expands in my chest. I don't need to be best friends with him. I just want some peace. He takes the coffee from me and sips it.

That's all I need. Him to drink the coffee, play terribly, and lose the game. But also, if we're offering a tendril of peace between the two of us, I wouldn't turn my nose up at it.

It would be a step back in the right direction, wouldn't it?

"Hmm," he finally says, his finger tapping on the cup. "No, I don't think so."

He slams the door shut in my face.

I blink rapidly a few times, my nose way too close to the wood for comfort. But it does justify the laxatives a little, so... I shake my head and frown, just in case he's watching, and head back to my condo.

Now I just need to hope that's enough to derail his game.

———

"Are you watching?"

"Yes, Aurora," Dad answers patiently. "What's going through your head?"

"Just that Knox is playing better than expected," I grumble.

Dad and I haven't talked hockey in a while. I was hesitant to even tell him about Joel, and then after he proposed, it seemed kismet to get back into the sport. Until Knox was traded to the Titans, of course. Then it felt more like the universe was giving me the middle finger than anything else.

When I asked Dad if he'd want to chat on the phone while watching a game, he was surprised. But then, it became normal. Part of the routine, in a way, but one of the best parts of it.

On the inside, I'm sweating. He doesn't look any worse for the wear, and I'd swear he drank that whole coffee. Even a few sips should've done the trick, maybe... I put in enough to give a horse diarrhea for a week.

I'm on my couch, wrapped in approximately four blankets. In a row in front of me, on the coffee table, is the extra cell phone, a bottle of tequila, margarita mix, and a half-empty glass. Because I've been drinking straight since the coverage started, and nothing has dulled my growing anxiety.

I mean, he *threatened* me. Luke, not Knox. Knox just ate me out 'til I *blacked* out. They're different.

The third period just started, and they're showing the bench of Titans. Knox has his helmet off, and he wipes at sweat dotting his brow. He looks pale, which gives me some comfort.

But he's scored already. Once in the second period.

The score is 3-1 in favor of Boston.

Suddenly, Knox is back on the ice with the line change, and he almost immediately is given the puck. I cover my face with my hands, peeking between my fingers, as he races for the goal.

It becomes a 2-on-1 race, and *bam*, he shoots and scores.

I swear.

"You're supposed to be a Titans fan." Dad laughs.

"Yeah," I mutter. "How's Ashley?"

Mom died when I was nineteen. It's been four years since her death, and Dad just started dating in the last few months. It was a bit upsetting at first, but then I met her. She's actually really nice. She seems good for him.

"She's coming over for dinner tomorrow," he says. "Her parents are in town from San Diego."

"Fun," I murmur. "Tell her I say hello."

"She misses you. I do, too, kiddo."

A lump forms in my throat again. "I miss you, too, Dad. I'll be back for Christmas."

That was always the plan. When I moved here, I

promised I would visit for at least one major holiday. And they're supposed to come here for Thanksgiving or Easter, depending on what they can get off of work.

The time on the third period slowly ticks down.

The score is still 3-2 Boston. And although Knox gets the puck again, the goalie comes out of the crease and checks him. *Hard.*

I cover my mouth. Knox goes down in a heap, sliding across the ice, and a whistle blows. Players fly at each other. It's bedlam for a moment. Fighting breaks out, and the camera zooms out to keep everyone in frame. Everyone except Knox.

Fucking camera angles.

Dad whistles. "Wow."

The refs finally get them separated. We get a shot of Knox being helped to the bench, blood pouring out of his nose. I let out a breath.

"He's always been tough," Dad advises. He can pick up on my worry easier than anyone else. Why wouldn't he? He's my dad. He's been with me through thick and thin, through the good times and the worst times.

I grimace. "He's the least of my concerns."

Dad snorts. "Okay, honey. Oh, Ashley is calling."

"Okay, I'll catch up with you tomorrow. I love you!"

"Love you, too. Hang in there, kiddo."

I set my phone aside and focus back on the TV, turning up the volume. The announcers are talking about some Boston rookie who went to college with Knox. I perk up as they zoom in on a roguishly hot guy—purely from an observational stance—with a scrape on his cheek. He seems to look straight through the camera, then turns and steps up into the bench.

Devereux, the back of his jersey reads.

A friend of Knox's, I think.

And yet, their teams are fighting.

If he went to school with Knox, then he must know Jacob, too. Now I find myself wishing I had gone to the game, if only to watch their interactions more closely.

Play resumes, and it feels like I'm holding my breath the whole time. Devereux scores with a wrist shot to the top corner, the puck getting past Joel on his glove side. It's a beautiful shot, I'll give him that much.

The final buzzer sounds.

I close my eyes. Boston wins, 4-2. But Knox still played well. Not enough of an upset... I couldn't actually tell if anyone was giving the game away.

Is it one player working with Luke?

Or someone more insidious, like the equipment manager messing with their stick lengths, or... I don't know. *Something.*

I doze off on the couch, twisting the questions around like a puzzle with no solution, and wake up abruptly to the sound of knocking on my front door. It takes me a minute to right myself, to rub my eyes and focus. I wrap one of the blankets around my shoulders and go to the door, peeking through the peephole.

There's no one there.

Frowning, I unlock the door and crack it open.

Immediately, someone out of sight shoves it inward. The door smacks into my face. I stumble backward, and a man steps inside.

"What the hell?" I try to stand tall, but my nose is smarting. "Get out of my—"

He moves faster than I expect.

His fist smashes into my face. Pain explodes through my head, and I hit the floor hard. He's on me in a heartbeat, his knee digging into my stomach as he hits me in the face again. Blood fills my mouth.

I try to raise my hands to cover my face, and he moves his assault to my torso. He kicks me in the stomach once, twice—

I let out a moan. Trying to beg him to stop, but I can't get the words out.

What is minutes or hours later, he stops. He nudges me onto my back, and I feel his gaze on my face. I crack my eyes open.

"Listen to directions next time," he says gruffly.

I've never seen him before, but the chill of *why* he just attacked me crystalizes.

He leaves without another word. The door clicks shut like it wasn't just complicit in the crime. My hands are shaking so bad, it takes me a moment to press them flat to the floor on either side of my body.

I'm going to throw up.

Everything hurts, but at the same time, I'm starting to separate from it. To keep the pain in a box in the back of my mind. Or maybe to leave my conscience there.

I roll onto my side and spit out a glob of blood. A tooth comes with it.

I cough and gag, covering my mouth with the back of my hand. I just spit out my *tooth*. I reach in my mouth and probe my molars, finding the broken one. I cough and spit again, resting my head on the floor.

My eyes burn, along with the need to just... I don't know. Lie here in misery. But if they did this to me, what would they do to Knox?

Luke knows we're married. And while he probably doesn't know the extent of our relationship, I can assume he thinks it was a mutual thing.

Which means Knox just became leverage...

Or maybe I'm the leverage?

I throw up without warning, barely leaning to the side. I haven't eaten much, so it's just the margaritas and bile. It burns worse coming up than it did going down. My stomach cramps. I groan, curling my arm around my ribcage.

Fear pricks at my skin, urging me to move. Above all else, I know I can't stay here. Not when he could come back and finish the job.

An unlikely scenario.

Rationally, unlikely. Emotionally? Terrified.

I force myself up. I'm not wearing shoes. The blanket I had around my shoulders is on the floor, and I bend to get it before the agony in my stomach stops me.

Fine.

After careful consideration, I go without. I only grab the fob to work the elevator and the key to get into my unit. I limp to the elevator and ride it up to Knox's floor, then make the long walk down to his end unit.

By the time I get there, I'm winded. I lean against his door and knock, already knowing that he's not going to be there. I hold my stomach and slide down the door. My watch captures my fast pulse.

I try to breathe regularly. In through my nose, out through my mouth.

He'll be back soon.

Maybe.

But I do think he would help me. Besides, I don't have anywhere else to go.

17
KNOX

I'm not sure how I'm going to live down nearly shitting my pants. *Nearly*. Jesus, I'd never run off the ice to the locker room bathroom so fast. It felt like a jet missile was trying to fire out of my asshole.

When I returned to the ice, I got some laughs and helmet pats. Because my teammates know the only reason you sprint off the ice in the middle of the game is for one reason.

Anyway.

I spent most of the flight home locked in the bathroom, emerging pale and tired and *pissed*. I ate my same game-day-ritual meal, chicken fettuccine alfredo approximately three hours and forty minutes before the first puck drop. I did my same warm-up, same *everything*.

Except...

Aurora gave me a coffee this morning. That deviated. Not that I don't normally get coffee, because I do. But... she gave it to me, and I should've flagged her niceness as something more nefarious.

"You okay?" Jacob asks, glancing over at me with a

small smile. "You need me to pull over?"

"Fuck off," I grumble. "Aurora poisoned me."

"That's quite the accusation."

We played one of our best friends, Greyson Devereux, tonight. I miss that quick-footed fucker, and it was nice to check his ass into the boards a few times. But only when his chirps got out of hand.

They won, which put most of us in a shitty mood.

Pun not intended.

"It's the only thing that makes sense," I insist. I explain about the coffee. And the previous coffee incident, in which I ended up wearing it.

We turn into the parking garage under the building. I have yet to buy a car in Denver. I had a sweet one in New York but ended up selling it instead of transporting it. Besides, I have Jacob.

"Come on," he sighs, shutting off the truck and hopping out.

I follow, slinging my bag over my shoulder. "My asshole burns," I complain.

"You shouldn't have taken a drink from her, then." He laughs. "She shows up on your doorstep with a wide smile and an offering? Assume it's poison. From now on."

Ugh.

He scans his key fob and hits the buttons for his floor and mine. We ride it up in silence, the doors opening smoothly on his floor. Where Melody most certainly waits for him in their condo, maybe naked. Not that I want to think about my best friend naked.

Speaking of which.

I lean into the opening. "You, me, Melody. Dinner tomorrow."

Jacob waves me off without looking back, and I smile. I

take that as a *yes*. Which is good, because I really need to ask Melody more questions about Aurora's book. I still haven't cracked it open.

The elevator doors close again, and I glide upward. I'm tempted to hit the button for *her* floor, but in the end I manage to resist. I'm angry, sure, but there will be time to get revenge. I'll concoct the best thing I can think of, a mastermind plan of agony for dear, sweet Sunny.

With that in mind, I practically skip out of the elevator and down the hall. Around the corner. My condo is at the end, a corner one with excellent windows on two sides. Aurora's doesn't have *that*. Hers is nicely decorated, but decoration can only go so far.

But there's someone slumped against my door.

My brows furrow, my steps slow, until I get closer.

Dark, red-brown hair. A slender figure.

Aurora.

But her face is bruised and swollen, her lip split. There's blood in her nostrils and chin, and her eyes are closed. Her chest rises and falls shallowly. Her arms are looped around her stomach.

"Sunshine," I breathe, suddenly rushing forward.

I fall to my knees beside her, not sure where to touch her. God, she looks *awful*. My hands hover over her, and my fucking stomach knots. This is a lot. I clench and unclench my fists, but she doesn't magically wake up at my presence.

How long has she been here?

"Aurora," I try, finally placing my palm on her shoulder and shaking it.

She jerks awake. Her eyes are swollen, nearly shut, and she blindly swings at me.

"Hey, hey." I catch her wrists as gently as I can. "It's me."

Her green eyes, the one with the splotch of blue that seems so much darker lately and her all-green one, burn into me. They seem more vibrant against the reddish-purple color of bruises.

"Knox," she tries. "I'm—"

"It's okay, you don't have to explain." I unlock my door, keeping her from falling inward. "I've got you, okay?"

Without waiting for her consent, I lift her into my arms. She goes tense for a moment, a groan hissing out through her teeth. I can only imagine what hurts. I need to see it, though. I need a clearer picture. I need to see what they did to her.

I carry her to the bathroom, setting her on the counter and maneuvering her so she won't fall forward.

"Hold on to me," I advise. I take her hands and put them on my shoulders.

Her grasp is weak. I sidestep and grab a washcloth, twisting the tap to hot water. Her hand slips around to the back of my neck.

"What are you doing?"

"Cleaning you up to see the damage." I touch her nose, feeling from the bridge down to make sure it's not broken. It feels okay, which is good. I'm shit at resetting noses. My mom had to do it to me once, and my coach another time.

No thank you.

She sighs and leans back against the mirror. "I lost a tooth."

I pause.

The rage that overtakes me is like a windstorm. She's in shock. It's obvious because she's not trembling or scared. She's just staring blankly at me, her eyes dull. And the rage reminds me that someone did this to her. She didn't trip and fall down the stairs.

Someone hurt her.

I grip the counter with both hands, leaning forward and practicing my deep breathing. Because this fickle emotion is irrational and all-consuming, and I don't want to do something stupid.

Now I understand why my brother did what he did when someone threatened Willow.

A pinprick of guilt stabs me.

Now I'm Miles in this situation, having driven Joel away to claim the girl for myself. And obviously I didn't really give a shit about Willow... I mean, I dated her for a year because I wanted to win a bet.

And I wanted to get back at my brother.

But now Aurora is in front of me, awakening all these feelings I'd been repressing. Not just toward her, but toward everyone.

I don't like it.

"I didn't know where else to go," she says in a weird monotone. "I'm sorry."

"Who did this to you, Sunny?"

She flinches. Just a little. I grip her chin and force her to look at me, ignoring the pain in her eyes and the hiss of breath she lets out. Then, something changes.

"I don't know," she lies.

I know her, and I sure as shit know her lies. She doesn't want to tell me the truth?

"Fine," I bite out.

I wet the cloth with hot water and, keeping hold of her chin, clean her face. She cringes or winces every time I brush it across her skin, but eventually she just squeezes her eyes shut and lets me get the blood off her face.

"Take your shirt off," I order.

She tries, but her face contorts as soon as she tries to lift her arms above her shoulders. After watching her struggle for a long moment, I knock her hands away and grip the collar.

Her eyes widen. "Don't—"

Rip.

"Again?" She sighs. "Stop ruining my shirts."

It's satisfying, though. Her heavy, full breasts are bare to me, and my breathing stalls out. Her nipples tighten, pebbling in the cool air. She's not thin, exactly, but soft in all the right places. Which I knew from the revealing dress she wore the other night, and seeing her naked in her bed, but my brain has gone all fuzzy. It takes all my willpower to force my gaze away from them. Away from the vertical scar between her breasts, too, and the healing scabbed line beside it.

Her sides and stomach are already an ugly motley patchwork of green and purple.

"Kicked." She clears her throat. "I'm actually feeling better."

I'm going to track down whoever did this and flay them alive.

"Can you just…" She slides off the counter. "Help me back to my condo? I didn't want to stay there alone, but I shouldn't have come here."

"No." I don't move, and it puts us chest to chest.

Fuck, her bare chest to mine. I look down at her. She could be internally bleeding. She lost a tooth. She's—*she's terrified*. She might hide it well, but there's no part of her that wants to go home.

"I know what you look like when you're scared, Sunny," I whisper.

I take her hand, a little shocked to find she's still wearing my ring. She wasn't when I tied her up the other night. I run my finger over it, then step back. Putting breathing room between us so my mind will work again.

"You're staying here so I know you're not going to die." I eye her like she might just collapse in front of me. "Did you bring your key?"

She nods, pulling it and the fob from her shorts pocket.

I palm them. She follows me to the living room and sinks onto the couch gingerly. It's late, well past midnight, but neither of us acknowledge that. Her shirt is still hanging open, not that she seems to care about that either.

In all honesty, she seems out of it.

Do I call the police? Why didn't she?

"Are you involved in something that's preventing you from calling the police?" I ask.

She twitches.

"Aurora."

"Don't call the police, Knox." She meets my gaze. "Please."

We stare at each other for a long time. A minute, at least. It's not really that long in hindsight, but it is a long time when you're not blinking. And sometimes I feel like I just need to keep my eyes open wide whenever she's around, one, because I don't trust her not to stab me the millisecond my eyes are shut, and two, because I don't want to miss a thing.

Her face is going to be worse in the morning.

"Ice." I snap my fingers. Ice always helps after fights, and this was a fight. A one-sided fight, but still. I wrap a bag of frozen peas in a hand towel and place it in her palm. "Put it on your face. I'll be right back."

She nods and rests her head against the back of the

couch. I stand there and watch until she lifts it and gingerly presses the makeshift ice pack to her cheek.

Then I head to her condo.

The door seems intact. Meaning it wasn't kicked in, the lock wasn't picked. She might've opened it to her attacker, or at least left it unlocked. Inside appears the same as the last time I saw it, too. Minus the key details: blood on the floor. A streak, a glob. A tooth.

My stomach churns.

She threw up, too.

I dial Jacob's number.

"What?" he asks. "You run out of TP?"

"Funny. No. Someone attacked—" My throat closes before I can get her name out.

"You? Are you okay?"

"Not me. Aurora. I'm standing in her condo." I give him the number, knowing I only have to wait a few minutes. That's a perk of living in the same building as my best friend.

I stash my phone and don't move any farther into her space. Everything is brightly colored. The deep-blue velvet couch with a pale-yellow, knit blanket folded over one back cushion. It's so... well, *sunny*.

How I manage to smile at that is a miracle.

Jacob enters and stops short. "Damn."

I glance back, my smile quickly fading. He changed into shorts, a plain t-shirt, and slides. With socks. His hair is messed up, which means I probably interrupted something.

Sorry, Melody.

"Who was it?" he asks me.

I wish I fucking knew. All I can do is shake my head, and then an idea—that there is someone who *would* know—bursts to life. I leave the condo in a hurry and jab my finger to call the elevator. At this time of night, no one's used it since Jacob. It opens immediately.

He joins me, raising an eyebrow.

"Jerry," I say gravely.

"The doorman? I don't really interact with him. Is he on the night shift?"

Oh, fuck. "Probably not."

Still, we make the trip down and talk to the overnight guy and determine that Jerry clocked out at eleven-thirty. There was a little overlap between the two guys, the latter being more security than doorman. He sits behind the receptionist desk with a radio strapped to his hip and shrugs when we try to question him further.

Back in the elevator, Jacob slaps my shoulder. "Go take care of Aurora. There's nothing else we can do tonight. We'll talk to Jerry tomorrow."

Right enough.

Except, I hesitate outside my door.

Like she's going to bite?

No.

Shaking my head at the irrationality, I unlock the door and drop my key and hers on the side table. I kick off my shoes and find her passed out on the couch, the bag of peas resting on half her face.

Her breath whistles with every exhale, her sleep apparently deep.

Which means she feels safe here?

I slip past her and into the bathroom, showering and doing my best to ignore the bloody washcloth in the sink. I pull on clean sweatpants and flop in bed.

Then get right back up again.

Because... well.

I can't just leave her out there.

18

AURORA

Everything hurts.

This is worse than waking up after the emergency surgery, because at least then I had drugs. Right now, the vibrating pain radiates through my whole body. There's a noise buzzing in my ears.

"Pain meds."

Knox's rough voice overrides the buzz.

That gets my eyes opening. Well, one eye. The other cracks a little, but I can't see much through my eyelashes. And the rest of my face refuses to cooperate.

"You look like you went through a meat grinder, sunshine." He cradles the back of my neck and guides me up without asking. He runs his thumb along my lower lip, pulling my mouth open. In goes a few pills, and the cool rim of a water glass touches my lip a moment later.

I swallow, covering his hand holding the glass and tipping it higher. My throat is sore, although I don't remember being choked... or screaming.

"Enough," I finally mumble. I push his hand away. "I'm fine."

"You're the opposite of fine, and you're going to talk to me. Right now."

Okay, maybe I am the opposite of fine, but that doesn't mean I'm going to tell him everything that's happened.

"I don't want to drag you into it," I eventually say.

"Consider me dragged." He plants his hands on his hips. "Either you tell me now, or I'm going to keep you here until you do. And trust me when I say I think I'd prefer the second option. There are so many more ways to torture you when we can get up close and personal... don't you think?"

I shudder. "Um... Yeah. No, you're right. It was some guy I met on a dating app."

"You're such a bad fucking liar," he snaps. His gaze drops to my chest, then back up to my face. "Well, you're asking for it."

I shake my head and push the blankets off, belatedly realizing I'm not wearing pants. Thank God for full-coverage panties. And then the memory of Knox ripping my shirt in half comes back, and I automatically cover my chest. My fingers touch a zipper.

I'm in a zip-up sweatshirt. Oversized.

Knox-sized.

My face heats. And with it, the ache increases.

"I'm going home now," I say. "Get out of the way."

"You're going to go like that?" He ogles my legs.

"Yes," I snap. "I don't give a shit. And you're the one who took my clothes anyway."

He grunts. "You had blood on your shorts."

I tip my head back and squint a little, trying to judge what emotions are hiding under his stoic expression. He hasn't changed that much—and even though he may hate it, I can still read him.

Angry.

Worried.

Confused.

"You're wondering why I came to you?"

He shrugs. "You could've called anyone."

"My husband was only one floor up." I glance away. "I didn't want to explain to the police and make it worse."

"Make *what* worse, Aurora?"

I don't like him saying my real name. It's too serious. And yes, this is a serious situation. But he's never really called me by it before. It scrapes against me the wrong way, and he seems to notice the reaction.

"Aurora," he repeats.

Jesus.

"I saw something I shouldn't have," I hedge. "And they wanted to drive a message home."

"Uh-huh."

"Yep." I move past him.

Try to, anyway.

He blocks me, gripping my upper arms and walking me backward. Until my legs catch on the bed. He releases me with the tiniest shove, and I fall. It doesn't hurt completely, but my ribs protest my sudden gasp that accompanies it.

I curl my arm around my torso and glower at him. "Not funny."

"Totally not funny," he agrees.

"You're a blabbermouth." I point to him. "If I tell you this, you're going to tell all your friends. And then you'll end up telling everyone else, too."

He glowers at me. "My friends are actually helpful in situations such as this." He checks his watch. "Actually, we need to go."

He grabs clothes from his dresser and flings them at me. "Put those on."

Sweatpants that are guaranteed to be too big. I glance down at my chest and zip up the sweatshirt the rest of the way, to my throat, scowling at him. But I put on the pants and roll the waistband down until I'm not drowning in fabric.

"Great. Come on."

"Where?"

He sighs. "You didn't even bring shoes." He tosses flip-flops down in front of me. "We're not going out, if that's what you're worried about."

"I'm not worried at all," I argue. But I'm moving, sliding my feet into the oversized sandals. I lead the way out of his bedroom, into the main part of his condo. That seems an awfully lot like mine, just in reverse. And way more windows.

I didn't notice that last night. But now, sunlight streams in through the huge floor-to-ceiling windows on two sides.

Corner unit. Should've known.

"Lucky," I mutter.

"Not so lucky when even the sun reminds me of you," he replies under his breath.

I ignore that.

We head down the hall to the elevator, and I glance up at him. His hair is a mess of curls, like he's run his fingers through it a million times. There's scruff on his cheeks and shadows under his eyes.

I haven't looked at myself in the mirror, and I don't really want to know.

It's really fucking tempting to ask how the game went. But I'd rather not remind him of the laxatives he's no doubt pinned on me. Rightly. But still.

He loops his arm through mine, pulling me toward the door.

And the door*man*.

"Jerry," he calls.

I gulp. A lump forms in my throat, and I suddenly have a feeling I know exactly why we're here. I dig my heels in, but I have no traction with these stupid shoes and the fabric that's swallowing up my legs.

The doorman turns to us, and immediately his normally tan face goes a sickly shade of green. He steps back on reflex. "Ms. McGovern, are you—?"

"Save it," Knox snaps.

"I must really look like shit," I joke.

Knox steps in front of me, so I can only see Jerry's face over his shoulder. I huff at his back, but he ignores it.

"You let someone in yesterday," Knox says to him. "Maybe they asked about Aurora's condo? Which one it is?" He glances over his shoulder at me. "You're known to give out condo numbers, aren't you, Jerry?"

Jerry shakes his head frantically. "No, no, I didn't—"

"Does her face say you didn't?" His voice is colder than I've ever heard it. "Did you have any inkling of what the man was going to do when you let him go up to her condo?"

"I—"

"Is there a problem?" The manager has appeared, hurrying forward with a slight frown. And then he sees me, and he, too, goes pale. "I heard you were inquiring about Gerald's next shift, Mr. Whiteshaw, but are you accusing...?"

"I'm accusing *Jerry* of letting up someone with malicious intent toward my wife," Knox growls. "And I will not stand for it. We live here. We pay a lot to be here. I expect, at the very least, a decent measure of security. Give me one good reason not to involve the cops?"

The manager's mouth gapes. Open, closed, like a fish out of water. Finally, he seems to make a decision, because he clears his throat and straightens his suit. "Jerry, take a fifteen-minute break. Mr. Whiteshaw, if I see a single hair on his head misplaced, you will be stonewalled. I promise you that."

Knox considers it, then nods. Jerry seems slightly green, but he steps outside.

And I... don't follow.

Because I don't want to know if my doorman was involved in letting Luke's lackey up to my condo. I don't want to know what Knox is going to threaten him with, although I could certainly use my imagination.

Instead, I do what I've wanted since I woke up: I go home.

19
KNOX

"Here's the thing, Jerry," I say, leaning one shoulder against the cold brick of the alleyway. He led me here, but I'm more than happy to use it to my advantage. He's blocked in at this angle.

And while I'm not the greatest goalie, I can keep one man from passing me.

"You know him. You saw him. And the sooner you start talking—"

"I got a call," Jerry says. "To let him up. He didn't say anything about Ms. McGovern's place. Didn't even ask. I just got a call saying that it was okay to use my fob and send him up to the fifteenth floor."

"Which is *Aurora's* floor, Jerry."

He shrugs helplessly. "This was way above my paygrade, Mr. Whiteshaw, I assure you."

He's sweating.

"Tell me about this caller. You know them?"

"I do."

"And they have the authority…?"

"Yes, yes, of course. Please, I didn't realize—I feel

terrible about what happened to Ms. McGovern. But I had no idea."

"Who called?"

He stills. "I can't—"

"I don't give a shit about what your manager said, Jerry. Who. Called?" I step forward. For once, I wish I took after Miles and carried around a damn folding knife. Not that this situation really calls for it. I'd be an idiot to threaten him with a knife in broad daylight. And what if that just made him clam up instead?

My movement is intimidating enough, I suppose. Because he stumbles back and raises his hands in surrender.

I just eye him. I mean, jeez, he's terrified. And I haven't even done anything.

"Why are you scared of me, Jerry?"

"I like you, Mr. Whiteshaw. But after I tell you, I'm going to either lose my job or my life. And I'm sorry for that. I'm so sorry—"

"Who called you?" I interrupt. "Focus."

"Luke Abernathy."

Well, fuck my uncle.

He's the Titans' owner's son—the one I caught Aurora talking to the other night. He doesn't really have a hand in the day-to-day business of owning a team. Neither does his dad, for that matter. They're the money, and our coach is the true talent.

But if he's meddling around with Aurora, it means she knows something she shouldn't.

So what is Luke Abernathy up to?

"He wasn't the one you let in, though, right?"

Jerry shakes his head quickly. "No. No, sir."

I bite my tongue. "Anything else?"

"No—"

I turn on my heel. Aurora's injured because she got herself into something. I don't know what, but I do believe she probably walked into shit.

Speaking of shit...

Can I really take revenge on an injured girl?

With a sigh, I realize: *nope*. I'm not that much of a monster.

But then I take my keys out, and I thumb the newest addition. The bump key that will get me into Aurora's. And I smile to myself. Because I can wait, and then it'll hit her when she least expects it.

20

AURORA

The following weeks pass in a blur of writing, hiding, and little travel. I don't leave the building much at all, just quick walks to get coffee or groceries, then right back inside.

Thanksgiving came and went. Dad wanted to fly out, but I insisted that it would be better if I came home. He and his girlfriend were doing some lowkey meal, and I confessed that I missed my old bed.

He laughed at that. And sure, it was a tired twin mattress in an outdated room that was last decorated when I was fifteen, but it was mine, and I needed some better nostalgia than Knox Whiteshaw.

So I went home. I ate turkey and helped Ashley make mashed potatoes, stuffing, cranberry sauce, green bean casserole. I forced myself to laugh at the yellowing bruises lingering on my cheeks and abdomen and wave off their concern.

We went to the doctor, who made sure I wasn't bleeding internally or dealing with a broken nose. Then to the dentist, who was able to fix my tooth. The full thing didn't fall out—it *broke*. They had to special order a crown, but once it came in and was secured, the dentist called it good.

And when I flew back to Denver, stepping into my empty condo felt... odd. Home and not, all at once. I couldn't swallow for the longest time, just standing in the foyer and wondering what the hell happened to me.

The blood and vomit from my attack is gone. Not even a trace on the floors. The manager had a professional cleaner come out and take care of it while I watched from the couch, blankets curled around me.

But I can *feel* the memory of it, and I can't seem to shake it.

So I go from never leaving my condo to not being able to stay in it for longer than a few hours. I get a hotel room after Thanksgiving. I spend my days at coffee shops or in the lobby of the hotel, my clunky, pink typewriter and stack of paper slowly becoming a grievance to lug around.

My book is still selling. My inbox is cluttered with unanswered emails, a thousand people wanting a thousand different things. I don't know how to keep up with it, so I don't. I let the guilt fester every time I close the app without reading or answering a single thing.

The first week of December, I meet Beth at her apartment for coffee. My bruises are mostly gone, my ribs mostly healed, my ego mostly intact.

We catch up. I omit anything about being injured, although she asks if I had a nose job.

Nope, I answer, then change the subject in a hurry.

The weather officially turned. We had our first big snowfall, almost a foot of crisp white snow coating Denver. For a few days, the city sparkled.

And all the while, I don't see Knox.

I've thought about him, though. It seems like all I'm doing is living in the past, picking through every memory I can of the two of us. Every stage of the game, up until the end.

But I don't rush it.

When I try to shift toward some other story, like a sequel to my breakout hit that focuses on a side character, I can't do it. The words just halt.

Until I go back to *him*.

I guess saying I haven't seen Knox is a lie. Because I've seen him every few nights for the past month on my television. The phone Luke gave me has remained quiet. I half expected him to show up and say something to me.

But that would give it away, wouldn't it? That he's part of the plot.

So while I write, I also muse about the inner workings of his operation. I keep it circulating in the back of my mind, then finally draw it on a piece of paper.

At the center is someone I don't know. A big question mark, because Luke referred to a boss. Straight out from the boss is Luke. Luke's connected to the guy I saw at the club, who supplies money? He said something about getting money together.

Under him, I write: *Bank?*

Also connected to Luke is the assistant coach. Whether or not he's actually the man Luke has on the inside is up for debate, but I saw them talking to each other in the hallway that one time. So he's messing things up for the Titans, but clearly not enough to cause losses anymore.

Unless the betting has swung in the other direction, then they're letting the Titans win again.

I tap my finger against my chin, then fold the paper and shove it into my bag.

When I arrive back at my hotel at the end of the day, my door is cracked open. I stop and drop my heavy, typewriter-laden bag in the hall and fish the pepper spray out of my purse.

I push the door open as quietly as possible, creeping in. My thumb is on the spray, ready to press—

"It's just me." Knox flicks on the bedside lamp, illuminating the room. "Jesus, Sunny, were you going to Mace me?"

"Better than the Taser." Which is also in my purse. I go and retrieve the bag I left in the hall, then move the lock so the door can fully close. "How'd you find me?"

"Well, it took three weeks." He frowns. "Don't you ever go home?"

"No."

"Oh." He stares at me like he can't fathom it. "Why?"

I cross my arms. "You're not seriously asking me that question."

He nods, accepting that. Accepting my answer, or whatever he assumes my answer is. I mean, I got beat up there. My face looked like it went through a meat grinder, my dental bill was insane, and *yeah*, the nightmares that were plaguing me were enough to make me run away.

If he doesn't understand that, he doesn't have to. Although it would be nice if he did without asking in the first place.

Until he opens his mouth and says the one thing I don't expect.

"Luke Abernathy."

I stop.

"Yeah, thought that name might get a reaction." He narrows his eyes. "Or a non-reaction." He lifts the black flip phone I had left charging. "He texted, you know."

Shit. Everything in me goes hot and cold all at once. A little *danger* siren screaming in my ear. Warning me not to drag Knox into this. Not to drag *anyone* into this.

I scramble for the phone, but it puts me in close proximity to Knox.

And that's my mistake.

He wraps his arm around my waist and flings me onto the floor. He's on me in an instant, wrenching my arms behind my back. My cheek presses into the rough carpet, and I try to remember to breathe.

It's not painful.

Uncomfortable, but not *painful*. I don't think I could escape his hold if I struggle, so I just freeze. Fight or flight, I pick the third option. The one that immobilizes me.

"'Time to pull more strings with your husband,'" he reads, leaning over me and running his lips across my ear. "Now why is Luke Abernathy, the Titans' owner's son, asking you to pull strings with me?"

I can't answer.

I press my lips together.

"Are you in danger, Sunny?"

Tears burn the backs of my eyes, and I swallow hard around the lump in my throat. "I don't suppose you're going to ride in and save the day again."

"I'll save you and condemn you," he replies. His tongue flicks out, licking the sensitive spot just behind my earlobe. "I promise you that, sunshine. You're going to know true darkness when I'm done with you. But you'll be safe from all the demons in the world. Except me."

21

KNOX

"I got you to break things off with the fiancé."

Joel. I don't want to think his name, let alone say it. I trace my finger down her spine. I've got her wrists in one hand, my grip strong enough that it must be on the painful side. Her cheek is flat on the hotel carpet floor, and I don't even want to think about how many germs are down there.

"You walked into Blood and Cherry and told my whole team that you were Mrs. Knox Whiteshaw."

The bar the Titans always go to. The one owned by her friend, Beth. In high school, she was always hanging around Sunny with her low-cut shirts and push-up bras, trying to attract any attention she could. How those two ended up friends—and somehow *stayed* friends, knowing what I know about Beth—is beyond me.

"Dear wife," I continue, tracing the back of her shirt collar. "You made a mistake when you told everyone that you're married to me. Because now I'm going to claim it, too."

Her breath hitches.

I sweep her hair off her neck and lean over her. She's not as slender as the girls who typically chase the hockey team. She's got a softness that I haven't felt in a while. A little padding on her hips and waist, her breasts full but not large. I shift my weight and roll her under me, sitting back down on her hips. Leaving her hands free.

She stares up at me, her auburn hair fanned out around her face, and her lips part. "I don't really know what you mean by that."

She tried to disappear on me. For weeks, she's been *gone*. Evading our building. She even went home for Thanksgiving. My mother called me, said she'd seen Aurora home with her father. I pretended not to give a shit, although I can say with certainty that my mom saw right through me.

But how could she just leave?

It makes me realize how much I crave being around her. The glimpses of her over the past month were micro doses of her toxin. I'm thoroughly addicted, and my willpower is not strong enough to keep away from her.

To be fair, I held out for almost a month.

There's a tracker in her tooth. Our local dentist back home required a little persuasion, and a lot of money, but in the end he did it. So while she was home, and then later at hotels and coffee shops and the library, I watched her movements on my phone.

Obsessed doesn't cover it. I feel sick, inside and out.

I push up her shirt, exposing her sports bra. Instead of cutting through it like I did the other one—I'm fresh out of box cutters anyway—I shove it up. Everything to her neck. She squeaks, the reaction belated, and tries to knock my hands away.

She's mostly healed. The cut that I gave her is gone, just

a thin pink line beside the thicker surgery scar remaining. The bruising around her torso and stomach is all gone except a vague hint of greenish-yellow across her ribs. Her face is clear.

Maybe it's just a mental thing?

Which wouldn't be the worst thing in the world. I can break her of that fear... or lean into it. I run my hands over her ribcage.

"This is improper, Knox," she breathes. She's doing a poor job of struggling against me. In fact, she's really not struggling much at all.

Curious creature.

I've put my hands on her breasts, and damn. Nothing is going to pry them away.

My dick thickens in my jeans, trying to stand up straight. Not that I'd fuck her. She can choke on it any day, but her pussy can grow fucking cobwebs before I touch it. The rest of her, though... *fair game.*

I pinch her nipple. Her eyelashes flutter, her back arches slightly. Even though she doesn't want to be, she's okay with me touching her. Manhandling her. It's evident in how she doesn't resist me.

I move one hand higher, until it's wrapped around her throat.

Her pulse point is oh-so delicious. The rapid beat is enough to set my adrenaline on edge.

And that's why I squeeze. Cutting off the blood flow to her brain.

Her mouth pops open. There's the fear I need.

I push two fingers into her mouth, pressing down on her tongue. "Suck my fingers like you'd suck me off."

My voice is husky, I'm turned on to the millionth degree. By *her*, yes, but also by the panic that's widening her eyes. She looks at me with those eyes, pleading with me.

Like I'm not serious?

I am.

"Suck, sunshine," I order. "Or pass out, and you won't know what I do to your body. You'll just wake up alone in this hotel room..."

Tied to the bed, waiting for someone else to discover her and set her free.

Vicious lust rushes through me.

And then, just when I think she might bite my fingers off, she closes her lips around them. Her tongue laps at the pads of my fingers, tentatively exploring my two digits. Her cheeks hollow with the force, and it makes me hard as stone.

Her eyes roll back in her head, and she goes limp.

Whoops.

I release her throat and lean over her, touching her cheeks. Then patting them harder. This is what I wanted, right?

Her eyes snap open, and she jerks up.

I just barely dodge, and her forehead clips my jaw. I let out a hiss, but at least she missed my nose, which she was probably undoubtedly going for. Or my teeth. Not that I'd have a problem losing one of them.

Like hers.

Speaking of that.

I grab her jaw and force her back to the floor. I squeeze until her mouth opens, avoiding the pressure, and I lean down over her face.

"How's the new tooth?"

"W-what?" It comes out a bit mushy, seeing as how I'm holding her mouth open.

I spot the new tooth in the back.

"It cost a pretty penny," I murmur, releasing her jaw. "To bribe your dentist into installing the tracker."

Maybe I wouldn't have told her if I wasn't faced with her naked breasts.

Her eyes widen. "And it took you three weeks to find me?"

"I was exercising some self-control." I stick out my lower lip. "Did I not do a good job?"

She squirms under me, her expression stricken. I don't know if she wants to throw up or rip the tooth out—or both.

But feeling the need to prove it, I open the app on my phone and flash her the screen.

"No hard feelings, sunshine. I'd just rather know where you are at all times."

"Because you're insane," she spits. "Get *off* me."

"Get off?" I nod slowly, undoing my jeans. "Good idea."

"Knox." She narrows her eyes at me. "You're a grade-A asshole."

"Tell me something that'll make me soft." I grip my dick through my boxers, and her eyes go down to it. "Try talking down to me again. I dare you. See if it makes a difference."

"You're fucking crazy."

"You'll be calling me other things when I'm taking your mouth in the middle of the night. Actually, scratch that, because you won't be able to talk at all." I grin at her.

I spit in my hand and get to work. It's kind of a surreal experience, jacking myself off in front of Aurora like this. I mean, we've come a long way since mutual masturbation as teenagers. And making out in cars.

"I'm not sure why you think you'll have access to my mouth," she whispers, trying to wiggle free. "Your cock should come with a warning. You know, like those tiny kid toys. Choking hazard."

"You know all about that," I groan.

I beat my stick until precum oozes out, and I take it and smear it across her lips without thinking. She exhales sharply, twisting her head away.

"How's your heart, Aurora?"

"Fine."

My gaze drops to the scar in the middle of her chest.

Fine.

Doubtful.

"How's your brother, Knox?"

I stop.

And stare.

And try to figure out if she's *fucking serious*.

But the more we glare at each other, the more I realize that she's succeeded in fucking with my head.

Because I lose my erection as fast as I lost any desire to play nice with Aurora McGovern.

So this time, when I wrap my hand around her throat, I don't stop squeezing until she's unconscious.

22

AURORA

I wake up in a weird position.

I never sleep on my back, with my legs outstretched and my arm above my head. My other one is curled over my stomach. I shift and roll, and there's a clinking noise that follows me.

How did I get to bed? The last thing I remember is... asking Knox about his brother. Which just kind of came out of me. Mainly because his brother and him are so fucking competitive, and I figured thinking of Miles would be like thinking of a grandma while trying to get off.

It worked, but then he apparently didn't like that. I swallow carefully, although my throat doesn't really hurt. Not as much as it does after waking up from being under anesthesia.

I open my eyes, blinking in the darkness.

When I pull my wrist, it doesn't move. I draw my feet up, but they barely come. I can bend my knees, and then they're stopped. With my one free hand, I lift the blanket and try to find out what's trapping me.

Cuffs. Leather ones locked around my ankles. I try to

adjust my eyes to the darkness faster, but it's too much. Just oppressive black that quickens my breath.

If there's one thing I didn't count on, it's the sudden claustrophobia.

There's a flash of brilliant white. It fades back into darkness, and my eyesight is worse off than it was. I let out a whimper, covering my face with my free hand.

"I knew you were awake."

I cringe.

The edge of the bed dips, and I unwillingly shift toward Knox. He takes my hand and guides it above my head, strong-arming me when I resist.

"As we speak, movers are boxing up all your shit and delivering it into my condo. They've been instructed to ignore any moaning, though. Don't you worry."

"What—"

The intense *buzz* cuts me off. I jerk, although nothing touches me. Just his one hand lingering on my wrist, his nail running under the cuff.

"Scream all you want. No one's coming to help you." He pulls at the edge of my panties.

I flinch. I hadn't realized I was wearing anything—there's a whisper of sheets against the rest of my skin, especially my bare breasts. The thought should make me panic, but instead I just... curl my fingers into my palms and try not to give him what he wants.

Which is, arguably, any reaction.

"Oh, one more thing."

He puts something over my ears. Headphones? They're thick, and there's a band across the top of my head, and after a second, everything goes silent.

I can't hear anything—not even Knox.

He touches my panties again, shifting them aside. My

body breaks out in goosebumps at the cool liquid and object that fits almost perfectly against my clit. I'm afraid he's going to push it inside me, but it doesn't go in. It's just held in place by my underwear.

It buzzes to life. I don't hear it—*I can't hear anything*—but I feel it. It's concentrated directly on my clit, a powerful sucking force I have never felt before. My back comes off the bed, and only the restraints keep me from falling off it.

I come too fast. It's like a steam-engine train blasting through me, pleasure turned up to level fifteen. I think I make noise. How could I not? I feel the groan vibrate in my throat, my chest. I've never used a vibrator before, but now I'm regretting it. Because *holy shit.*

When I eventually sag back down, he doesn't shut off the toy like I thought he might. Or rather, like I hoped he would. It stays steady against my throbbing, newly sensitive clit.

The bed lifts.

He's leaving?

There's a crack of light, and I latch on to the sight of him slipping out into the hall.

The door closes again, leaving me to... *this.*

I don't know how long it takes me to come again. I think I make more noise, pleading screaming nonsense. Stops and oh no's and endless moans. I don't know how loud I am, if my voice is just above a whisper or a yell. The toy presents never-ending pleasure that's pressing more toward pain, but it's all wrapped up together.

One without the other wouldn't work.

And then again.

On the fourth, I'm shouting curses. My throat hurts with the strain of volume. Sweat coats my skin, I can't keep from panting, and my wrists are sore from yanking on the bonds.

Five.

Six.

Seven.

The toy dies on the cusp of number eight, and I collapse in a puddle of bones and jelly muscles.

But not for long.

The door opens, the light comes on. I blink drearily, glancing around to get my bearings. I'm not in Knox's room, like I thought, but *mine*. My wrists secured to *my* headboard, the foot restraints disappearing past the bottom of the mattress. To attach to the bed frame, probably.

He comes around and pulls the headphones off. "Enjoy that?"

I wet my lips, ready to curse him out for real—until the sound of other people in another part of my condo reaches us. Male voices.

He was being serious about movers?

"They're coming in for the bed next," he says. "Hopefully they don't mind the wet spot you've left behind."

"You—" I lick my lips. "This is—"

Improper. Insane. Unjustified.

Wholly exhilarating.

He undoes the ankle restraints. Then my wrists.

When he reaches into my panties to remove the toy, he drags his finger across my clit. He stays there, his gaze on my face, until I come again. I groan through my teeth, refusing to make more noise. Finally, the feeling—and his finger—leaves me.

"Wow," he murmurs. "Do you want to know what the guys in the other room said?"

"No." My face heats, and I sit up slowly. "But you're going to tell me anyway."

"They said I was a lucky guy, having a screamer like you. I told them you were doing it to show off, and they got all flustered." He leans forward. "But you know the truth of the matter?"

I shake my head.

"My wife might be the most fuckable woman in the room." His gaze drops to my breasts, then to my lap. "Might have the best ass and lips and strange, alluring eyes... but you're never going to know what my dick feels like sliding into your cunt. Because that is so beyond what you deserve, it's almost laughable."

Why?

The question is on the tip of my tongue.

But instead, I just grit my teeth and nod. Accepting that he hates me for something bone-deep, and it's just another mystery I'm going to have to solve on my own.

"Anyway." His tone changes. Lightens. "There's an outfit for you in the closet. We're leaving in ten minutes, whether you're ready or not."

I shiver. He pats the bed next to him, then hops up and leaves me in the room. Keeping the door open, the voices still out there now getting louder as Knox rejoins them.

Someone passes by the door, and I yank the sheet up with a quiet gasp.

Asshole.

Before someone else can pull the same stunt, I hop up and slam the door. Then cross to the closet, which has *one* outfit in it.

The tight black dress I squeezed into when I declared myself his wife in front of everyone at the bar. Tall black heels with red soles—freaking expensive shoes, is what those are. I turn away from it and scour the rest of the room for *anything* else, but I barely recognize my bedroom. It's been cleared out except the bed.

"I hate him," I whisper. Letting the loathing crack my chest open and fill me with ice.

It's what fuels me. What gets me into that dress and heels. I run my fingers through my hair and smudge out my eyeliner, but that's the best I've got under the circumstances.

And yeah, maybe it does look a bit like I was just fucked.

All the better to convince whoever Knox wants to show me off to that we're... something other than enemies.

When I write about us, I vow not to skip out on the ugly parts. I'm not going to shy away from the darkness in him, the things he hides away. The sick gleam of joy in his gaze when he's twisting the knife in my gut. How far we've come from where we began.

Two kids who didn't know any better.

But now we're putting on an act, and I am blind to our direction. Which means the direction is mine for the taking, isn't it?

Whatever Knox thinks about me, however he envisions this going... I will derail it.

I guess, in a way, *let the show begin*.

23
KNOX

Knockout.

Fuck.

She's so fucking pretty I just can't stand it. In the pettiest of ways, I want to drag a knife down her cheeks and permanently scar her, just so only I find her beautiful.

So no other guy is tempted to look at her.

She doesn't ask questions when I hold the door open for her, ushering her first into the hall, then the elevator, then out past the doorman.

The new doorman, might I add. After a little chat with the manager, we determined that Jerry's best plan of action was to leave the country. I know a lawyer or two, and I threatened every lawsuit I could come up with. Some might've been made up, but whatever.

It was a fun conversation nonetheless.

Jacob was there to back me up, the dark-haired, big-muscled scary guard dog to my more friendly face. Sometimes people don't take me seriously because I seem so nice. Charming. I mean, it's how I got Willow to fall for my bullshit for a whole year. Convinced her to love me.

I get an unexpected twinge of guilt over that. But it dissipates when I focus back on Aurora. My heart goes all cold and frozen again. Back to our regularly scheduled broadcasting.

We sit in silence in the back of the hired car. She looks out the window, I scroll my phone. Through the hundreds of numbers I've collected over the years. Girls, mainly. Sometimes the random guy tried to pick me up, and I humored them just long enough to flirt via text. But dicks aren't really my thing, so... polite pass. Or, most of the time, *polite ghost.*

Without warning, Aurora snatches my phone from my hand.

"Mandy Big Tits," she reads.

I roll my eyes.

"Marcy Blue Hair. Maria the Columbian. What the fuck, Knox?"

"Maria was particularly good at speaking Spanish while being fucked from behind." I smile at her. "You can put that in your next book."

She scrolls. "Rebecca Christmas Lady. Sandy Sugar Rim Margaritas. Serena Folded Chair. What does that even mean?"

"She sucked me off in one of those folding metal chairs. It was at some event." I shift. "No need to get so defensive."

"And what am I under?" She zooms up to the top of my contacts—it takes her a good minute—and starts typing.

Aurora—*nope.*

Rory—*not a chance.*

Sunshine—*getting closer.*

Aw, sweet little devil even types in *wife.*

"Come on, Sunny, I thought you were smarter than that," I whisper in her ear.

She shudders.

Then types in the name I just called her.

Sunny the Betrayer.

A nice name for what she did. I wanted to go more drastic, but I couldn't help it. I felt guilty. I felt freshly heartbroken, and for the first time in my life, I was devastated. I didn't know what the word meant until I headed back to college right after winter break, knowing I would never talk to her again.

I focus back in on Aurora.

She's shaking her head slowly, clenching my phone so fucking tight her knuckles are white. Her hand is trembling.

"This isn't fair," she says. "You think I betrayed you?"

My mind goes to Willow again.

And then my brother.

I've tried so hard to repair things with him. After my mother tried to talk sense into me, into shoving reason in my face. I know I fucked up with them. Willow and Miles. More Miles than Willow, though.

"Knox. How did I betray you?"

My lip curls. "It's funny that your memory is so poor, Aurora."

She flinches. She doesn't like me calling her that any more than I do. She can't make up her damn mind when it comes to me.

But she does decide something, because she hits the button to roll down her window—and then out goes my phone.

I open and close my mouth.

She rolls it up and sits back, staring straight ahead. Her lips are pressed in a firm line. I shouldn't have made her wear that dress with no bra. She crosses her arms under her breasts and lifts them, practically forcing me to stare at them.

Never mind that she just threw my phone out the window.

Or that she doesn't seem remotely bothered by my impending reaction.

Except, I'm not having a reaction. Nothing except... humor.

A laugh bubbles out of me, and once the dam breaks, I can't get it under control. The driver must think we're crazy. He glances back at us once, twice. I laugh to myself about the absurdity of what we're doing.

I just heard her scream every curse under the sun as she orgasmed. Eight times, if my count is correct. Only once by my finger, and that was kind of an accident. In fact, I'm not sure how she even has her wits about her.

"You're insane," she mutters, finally meeting my gaze.

"You threw my phone out the window. You're insane."

"You had someone in your phone named Mandy Big Tits."

I smile. "She had honkers."

Her nose wrinkles. Have I ever thought noses were cute? Not 'til Aurora fucking McGovern. No. Aurora fucking *Whiteshaw*.

I'm just captivated by everything about her like I'm seventeen again.

"Did you ever have a meaningful relationship with any of them?" she asks.

My smile fades fast. "No."

Her witch eyes stare at me. That's what they are. Mostly green, the splotch of blue. They fascinate me and ensnare me and bespell me. It's dangerous to look her in the eye for too long.

"You haven't had a relationship? Ever?"

I wave my hand. "Well, there was one. But it wasn't real."

"Why?"

"Because my brother was in love with her."

I don't look away. I want to see her reaction, to absorb the flinch that comes along with my brother being in love with someone else.

She doesn't flinch, though. Her brow furrows, and she slowly tips her head to the side.

"You dated a girl your brother was in love with?"

"Yeah."

"Why?"

I lift one shoulder. "To win a bet. You know me, Sunny. Everything's a competition."

And this one, this battle between us, is the greatest competition of all.

O ur conversation ends when we arrive at our destination. Which seems to be a red-carpet event, judging by the, well, red carpet.

"One more thing," Knox adds, leaning over me and pulling my door closed.

I had barely got it open, letting in the clamoring sounds of photographers behind partitions. Just as quickly, we're back in our silent bubble. His broad shoulders block the view of the driver, who hops out anyway. Rush of noise, then quiet.

He reveals a slender thing from his pocket. It fits in the palm of his hand, and he shamelessly pushes my dress up.

I swat at him, gasping.

"Get away from me," I snap.

"Just a little something to manage you." He winks. "It's either this or I flip you over my knee and spank your ass raw so sitting becomes the management."

I glare at him. Spanking sounds... intriguing. My stomach does a somersault at the thought. But as much as I want to call him out on that, I also have no intention of letting him near my ass.

So I drop my hands, and he slips the object into my panties.

It brushes my still-sensitive clit. I inhale sharply and dig my nails into my palms. It seems to fit perfectly in place, and he carefully readjusts it. He leaves me to yank down my dress just as the driver pulls open my door.

Knox hops out of the other side. Now his tux makes sense. My dress feels much too short, though. He circles around and offers his hand, the driver standing back to allow him the space to do it.

I swallow. His hand lingers in the air, and I swing my legs out together. Then take his cool, dry hand, and allow him to help guide me up on the heels.

Cameras flash in our faces.

He adjusts our arms smoothly, looping my hand around his arm. He pats my fingers, touching the ring on my finger.

The ring I forgot I was wearing.

It takes me a moment to realize that he's wearing his, too.

My heart does this funny flutter. And then we're moving. I know what he wants and I smile brilliantly at his side, my charm only adequate compared to his. We go up the steps and into the huge foyer, and it's only when we're inside do I register that it's a museum.

"Charity gala," he finally says. "Raising awareness for sports-related injuries in youth. The importance of proper head protection, et cetera."

My fingers tighten on his arm.

"Don't you usually have to buy tickets to these sorts of things?"

"Yeah." He frowns. "I was going to take a date anyway. Don't read into it."

I scoff. "You were going to call up Mandy? Or Sandy? Or—"

"Stop, Sunny." He does something. His hand dipping into his pocket.

All of a sudden, the object between my legs buzzes to life.

I almost fall over. It's not the same as the other one. This is deeper, going straight through my abdomen and making everything clench in a wicked way.

"It's not so bad that you can't walk," he scolds. "Be a good girl and maybe I'll give you a respite."

"I think I hate you more than I did an hour ago," I force out.

The vibrations cut off almost as soon as I stand straight again, and I breathe a sigh of relief. My gaze cuts to him. To his styled hair, the black bow tie, and crisp white shirt under his black tuxedo. I'm not as put together by a long shot, and my insecurities flare.

Why am I here?

Why didn't he sneak me in the back?

Instead, he led me in past photographers wearing our rings. Even drawing the subtle attention to them. So what are the headlines going to say in the morning? What kind of lies will they spit about me?

We continue into the main ballroom.

I expected him to take me to a club or a bar—but this is luxury. Rich people. Famous people. Some in floor-length gowns, their hair and makeup immaculate.

It's another way I'm a fish out of water. My bank account might be blossoming from my book's success, but it doesn't hold a candle to some of the men and women in the room. I rake my fingers through my hair again, cursing that he didn't let me prepare.

But this is Knox, and it seems to be just another thing he does to keep me off-balance.

We collect drinks from an open bar. Wine for me, whiskey for him. I don't even open my mouth, he just orders. Another bullet point to hate him for. The fact that I quite enjoy the wine he selects is irrelevant.

Finally, we end up at a large round table with some familiar faces.

Camden Church, captain of the Titans, for one.

He's sitting with a girl at his side, her dark hair in an elegant bun. Her dress is also long, covering her legs.

"Whiteshaw," he greets his teammate, rising as soon as he spots us. He's one of the hotter Titans, I'll give him that. "And Ms. McGovern. Or is it Mrs. Whiteshaw? I didn't catch that the other night."

"I kept my maiden name—"

"She's actually in the process of changing it," Knox interrupts. "It's long overdue."

My face flames, and I gape at him. "I'm in the process?"

"Of course." Knox's eyes gleam.

The vibrator starts. A low vibration that awakens a warmth inside me. Unlike the last time, it doesn't make me double over. Good thing, because I think I'm expected to speak.

I tighten my grip on Knox's arm.

He continues, "We filed the paperwork yesterday. It's been an undertaking. Getting your birth certificate, filing to change your name with social security..."

Jesus, he's serious. I don't have the bandwidth for this right now, so I try to ignore him and focus back on Camden.

It's hard, though, when all my concentration keeps slipping back between my legs.

"Aren't you going to introduce us to your date?" I ask.

He makes a face. "Aurora, Knox, this is my sister. Sister, meet my teammate, Knox Whiteshaw, and his wife, Aurora."

Now that he says sister, I totally see the resemblance. Same hair, nose, mouth. I bet they have the same smile.

"Grace," she says.

"Pleasure," Knox says.

The vibration increases.

I raise my eyebrows and manage to squeak out a hello, and then we're in motion again. We circle the table, greeting his other teammates. Royal Lawson, who appears to be flying solo. Dawes, with a girl hanging on his arm in a similar way I'm clutching Knox's.

I see how it looks and immediately retract.

The vibrations increase. I don't bow over like I want to. I go stiff, trying not to react. But it's like an electric wire is lit up along my spine, drawing all my attention down to my core.

"Rule number one," Knox says, pressing his lips to my ear and threading his fingers through mine. "You don't pull away from me. Not tonight."

"Great."

"Great," he repeats, watching my side profile. "Rule number two, you tell me when you're on the edge."

I grit my teeth. "Is this a lesson in edging, then?"

"I gave you your fill of orgasms earlier." His grin is positively evil. "Was eight not enough for you?"

The vibrations increase. I can barely think, but my feet are moving. Knox is guiding us. To two open chairs. I sink into one, squeezing my thighs together and willing myself not to let this affect me.

"I'm there," I manage, my back arching. "You're an asshole."

My damn nipples are hard enough to cut glass. They're definitely visible through the fabric of the dress. He makes me go another five seconds, and I'm just about to actually come in public when it stops.

I sag.

My face burns, and I blink rapidly as the feeling fades. I look around the table, but no one's paying us any attention.

"Okay, let's go." Knox stands and tugs on my hand.

Which he's still holding.

We go toward another table, where we find Jacob Rhodes and a curvy, gorgeous woman beside him. She's got dark-rimmed glasses, and light-brown hair loose and curled around her shoulders. Her teal dress is stunning in its detail, and it shimmers when she moves.

"Hey, Mel," Knox says, his voice a thousand times lighter than any time he's said my name. He drags me forward and throws his arm around her, hugging her awkwardly. Since I'm still attached to him. "This is Aurora."

"McGovern?" Mel questions, her gaze bouncing from me to him.

"Soon to be Whiteshaw," Knox inserts.

I roll my eyes. "Nice to meet you."

"Melody," she says. "Jake's... person."

Jacob Rhodes snorts behind her, snaking his arms around her waist and pulling her into him. "My person, huh?"

"We've gone over the fact that girlfriend is too weak," Melody mumbles. "So, yeah. Person."

"'Til he puts a ring on it." Knox waggles his eyebrows. "I'm going to be your maid of honor, right?"

I snort. "You're laying it on a little thick, *babe*."

"Well, Melody and I are BFFs. It's only right—"

"Knox," she interrupts. "If I have a maid of honor, it's going to be Lucy. We've talked about this."

I groan and smack my forehead. "He's brought up being a maid of honor before?"

She cracks a smile. "Once or twice."

"I didn't even have a maid of honor," I say under my breath. "My mom doesn't count. I mean, she does count, but... she was there as my mom."

And suddenly, that's it.

That's the line I can't cross.

It isn't that I'm married to him. I accepted that a long time ago. And it isn't that he won't fucking sign the divorce papers.

It's that my first marriage turned out to be a sham, and my mother is gone, and she'll never get to see me walk down an actual aisle toward someone who really loves me.

Instead, she saw me and Knox at a courthouse, a storm raging outside—like even the weather disagreed with our decision—wearing a white dress that was guaranteed to go see-through as soon as we stepped outside.

She stood with his mom and they were our only witnesses, and she died two and a half years later.

I don't think about her much.

Okay, no. That's a total fucking lie.

I think about her like she's still alive. I think about what she might be doing—at home with Dad, for instance, or out to lunch with her friends—and then I think about the things she might say to me. About my career, my cross-country move.

What would she have thought of Joel?

And how would she react to Knox's behavior?

It doesn't even fucking matter, because she's ashes in an urn on my father's mantel.

Because where else do you put her? Not in the ground. Not when she was secretly afraid of the dark, and didn't like bugs, and was more of a city person than me or Dad. Concrete and skyscrapers over endless fields of grass any day. So putting her in the ground, *alone*, seemed so wrong.

There's a ringing in my ears, but his voice breaks through it.

"Aurora?"

I yank my hand out of Knox's grip and bolt.

25
KNOX

"What did you do?" Jacob questions, watching Aurora flee.

Melody just seems sad, so I focus on her. Because Jacob is a guy, and he knows Melody but he's kind of shit at reading other women. But Mel is a girl's girl, and she'll give it to me straight. Maybe. Hopefully.

"Her book was dedicated to her mom," she eventually says, her gaze on me. Not too mean, just honest.

"Yeah, her mom's pretty cool." I lift my shoulder. "I mean, I haven't seen any of them in a while. When I go home, the timing always seems to be off."

"Knox..." Melody shakes her head. "Aurora's mom died."

My brain turns off.

I hear it. I know I hear it.

But fuck if I believe it.

Because her mom was always this vibrant person. She liked to bake when they had the money for it. Things were a little tense for a while, sure... she worked two jobs to pay off the medical bills and keep their family afloat while Aurora's dad pulled as much overtime as he could get.

It left Aurora with our family a lot of the time.

But before, when we were kids, she was a bright presence. It's where Aurora gets her nickname from. Her mom once told me that Aurora means dawn, and dawn is when the sun first rises. I liked that Aurora represented the first few rays of sunlight in the morning, beating back the darkness.

Over and over.

And she's been without her mom? For how long?

"Knox—"

I ignore them. They're behind me now, anyway, as I stride after Aurora. I don't know exactly where she went, but I follow the path, nonetheless. The hallway isn't empty, but no one seems to have seen her.

I check the restrooms, even stepping in and looking under each stall door when she doesn't reply to her name.

Nothing.

Well, there's an old lady who emerges from the last stall and hits me with her handbag, but that's just a misunderstanding.

Properly scolded by the ninety-year-old, I pick a hall at random. There's a roped-off staircase off to the side, and if I was Aurora, I'd definitely step over it. It's barely knee-high, so I do just that. And hold my breath for a moment, waiting for an alarm to go off. When nothing does, I jog up the steps and into a new exhibit.

It's decorated for Christmas. No, like Christmas exploded. There are trees everywhere decorated in all different styles, and paintings on the walls, and I try to not get caught up in gawking at the trees when I need to find Sunny.

Aurora.

Same difference.

But I'm struck with the thought that she hasn't been Sunny in a long time, even though I've been calling her that. Even though I thought—

How can she be Sunny when her mom died?

I pass through it and finally enter a calmer, albeit a bit dark, room with just paintings and benches.

And there she is.

On a bench, her face in her hands and her hair hanging down like a curtain to hide even more. She's not crying, I don't think. She's not making any noise at all. If the room was any darker, I'd have passed right by her.

I blow out a slow breath.

The ring I put on her finger when she was passed out—I found it in her jewelry box when I started getting things together to move her into my condo—is on the bench beside her.

"When did she die?"

Aurora flinches.

"Your mom," I pry. "I could look it up, but..."

"When I was nineteen," she whispers without lifting her head. "Four years ago."

I digest that.

"I'm so sorry for your loss, sunshine."

She drops her hands and sits up a bit straighter. "You didn't know?"

I shake my head. "No."

"Your mom—" She scowls. "Your parents came to the funeral."

"I wasn't really talking to my parents much, then, either," I admit. "I was dating Willow. Miles' girl."

"So you ostracized yourself."

"Something like that, yeah."

"Fuck off, Knox." Her eyes are full of unshed tears. Not crying, but on the way. "I don't want to talk about you. I don't want to talk about any of this."

She picks up the ring and shoves it at me. "I don't want to wear this. I don't want to look at it, I don't want to think about it—"

"You kept it, though." I catch it and her fingers, keeping her palm pressed to my chest. "You kept the ring I gave you. For fucking years. Why?"

She blinks at me. "Because I didn't want to believe the worst, Knox."

"What did you want to believe?"

"You're so good at *talking*, but you suck at communication." She stands, tugging her hand free. "You think I did something to betray you? Why didn't you ask me? Instead of just accusing me and ruining my life?"

"I didn't ruin—"

"It's that betrayal that's making you hold on to our sham of a marriage," she snaps. "It's that one moment, whatever happened when we were seventeen and eighteen, that put us on opposite sides. And when I needed you, you weren't there." Her voice cracks.

And the tears spill over.

"You wanted me at your mom's funeral?"

"Yes." She lets out a laugh. "Yes, Knox, I would've wanted you at the fucking funeral. But instead, you didn't even know she died."

I didn't.

I'm standing on a razor wire's edge, debating which way to fall. Staring at the one girl I thought I'd do anything for and questioning absolutely everything that's come out of her mouth since I met her.

Like I've been doing on repeat since I left for good.

"If you wanted me in your goddamn life so bad, sunshine, you shouldn't have slept with my fucking brother."

I point in her face. Forget the fact that I was going to be nice. I can't seem to keep it together around her, and she's *asking* for this. She wants honesty.

Well, here's the honest truth. "You did this to yourself, Aurora. I didn't ruin anything. *You did.*"

26

AURORA

"Hello?"

I bite the inside of my cheek. This is one of the stupider things I've done. Especially since Knox is asleep. I went as far as I could go in his condo, caught in the corner of windows on the opposite side of the large space.

I still feel hollow. Crying never sits well with me. And I had prided myself on not crying since my mom died. But apparently thinking about her, or having anything to do with Knox, has unleashed the tears.

Years' worth of crying is all coming out now.

I slipped that vibrator out of my underwear and threw it back at him along with the ring. Because I wanted none of it. I didn't want to touch him, I didn't want to follow his rules. I just wanted to sit in silence and wait until we could go home.

My unit is empty of all my personal possessions. The only things left are the big furniture items that didn't fit in his condo. The bed, the couch, et cetera. We went there before coming up to his, and I stared in shock at how much work the movers did in so short a time period.

Now, my clothes are in Knox's bedroom. There's space in the closet for me, and my dresser was just hauled up and set next to his. My office was boxed up and put into his spare room, creating some sort of disaster.

The pink typewriter survived, though.

So did my desk, locked drawers and all.

And apparently, I'm well on my way to a name change. That thought makes me slightly sick, too. Mom did it when she was younger than me. She and Dad got married young, after all. I didn't talk to her about that. If she had help or if she figured out everything on her own.

"Is anyone there?"

Right. I made the phone call, now I need to live with the consequences. I can't just stay silent. So I gather my courage and blurt out, "Why does your brother think we slept together?"

Silence.

Then, "Aurora?"

I exhale. "Yeah."

"Why are you calling in the middle of the night?" Miles asks.

"I—" Shit. "Sorry. We were at some charity thing—"

"We?"

"Knox and me." I wince. "I'm sorry, this is coming out all wrong. And I'd start with pleasantries, but it's late. Not really when you want to small talk, right? Jesus, I'm rambling. I've been around Knox for too long. Anyway. Can you just fill me in on why he thinks I slept with you, of all people?"

Miles Whiteshaw, Knox's younger brother and one of the best damn goalies I've had the pleasure of practicing against, whistles. "You know, I don't actually have a clue. He never said anything to me."

"Because we didn't."

"Obviously." His voice is dry. "Hang on a sec."

There's a voice in the background. Sleepy, melodic.

"Aurora McGovern?" a girl asks.

I find myself smiling. "Are you Willow?"

"Yeah."

The one who Knox dated. *My brother's girl.* I want to know more than just the surface-level story he told me. I'm sure there's more there, more hurt buried between them. Knox can't seem to go anywhere without hurting someone.

Usually it's me, but sometimes it's his brother, too.

"I'm sorry for whatever Knox put you through. He hasn't said much, but... I'm sorry."

Even though I don't have the details, I feel in my bones that it's the right thing to say. I don't want to apologize *for* him, but I don't want to be awkward. Or ignore it.

"Oh. Wow. Um, no, you don't have to apologize for that. I just wanted to talk to you to see if you were okay."

"Me? I'm fine." It's a lie. Will I ever stop lying?

"Knox is a lot," she says. "And no offense for what I'm about to say, but he never mentioned you."

"I was banished from being in his physical presence and his mind," I joke. Eh, okay, maybe it's more truth than jest. "Nothing new there. Anyway, I just wanted to confirm with Miles that I didn't, uh..."

"Sleep with him."

"Yeah. Wow, that sounds awful. I'm so sorry. Again."

It occurs to me that she's slept with Knox. The thought turns my stomach, and I almost hang up. I'm not petty, but that's a lot. Especially since the asshole refuses to sleep with *me*.

She laughs. "It's okay. We're playing the Titans on Tuesday in Denver. I don't suppose I'll see you there? Jacob got us all a suite, and you're welcome to join."

"That would be..." I have a damn lump in my throat. Whether or not she slept with Knox is irrelevant. "That would be really nice. Thank you."

"Great. I'll snag your number from Miles' phone and text you at a reasonable hour tomorrow!"

"Cool. Thanks, Willow."

The line goes dead, and I cover my mouth. Of all the ways I thought that would go, ending up with a girl-date for the Tuesday game is not at all how I pictured it.

Instead of going back to bed, I sit at my desk in the spare room. He has a twin bed shoved in the corner for visitors or something—but the rest is a similar mock up to my old office.

I run my hands over the shiny typewriter, vowing to replace it with something more similar to the one I used to own. I have a lot of conflicting emotions. About Knox and Willow, and about people touching all my stuff, and him taking over my life to move me up here, and... Well, let's just say that sleep is the last thing on my mind.

So I try to write about all the ugly things Knox and I have done to each other. But what ends up coming out is a bit nicer than that.

27

MANUSCRIPT

CHAPTER 3

We're drowning.

I'm not sure when I realized it. Maybe when Mom got another job in the evenings, and Dad started working overtime so much he was barely home. The Whiteshaws had me over for dinner more often than not, since I was left home alone after school.

Not that I minded.

Miles, Knox's brother, teaches me how to play video games. They only have two controllers, so Knox watches. Or ignores us completely, depending on his mood. Sometimes, if I'm persistent enough, we go into the basement and take shots at the goal. They converted part of the mostly empty basement for hockey practice. Sometimes, if we all beg hard enough, in the winter our dads get together and make an ice rink for us in the flat part of our backyards.

Either option is better than their summer outdoor setup.

They only let me take a shot or two before I'm forced to

sit aside. My lungs ache anyway, and my breathing comes harsh and shallow after any amount of exercise. It's the recent surgery, the healing incision, my heart getting used to a new device inside it.

I hate all of it.

They watch me like I'm going to collapse, even when I wave them off. Even as I dream of playing in the Olympics, knowing now that it's impossible.

But I'm getting closer to the Whiteshaw boys. I was already close to them, but now Knox takes me for drives in his car, going out for ice cream or around the block with all the windows rolled down just to get some fresh air. When we return, our hair is windswept and our smiles are huge.

He's going to college soon. While my parents seem to never be home, I sit with his parents at the high school games. I'm with them when Knox opens his acceptance letter to Crown Point University. And then a personal letter from the hockey coach, Roake, arrives. He's 'thrilled' to welcome Knox to the team.

Miles watches with envy, leaning forward over the dinner table like he wants to take the letter and read it for himself.

Meanwhile, I sit and stew, grateful that Knox has been given an opportunity to continue hockey and insanely jealous that I can't. The girls on my juniors team faded away as soon as my dad told them I was no longer able to play.

The ones I thought were my friends vanished, leaving me with just Beth. Her interest in hockey is nonexistent, though. We only get together outside of school or our houses if I want to do girly things, like wander the mall or get our nails done. Which is rare.

I'm not sure what the tipping point is for my family,

though. One night, waiting for Dad to get back from a business trip and Mom to return from her shift at the local restaurant, my heart seems to beat extra hard.

Worry pricks at me, and I go downstairs to the phone on the wall.

My hand hovers over it, wondering who to call.

Mom?

Dad?

9-1-1?

I close my eyes and breathe as deeply as I can, although it isn't very deep at all. When I open them, the room spins a little. But my attention snags on the pile of mail on the table. Most are opened and left, and although it never has before, my curiosity tugs at me.

Ignoring my symptoms, I slide the mail out of their envelopes.

Overdue bill.

Overdue bill.

Overdue bill.

Final warning, some of them say, in large red letters.

Water, electricity, gas. The mortgage, the internet. We don't have a fancy television with all the channels. We don't really have anything extra, now that I think about it.

And then I find the medical bills from the heart surgery.

I don't know what all these numbers mean or why the figure is so high.

I needed the surgery or I was going to die. And now they're charging... so much money.

Headlights swing across the front of the house. I scramble to put everything back the way it was, neat and orderly, and hurry up the stairs. My heart pounds like it's about to quit on me by the time I reach my bedroom, and I close the door and sink to the floor.

I will myself to calm down. To breathe normally, to slow my pulse.

Panic will escalate the problem of my heart.

But tonight, panic just seems to be it for me.

The thought of burdening my parents with my panic, when they're already dealing with enough, nearly suffocates me. I blindly reach for my cell phone, a gift from my parents last year, and dial Knox's number.

He answers on the first ring.

"I can't calm down," I wheeze.

"Sunny? What's going on?"

"Panic—"

"Okay, okay." There's rustling. "I see your mom's car in the driveway. Are you in your room? Do you want me to get her?"

I choke out a sob. "I can't talk to them. Not about—" They would just assure me that it wasn't my fault, that they're doing everything they can, that things will be fine. When I know the opposite will be true.

He swears. "Okay, hang on."

He doesn't hang up, but he stops talking. I grip the phone hard and focus on his ragged breathing, his muttered swears, and less than five minutes later, he's shoving open my bedroom window and climbing through.

I drop the phone.

"Sunny," he whispers, crawling to me. He cups my cheeks with both his hands. They're cool and wet from being outside, from climbing the tree beyond my window. "What's wrong?"

I just shake my head and dive into his arms. Never mind that we're strictly just friends, that we've been friends since I kicked his ass in a slap shot competition when we were eight and ten. After the pushing-in-the-mud incident, of course.

Because no great hockey player would just lie down and take that.

"We can't afford the surgery," I finally admit.

"The one you just had?"

I slowly nod. But I've got this feeling that my heart just wasn't made to last. That I'll need another surgery sooner or later, that my parents will have to declare bankruptcy— or worse. What sorts of things can we trim from our lives that we haven't already?

Knox seems to read my mind. "You think you're going to need another one."

I swallow and press his hand to my chest. "Do you feel that?"

His gaze drops down and lingers on our fingers. Belatedly, it occurs to me how intimate this position is. I let go automatically, just as he leans in.

When his lips brush mine, it's like everything goes still.

Even my heart.

I press up and into him, gripping the front of his t-shirt with both hands. His go under my elbows, holding me steady.

"Aurora?" Mom knocks on my door and opens it without warning.

I shove away from Knox, practically falling over backward.

Knox doesn't move.

Mom pauses, her gaze ping-ponging from me to him and back again.

"Well," she murmurs. "No closed doors with boys around, Aurora, you know that." She tries and fails to hide her smile, slowly backing out of the room. "Not too late, you two. It's a school night."

I wait until the door to her room clicks shut, and I whirl around. My face is on fire, and Knox... the jerk is silently laughing. He wipes away tears, shaking his head at me.

"Excellent timing," he finally manages.

I punch his shoulder. Because what else am I going to do. Kiss him again?

28

KNOX

Aurora is gone by the time I wake up.

We didn't have the best night. After the mom death chat, and then me blurting out my long-kept secret about her sleeping with my brother, we proceeded to get drunk, stumble into the car, and fall into bed. On our own sides, with a gulf of space between us that may as well have been a mile.

I wander into the office-slash-guest bedroom, where we put her things up in the best imitation of the way she had it. There's a paper in the typewriter, queued up and ready to go. Beside that is a stack of papers facedown.

Already typed.

I pick up the stack, noting that it starts on chapter three. It starts with: *We're drowning.* And it takes me approximately four seconds to register my name in the same paragraph.

Interesting.

So naturally, I go digging for the first two chapters.

They're not in the first drawers I check, and the last one is locked. Which piques my curiosity and convinces me that they're hiding there. I could break the lock, or I could attempt to pick it.

Or...

As soon as my new phone arrives, I rip it open and download my stored memory. Then I dial Jacob.

Five minutes later, he's kneeling in front of the heavy desk with his lock picks, and the drawer makes a nice little snick as it unlocks.

"Thanks." I pat his shoulder and grab the pages, confirming I have chapters one and two in my hands. "That's all."

"Okay—"

"You've got to go. We can chat later. Breakfast with Melody! Don't forget!" I herd him toward the door, my excitement bubbling. Because Aurora's been writing about me, and I need to know exactly what she thinks of me.

It's conceited, but whatever. The girl's not exactly an open book otherwise.

"You're welcome." Jacob snorts. "And yeah, sure."

"We were supposed to do dinner and we didn't," I point out. "You owe me. You owe me breakfast for that one time you left me with the bill—"

"I got it," Jacob interrupts. "Go read, or whatever. I'll talk to you later."

I close the door behind him and flop on the couch, then start reading. And the nerves that hit me come only a moment after the first line. Because once I read this, I don't think I can go back.

But then again, I don't want to. Knowledge is power, after all.

I spend my sixteenth birthday in the hospital.

We were on our way to Dad's summer hockey intensive—he took a job as the assistant coach for the ten and ups—when this weight pressed down on my chest. I couldn't breathe. My heart raced, but no matter how hard I gasped, nothing brought air into my lungs.

The last thing I remember is my dad's shout.

And then I wake up in the hospital bed, a monitor attached by cords to my chest, another clip on my finger reading my blood oxygen. It's quiet before I open my eyes.

I remember the near-silence, the hum of the equipment around me, and it dissipates faster than snapped fingers as soon as I open my eyes.

My parents are on either side of me. Mom is always worried—Dad's the calm one. But he's anything but calm now, his brows pinching in, his lips in a tight little line. His normally tan face is pale, and his palms are sweaty. He's holding on to my hand with both of his in a death grip.

The pages are ripped from my hands.

I look up, shocked to be caught by surprise. Aurora stands over me, positively seething. She snatches up the rest of the pages and cradles them to her chest. Her V-neck sweater clings to her, and her jeans make her hips a focal point. Her cleavage, too, probably, if it wasn't hidden behind the pages she's attempting to save from me.

"No," she yells at me. "No, you don't get to read my personal thoughts on what happened to us, Knox. You don't get to torture me and invade my privacy, too. Pick one."

I stand, ignoring the way blood is rushing to my groin. "I want to know what you're saying about me."

"I want you to sign the divorce papers." She stands tall,

but her hands are shaking. The edges of the pages flutter against her. "And yet, you keep telling me no. So you should get used to the word, too."

"Our situations are different." I wave her off and stare at her lips. She's painted them baby pink, a little glossy. Everything about her is designed to test my willpower.

"Yeah," Aurora sneers. "You ruined my relationship. And your brother's. And Willow's, and Joel's—"

"Haverhill has nothing to do with this." I breeze past her for the bedroom. I need to get out of here. Getting caught has made me all itchy on the inside, and I kind of feel like I'm going to explode if I don't do something.

"Joel has everything to do with this!" Aurora yells, chasing after me. When she rounds the corner into the bedroom, the pages of her manuscript are gone. "I loved him! I was going to marry him—"

"No you fucking *weren't*!" I shout back. I grab her around the neck and tow her into me. Because she's been driving me crazy since her orgasm marathon yesterday. I stop an inch away from her lips. "If you were going to marry him, you wouldn't have just said love in the past tense. And you would've chased after him when he snatched his ring off your finger. Instead, you come to yell at me. You whine about how I ruined your life, blah, blah, blah. I saved you from a failing relationship, sunshine. You weren't in love with him. You might've married him, but that's just because you're afraid of actually falling in love with someone. Sooner or later you'll see the truth."

Her chest heaves. "I hate you."

"*Good*. Because I'm going to kiss you, and I expect you to fight back."

Her eyes light up an instant before I cross that final distance between us. As with all of our arguing that somehow ends in making out, it isn't gentle. It's more like war between our mouths. Our teeth clack together, our lips become bloody casualties. Her hands are in my hair, tugging and scraping.

I use my grip on the back of her neck and her hair to angle her head. We crash into the wall, lips fused together. I don't care about breathing or anything. I shift my hips forward, grinding my erection into her belly.

She gasps against my mouth. I want to fuck her, but I made a promise that I wouldn't. And now she knows why.

"Did he fuck your ass?" I pull back just enough to catch her expression.

Confused then *furious*. More so than before.

Her incoming slap is too predictable. I catch her wrist and use it to twist her, forcing it behind her back. My free hand goes to her ass, massaging through the denim. I release her wrist and reach around her, unbuttoning her jeans and dragging them down her legs. I take her panties with it, but she doesn't fucking stop me. I kneel behind her and lick her ass cheek, then run my fingers between her legs.

She doesn't stop me because she's too turned on. She doesn't care about my promise either.

"You want my cock, sunshine?"

"No." She looks over her shoulder. "Definitely not."

"You're such a bad liar."

I rise and spit on the crack of her ass. My saliva drips down, and I spread her cheeks to let it go even farther. She makes some noise in the back of her throat, and I chuckle. It comes out dark, though.

"Brace your hands on the wall."

She does what I say. A thrill goes through me. I undo my pants and free my swollen cock, stroking it a few times before sliding it between her legs. Not in her—*a promise is a promise*—but getting wet with her arousal. It's not as good as being in a pussy. But if I wanted to fuck her, I would've done it already.

My dick is *so fucking close*, but my self-control won't let me break. Not now.

She huffs. "You think this is fun for me?"

"This isn't about you." I change my angle a little, sliding through her slick arousal and hitting her clit. Judging from her sudden squeak, it works for her, too.

I nudge the outside of her foot, bringing her legs in closer. And making what I'm working with tighter. All because I chose not to fuck her.

And I won't. But I do a fantastic job of torturing both of us until we're panting, sweating messes.

She spins around and drags me into her, pressing up on her toes. Our lips meet again, and I slam her into the wall. She lets out an *oof*. The kiss only lasts a moment before I drag my mouth down her throat. I bite her shoulder hard enough that she screams.

The sound bounces around in my skull.

She tears at my shirt, my abdomen, shoving it up and parting only long enough to get it over my shoulders.

"Fuck your abs," she groans. "Fuck your stupid body, I hate it so much."

I bite her neck and grope her ass, pulling her body up. She automatically wraps her legs around my waist. Her hand travels farther down, from my stomach—that, yeah, I'm fucking flexing—to my dick.

She wraps her fingers around me, and I see stars.

"Hope you last longer than your shifts on the ice," she whispers.

I groan. "You're not very nice, you know that?"

She redirects my mouth back to hers, nipping my lower lip. "That's what you like about me."

"I don't like anything about you."

"Right—"

I shift my dick, pushing through her hand. The tip slides against her core, and her words stop coming. That's the only thing that doesn't come. I tease her like that, tease *both* of us, and my control is fraying.

Which is not allowed.

I yank back and drop her legs. She barely catches herself, then blinks up at me with those big eyes.

"God, you're the worst," I manage. Which is so fucking lame.

She blinks again, and this time it's like she somehow erases all traces of lust from her witch eyes. "I am," she agrees. "You think I slept with your brother. After we got married, I presume?"

The memories come roaring back. I literally hate her so much, it takes all my willpower to step away from her. I tuck my still-hard dick back in my pants. It's throbbing, the only thing not giving a shit about our argument. Because who else could turn some lust-driven craze into a fight? Aurora.

"You couldn't even break things off with me, first," I snarl. "I mean, where's the decency? If you're going to fool around—"

"What, did I just go from fucking him to a full-blown relationship?" She follows me. "That's insane, don't you think?"

"Insane?" I grab her by the throat and force her down to her knees. "Open. Your. Mouth."

She laughs. "What, you're not going to lose your erection when I mention Miles?"

"I'm going to bruise the back of your throat so you hurt every time you try to talk," I growl. I grip her chin, my fingers and thumb pinching her cheeks. "Take my dick out."

We glare at each other.

And then... she does it.

It turns me on that she follows directions. "Good little slut," I croon, exhaling when she cups my balls. "Now beg for my forgiveness."

"I don't need your forgiveness," she spits. Her words are distorted, because I'm still pinching her cheeks together, keeping her mouth open.

I run the tip of my dick along her lower lip. "Do you still want a divorce, sunshine? Do you still want to be free of me? Even knowing that this turns you on?"

She scoffs.

I release her. She falls back to sit on her heels.

"Show me you're not wet." I raise my eyebrow.

A dare.

She's a sucker for a dare.

Which is why I'm not really surprised when she slides her hand down and her fingers return wet.

I smirk. "What now?"

She scowls. "I don't know."

"Do what you want. Do what you think you might want." I wait for a moment. Then another. A span of heartbeats, in which I cannot fathom what she's actually going to choose.

And then she's rising on her knees and coming forward, and my brain explodes when her lips wrap around me. She's glaring and sucking, and I'm addicted to her fight.

This is why she's not allowed to leave.

This is why she's going to become a damn Whiteshaw, whether she wants to or not.

No one sucks dick like her. No one argues with me like her.

I tangle my fingers in her hair. Not to control her, but to feel the silky strands. To make sure she's not going to quit on me early. When she reaches up and cups my balls, I groan. Her tongue swirls under my tip, and then she pushes me deeper. I hit the back of her throat, and the most miraculous thing happens—she relaxes. She takes me deeper, until her throat contracts around me. Her gag is a beautiful soundtrack, as are the tears that form in her eyes.

"That's it," I urge. "Just like that."

I'm going to come.

"You're going to be good and swallow, yeah?" My grip tightens ever so slightly in her hair.

Her gaze is cutting. I can't decipher it. Don't really want to. And I'm not giving her a choice anyway. I get closer to the edge, and my hips jerk. She makes a noise in the back of her throat, a low groan. I mirror it.

When I come, it's on her tongue, with her lips wrapped around my shaft. And she swallows.

I finally release her, and she falls backward. She licks her lips, then wipes her mouth with the back of her hand.

"Well? How was your dessert?" I ask.

She sniffs and picks herself up. "I expected it to be a bit dusty, since you spend so much time on the bench. But it wasn't bad."

My jaw drops. She smiles sweetly.

This fucking girl.

29
AURORA

I inspect my tooth in the mirror. There's a tracker in it, according to Knox, which means he knows exactly where I am right now. If he cares.

While Knox was in the shower, I got dressed and went to Beth's house. I made up some lie about the pipes being busted in my condo and not having water 'til it's fixed. Which could be later today, depending on how I'm feeling, or... a few days?

Because that's easier than telling her about Knox. And that he thinks I slept with his damn brother.

Beth leans on the doorframe. "What are you doing?"

I pull my hand out of my mouth. "Just making sure the dentist didn't fuck up my tooth."

I lie.

And lie.

And lie.

"So, are we going out tonight?" She brushes my hair off my shoulder, and her gaze drops to the bite mark on my neck. It seems like whenever one heals, Knox gives me another.

Shit.

"You dog," she laughs, leaning in to inspect it. "Did you get back with Joel?"

My heart gives a little flutter at his name. A flutter of fucking guilt, really, but whatever. I've tried not to think about how I left things with the Titans' goalie, and it's been over a month since I've even seen him.

Face to face.

Because God knows I can't stop watching the Titans on the television, no matter where I am. My condo, now Knox's. Beth's apartment this afternoon. I texted my dad during them, shit-talking about the players. He takes particular pride in knowing two NHL superstar rookies. Miles and Knox.

He was their original coach.

He even confided in me today that a reporter for a big-time media outlet reached out to get a quote from their former coach. They wanted to know what he thought of the boys playing pro, yadda, yadda...

"They even mentioned you," he added. "Asked if I would comment on you being married to Knox."

I was expecting dirt to be dug up on me since we went to the charity gala, but maybe Knox buried it. It's only been a day. They could be waiting for the next weekend news cycle...

Are they going to write about how I can't play hockey anymore? How I grew up schooling the Whiteshaw boys on the ice, only to be ripped off of it at sixteen?

"Was it someone else?" Beth squeals, pinching my arm.

I jump back to reality, rubbing the sore spot. "What? No!"

"You're allowed to have a fling, babe." She tuts. "It might loosen you up a little."

"I'm loose," I grumble.

She makes a face, then straightens. "Oh, by the way. Do you have a second phone?"

I meet her gaze in the mirror, drawing a big fucking blank for a minute. Then it occurs to me that I grabbed the phone Luke gave me, tossing it in my purse on a whim, and my heart goes all weird again.

I press my palm to my chest and take a deep breath, then move past her. "Yeah, uh, it's just... A work phone. Because all the notifications were driving me crazy, you know?"

"Because you're a big famous author," she teases. She drifts after me. "How's that going, by the way? I noticed you didn't pack your typewriter."

I grimace. "It's big and clunky and annoying and I hate it."

"Oh."

"Yeah." I dig through my bag until my fingers brush the edge of the phone. I pull it out and scan the text, then drop if back in my bag. Because fuck this. Fuck all of it.

He left me alone for the most part. After that beating, I mean. Like we were taking a break... maybe he knew I had gone home for the holidays. Maybe he's keeping tabs on me at all times, like Knox.

I never told Knox why he was texting me about pulling strings with him. I never admitted any of it, because the pain of being beaten up was a little too much to bear. And while the doorman who let Luke's guy into the building and up to my condo is gone, the memory of it is too real.

Being back here has been interesting to say the least. At home, I convinced myself that I was safe. The hotels made me feel safe, too, until Knox burst in and ruined that.

If I close my eyes, I can taste the blood on my lips. The

feel of my tooth coming loose, my stomach aching, the pain so bad I couldn't help but throw up right where I'd lain.

It's humiliating to relive.

"I've got to go," I tell my best friend. I slip on my coat and flip my hair out, and Beth frowns as I make a beeline for the door. "I'll see you later, right? We're going out. I'll meet you at Blood and Cherry."

"Of course," she murmurs. "But, Aurora—"

"I'll explain later. Thanks for letting me hang out here this afternoon!"

Another lie. I have no intention of explaining anything to her. Or anyone.

I make it to the arena in record time. There's a text on my real phone from Willow, Miles' fiancée, with a pass to get up to their suite in two days. We've got a complication with this game, first—then we'll worry about facing Miles' team on Tuesday.

Right now, I need to convince Knox to win this game. By *two*. But it can't be any two, it has to be his two.

This is not exactly what I thought I'd be doing on a Saturday afternoon, storming into the players' area of the arena. And yet, all my years following my dad around has me feeling not as uncomfortable as I would've thought. It'd actually be kind of nostalgic if I wasn't so anxious.

Guys are playing a game with a soccer ball in a huge open space, kicking it around without letting it touch the floor. I don't spot Knox among them, and I almost move on.

Until my gaze catches on Joel.

He spots me immediately, and the ball sails past him.

There's a chorus of groans, but he ignores them all and approaches me.

I hoist my purse up higher on my shoulder, gripping it tight, until he stops in front of me.

"Aurora," he greets me. "What are you doing here? Are you okay?" He reaches out, then drops his hand before he can touch me.

"I'm fine." I clear my throat. "I, uh... Listen, Joel."

It actually hurts to look at him. And Knox's accusation that I never really loved Joel, that I didn't fight for him, float up in my mind. I don't want it to be true, but it's shocking how fast I got over it. Over *him*.

"What is it?"

"I need to apologize." I look down. "I'm so sorry for how things happened and that I lied to you. I didn't mean for it to escalate, and Knox—"

"It's okay." He shifts. "I don't think I'm built for marriage. It's just one of those things that I thought would work for me, but the idea of tying myself to a person forever is kind of claustrophobic."

"Oh." Well, that's good... I guess. "At least you figured that out now."

"Yeah." He pats my shoulder. "I appreciate our time together, Aurora. Take care."

And with that, he heads back to the game. I stare after him for only a moment longer, then shake it off and continue to the locker room.

It's quiet inside. The fun and games are out in the hall, clearly. Sitting on a bench in front of a locker is Camden Church, headphones in place and eyes closed.

And he's alone.

I let out a huff and plant my hands on my hips.

Of all times for Knox to pull a freaking disappearing act.

I march forward and yank off the headphones, jumping back to avoid Camden's surprised lurch. He focuses on me, and his gaze narrows.

"Where's Knox?" I question.

"I don't know."

I roll my eyes and dangle his headphones from my fingers. "Like hell. You're the captain, you know everything."

"He's probably on the roof." Camden tips his head back. "Are you afraid of heights?"

"No." I mean, *yes*, but he doesn't need to know that. "Is that, uh, where?"

"Take a left out of the locker room, stairs go all the way up."

Great. I toss the headphones back to him and stride out. I guess I just need to be honest with Knox. Because otherwise, I'm not really sure how I'm going to pull this off.

Staircase located.

By the time I hike up seven flights, I'm sweating and gasping for air. I press my hand to the wall and lean forward, taking slow, deep breaths. I like to stay in shape, but this is pushing it. Plus, we're in Denver. The fact that it's a higher altitude just *sucks*.

Lungs reined back under control, I exit the stairwell onto a concrete roof. It's not big and open, like how I expected. There are air-conditioning units and all sorts of stuff. Duct work, whatever. It takes me a solid minute of wandering to find Knox.

He's sitting on the ledge with one leg hanging over the edge.

"What are you doing?" I shout.

I rush forward and grab him, practically falling backward with his arm in my grasp. He comes with me easily—probably because there's not much else holding him up—and we fall in a heap to the ground.

Ow.

He's mostly on top of me, and he rises a little to look down at me. He brushes my hair out of my face.

"Aurora?"

"You idiot." I push at him. "Get off me."

"I wasn't going to jump." He doesn't move.

"No, but you could've fallen." Tears burn the backs of my eyes, and I try to will them away—without success. My eyes flood. "Damn it. Get *off*."

"Oh my God, you care whether I live or die." His voice is full of something like *wonder*.

"What the fuck is wrong with you?" I shove at him. "Of course I do! You are the world's biggest idiot and hypocrite and jackass all wrapped up in one hot skin suit."

He laughs.

This is not a laughing matter.

"Knox Whiteshaw," I say firmly, ignoring the tears still blurring my vision. Ignoring the way my heart is beating way more frantically than I'd like. "What the fuck is wrong with you?" I don't care that I just asked him. It bears repeating.

"A lot of things," he answers. "But mainly? You."

Ugh.

Except he's looking at me like I'm not really something *wrong* at all.

And that's confirmed when he kisses me again.

I think I could drown in Knox Whiteshaw's kisses. I thought that when I was sixteen, giddy and high on teen love. I thought it when we kissed in the bar, when I straddled his lap and wore his ring. It's definitely on the forefront of my mind now as he sucks all the oxygen from my lungs.

He pushes my shirt up, and then my bra. His cold

fingers cover my breasts, pinching and tugging at my nipples without once removing his lips from mine.

Heat and a flood of desire flood straight between my legs.

He shifts his hips forward, his erection—bound by his jeans, blocked by mine—hits *almost* just where I need. He does it again and again, until I move and spread my legs wider, fixing the angle. And then it's *just right*.

Call me Goldilocks, I guess.

He nips my lip. Sucks it. Kisses every inch, my upper lip, my lower lip, the corners. Paying attention to the little details that I wouldn't have thought matter, but each one sends a rush through me.

But he learned how to kiss somewhere, because he didn't kiss like this at seventeen.

I turn my head away, more tears falling.

"Why are you crying, Sunny?"

Because you went off and had a whole life between us. Because you think I betrayed you. Because there's only one way you'll believe me, and I don't know if I can do that.

Instead of vomiting that truth, I go with something else.

Another twist of lie and truth all wrapped up tight enough so Knox won't be able to tell the difference.

"I need to tell you about Luke Abernathy."

He groans. "Why do that when we could do this?"

He moves his hips again, nudging that spot between my legs that's fucking electric. But I shake my head and rise on my elbows, bringing me face to face with him. My vision is taken up completely by his face, his blue eyes. And that's how I admit what I need to tell him.

A truth that could get us killed.

"Betting fraud," I whisper.

He stops. "What?"

"Luke Abernathy is working with people to commit fraud. They're rigging the games—"

Knox covers my mouth with his hand. "Stop, Aurora. Stop talking."

When I press my lips together, he removes his hand and hops up. He takes me with him, his grip on my wrists sure and steady. One minute I'm under him, the next he's making sure I don't tip over sideways.

"Knox—"

"He had someone beat you up because—"

"Because I was supposed to make sure you didn't play well."

He narrows his eyes. "That's why you spiked my coffee."

My face heats. "Well... yeah. Sorry."

And while I wish I was there to witness his dash to the locker room in person, the television cameras made sure to pick it up. I watched the replays, having missed the live version, when I was holed up in a hotel room the week after.

"He had someone beat you up because I played well."

I've seen this expression on his face before. Stricken. In a way, hopeless. Like he doesn't know what on earth he's going to do to get us out of this mess.

Wait. There's no *us*. There's me and the consequences of my actions, and there's him and the consequences of his.

And maybe they're related, but we're not in this together.

"Stop thinking," Knox snaps.

I rear back. "Excuse me?"

"Your thinking got us into this mess. You *thinking* that you could keep this from me—" He chokes. "You got *beat up*. Attacked. That's not going to happen again, do you understand me?"

Do I?

"I didn't think you'd care that much," I mumble. "I just didn't know where else to go."

He glowers at me. "Damn straight you come to me."

Oh.

My heart skips a beat.

"What does he want you to get me to do tonight?" he asks.

I fish out the phone and show him the message. It's a photo of me on the floor—I don't even remember the guy taking a picture. I look *awful*. But with it are the words: *Whiteshaw – two goals or we'll repeat this.*

"Like fucking hell," Knox growls.

"Right." I laugh, but it comes out nervous. High. "It's fine. Do whatever—"

"Fuck that." He takes my hand.

I start, but he ignores it and pulls me back down the stairs. Faster than I'd like, but whatever. It isn't until we reach the bottom, and I'm gasping for breath, that we slow slightly.

"Rhodes!" Knox yells.

Jacob passes the ball and bows out of the game. The guys close in his spot in the circle, and he jogs over to us.

"We've got a problem," Knox tells him.

He drags Jacob—and me—to a secluded corner and proceeds to explain *everything* to him. Even when I open my mouth to stop him, he just pulls me closer and wraps his hand around my face. His palm covers my mouth, his fingers digging lightly into my cheek.

Like honestly.

Does he ever *not* tell everyone *everything*?

"Okay," Jacob says when he's finished, his gaze bouncing from me to his best friend. "Well, shit."

Yeah. That about sums it up.

30
KNOX

It's kind of hard to score two goals when your wife *isn't* being threatened. Add in the violence, and it's damn near impossible.

We're playing Vegas. They made the playoffs last year, too, and went a hell of a lot further than either the Guardians or the Titans. Which kind of sucks, because they're cocky little shits who won't stop running their mouths.

Normally that title goes to me.

But Jacob and I have been trying to work together—difficult as that is, since he's a d-man and I'm a center. So, not quite playing in the same place on the ice. Already, Church has yelled at me from the bench about if I need a map to find the right position.

Ha, ha.

A Vegas player comes flying at me a second after I'm passed the puck. I dig into the ice and let him career past me, passing the puck across the ice to Scofield. It's a little choppy, caught on snow from our blades, but he cradles it easily and rockets down the far wall. He sends it back to me.

I'm covered, though. I throw an elbow into the Vegas player crowding my ass, immediately passing to Jacob at the top of the zone.

We play a game of pass-the-puck, until I finally get it and take a slap shot. The puck soars like a bullet toward the Vegas goalie, but the fucker stops it off his arm blocker at the last second.

Fuck.

Vegas takes possession. We change shifts, and I squirt water into my mouth from the bench as they take it toward Haverhill.

He and I haven't talked much, which is just fine.

And a second later, they get the puck past him.

My attention turns toward Aurora. She's sitting stone-faced in the stands, her arms crossed. And Luke Abernathy is sitting beside her.

I stiffen, gripping my stick harder. What the fuck is he doing? Why is he sitting next to her? Why is he—?

He waves.

At me.

I grit my teeth and look away, pretending not to notice. I just need to be Mr. Calm, Cool, and Collected.

"What the fuck is wrong with you?" Church demands. He pops his mouth guard out and sits beside me.

"That's not the first time today I've been asked that," I reply.

The game is restarting in a minute, our other center, Dawes, lining up for the face-off.

"Is your wife distracting you?"

"No." Now I'm like her, lying through my teeth. "It's just an issue with someone threatening her and ruining the sport of hockey as we know it." I grimace. "I shouldn't have said that."

Church stares at me.

"What? I mean, if there was a little conspiracy to rig games and, uh, betting... potentially stealing millions of dollars, I wouldn't know anything about it." Shit. I clear my throat, but it's not making it any better. *Shut up, Knox.* "I'm just saying, the likelihood of me having knowledge of *that* is so low, it's like, practically nonexistent."

"Whiteshaw!" Coach slaps the top of my helmet. "You going to sit here all night or are you planning on playing?"

Aurora's duster comment pops into my head.

"Okay, yep, going!" I stand and shuffle down the bench with the wingers in my line, swinging my leg over the boards in preparation to get on the ice.

I wait for the first line to return. Dawes grins at me with his mouthguard hanging out. I take off the minute he's within reach.

I just need to freaking score.

The stars somehow align, and I take a wrist shot through a lot of traffic, shocked when the puck floats straight into the net.

Thank fuck. I throw my arms up and skate around the crease, going to the boards just as my teammates collide with me. There are love pats to my helmet, my back, and I head down toward the bench to collect the fist bumps from my teammates.

That's the best part, really. The rush of adrenaline, the cheering of the crowd. Our goal song, which is cheesy but ultimately pretty perfect for the Titans.

One more to go.

I glance up at the screen and watch the replay, grinning to myself. It cuts to Aurora's reaction, and my smile freezes on my face.

Luke is whispering something to her when I score, and

while she appears to be listening, she's definitely not focused on him. She's watching *me*. She leaps to her feet and throws her hands up, jumping in place.

I glance over to where she's sitting.

Luke is gone, and she's smiling.

See? I can do something right.

"One more," Jacob says.

Yeah. There's an unspoken *or else* following that sentence, although I know he doesn't mean it like a threat. He's not the one threatening Aurora.

On my next cycle, I get the puck and somehow, I score again.

And in the third period, I score again.

It's accidental, though, a deflection when I just meant to get the hell out of the way.

And Haverhill can't seem to get his act together. Because with four minutes remaining, we're still losing by *three*.

"High-scoring game," Church says to me. "What do you make of that?"

"I don't make anything of it." I pour water on my head. I'm burning up, but I'm glad I don't have the urge to shit my pants. Because that was fucking embarrassing. "I just think it's a high-scoring game."

"Uh-huh."

Lawson collides with a Vegas player. It's a nasty, uncalled-for hit from the Vegas side, and the whole crowd immediately dials in on them. There's boos and jeers that float up around us, the low tone going straight through me. It's nice when we've got the home team rooting for us.

They shove each other, and the whistle blows. Play comes to a halt. They're smack-talking, normal shit, but

Church and I automatically lean forward. Forearms on the bench, ready to leap into action if needed.

It wouldn't be the first time we've flung ourselves over the boards to get our skin in the game.

Their gloves come off.

"He's been itching for a fight," Church mutters.

"Good," I reply.

The refs are circling, but they don't interfere while Lawson and the Vegas player latch on to each other. They get some hits in, playing the fun game of trying to stay out of reach and hit the shit out of the other guy. Their helmets are knocked off.

"Come on," I yell. "You beat your dick harder than that!"

Another few seconds pass, and then Lawson seems to have had enough. He does some twisting move, dragging his opponent in closer and getting him off his feet.

The crowd, our bench, everyone goes mental.

The linemen step in, pulling Lawson away to the sin bin, and the Vegas player staggers to his feet. He spits blood on the ice and is guided away.

Good.

Three minutes left, and it's four on four. But we're losing so bad, I don't think it matters.

At a minute thirty, Church and I get back on the ice with Jacob. I don't want to score again, mindful of the threat against Aurora. I give the puck away as soon as I get it. Church shoots me a weird look. My passes are intercepted, and even with a man down, Vegas rushes the puck toward our goal.

And they fucking score.

I check the time and shake my head.

Two seconds left.

The refs organize us after Vegas's quick celebration. I take the face-off, bending low and ready. Although it's pointless. There's no way we're going to catch up after *that*.

We just got our asses handed to us.

And sure enough, the Vegas center seems to *let* me win the face-off, sending the puck to Rhodes. But the horn blows, and the game is over.

Seven to four.

What. The. Fuck?

There's a weird lingering sense of shame hanging over my head as we head to the locker room. I throw my helmet into my cubby. Everyone is quiet until our coach comes in.

"Everyone back on the ice," he says in a low voice. "*Now*."

Jeez.

We go without a word. I barely remember to grab my helmet and stick. Some guys have to re-lace their skates, which they do with quick, jerky movements. Our coach is bag skating us, I can feel it in my bones.

Which means he's going to run us into the ground to prove a point.

The arena is still slowly emptying when we hit the ice. His assistant coach blows a whistle, and we skate to the goal line.

"You know the drill," Coach says quietly. "Begin."

The whistle blows again. One sharp blast.

We push off, doing stupid suicide sprints to each line and back. Farther and farther, until we're crossing the whole rink. We make it back to the goal line, and I dig into the ice. I look over at Jacob, who frowns.

And Church, who's gritting his teeth like he expects this to go on all night.

Great.

We go again.

And again.

And again.

I puke, but I'm not alone. I press my hand to the boards and cough and choke, then swallow my pride and get back on the line.

I spot Aurora. She's still sitting in her seat, her arms folded tightly over her chest. Her expression is pinched, but she doesn't react otherwise.

Haverhill takes a tumble on the final turn, sliding into the wall. He's not the only one starting to fall over his feet. I can barely keep my skates under me.

By the time Coach calls it, we're drenched in sweat.

"In the goal, Haverhill." He knocks a pile of pucks onto the ice. "Two-on-ones."

Jacob takes his position in front of Haverhill. Church and I lock eyes, and we trade a nod. We move wordlessly toward him, Church cradling the puck and taking it down along the boards. When Jacob moves to intercept, he passes to me.

I know my best friend. He skates backward almost as fast as he does forward, and he races to meet me. I take a wild snap shot.

Haverhill catches it in his glove.

"Next," Coach yells.

We move aside, but before long we're up again. My legs have long since gone numb. I start our run, and Church shoots. It's blocked. *Again.*

"Next."

"Next."

"Next."

In the end, it's Lawson who slips the puck past Haverhill.

And Coach stops. He opens the door to allow us off the ice, stepping away to let us pass.

Without a word, we go. Silence rules the locker room. We strip and shower and re-dress, then exit and head our separate ways.

Aurora waits for me outside, leaning on the hood of Jacob's truck.

And suddenly, I'm not really tired anymore.

31
AURORA

"That was brutal," I comment.

Dad never really bag skated us like that. I mean, he coaches kids, and his focus tends to be more positive. He'll tell you when you don't play your best —and by *you* I mean *me*—and he put a big stress on fitness.

But that's different.

Knox's hair is wet when he finally emerges from the arena. Jacob is right behind him. Their bags are slung over their shoulders.

"How'd you know this was my truck?" Jacob questions.

"I guessed." I didn't guess, but saying that I'd seen him drive it would be a little weird. "So, who's hungry?"

"Me." Knox groans. "I need a full-body massage and a five-course meal."

"Weird combo, but I can see it."

"You volunteering to massage me?" He raises his eyebrows. "I wouldn't turn that down."

"I'm volunteering to be one of your five courses," I counter.

Jacob snorts and unlocks the truck. We pile in, me in the

backseat with the gear and them up front. It's actually kind of reminiscent of driving home from practices with Knox and Miles after school, me always in the back with the hockey bags. Knox drove. Miles liked to ride as a passenger princess with his hand out the window, even in the winter.

Watching them all skate for their lives was kind of satisfying. Their loss was abysmal. If I didn't know any better, I'd think Joel had a hole in his glove. Or maybe someone poisoned him, because his reaction time was not what it usually is.

Everyone has a bad day, but... yeah, the whole team was a mess. Vegas played good defense and even better offense, and it's reflected in the score.

"What was Abernathy talking to you about?" Knox twists in his seat. "Why was he sitting next to you?"

My cheeks heat. "Clocked that, did you?"

"Always."

I focus on the dark scenery rushing by. The traffic isn't bad now, not like right after a game. They were on the ice for over an hour. I don't really want to think about Luke's threats. He sat with me, quizzing me about Knox's knowledge. If I told him anything. If I gave anything away. If I was planning on looping him in.

Nothing, no I didn't, I'm not going to tell him anything.

He said a new doorman is just as easily bribed as an old one. Except next time, his lackey would bring knives. And maybe he wouldn't go as *easy* on me.

A chill slips down my spine, and I force the thought into a box in the back of my mind. I'll open it later, when I'm ready to digest it. But right now, I just... can't. Not when the pain is still so present in my mind.

"Sunny."

I flinch. "Don't."

"You don't like it when I call you Aurora, you don't like it when I call you Sunny. What am I supposed to call you? Wife?"

A strangled noise comes out of my throat. "No."

"That's what you are." He glances at Jacob, who's studiously ignoring us, then unbuckles. And the next thing I know, he's climbing in the backseat with me.

"What are you—?"

"Stop." He presses his finger to my lips. "Just shut up."

And then he kisses me.

I hate his kisses because they make me forget the six years between *then* and *now*. They make me forget that we don't get along, that he told me he never wanted to see me again. That he's refused to let me go and refuses to believe me.

In two days, we're playing Miles' team.

There's one way to prove that Miles and I didn't sleep together, but Knox isn't going to like it. Not that that's ever stopped me, but still. The thought is a little nerve-racking. Like I'm going to give up something just to prove a point.

Actually... Yeah, no, I'd absolutely do it to prove Knox wrong.

But anyway, he's kissing me, and I'm thinking about his brother—not exactly strong evidence to the contrary. I cup his neck, my thumbs on his pulse points. It's quick, and I smile against his lips. Because he's affected by me just like I'm affected by him, and I just can't contain my satisfaction at that.

The front passenger door opens, and I break away long enough to spot Melody sliding into the seat. But before I can say anything to her, Knox pulls my face back around to his.

And God, why does that turn me on?

Even as Jacob greets her, I can't focus on the words. I just taste Knox. And the slide of his lips on mine, the sweetest seduction in the form of wicked promises. Gosh, it's hard to remember that I hate him when his tongue moves against mine like this.

And why is he kissing me anyway?

Why can't he keep his tongue to himself?

He's pulling at my hips, and I slide onto his lap. I wrap my arms around his neck, my chest brushing his. We're glued together from hips to shoulders, to our open mouths, and if we weren't in a half-public place, with his friends literally a foot away, I'd be tempted to push us further. As it is, I grind myself on his groin. He's hard, although his pants do a somewhat poor job of containing it.

"Don't have sex in my truck."

Knox lurches, and I glance over my shoulder at Jacob. He's twisted around, slapping Knox's knee.

"Too close to her ass, dude," Knox murmurs, tugging me closer.

Because we're doing this, apparently. The whole possessive thing.

I don't mind it.

It takes me another second to realize we've arrived at a twenty-four-hour diner. Jacob and Melody get out, and it takes me another moment to disengage from Knox.

The fucker smirks at me, tired but *satiated*, like he just got his fill of me and can die happy. Although he can't, because he hasn't actually gotten off. And he won't. That's not in the cards for him. Not when he scored three goals instead of the agreed-upon two.

I already foresee my punishment coming from a long distance. The echo of a train when I'm tied to the tracks.

I slide out of the truck, landing on wobbly legs. Knox is

there a second later, brushing my hair off my shoulder and kissing my neck.

"You're in a mood." I tip my head to the side.

"You stayed."

"You were my ride home."

"You could've ordered a car," he replies. "But you stayed."

"I wanted to watch you suffer."

He pauses. "Me, too."

I don't know if he means me watching him or him watching me. But I don't get a chance to ask, because he moves past me and trails Jacob into the diner.

I sigh, straighten my shoulders, and follow.

———

Knox orders everything off the menu.

Melody Cameron, Jacob's old professor turned obsession turned love of his life, sits in the booth with Jacob. Her light-brown hair is caught up in a bun on top of her head, and her dark-rimmed glasses are perched on her nose. She's wearing red lipstick, a black Titans sweatshirt, and jeans.

She's dressed down compared to our last brief meeting at the charity gala.

"I've read your book," she confides to me.

"Oh?"

She glances at Knox, who's still chatting with the waitress. Customizing everything, or something. I don't know—and either way, I'm trying to ignore him because it's embarrassing to be that picky.

"Yeah, well, he asked me to."

My brow automatically furrows. "Knox did?"

She smiles. "It was kind of adorable. And very cloak-

and-dagger, you know? He didn't want me to know why he wanted me to read it, and then he asked my opinion on it—"

I stop her with a raised hand. "I get a lot of backlash on that book. Reviews to my face aren't really my thing..."

"No, Aurora." She grabs my hand and squeezes my fingers. "It was fantastic."

"Oh." I narrow my eyes. "Did he pay you to say that?"

"It's my honest opinion."

"You're out of *sausage*?" Knox exclaims to the waitress. "How? What? We have a very important, secret mission we're trying to carry out here, Cathy. We're trying to take down a fraudulent betting ring—"

"Okay, enough." I roll my eyes and pat his hand. "Poor guy, we took him out of the mental hospital across town to see the hockey game. And now he thinks he's a player and a spy."

The waitress blinks at me, then laughs nervously. "So, do you want all the food he ordered, or...?"

"Yes, of course," Knox snaps. "We're hungry. We're spies."

Jesus.

She nods and hurries away, and I shake my head.

"You're not helping our case here, babe."

He snorts. "Yeah, right. I didn't tell her anything—"

"You would've told her everything," Jacob points out. "I mean, it's your track record."

"And we're not actually spies," I point out.

Melody chuckles. She doesn't seem put off by his behavior, which is just weird in and of itself. I want to know more about her. She's kind of intriguing. There's paint in her nail beds, and Jacob keeps his hand on her thigh.

It makes my throat go all tight.

I already got the story of how they met. She was his professor, he was failing her class. Kind of cute, in a way. And then she was taken by her ex-husband, Jacob thought she ran away... cue years of misery on both their parts.

Until she showed back up with no memory.

We keep the chat light until the waitress returns. I didn't even order food—I was a little distracted—but the waitress *fills the table* with plates. So many plates. We have to push our drinks all the way to the side, and we stare as literally everything on the menu is set down in front of us.

Except the sausage.

I take a bite of bacon. It's extra crisp, just the way I like it, and Knox elbows me.

"You did not remember how I like my bacon," I mutter under my breath.

"Yes, I did."

"And you tape your stick the way I used to."

"Maybe I do that, too."

"You're evil," I snap.

"You're not so saintly yourself, sunshine."

Ugh.

Still.

Pancakes with different fillings, waffles, French toast, every kind of egg imaginable. Benedict, fried, scrambled... okay, maybe I'm not up on all my egg terminology. But it's a lot. I pick a plate at random and scoop some scrambled egg onto it, next to the waffles and bacon. Ketchup on the egg, maple syrup on the waffles. Nothing touching my nearly burnt bacon.

Coffee with just a dash of cream and a spoonful of sugar.

It's a good breakfast for it being almost midnight.

"Have you met the other girls, Aurora?" Melody asks.

She picks at an omelet. "We're all going to the game on Tuesday, and Willow mentioned she invited you."

"Yeah, she sent me the suite pass."

Knox drops his fork.

I glance over at him, frowning. "What?"

"When did you talk to Willow?"

"The other day..." I narrow my eyes.

Then it dawns on me that I didn't tell him about my conversation with his brother. Because why would I tell him about that?

I tap my chin and pretend to ponder it. "Hmm, is this because you still think I slept with Miles?"

Melody chokes.

"How did you get her number if you didn't talk to my brother?" Knox faces me fully. "Were you hoping to undermine me even further?"

I glower at him. "Yeah, Knox, my one goal in life is to sabotage you. *Oh, wait*, that's been your mission. You conceited asshole." I push at his arm, ignoring my odd heartbeat. "Let me out."

Stupid booth.

"No." He crosses his arms. "Miles always wanted to get back at me—"

"You petulant child," I seethe.

"If you think he'd do something as stupid as cheating on Willow, you've got another thing coming," Melody interjects. "He loves her more than anything. So adjust your attitude, Knox Whiteshaw, and stop letting your insecurities rule you."

Oh God, I think I'm in love.

With Melody freaking Cameron.

Knox stares at her for a second, shock flickering across his expression, and I smile.

"I'm so glad you found someone else to put you in your place," I say on a laugh.

But I'm still not staying.

I scoot to the side enough to draw my legs up, and I stand on the seat. I step over Knox, ignoring his expression, and hop off the bench.

"I'll call a car, as you oh-so graciously pointed out earlier I could do," I say sweetly. "I'll crash at Beth's place. Wouldn't want to ruin your night."

He frowns.

I tap my cheek, mind on the tooth with the tracker. If he's to be believed, which, you know, sometimes he can't. "You know where to find me if you want to apologize for your asshole behavior."

Shame we never got around to discussing the betting debacle.

Once outside, I press my palm to my heart and will myself to calm down. Fighting with Knox gives me a boost of adrenaline, but it's not good to get so worked up. Especially since it feels like I just ran a mile.

But I'm not turning around and going back. No way.

All that, and I didn't get to finish my bacon.

My heart feels funny.

I try to tell myself it's nothing. After leaving the diner, I swung by Beth's bar to get her key. She's still at work, and I'm crashing on her couch. It's almost two in the morning, and my worry keeps me awake.

I periodically press my index and middle finger to my throat. I count the beats and try to convince myself that I'm just being paranoid.

But my pulse is quick, and maybe a little uneven, and I'm not a hundred percent sure that I am okay. Which is why I end up caving. I call Beth and ask her to bring me to the hospital. She's got a car, the bar isn't far... She offers to stay once the ER doctor decides to admit me, but I wave her off.

They do tests, an EKG, all things that I've had done before and don't want to relive. My phone sits untouched on the rolling side table, alongside a cup of water. I don't want to call my dad. I don't want to freak him out or make him decide to get on a plane and fly out.

Because it's most likely just anxiety.

Or stress.

After Luke left me at the game, I searched betting apps and downloaded the more popular one. I scanned it for odds on the Titans winning by two, or Knox scoring two goals, or *whatever*. I didn't come up blank, per se, but I didn't find what I needed.

In the end, though, it didn't matter what I thought I was searching for. And it just goes to show that I can't begin to fathom the web of this organization and the planning they put into it. I'm assuming millions of dollars are at stake.

Was it Luke's intention to have Vegas win?

Or was Joel just not on his game?

"We're going to keep you under observation," my new doctor informs me. "Our top cardiologist will be in tomorrow morning, bright and early, to chat with you. But it's not a heart attack or anything we're deeming emergent. The best course of action is to wait and see."

I don't think I'd be able to handle another emergency. Although coming to the hospital in the middle of the night feels like one, I'm glad that I'm not actively dying.

How dramatic, right?

As soon as I'm alone, I sag back against the pillows and touch the scar on my chest. It used to be slightly raised, but it's faded in the last six years. Since my last emergency surgery.

Thinking of that sends a shiver down my spine, and I screw my eyes shut tight.

"This isn't that," I whisper to myself.

I try to ignore the lit-up monitors behind my head. They've quieted the beeping, and I close my eyes...

Only for my narrow bed to dip some time later, dragging me out of my half-dream.

When I crack my eyes open, I can't quite tell if I'm still dreaming.

Knox sits beside me, his black cap backward on his head. Gray sweatshirt, black sweatpants. He looks like he did at seventeen, the familiar worry lines furrowing his brow. He used to sneak into my hospital room and keep me company.

"Sunny," he whispers, more of an admonishment than anything else.

And before I can say anything, he kicks off his shoes, ditches the hat, and peels back the blankets. He crawls in beside me, curling his body around mine.

"I know you hate hospitals," he whispers.

Yeah.

"So just this once, we can call a truce."

Just this once.

33
MANUSCRIPT

CHAPTER 4

"Sunny!"

Knox catches up to me in the hallway, slipping my bag easily off my shoulder. He hooks it over his bag like it doesn't weigh a million pounds.

"So, I did some checking."

I eye him. "Checking on what?"

He glances around, then lowers his voice. "Insurance."

"Okay…" I don't get it. And my face probably says that.

It's been three days since we kissed in my bedroom. Three semi-awkward days where I did my best to keep Knox at arm's length. Making sure someone was always in the room with us, be it his brother or a parent.

Because I can't stop thinking about the kiss. And kissing him again. And touching more than just the front of his shirt.

He runs his fingers through his hair. "Listen. Some insurances are better than others, and they cover more. So you leave the hospital with a bill of five grand instead of a hundred grand." He stares at me.

"That's great," I offer. "I don't really understand what you're getting at, since my dad can't just switch insurances. He already looked into it, and it's way more expensive to do it out of pocket. His employer—"

"No, I know." He goes quiet.

Which is very un-Knox-like.

"Can I give you a ride home?"

I make a face. "No, I don't think so."

"Okay, I'll just hold your bag hostage, then." He winks at me and strides off. "You know where I usually park, sunshine!"

I stop. Beth comes out of a side hall and pauses beside me.

"What's up with that expression on your face?" she asks. "Like you just tasted something... deliciously sour."

"That's weird, Beth."

She shrugs. "So?"

"Knox is being weird." I sigh. "I mean, we kissed in my room—"

"*Hold up*," she screeches, grabbing my arm and pulling me into the girls' bathroom down the hall. "Spill. All the details."

I wave my hand. "I had a panic attack and called him. He climbed in through my window. We kissed. Mom walked in and interrupted."

"Before tongue or after?" Beth demands.

She's the one who's had three boyfriends. She knows all about kissing and tongue and other *stuff*, like the mechanics of blow jobs and sex. She's the one who gave me instructions last year at a sleepover, barely getting through it without giggling.

"Before," I mumble. My face is getting hot again. "And now he has my backpack, so I've got to go retrieve that. I think he's going to drive me home..."

She was going to do that.

But clearly, the prospect of him kissing me again is all she can think about, because she's practically giddy. She pushes me in his direction, clapping loudly. "You got this!" she calls. "Kiss him with tongue!"

Jesus.

I find Knox's car pretty easily. He's leaning against the back bumper, smiling like the cat who just caught the mouse.

"Get in, sunshine," he says.

I roll my eyes, but I do as instructed. I try to breathe normally, to focus on the fact that this is just my neighbor giving me a simple ride home.

But all that goes out the window when he gets in, starts the car, and pulls onto the street, then puts his hand on my thigh. I stare at it for a long moment. The heat from his palm is incredible, seeping through my jeans at an alarming rate.

And then he heads in a different direction. One we've been before, that leads to the lake. Away from home. We're silent the whole way there. Also not very Knox-like. The hand on my leg, the quiet... it's making me nervous.

"Say something," I blurt out, just as he turns into the parking lot for the lake's boardwalk.

He parks and kills the engine.

"I'm going to kiss you again," he warns, twisting toward me.

I mirror his movement, swallowing hard. "Okay."

This kiss is guaranteed to not get interrupted.

And it isn't. Not when he slowly reaches for me,

cupping my cheek. Not when we both lean forward, drawn together like magnets. Not when our lips touch for the first time, sliding tentatively together. Or when his tongue sweeps along the seam of my mouth, a tentative ask to open. Which I do.

And the taste of his tongue suddenly in my mouth, playing with mine. His kiss morphs from slow and shy into something much more aligned with his personality. Friendly and open and full of passion. I feel it, too. I'm caught up in the desire coursing through me, zapping all over my skin, I barely register his hand on my hip. Then his thumb on my bare skin just above the waistband of my jeans, under my shirt. Dragging lines across my skin that leave me tingling.

Eventually, we break apart. My breathing is ragged, my heart pounding. Usually when it beats this frantically, I get worried.

But right now, all I want is *more*.

More Knox. More kissing. More, more, more.

"Your dad's insurance sucks," he says, the breath on his exhale hitting my lips. "That's why it costs so much. They're paying a fortune."

I blink at him. "How do you know that?"

"I did some research." He shifts slowly back into his own seat. "And, um, I have a solution."

"Okay..."

"Marry me."

There's this moment where everything stops. Like, my heart, my thoughts, the world. Everything jars to a halt, and all I can do is replay Knox's last two words.

A two-word sentence.

Or was it a question?

"Um, Knox—"

"I know, it's crazy and stupid and it's not really how I wanted to ask you." He seems so sincere. He grabs my hands, squeezing both tightly. "If we're married, you can get on my family's plan. I already checked. And my parents have the top-of-the-line shit, like the best that money can buy. Because—well, I guess because they have money, right? I'm sorry if that's insensitive—"

"Knox."

He winces.

"You want to marry me... so I can use your insurance?"

"Well, yeah." He looks away. His face gets redder. "Yeah."

My gut is flipping. I just can't tell if it's a good or bad thing. "I'm sixteen," I point out. "I just... I mean, you're seventeen. We'd need parental permission, and..."

How do I tell him that I always thought I'd get married for love? Like the white dress, fairy-tale wedding, all that stuff? Good vibes only. Cake tasting and picking out flowers and colors, selecting my bridesmaids. Asking Beth to be my maid of honor, obviously.

"I would do anything for you," he manages. "And this is just the tip of the iceberg, Sunny. You and I could be endgame, but—"

But I have to survive to the end to be endgame.

I close my eyes. "It's a nice thought. I just don't know if I can do that."

He releases my hands. "Promise me you'll think about it?"

"I will." I crack my eyes open.

He's shifted back fully into driving position. It only gives me a moment to get righted before we're backing out of the parking spot and heading home.

To be talked about... never again.

Because marrying Knox Whiteshaw is irrational. Crazy. Insane, even.

All things I am not.

34

KNOX

I dream of sunshine. A glittering, outdoor ice rink, completely smooth. Ready to be carved up by skates.

Aurora.

She's standing on the ice in hockey gear, a stick in her hand and pucks spread out around her bare feet. Her toenails are painted pink, the skin around them turning blue. She doesn't look the least bit cold, though.

"Come on," she goads. "You wanna go?"

"Your bedroom or mine?"

Her cheeks flame. Pretty little thing. Her red hair just makes her flush stand out more. The cold is creating a beautiful dichotomy on her skin. Pale and cherry red. She adjusts her stick and steps to the side, sliding on the ice like she was born for it. Even barefoot.

I step out onto the rink after her. The bite of cold travels up from the soles of my bare feet, zinging straight up my legs.

"It's not that bad," she whispers, suddenly in front of me. "It's like an elephant sitting on your chest."

I blink at her. "What is?"

"The ice. If you get used to breathing with the elephant, it just helps life go on. Instead of thinking you're abnormal, or…" She laces her fingers with mine. "Or *cold*."

"I'm not cold."

She cracks a smile. "I thought I was the liar."

The sunshine fades. The sky grows dark around us. "You are the liar."

She slips away from me, taking a puck and shooting toward the far side. There's a goal I hadn't noticed there before. And a boy in the goal. He's younger than both of us, closer to how I remember leaving him when I went to college.

He blocks her shot and takes off his helmet, shaking out his hair.

"Nice try, Sunny."

That's what I call her.

Nice try, Sunny. It echoes in my brother's voice, coming at me from all sides. Even as Aurora drifts closer to him, shooting again. And again. And again.

He doesn't stop them all, but he tries.

She can skate circles around us.

I follow her. There's a stick on the ice, and I pick it up. It's got her style of tape on the handle, something I used to hate but now can't skate without. It freezes my fingertips. "Is this what you feel?"

"No," she calls back. "I feel the elephant."

I don't know what that means.

Not until something knocks me flat on my back and a heavy weight lands on my chest. I can't breathe. I lose the stick, flailing helplessly on the ice. I gasp, but no air comes to my burning lungs.

"Like that," she says, stopping over me.

Miles looks down at me from her other side. "He can't breathe."

His tone is clinical but not alarmed.

"I know," Aurora answers. "But he'll get used to it."

———

I wake up in a sweat, gasping for air.

"You're okay." She brushes my hair off my forehead. "Breathe, Knox."

My lungs finally cooperate. I inhale sharply, coughing and rolling onto my side. I gag, almost throwing up, but manage to not make that big of a fool of myself. She pats my back until I twist toward her, then scoot into a sitting position like her.

"You been up long?"

"Just enough to watch you squirm in your sleep." She points to the tray. "A nurse brought two breakfasts. I managed to convince her not to kick you out at four o'clock this morning."

I rub my eyes. "Thanks."

"It's eight," she supplies before I can ask. "And the doctor is discharging me."

"You had a whole conversation with him while I slept?" I squint at her. I didn't think I was that deep of a sleeper, but... jeez.

"You had a long day." She waves me off.

That reminds me of my dream. Her hand anyway. I take the blanket and flip it off our legs, exposing her bare feet.

And her pink toenails.

I shiver.

"Are you okay?"

"Just a weird fucking dream," I reply. "Um, I'm going to

go check on that discharge paperwork. And see if you can fly."

"We're not flying," she points out. "You have a home game. Melody and I are driving."

I stop, realizing she's right. "But eventually you'll need to fly."

Melody is picking her up? Are they that close? I mean, they met twice, but probably a grand total of under an hour spent together.

She sighs. "Stop trying to figure out my ulterior motive. It's exhausting."

"You're exhausting," I retort.

I put my shoes on and find my hat on the floor. After a quick detour through the bathroom—they even have a toothbrush, which I'm pretty sure is one Aurora keeps in her purse like a psycho, although it doesn't stop me from using it—I head to the nurses' station.

My mission?

To get the *real* story.

One of the nurses recognizes me. I lean on the counter and give her my best, most charming smile. Once Miles was born, I had to rely on antics to get the attention I deserved. Which usually resulted in being labeled *class clown* or some such monstrosity. I got the laughs I wanted, though, and the focus from my parents that I needed.

Miles was always the quiet, calm one. He had boundless energy on the ice and a bit of a toxic behavior when it came to competition. I mean, *I'm* competitive, but he took it to a new level. It was him who escalated things when we were on the ice together.

He was just too good. Naturally. I needed to take him down a peg or two. It resulted in fights, smack-talk, just regular brother shit but spiked by adrenaline and blades attached to our feet. And padding. Because no matter how hard you whack someone with a stick, it's not going to hurt as bad if they're in full hockey gear.

They essentially ended our feud when they put him in the goal.

I tried to goaltend, but I hated it. Hated being confined to the crease, to going from standing around to a hundred percent alert. To wearing the weight of the game on my shoulders if I let a puck in, if my playing wasn't perfect.

Miles never sweated that.

So he could take that crease and all the glory that comes with being a goalie.

Me? Center. Aggressive, charming, lethal in a face-off. It's where I shine.

Anyway, back to the nurse. She's watching me like she's never seen a hockey player with all his teeth before.

I refrain from making myself more human by detailing the almost-shit-my-pants scene.

"I hope you can help. I just want to talk to Aurora's doctor, see if there's anything I should keep an eye out for..." I lean in and lower my voice. "She had emergency open-heart surgery a few years ago. I'm sure that's in her chart, but it makes me worry."

Her attention drops to the ring on my finger.

It's been on a chain around my neck for six years. I put it on for the charity gala, and I haven't been able to take it off since. Not that I'm reading into that at all.

"Please," I say.

She types something on the computer. "We have Aurora's history. If the doctor saw anything alarming—"

"Aurora doesn't freak out," I interrupt. "She wouldn't have come in if she didn't feel something that made her worry."

"There was a murmur," she admits. "When Aurora first came in, the ER doctor noted a heart murmur. But all the tests came back normal. They've scheduled a follow-up—"

"Okay." I frown. "Thank you."

I head back to her room and stop. I need better people. Better doctors. The best that money can buy. Except, I have no idea where to start, and I'm terrified of getting it wrong.

She's in a new state, after all. My insurance would've come with her, if she transferred it... if she's still using it. I signed the paperwork on autopilot when I joined the NHL, and then again when I was traded to the Titans. I didn't think about it, because Aurora was one of those things I would've rather never thought of again.

Doesn't mean I was willing to *abandon* her, as the lawyer tried to argue.

Speaking of which, I should make sure that's squashed. She's back to living with me, financially dependent... maybe. I don't know how much she makes on her book, actually. But she's living with me, and we're sexually *something*, so she doesn't have a leg to stand on.

Not when I want to stay married.

I do want to stay married, right?

But like... not just to torture her. Because I think I might actually be falling for her. *Again.*

35
AURORA

Tuesday.

Game day.

We got almost a foot of snow overnight, which was unexpected. I ripped the tags off the boots Dad sent back with me a few weeks ago, grateful for the warm, fake-fur-lined interiors. I wiggle my toes and zip up my jacket, carefully fixing my makeup and my winter hat.

I get into Jacob's truck with Melody, armed with two coffees. She smiles at me and takes one, sipping it carefully.

"Delicious. Hazelnut?"

"A little birdie said you might like that flavor." I smile. "And I happened to have it in my fridge." I pull out a pack of gummy bears. "And I brought sugar."

When I was a teen and traveling with my dad to hockey camps and games, he always had coffee in the cupholder and gummy bears tucked in the center console. I'm not really sure why I even grabbed them. But I saw them in the store yesterday and just... had to have them.

It's not a long drive—well, it's not supposed to be. But

with game-day traffic on top of the snow, we inch our way toward the arena parking garage.

Knox and Jacob left a few hours ago. They have their rituals, and I can't begrudge them for those. Besides, I think I'd throw up if I had to watch Knox house a plate of chicken fettuccine alfredo in under five minutes. At eleven o'clock in the morning.

Game-day-ritual meal, my ass. He just likes pasta.

Even still, the conversation with Melody comes easily. Even though she's just over ten years older than me, we click better than I have with almost anyone else my age. Except Knox, I guess. But do we click, or do we just *argue*?

Even Beth and I have a disconnect sometimes.

I learn that Melody is a painter. She just sold her fifth painting to an art collector in Seattle. With some help from Jacob, she bought a space for a local gallery here in town. They had a show for her a year or two ago, and since then she's been in love with the space.

So now she owns it, although she has people to run it for her. She spends her days painting, yes, but also curating her own collection of art to sell and helping others get off the ground. She teaches an English Lit class at the local college, too.

I tell her about my book, the one she read. She has questions about publishing, coming from an English degree, and then about the characters. It's kind of surprising that we go there, because I just assumed that she said she read it to be nice.

I wasn't going to quiz her on it.

"Give me the rundown on the others?" I ask.

"Violet and Greyson are married. Violet's a ballerina with the Boston Ballet Company, and Greyson plays for Boston.

She's nice, a little quiet until you get to know her. Willow is her best friend and more of a socialite than Violet." Melody glances at me. "She's sober, just so you know. She and Miles are engaged, with a wedding planned for next summer. They just adopted a dog, and her sister watches it while they travel."

"That's nice," I murmur.

"Willow sings," she adds. "Um, last I heard she was talking to a record label, but I don't know what's happening with that."

"Wow."

"Then there's Aspen and Steele. Aspen's mom married Steele's dad, so their family is a bit jumbled. Kind of funny, if you think about it..."

"Uh-huh."

"Aspen is nice. She plays the piano, and she can come across as tough sometimes, but underneath she's a sweetheart. You'll like her."

"Okay." I mean, I'm sure she's right. But I'm also fucking nervous.

I have Beth.

And that's... it.

"You played hockey?"

I glance at her. "How'd you know about that?"

"Knox was saying how you used to skate circles around him and Miles. As someone who's not good on skates and has two left feet, I find it inspiring."

I sink back. "Yeah, well, Dad's a coach for squirts. Like ten-year-olds. At the time, I had way too much energy, and Mom was more than happy to let me go race around on the ice to get her few minutes of peace and quiet."

I shouldn't talk about my mom. An ache forms in my chest, and I try to rub it away. Not that it works. I just feel the lingering tingles of disrupted nerve endings along the scar, and it reminds me that I'm not normal.

That most things in life I've cared about have been ripped away from me.

"Your mom?"

"Died," I murmur.

"I read your dedication to her in your book. I'm sorry for your loss." She hums. "Mine wanted me dead."

I stare at her. Melancholy mood officially *broken*. "I think I want to hear this."

Her telling the story gets me out of my funk, and I find myself enraptured. I mean, I write about twisted things—and sometimes I don't know where that darkness comes from. But this is a whole new level.

Meanwhile, Knox is convinced I'm worse than my characters.

And Melody's mom could be a villain right out of the book.

"You've dealt with a lot."

She shrugs. "You have, too. Don't feel like you need to compare our stories."

"That's all I do, really." The quiet admission stings a bit.

"Well, we don't." She parks and zips up her coat. "We support girl power."

With that, she turns off the truck and hops out. An icy wind sweeps into the cab, and I shiver for a split second. Considering her words. Girl power is important. The romance industry is dominated by women, and yet, I don't help anyone. I don't talk to anyone.

I figured out a way to market my book, and when it blew up, I shut down.

That's not very *girl power* of me.

But at the same time... what if I don't have the

capacity for it? What if writing these twisted characters and pushing it out into the world made me tired and bitter, and then my life just kept imploding more and more?

What if there's only so much I can do, and being nice is the first to go?

What if I'm not a nice person?

I follow Melody into the arena, to a special booth where an older man greets her by her name. He scans her phone, then turns to me.

"I don't think we've met, young lady."

"Aurora," I say.

"Knox Whiteshaw's wife," Melody interjects. "He was the recent trade."

The older man waves her off. "Yes, yes, the people who come through can't stop yipping about him. Not undeserved, your husband has a killer wrist shot."

"I'll make sure to pass that along." Because I specifically remember helping him with that when we were thirteen and fourteen. He was miserable at those technical shots. Slap shots? No problem. Snapshot? Not as good but not anything to complain about.

And now look at him.

My phone rings on our way upstairs. Dad's face fills my screen, and I motion for Melody to go without me. "I'll meet you up there."

"Okay," she says softly.

"Hey, Dad," I say. "What's up?"

"I got a phone call today." His voice is tight, and he skips our usual greeting. "I just need to know what you're involved in, kiddo."

"What?" My heart gives a thump, and I close my eyes. Now's not the time for my *heart* to be reacting like this. I lean my shoulder against the wall. "I don't know what you're saying."

"Do you need help? Are you…?"

"Am I what?"

"Are you betting on the games?"

My vision goes white-spotted. I slide down the wall and sit hard. "Dad, what? No, I'm not—"

I mean, I am. But it's the only way to try and foil this stupid betting fraud, to put some skin in the game. I mean, it's not like I know what the outcome is going to be. I just have what Luke tells me to get Knox to do.

And I have.

Well, I've tried.

"I'm not addicted to gambling or anything, if that's what you're worried about," I whisper. "Who called you? What did they say?"

"It was a man concerned about you. He said you've been using your friendships with the guys on the team to get favorable outcomes. Aurora, I don't have to tell you that that is *illegal*."

What?

"No, Dad—"

"Honey, if you're having money problems—"

That's laughable. I'm making more money than I ever have with the book, which has taken on a life of its own, and he thinks I'm gambling away my last pennies.

"You have it wrong. The guy on the phone was just trying to scare you. I promise. It's probably a scam or something. I made a few low-risk bets that paid off, some that didn't, but nothing major. And I did not *rig* anything."

He's silent for a moment. Then, "Am I going to see you for Christmas?"

"I…"

"I ran into the Whiteshaws. Knox told his mother that you'd both be traveling back. She was surprised to find that I hadn't heard the same from you." Now his tone is hurt.

I'm going to kill Knox.

"Sorry, it's, um… I don't know. I need to talk to Knox about it, apparently. But yes, I'll be home. We'll celebrate Christmas."

"Are you all right, Aurora?"

Am I all right?

Well, *no*.

"I will be," I promise. Never mind that I didn't call him about the heart scare. No need to freak him out *that* much. Especially when I'm going to see him in a few weeks.

Something Knox could've told me about.

I hang up with him and hurry to the suite.

But in the doorway, I stop.

Melody is standing with three other girls, laughing about something. She looks at home among them.

And I'm a complete fish out of water.

I'm not a girl's girl. I'm not anything other than someone who'd rather be in her own head than socializing. Beth has condemned me for that before, although she insists that she still loves me. Knowing she's working at the bar while I'm here fills me with guilt.

"Aurora!" Melody waves me in. "Meet the girls."

I swallow and nod, forcing a smile.

"Aurora, this is Aspen, Violet, and Willow. And Steele and Greyson are in the corner." She hooks her thumb over her shoulder.

Two guys, familiar in a distant, weird way, are standing by the glass talking quietly. They both glance my way, brows furrowed, then go back to their conversation.

Shit. I shift my weight. "So, um, what has Knox said

about me? Poisoning the well, I'm sure." I cross my arms, then uncross them.

Damn it, I'm *fidgeting*.

Willow's brows furrow. "Poisoning the well? He hasn't said anything to us. He really only talks to the guys and Melody."

They're all so pretty. And they're friends.

And I'm not anything, particularly friend*ly*.

"Excuse me." I hold up my phone, like it's ringing, when really it's never been so silent. Doesn't stop me from rushing out and down the hall, into a stairwell, and dialing the first number that comes to mind.

"What's wrong?"

I suck in air, but it's hard to breathe. Hard to talk. I sit heavily on a step and put my head between my legs, but it's not working. So he just listens to me gasp for a solid fifteen seconds, wheezing a little, before the line goes dead.

Less than five minutes later, a door far below bangs open. Footsteps pound on the concrete steps, and when Knox rounds the last landing, he doesn't stop. He rushes up and drops to his knees in front of me, forcing me to lift my head.

"Is it your heart? Can you breathe?"

I shake my head. "Panic," I wheeze. "I can't do this. I can't be your wife."

He narrows his eyes. "You're panicking because you're having cold feet *now*? Six years after you actually married me?"

Well, *yeah*.

"Jeez, Sunny, I didn't realize you cared." He touches my cheek, then brushes his thumb over my lips. "Just breathe. You're okay."

I try.

He puts his hand on my chest, grabs mine, and puts it on his. I feel his heart beating steadily, the rise and fall as he inhales and exhales. I follow his lead. My gaze is stuck on his lips, on the way he makes a *whooshing* noise on the exhale.

"Okay?" he asks.

I bite my lip. "I just don't have very many friends. They're *your* friends."

He blinks. "Who? The girls?"

"Obviously."

He laughs. It bursts out of him, so loud that I almost flinch. *Almost.*

"They're not my friends. Not after what I did to Willow. You want me to prove it to you?"

I raise my eyebrow. I don't have that feeling of suffocating anymore, and I let him help me to my feet. "That sounds like a challenge."

"You know it." His gaze gleams. "So, how about it?"

"What do you have in mind?"

36

KNOX

Aurora doesn't have very many friends? She's a world-famous author. And she's still carrying on her relationship with Beth, even after all they've been through. But, *sure*, I'll prove to her that I'm not close with my best friends' girls. If it makes it easier for her to sit and watch the game...

Plus, Greyson and Steele know what's up with us. They got the lowdown the other day, a whole long-ass text message—or six—that explained the who, what, where, and why of my marriage to Aurora. So consider them, plus my brother and Jacob, all filled in.

Whether they shared that info with their ladies is beyond me.

Greyson and Steele are also charged with running interference between Luke Abernathy and Sunny. So if he tries to get close to her, or threaten her, then they'll step in. Which could be a good or terrible thing, depending on... well, on Luke Abernathy.

And how far he'll go.

I take Aurora's hand and lead her to the suite, pulling her in with me.

"Ladies," I call. "Aurora was feeling a bit out of sorts. Worried about my wellbeing against my brother."

I glance at her, and she frowns.

"She's got a soft spot for Miles," I continue. "She's seen his dick, after all—"

Aurora yanks her hand out of mine. "You're relentless, aren't you?"

"You're the one who wanted to make friends, sunshine. I'm just helping—"

"You mean sabotaging," she interrupts.

"Oh my God." I shrug and pretend to pick lint off my jersey.

I was in the process of getting my pads on when she called, and I dropped everything to get to her. Which makes me feel a bit like a damn fool. I mean, did she even need me? Or did she just want to see how fast I could get to her?

"Anyway. Willow, you keep an eye on this one." I slap Aurora's ass.

She jumps a foot, and I smile.

Wickedly.

"See you later, *baby*."

She scowls at me, and I salute my friends. Out I go, leaving her to clean up the mess I made for her.

Downstairs, I almost crash into none other than my brother. He holds up his phone, where a text from Willow on his screen reads: *He's out of control.*

"What are you doing to fuck up my life now?" he goads. "Have you not done enough? Do I need to break your nose again?"

I scoff. "You didn't break it in the first place."

"Knox."

"Miles." I roll my eyes. "Your other girlfriend is upstairs with Willow. You might want to get your story straight with her—"

He stares at me. "She said you thought we slept together. I didn't actually think you meant it."

"Well, I do." I know what I saw. And what I heard. "I have evidence."

Miles crosses his arms. This is the most we've talked since, well... since the Willow debacle. And that was years ago.

"You have evidence," he repeats. "Evidence that you've somehow managed to keep to yourself for six years?"

My anger spikes. I step in closer, grabbing the front of his shirt. "Yes, baby brother, I decided to keep it to myself. Because I love you, I'd do anything for you. Even if that means not blowing up your world when you blew up mine."

He shoves me away. "Fuck off, Knox."

Yeah. Conversation *over*.

"See you on the ice," I snap. "Let's hope you remember how to play against me. It's been a while."

I storm past him and into the Titans' locker room, my stomach flipping. I hate it when we fight. I've hated and regretted the years following what happened with Willow. Not because of her, but because of just how strained my relationship with my brother became.

Mom tried to get us to fix it. She pushes us closer at every holiday, watches our stiff interactions with sad eyes, but she's like me. She doesn't know how to make it right.

"Whiteshaw."

Church stands in the doorway, and he motions for me to follow him. We've got forty-five minutes until we need to be on the ice to warm up, and about an hour and a half until game time. I was slowly getting ready when I got Aurora's call.

She called *me*. And of course, I messed that up, too.

There's some part of me that relishes it. That wants to mess her up all the time, like smearing red paint on her white walls.

We end up in an office down the hall. Church closes us in and leans against the door.

"I was thinking," he starts.

"That's never a good sign."

"There's something going on with the games. You said... hypothetically, of course, that you're being told how many goals to score?"

I cross my arms. "I didn't mean to tell you that, Church. These guys are serious. They already attacked my wife once, and fuck if I'll give them an excuse to come after her again."

I'm somewhat regretting opening my mouth. Jacob warned me about this. Telling people. What if Church is in on it?

"They're rigging the whole game," he says.

"Probably."

"How?"

I shrug. "No clue."

He eyes me. "It's not just you, then. There's someone else."

I consider that. The idea that Luke Abernathy got to another player. He might not be threatening them like he is us—he could just be paying them. Bribery works just as well as threats. Maybe more so if it's a high enough payout.

"Who would do that?" I shake my head. "A d-man letting the other team through? Someone just underperforming?"

Church makes a face. "I don't know. But we need to figure it out. Who's in charge of the operation?"

"Oh, um..." I hesitate. "I'm not going to tell you that."

Besides, it *has* to be bigger than just the owner's son. It has to be more widespread than just the Titans. Especially since he doesn't contact Aurora all the time, for every game. It's sporadic. And that's either to try and not draw attention, or...

"We're not going to make the playoffs at this rate," Church says quietly. "If you keep sabotaging us—"

"I'm not," I snap. "I was told to score twice—"

"And you got a hat trick."

"Well, the third was an accident," I hedge.

"They ran all over us," Church argues. "How?"

The door opens, knocking Church aside. Jacob slips inside and flips the lock, scowling at his captain.

"If you're going to hold a secret meeting, for fuck's' sake, lock the door."

Church sighs.

"What about the assistant coach?" I straighten. "He was talking to—"

Jacob shoots me a look.

"Someone," I finish lamely.

Church's gaze bounces back and forth between Jacob and me. "Fine," he finally says. "You don't trust me. That's fine. Just figure out who's sabotaging us under orders, and loop me in."

"Yes, boss," Jacob says. A bit sarcastically. He even salutes.

Camden Church frowns and leaves us alone in the office, the door closing softly behind him.

"Well?" I question. "I mean, I didn't expect him to believe me..."

"We don't know who to trust," Jacob points out. "You can't just tell people. What if he's working with Abernathy?"

"Then we're fucked."

"Right. So shut up and keep your eyes peeled." He yanks the door open. "We've got a game to win."

With no restrictions on us, I find the weight coming off my shoulders. We don't have orders to lose—which means we can play our best.

And I'm relishing getting one over on my baby brother.

"Think I can repeat my hat trick?"

37
AURORA

Plan Prove Knox Wrong is about to go full throttle. I decided it after he told the whole suite I slept with his brother, then left me to defend myself.

As soon as he was gone, though, Willow burst into laughter.

And the mood considerably lightened.

Now, I'm sitting between her and Melody, who's on her phone and not really watching the game. The other two, Violet and Aspen, seem more into it.

"Not a fan?" I ask Melody.

She winces. "It's just... bloody."

I grin. "Yeah."

"You played," she says. "What position?"

Willow perks up. "You grew up next to the Whiteshaws, right?"

"I played winger. A forward position," I say for Melody's sake. "And yeah, my family moved in next door to them when I was five or so. My dad coached their team for a bit. Until they outgrew it."

"Cool," Willow murmurs. "And this rumor..."

"Is going to be put to rest," I assure her. My gaze drops to my lap. "He keeps bringing it up. I think it bothers him more than he admits."

Or maybe this is his way of admitting it.

"You two got married young," Melody says. "I mean, that's a lot of pressure. You were how old? Sixteen."

"Yeah." My throat tightens. "I was sixteen. And it wasn't love, really. I don't know. It was more necessity than anything else."

He saved my life. It sounds dramatic, but it's true. My family was drowning in debt. The medical bills kept stacking up, on top of their regular bills and the mortgage, food, and clothes, and *hockey*. Before they snatched that away from me.

It wasn't a good situation in any way, except the distraction of the Whiteshaw brothers next door.

"Anyway," I say, casting a glance around to change the subject. I find Greyson and Steele watching me, too. "Devereux. I saw your game against the Titans last week."

He cracks a smile. "Oh, yeah?"

"Yeah. Hey, did your coach know you were out on the ice?"

Steele snorts.

"Like you could do better?" Devereux challenges.

Oh, I love a challenge. And I miss skating more than I miss anything in the world. I pretend to consider it, then shrug. "Yeah, I probably could. I mean, the bar is kind of low."

He whistles. "Okay, game on."

"Game on," I echo.

"I want in on this," Steele interjects. "Tomorrow. Before we fly home."

Knox is going to kill me after the hospital scare.

"Deal," I agree anyway. "Miles can goaltend."

"And Knox?"

"Can fuck off."

They laugh. Even the girls. And I smile, settling back in my chair. The teams have left the ice, their warm-up done, and the game will be starting soon. But now I have a nice, warm feeling in my chest. So maybe I *can* make friends.

Until I look at Willow and bite my lip. "Will you tell me what happened between you two? Or... the three of you, maybe?"

She meets my gaze. Steady, steady, steady. "Of course, Aurora. But it... it's not pretty. Maybe some things are left unheard."

"No." I stare her down. "No, I need to know all of it. The good, bad, ugly. I don't trust that he'll be honest about it."

She nods. Aspen holds her hand.

"Knox and I started dating our junior year. We went from hooking up to something more committed within a few months, and were together for a year."

I try to control my face. He was with her for a *year*?

"I have—*had*—issues with love. Unbeknownst to me, he was waiting for me to admit it." Willow frowns. "He was adamant. But he never said it to me. He made me believe he did, but when I told him I loved him... he laughed in my face."

Ouch.

"It was at a party. Everyone saw my humiliation."

"There was also the matter of Knox choosing to save his brother over her," Aspen interjects. "Which we're still pissed about."

"He—what?"

Willow takes my hand. "That's not important. They're still mad, but I understand his motivation. We were in danger, but there wasn't a win-win scenario. Someone had to lose, and to Knox, nothing was more important than his brother."

I understand that, too.

"That's the gist of it," Willow finishes. "Kind of a quick story for what felt like a decade of my life."

I clutch her hand tighter before she can pull away. "Thank you for telling me, Willow."

She manages a sad smile. "Yeah, well. It's good to know, so he doesn't do something similar to you."

"What, sacrifice me for Miles?" I laugh. "He'd gladly burn me at the stake for no reason at all."

And I'm pretty sure *that's* the truth.

———

I spend the majority of the first and second period explaining things to Melody. Like an announcer rapid-firing play-by-plays in her ear, but made a little more digestible to someone new to the sport.

Willow leans forward every time the Titans go on the offensive, circling Miles in the crease like sharks out for blood. Violet sits between Willow and Greyson. Steele and Aspen are on his other side, his arm wrapped around her shoulders.

I have to admit, today the Titans are a new team. They come out swinging, with an aggressiveness I haven't seen in the past few games. They've gotten into a few scuffles, but nothing crazy.

Not until there's a breakaway play, and Knox charges at his brother.

I lean forward, too, my breath caught in my chest.

He dodges around a d-man and shoots, a perfect wrist

shot that soars like a bullet—

Into the net.

I jump to my feet, pounding on the glass and cheering. Because I could almost *taste* that shot and the sweet victory that follows it. Knox collects his congratulations and glances up at the suite. For a moment, it seems like he's staring right at me.

But then the moment breaks, he turns away, and I return to my seat.

I glance down to the far end of the rink, where Joel stands. He seems more composed today, and I chalk up their epic loss to a really bad day. Sometimes a little thing can get in the way of a hockey goalie's mojo. A deviation in their routine, a distraction...

I hope I'm not the distraction.

My phone goes off, and I pull it from my pocket absent-mindedly.

Bet confirmed, the notification reads.

It's from the gambling app I downloaded to watch the odds.

My *other* phone vibrates, and I scramble for it in my purse. I don't know what to check first—because I definitely didn't just make a bet on anything.

Luke: Throw the game or kiss your savings goodbye.

What?

I toss the burner back in my purse and open the app.

I placed—no. No, I didn't.

It's all of my money. The book income plus everything from my experimental gambling—and the wager was placed on the Titans losing. There are good odds on it because they've been projected to win.

And now they can't, or I lose everything.

The horn blows, signaling the end of the second period.

My gaze shoots up to the scoreboard, confirming that the Titans are in the lead. 1-0.

Fuck.

I open my bank account, my heart all but in my throat. There's a balance of five dollars left in my business account. A thousand or so in savings. Nothing major.

But hundreds of thousands of dollars—*gone.*

Unless they lose.

I go back to the app, but it needs a password to cancel the wager. And somehow, no matter what I try, the password is wrong.

"Are you okay?"

I cringe and face Violet and Aspen. "No," I answer honestly. "I need to get down to the locker room."

"Okay," Violet says. "Grey?"

He appears at her side, and she repeats what I need.

"Sure," he says. "Come with me."

I can't do this. And yet, my feet move, following Greyson down the now-familiar path to the locker rooms. He talks to the guy at the door, who opens it up. Violet comes with us, and I almost jump out of my skin when she takes my hand.

"Whatever it is, we'll get through it," she says.

Miraculously?

I believe her.

"Thanks for not thinking I'm some major slut," I whisper. "Um, you know, with Knox accusing—"

She waves me off. "Don't. It sounds like he doesn't know what he's talking about."

"He doesn't." So how am I going to convince him to throw the game?

We wait in the hallway while Greyson strides into the full locker room like he owns it, the open door releasing the low rumbling tide of twenty men conversing, and then silence again once it swings shut.

After a few minutes, Greyson, Knox, and Jacob appear.

Followed by Camden Church.

"What is it?" Knox demands.

I shake my head, my words stuck. It's embarrassing to even say it to him, much less with three other guys staring at me.

He glances back at them, then draws me away. "Sunny. You look like you've seen a ghost."

"He hacked into the account I made to—to watch the bets." My hand is shaking, the phone trembling as I hold it out to him. "That's all my money, Knox. He bet everything."

"On us losing," he says, scanning it.

I can't meet his eyes. "Yeah."

He swears and turns away from me. I don't know if he's mad at me or the situation, or maybe a little of both, but he suddenly punches the wall. *Hard*. His knuckles smack into the painted cinder-block walls, and I cry out like he hit me.

I grab his wrist. His knuckles are busted.

The three guys surround us, Camden Church leaning in and pressing on one of his knuckles. Knox winces, and Church curses, too.

"You're going to play with a busted hand?" Church asks.

Knox scowls.

"You were my only hope," I whisper.

His hard gaze locks on my face. "I'm not losing against my brother, Aurora. You can't ask me to do that."

"I'm going to lose *everything*," I plead. "Knox, please—"

"No." He grips my shoulders and physically turns me around. "Go back to your seat. Don't ask this of me."

"I'm asking for help." My voice is small.

He's still at my back, his fingers digging into my upper arms. "I know. And I can't do it."

Okay, fine. "Go away, then."

He exhales, but he doesn't argue with me. Instead, he does just that, the door to the locker room banging shut behind him.

Once he's gone, I face the others. I don't like asking people for help. I don't like depending on people, but honestly, I don't know what else to do.

I look from Camden to Jacob. "Will you help me?"

38
KNOX

Can't lose.

Won't lose.

But we do anyway.

I pat my brother on the helmet and leave the ice, trying not to lose my shit. Because Church, Rhodes, they seemed to be working against me out there. Getting in my way, drifting out of position, blocking my shots. But not overtly. Not in a way that would get them called out or cause coach to bag skate us again.

No, this loss was fucking subtle. 2-1, the last goal squeaking past Haverhill in the final minute of the game. When I was sure it was going to overtime and then confident that I'd be able to get the puck past my brother in a shootout.

I keep to myself and change quickly, leaving the locker room and catching a ride with Scofield. He and I haven't bonded yet, but he seems equally pissed about us losing. Which, if there's someone on the inside, probably isn't him.

Unless his acting skills are superb.

Either way, we don't talk much on the drive over. He

lives a block down. I hop out at my building and head up, waving goodbye. Aurora probably won't be back yet. Or maybe she is, and we will have it out.

That could make my mood considerably better. Yelling at her. Kissing her. Something along those lines.

Maybe both.

I nod to the new doorman and scan my fob in the elevator, allowing it to shoot up to my floor uninterrupted. I get into my condo and toss my bag down, then the keys, and check all the rooms for signs of life.

Nada.

My phone dings.

Miles: Our parents want to take us to lunch tomorrow.

Me: To celebrate your win?

Miles: Don't be an ass.

Me: I'm not, I'm allowed to be upset that we lost.

Miles: You're allowed to be whatever you want. But Mom will be sad if you miss lunch with her.

He's got a point. My mother is a ray of sunshine, too. Like Aurora... like she used to be.

Me: Okay. Let me know when and where.

I drop my phone on the counter next to the keys and take another shower. This one scalding. While I'm humming to myself and doing my best not to mope all alone like a miserable fuck, the bathroom door opens.

"You in here?" Aurora asks.

"No, it's a ghost taking a shower."

"Okay, great." The door closes.

I pull the curtain back and stare at the door like it offended me, waiting for her to return. Or... say something. But she doesn't. My gaze moves to the counter and the glass of whiskey she must've left for me.

That's nice.

I finish my shower and swallow the amber liquid in one go, letting the smokey flavor linger on my tongue and track a path down my throat. After I'm dry and dressed, I head to bed.

Because fuck this day.

Except when I get there, someone's already waiting.

Aurora, of course.

She's naked, lounging on the bed with her legs crossed and her arms over her head. Posing.

I lick my lips, my dick instantly rising to the occasion. It's been too long since I've gotten laid. Minus that waitress after the moment Aurora and I had in the bar. But beyond that... nothing. I didn't even realize I stopped until I was lying in bed alone, beating my own dick, when only weeks before I could've had a chick doing it for me.

That's the power of Aurora.

"Why are you naked?" I ask.

She spreads her legs. "For our mutual enjoyment."

My brow lowers. "I already told you—"

"You're not fucking me. I know." She lowers her arms and brushes her finger across her clit. She sighs. "Doesn't mean you can't watch, though."

Damn.

Her breasts are full, her body soft. She was all edges when she was younger. Elbows and knees and ribs. She filled out, not quite enough to be considered curvy, but enough to be considered *dreamy*.

Fuckable.

When I should consider her the opposite.

"Get on the bed, Knox," she whispers, her throat moving with her swallow.

I peel off my clothes. I sit beside her, leaning back on the headboard, and curl my hands into fists.

I won't touch her. Not after what she did.

But she doesn't seem to have a problem, because her hips are moving subtly with her fingers, until she comes quietly. Her back arches, her body turns away from me, and she shakes with it. Until it passes and she sags.

My dick is harder than it's ever been.

"That was hot."

"This will be, too." She rolls toward me.

Something's in her hand, and it doesn't occur to me that I should be wary until it locks around my wrist. Then the other one.

"Did you just handcuff me?"

I don't need her to answer—I'm fucking staring at the metal bracelets locked on my wrists.

She drags my arms above my head, and there's another click. I look up at the traitorous headboard.

"What the fuck, Aurora?"

"Your handcuffs came in the mail," she breathes. "You should do a better job of hiding them next time."

She swings her leg over me, sitting just below my dick. It twitches, oozing precum, and she leans forward carefully. My cock brushes her abdomen with how close she gets.

I'm weirdly turned on and not at all afraid. Part of me wonders if she's going to leave me here and burn down the room around me.

I wouldn't be mad at that. In fact, I'd understand.

"Is this some trick to get me to sign the divorce papers?" I laugh and jerk on the cuffs, testing their strength.

She shakes her head, pressing her lips to the corner of my mouth. "Tell me why you won't fuck me."

My gaze hardens. "Because you slept with my brother."

"And you have proof that I had sex with him." Her eyes harden. "You know for a fact that I fucked him."

Such vulgar language, but it's true. She fucked Miles. I saw him leave her house, adjusting his clothes. And then I got the actual confirmation. So I didn't see him actually stick his dick in her? So what?

Doesn't mean it didn't happen.

"And if I have evidence of the opposite?"

I tilt my head. "Seems to be pretty cut-and-dried, Aurora." No more *Sunny* for her. I yank on the cuffs again. The headboard moves the slightest bit, and the chains rattle, but everything holds fast. "I don't know how you'd convince me otherwise."

"Well, I guess you'll find out."

She kisses my jaw. My neck. Her fingers run down my chest, to my dick. She strokes it once, twice, and I thrust my hips up into her hand.

"Is that the only reason you hate me?"

"It's the only one that matters," I promise. "Is this an interrogation? Or are you going to suck me off?"

"Better." She lifts onto her knees, her hand on my dick tightening ever so slightly.

"Aurora," I warn.

"Don't worry, Knox."

She smiles, but she's shaking. Her free hand rests on my shoulder, steadying herself. And when she positions me at her entrance, I have to physically tense all my muscles to stop from thrusting up into her. Because then I'd be a fucking hypocrite, wouldn't I?

"It'll only hurt for one of us."

I squint, trying to make sense of that, when she lowers herself down on me.

She's so fucking tight—and then there's resistance. She

keeps going, lowering herself and exhaling hard, and then something gives way. She slides down the rest of the way, her inner thighs resting against my hips, and meets my gaze.

There's pain in her eyes, but triumph, too.

My eyes feel like they're going to pop out of my face.

"Guess you didn't count on your wife being a virgin," she whispers.

Yeah. No, I definitely fucking didn't.

Now I'm questioning everything. But most of all is the fact that I've been so fucking blind to Aurora. I stare at her some more. I wish I could unsee the lies I've put on her. Her muscles tense around me, even though she's not moving.

Her mouth isn't the same as a pussy—and now that I'm in her, I'll never fuck anyone else. Ever again.

"Unlock me."

She rises slightly and winces.

"Aurora, unlock me."

While she reaches for the key—which is apparently tucked under me somewhere, judging by her blind groping —I try to wrap my mind around the fact that she's never had sex with anyone. I have a million questions. Why? Why *not*?

Okay, so I only have two questions.

Why has this gorgeous girl never been fucked to within an inch of her life? Left satiated on the mattress—

She frees my left wrist, then my right.

The handcuffs fall and slip between the mattress and headboard, disappearing from sight. Although if we retrieve them later...

No, Knox, focus.

Instinct takes over. It's like a rushing in my ears, distracting me from anything else.

She's a virgin. She didn't sleep with my brother.

My anger is wholly unjustified.

Something falls away from me. A piece of my guard, maybe, or my grudge.

I grip her hips and roll her. She gasps, hitting the bed, but I don't lose my position between her legs. I don't slip out of her. I think I could actually die happy here, buried in her heat.

"You didn't put a condom on me," I say, flexing my hips the slightest bit. Making her mouth pop open. "Was that intentional?"

"I—" She shakes her head. "I didn't really think about it."

"Well, for your first time..." I delight in saying that. "It's only right that I fill your cunt."

She nods wordlessly and reaches for me. I slide my hands up her chest, cupping her breasts, and slowly pull out. She's slick from masturbating, but there's blood on my cock. And pain in her eyes.

"Does it hurt?"

"You're bigger than..." Her eyes shift away from me.

I grin, touching her chin to bring her gaze back. "Bigger than you remember choking on, sunshine?"

"Shut up."

I drop down on my elbows and rest my forehead against hers. Her witch eyes are right there, her pupils so wide with lust that the splotch of blue in the green is nearly gone. She presses up and steals a kiss, her hands moving from my arms to the back of my neck.

Her lips touch the corner of my mouth. Feathering across my cheek, to my ear. "I need you to destroy me."

I stop. I'm practically shaking with the need to move, and she's asking me to *destroy* her? She doesn't know what that means. She doesn't really even know what she's asking, does she?

"If you let me loose, I don't know if I can rein myself back in," I warn her.

She meets my gaze, her fingers tensing on my neck. "Do it. Show me what I've been missing."

Okay.

I pull out until just my cock tip is inside her. Her muscles clench at me, nerves or anxiety getting the better of her for a moment. She's so tight even without that added layer, I'm not going to last long at all.

It's kind of funny. I've thought about what she would feel like. The experience of having sex with Aurora. But after a while, I let it go. I didn't think it would ever happen, especially thinking what I did about Miles.

She digs her nails into my skin, ripping me back to the present. Grounding me in pain. I look down at where we're barely joined. And all I can think is that I could've had this *years* ago.

My control snaps.

39

AURORA

He thrusts into me so hard, my vision goes spotty for a second. My body jolts, and only his hand holding the top of my head keeps me from banging into the headboard.

"Wrap your legs around me," he urges.

I do. The sensation of him moving between my legs, *inside* me, is something I didn't know I was missing until right this moment. He stretches me out, and the feeling is pain and pleasure intertwined.

He leans to the side and slips his hand between our sweat-slicked bodies, stroking my clit in fast little circles.

"Knox," I pant, digging my heel into his ass.

Every thrust has us hitting the headboard. His hand keeping my head from experiencing the worst of it. But he doesn't soften. He's moving slow, pulling out with great care, then pushing in *hard*. Causing waves to crash through me.

"You're perfect," he growls, dropping down to kiss my neck. He licks and sucks at my skin.

"I'm going to come again," I manage. I'm seeing stars.

More than when he tied me down with the toy. My body is buzzing.

"Good." His fingers keep working me.

He picks up the pace, and I lift my legs higher. I raise my hips to meet him, our bodies slapping together.

It's everything I wrote about and nothing I knew how to adequately envision. Besides porn, and romance books and movies—but those can't always be accurate, can they?

This is.

I want to kiss him and carve my name into his skin and I *get it*, the girls who become obsessed with the boys who take their virginity.

Because I'd believe he's actively altering my identity.

"Come for me," he orders, watching my face with rapt attention.

He pushes me over the edge, and I have a hard time holding his gaze. My eyes close, body arching against his. I grab at his waist, scratching at his skin, until he finally pulls his hand up. He wraps his wet fingers around my throat and turns my head to the side with his thumb on my chin.

And then he really gets to work.

He releases his hold on the top of my head and lifts my leg up, spreading it higher, and pushes himself up off me. He stares down at where we're joined. I'm caught halfway in a daze, struggling to comprehend that we're having sex.

Because I waited.

I waited for *him*.

Although at some point, it became more than that. More than just him and me and this idea of us in my head.

"You're so wet for me, sunshine. You know that's a good thing, don't you? You write about dripping cunts in that book of yours, when you've never experienced a cock stretching you out."

I groan through my teeth.

His pace quickens. His fingers are bruising, touching my neck, my chin. His other hand on my thigh, holding me open.

Making me vulnerable.

I like it.

I want more of that.

The most important thing is knowing your kinks, right?

Knox in control like this, with that gleam in his eye, is undoing me in the best way possible. He's touching, and for once, he's not talking, but it's not because he doesn't want to. There's just this electric charge between us, like radio static and heat.

He stills, exhaling on a groan and spilling inside me. His dick pulses, and he releases my thigh. He turns my face back toward him, kissing the corner of my lips gently.

"You know what this means?" he asks.

I shake my head, suddenly jelly-limbed and exhausted.

"You can't ever escape me now." He kisses me again.

He slips out of me, and I cringe. There's blood on both of us, coating his groin and my inner thighs. I drape my arm over my eyes. With the haze of sex fading—except the slight smell of our arousal, which is something I'd heard about but can't say I was prepared for—the embarrassment settles back in.

My face heats.

"Don't do that," Knox says. He pulls at my arm and rolls me toward him. "Don't hide."

"Don't hide?" I laugh. "I just forced you to—"

"See reason," he finishes. "The rest was mutual. Trust me."

I didn't think I'd be able to do that.

"For so long, it felt like I was waiting for you to come

back," I whisper. The need to explain is bubbling up, and I don't want to hold back anymore. I don't want to lie. "But then you didn't, and you said you never wanted to see me again. Which I could've accepted, but you wouldn't sign the divorce papers."

"So..."

"It felt like cheating. Even thinking about it."

He traces my collarbone. "And Joel?"

"You can say his name without getting mad?" I joke.

"Yeah, now that I know he didn't get his dick anywhere near you."

"Anywhere near my pussy," I correct, blushing slightly. "I sucked him off plenty of times."

Knox groans, dropping his hand. "I did not need to know that."

"You're the king of oversharing." I somehow get up the energy to rise on my hands and knees, crawling over him. To the nightstand that has my phone and a water bottle.

He palms my ass. "We should shower."

I grab the water and sit back, uncapping it and eyeing him. He's stretched out, and he props his head under an arm, his biceps flexing. It reminds me of simpler times. Not quite this, uh, *sexual*, obviously.

But for once, things don't feel so jaggedly broken between us. He's not looking at me like I sliced him up on the inside.

"You sore, sunshine?"

My cheeks heat. I guess I should've expected the *after*, or at least considered it in the broadest of strokes. I write about it. I write about the before, during, after. But living it is different.

Slowly, my guard comes down. I slip out of bed and pick my clothes up from the neat little pile I left them in. Knox watches me. I feel it, I hate it. I already am too exposed—in both the literal and figurative sense—and I can't be.

"Sunny?"

I don't answer. He sits up, brow furrowed, as I turn to close the bathroom door. My expression might give away my emotions, I don't know. But he rises too late. I close it and flip the lock.

I blow out a breath, dropping my clothes and starting the shower.

"Aurora." Knox's voice goes straight through me.

"Just let me have this—"

"This moment to retreat?"

There's a thump against the wood, although I can't tell if it's his hand or his head.

"Yeah," I whisper.

"No." The doorknob rattles. "For fuck's sake, Aurora."

I step into the shower. The water is scalding, although that helps ground me. The pain of it. I guess that's a bad habit—I couldn't stop taking hot showers after my mom died. I'd come out with my skin too red, hot to the touch, the bathroom filled with steam.

This is like that.

Except a moment later, Knox hoots, and the door swings inward. He pulls open the door to the shower and steps in behind me, immediately wincing.

"You're going to burn yourself," he snaps, pushing the head of the shower away from our bodies. "What are you doing?"

My throat is blocked. All I can do is shake my head and half-heartedly shrug.

"Come on, it wasn't that bad, was it?" He touches under my chin, lifting my face, and turns down the temperature with his other hand.

"I don't know." I shrug. "How was your first time?"

He frowns. "I blew my load in under thirty seconds."

"When?" I redirect the water to hit my back, soaking my hair and rolling down my shoulders.

"What do you mean?"

"When did you lose your virginity?"

He stares at me for a beat.

Then another.

"College," he answers carefully.

My brows furrow. I don't know how to deal with the unexpected jealousy. Or the urge to get her name and hunt her down.

"Be specific, Knox."

"Approximately two days after I told you I never wanted to see you again," he mutters.

To his credit, he doesn't flinch. He doesn't hide it. It's obvious he doesn't want me to know, but he still said it. So I can't flinch either. I try to absorb it, pondering the mystery of Knox Whiteshaw.

There's the fact that he was a virgin when we got married, too. That he hadn't slept with anyone else, even though he flirted with other girls in high school. Even though it took him a while to come around to *me*, I'm the one who stuck.

But then, he was truly convinced I cheated on him.

And he stayed convinced, for *years*.

Devastation blows through me.

"You dated Willow..."

"I did."

My throat is tight. It seems like I *want* to flay myself open with this line of questioning. But not knowing stings worse. "Was she the one who—?"

"No." He strokes the side of my face. "No, it was some

random puck bunny, I don't know her name. I tried to forget their names as fast as possible."

I close my eyes. "Just tell me what you saw to make you think I would've done that. Please."

His hand on my cheek stills. "I can't."

"I can't do this, then."

"Do what?"

I open my eyes and slick the water out of my face, glaring up at him. "I won't do *this*." I motion between us. "Not again." I open the shower door and shove him. "Get out."

He goes, and I don't care if he stares at me through the glass. I just need space. Because he's still hiding something, and we're still in danger, and my heart is still a mess.

In more ways than one.

40

KNOX

I wake up thinking about Aurora.

Which, really, isn't out of the ordinary. Especially when she's sleeping next to me.

But now, for the first time, I feel like I have permission to touch her. Not from her—she made *that* clear last night —but from myself.

Her breathing is deep and even. I stayed up late and waited until she fell asleep, then just lay there and considered all of it. All of her.

I roll toward her and sweep her auburn hair away from her neck. I rise on my elbow and lean over her, kissing her neck. She barely stirs, so I scoot closer. Until my body is aligned next to hers.

This is strange, too.

Sleeping next to her.

It isn't the first time we've done this. I knew she'd be sharing my bed as soon as I made the decision to move her into my condo. And there were many hospital stays where I climbed into her bed...

I sigh.

Sleeping next to her is intimate. I couldn't sleep next to Willow. I refused to let anyone else stay longer than it took to climax—and, on occasion, there were some second and third rounds. But that never equated to *sleep*.

She's peaceful like this. The furrow that usually creases between her brows when she looks at me is gone, the careful mask she wears in public for once put away.

Maybe that's why I touch her.

We're not teenagers anymore.

She's not sick.

I pull her panties down and spread her legs, positioning myself between them. I bury my face in her pussy, inhaling softly. She's not bleeding anymore, but I bet she's sore. I lick her, getting a taste, and slowly insert one finger into her.

She's so fucking tight.

She comes awake at that, squirming at the invasion.

It must be new.

It must hurt a little—or a lot.

Her hand trails over my face. Into my hair.

"I'm dreaming," she mumbles. Sleep clouds her voice.

I flick my tongue against her clit until her fingers tighten in my hair. She tries to push me away, and I finally close my lips around the sensitive nub and suck.

"Knox!" She gasps, arching.

I pump the one finger in and out. She's slick with arousal, which wakes my dick up. I want to be inside her—but she needs to come first.

And she does. Tugging at my hair, her thighs closing around my head. I don't care, I just want to feel her explode. She tenses and cries out.

I lick my lips and crawl up her body, kissing along her stomach, biting her breast over her shirt.

"What are you doing?" she asks. "I said—"

"I don't really care." I shake my head and reach down. I line up at her entrance. "I've got to have you, Sunny."

Her eyelashes flutter when I slowly push into her.

"Sore?" I ask.

She focuses back on me. "And if I am?"

"Then maybe I'll be gentle."

She frowns. "And if I don't want that?"

I consider her words as I move. My dick is ruling my brain right now. She seems serious.

"Then I won't be."

"Good."

Okay, then. I watch her face as I fuck her. When her nose scrunches, pain getting the better of her, I put my finger on her clit and distract her with pleasure. She cups her breasts, pinching her nipples through her shirt.

"Fuck, you're sexy. Show me."

Her gaze smolders, and she slowly pulls her shirt up. How she can make it a strip tease when I'm *inside* her is a talent I'll gladly watch over and over again. Especially when she gets the shirt up over her breasts and her muscles clench around me.

I lean down, knocking her hand away and biting her tit. I suck her nipple into my mouth, my movements slowing. I want to savor it. Her.

She groans and wraps her arms around me. The bite of her nails in my back does something to me. I move faster, chasing my high. She's getting closer to the edge, her eyes shutting.

"No," I bite out. "Keep your eyes on me."

Aurora's lips part, and her hands grip my neck. I kiss her hard, biting her lower lip until we both taste blood.

This is definitely better than waking up mad. Although

she's probably still going to be pissed at me later for God-knows-what.

I'd take that over silence and cold shoulders.

When she tips over the edge, I pull back just enough to watch her face. Her climax spurs mine on, and for the second time in less than twenty-four hours, I come inside her.

Damn.

Okay, I could do that more often.

As in, never wear a condom ever fucking again.

She exhales shakily. "I'm still pissed at you."

"For having sex when we weren't talking?"

"For—yes. *That.*" She hits my shoulder. "Get off me."

"Nah." I drop all my weight down on her, burying my face in her neck. She smells sweet and floral. "I think I'll stay here for a bit."

She's tense, but she can't fight me forever. And eventually, she relaxes.

I relax, too—until my alarm goes off and ruins everything.

"Ugh," she groans.

"Come on, Sunny." I lick her cheek, and she squeals. "We've got things to do. People to meet. Plans to scheme."

———

Sunny and I shower and get dressed with no shenanigans. Okay, some shenanigans. Like feeling her up when she's trying to get her bra on, and slapping her ass on the way out the door, and just reveling in touching her without guilt. And kissing her breathless in the elevator.

Greyson and Steele stuck around after the game, along with Miles. And Jacob, obviously, isn't going anywhere. She had apparently challenged them to some on-ice competition, which I put an end to with a firm glare. So we settle for breakfast instead.

I leave Aurora with the girls at the table, trusting that they'll probably talk shit about me. Or at least help her cope with what happened last night. Maybe they'll share virgin stories. I would kind of want to eavesdrop on that, though.

But away from the girls, and in a fashion that's apparently very *me*, I explain everything to the guys. While I finish telling them about the mind-fuck of last night, Miles glowers at me, and the rest just sort of seem to be in shock. Maybe. It's hard to tell, because they're trading glances and looking back at me, and their eyebrows are raised.

"What?" I shrug.

"Is that why you went after Willow?" Miles demands. "Because you thought I slept with Aurora?"

"Well..." I fold my arms over my chest. "Presumably."

"*Presumably?*"

"Okay," Greyson interjects. "Okay. So, she proved you wrong."

I nod. "Yeah, and now I'm going to kill someone."

"Someone," Jacob echoes. "You know killing *someone* without a plan is not a great idea. Just ask Miles. Or Willow."

That's true.

"So, big brother, why don't you tell us what made you think I fucked her?"

I wince. Miles seems pissed, and I understand that it's dragging up a lot of shit that we've spent the last few years trying to put behind us. I mean, he's engaged to Willow, for fuck's sake! That's got to count for something.

I didn't do any lasting damage to her. Or them.

"Well..." I hedge. "I saw you, drew some conclusions, and then it was confirmed."

"By the someone you want to murder."

"Yes." I nod vigorously. "Yes, they need to go."

"Meanwhile, you're involved in betting fraud? Game rigging?" Greyson asks.

"I would not say I'm involved," I point out. "I just, you know, sort of ended up needing to throw a game or two in whatever direction they say. Because they attacked her. If they do that for one fuck-up, what would they do next time?"

"Who's the someone?" Aurora asks.

I stiffen and slowly turn around. She's the last person I wanted to overhear this conversation. But she's leaning against the wall with her arms crossed. She looks put together, whereas I feel frazzled. Coming apart at the seams.

"I didn't mean for you to hear that." I come at her with my hands out. I don't know whether to grab her or surrender. "It's no one."

"No." She shakes her head at me. "No, it's not no one. You wouldn't believe just anyone, would you?"

Well...

"We'll give you a minute," Greyson mutters, slapping my shoulder.

He leads the guys out, past Aurora without so much as brushing her sleeve, but I barely spare them a second glance.

"Knox, be honest with me. For once."

I should. I should just tell her exactly what happened. But... There's something to be gained here. Something I want just as much as she probably wants to find out the truth from me. So I say, "Not until you let me read your manuscript, sunshine."

Her brows furrow. "You've never wanted to read anything of mine."

"You wrote about *us*," I point out. "That's different. And I had Melody read your book. She told me about it."

Aurora glares at me. "No, she didn't."

No, she really didn't. She gave me her thoughts on the matter, but it wasn't a play-by-play. Although judging from her face, maybe I should've asked Melody for more details... or just read the damn book myself.

Okay, adding that to my to-do list. Even if I just skim.

I'll probably skim.

"Maybe I don't want to know that badly," she says, her tone dismissive. "I'll figure it out on my own."

"How?"

"I'm exploring that part of my life through writing. I'll get to it, and I'll put it together with or without you."

I wince. But I'm nodding along. It's true—it's right there for her to figure out. Someone in her life betrayed us, and when it comes to light...

She doesn't back away when I approach. I tug at her wrist, uncrossing her arms, and lace my fingers with hers.

"It'll be okay, Sunny. Promise."

She looks away. "Maybe not, Knox. Otherwise you would've told me already."

True.

"Either way, I'll be here to put our pieces back together."

41
MANUSCRIPT

CHAPTER 5

I think about the proposal.
And think about it.
And think about it.
But the more I think, the less my thoughts make sense.

Because for one—I shouldn't want to marry him. We kissed a few times, he's been a hopeless flirt for years (since I hit puberty, when my breasts came in and the braces came off), but... hockey stands between us.

The fact that he can play, and my parents insist on wrapping me in cotton.

I join Beth in the stands, bumping my shoulder into hers. "Anything exciting happen?"

"They do some funky stretching." She wrinkles her nose. "It's like, erotic and uncomfortable at the same time. Why are they miming fucking the ice?"

I snort. "Jesus, Beth."

"Well..." She sighs. "It made me feel something I didn't

think I'd feel in a cold arena, surrounded by sweaty yelling parents and students."

I elbow her.

"Knox looks good," she points out.

For the past week, I've avoided him. Because while I want to think about what he said, I also don't want to think about it. No, *him*. I want to think about hockey.

Beth doesn't know about his proposition. My heart thumps out of sync in the middle of the night, just an extra beat or a skipped one here and there, and I tense up all over. And I consider the impact of an emergency surgery without better insurance.

And without Knox.

God, it's hard.

Because I like him, and I want to kiss him some more, but I'm only sixteen. Getting married at sixteen is insane.

"Yeah," I finally echo my best friend.

Knox is on the ice. He's standing on the blue line with the rest of his teammates, and Miles moves into position. He leans over in the crease, then lifts his head and nods to Knox.

They start. Three of them, passing and shooting. A wrist shot from the right winger, which Miles blocks. A slap shot from the next trio. I lean forward, balancing my elbows on my knees, and watch their footwork. Their control of the puck. Their passes, which are sometimes better than others.

Miles eventually skates toward the bench. The warm-up pace increases, the guys cycling through and shooting at the empty net.

"Are you guys not talking?"

I glance at Beth. "What?"

"You and Knox. You've been weird all week at school."

"Oh, um, yeah. Just family stuff. And I don't know, I haven't seen him much."

She nods carefully. "Okay."

The horn blows, the skaters leave the ice, and Beth jumps up.

"Popcorn?"

"Sure." But I'm grateful to just sit here and stare at the empty ice. Because I can mourn it again, for the hundredth time, without her trying to make me feel better.

After the game, I follow Beth down to the hall where the players will emerge. I move a little slower than her, and she bounces out ahead of me when we spot them coming out. They're guys our age. A high school league. And yet, she flings herself at them in a way that confuses me.

Because they're just normal high school assholes, minus *maybe* the Whiteshaw brothers.

She hugs Miles, plants a kiss on Knox's cheek. Congratulates the rest of the players on their successful game.

Knox comes up to me. "Hey, Sunny."

I incline my chin. "They moved you to center?"

"Our other guy can't win a face-off to save his life. We're trying something new."

I appraise him. He's won more face-offs than is usual for our team. "It suited you," I end up saying.

"Hey, Aurora," Miles calls, coming over and draping his arm around my shoulders. "Thanks for coming. Beth said we're giving you two a ride home?"

Knox's eyebrow rises slightly.

"Her dad was supposed to come. I guess he got held up or something..."

"Yeah." Knox shoves Miles' arm off my shoulder. "That's probably it."

I feel like, these days, I'm always following. Beth returns

and drags Knox away. Miles is with them. And I, with my heart that can't keep up, trails. Until Miles drops back anyway. He and I have always been good friends.

After all, he's not the one who pushed me in the mud for touching his hockey stick.

"You good?"

I nod. "Stairs, the excitement of the game... it's just a weight on my chest, is all. I'll be fine." But I'm not walking out of here without another reminder of why I can't play hockey.

He eyes me. "Fancy a ride?"

"What sort of—?"

He drops his bag and crouches, his back to me. "Hop on."

If he insists...

I climb on, and he takes a minute to adjust his hold on my thighs, then retrieve his bag and stick. But he doesn't jostle me, and instead picks up a jog to catch up with Knox and Beth.

"You're insane," I say in his ear. "Running?"

"It's either that or—*damn*."

Beth is climbing into the front seat.

Knox watches us, his brow furrowing. Miles drops me to my feet and circles around, tossing his bag in the trunk.

"Are we going to talk about this?" Knox asks me. "It's been a week, Sunny. You don't have time—"

"I know," I hiss. "I know I don't. But I'm trying to decide if it's just the insurance or something else in me that wants to say yes."

He tilts his head, appraising me. Then twists his ball cap around, backward, and leans down. He kisses me before I can stop him or jerk away, and his lips remind me that I could say yes no matter the reason.

The car horn goes off.

I jump back, my face heating. "Well, right then."

"Is that a yes?"

We stare at each other.

And I want to. I really, really want to.

So I say: "Yes."

42

AURORA

Knox taps my thigh, drawing my attention to him.

I raise my eyebrows, because this is *weird*.

We're at lunch with Miles, Willow, and the Whiteshaws. Knox's parents are pretty much the same as I remember them. Warm and welcoming and smiling. His mom kisses both my cheeks when we arrive at the restaurant, and his dad hugs me tightly.

They're as much family as my own parents. Moving away didn't change that—although I could've been better about communication.

I try not to think about that now.

Willow and Miles are across from us, and I have to keep biting the inside of my cheek. Because she slept with him, right? She had him before I did.

Knox leans over, pressing his lips to my ear. His voice is barely audible as he whispers, "Jealousy is a good look on you, Mrs. Whiteshaw."

I elbow him.

He chuckles and straightens.

His mom asks Willow a question, something about

singing, and I try to turn my attention back to them. To the words coming out of her mouth.

I'm a girl's girl, I tell myself.

It's another lie. Before moving to Denver, I wouldn't have said I had a lying problem. But now... well, if the shoe fits?

"Excuse me," I murmur, sliding out of my chair.

Instead of going to the bathroom—which would probably be reasonable, you know—I head outside. I follow the sidewalk around to the parking lot and press myself up against the wall, taking slow, deep breaths.

Why am I suddenly a green-eyed monster?

"Aurora?"

I flinch.

Willow stands there, her arms folded across her stomach. "I, um... Are you okay?"

I clear my throat. "I'm totally fine," I lie. "I just, you know... there's a lot going on."

"Uh-huh." She comes closer and leans her shoulder against the wall. "You know how long it took me to get over Knox?"

"Not sure I want to know," I say on a laugh.

"A month. If that. I was a wreck for a long time after he humiliated me, but it wasn't *him* who I was mourning or broken up about. It was me. I opened my heart, and he didn't give a shit." Her gaze is steady on my face.

I don't know what she's saying.

"Are you trying to tell me not to fall for him?" I scoff. "Because you don't need to warn me. I've known him—"

"No, Aurora." She grabs my hand and pulls it away from my stomach. "I'm saying there's a reason he didn't give a shit about me. And it's obvious with the way he treats you."

"Well..." *Fuck.* "If you say so."

"I'm not saying anything concrete, one way or another. I'm just explaining that..." She blows out a breath. "You know what? I'm not even sure what I'm trying to say. I just felt the need to explain and apologize..."

"You don't owe me an apology." I yank my hand from her grasp. "Seriously. You don't. You couldn't have known about me."

Although, come to think of it, I'm kind of surprised that Miles didn't use the marriage as ammunition against Knox. He must've known Knox didn't sign the divorce papers.

Unless they aren't as close anymore.

"Knox loves his brother over everything," Willow says. "I told you that."

I roll my eyes. "I know you did."

"But I was wrong, Aurora. He would give anything for his brother—but he'd give *everything* for you."

My eyes fill with tears.

She waits for another second, but my throat is closed off. I couldn't say another word if I needed, let alone if I wanted. And when I don't speak, she pats my arm and goes back inside.

It's ridiculously cold out here. I should've grabbed my coat, at the very least. My breath forms little clouds in front of my face. I close my eyes and fight my emotions. Wrestle with them, really.

Hands tug at my shoulders. I open my eyes and look up at Knox, but he doesn't say anything. He just pulls me into the hug that I desperately need.

We stay like that for a long moment, until I can swallow normally.

"You came for me?" I ask.

"Willow wanted first crack at it," he says, rubbing my

back. "But, you know. No one can cure an Aurora thunder-cloud quite like me."

That's true.

Through panic attacks and hospital stays and recovery, nightmares and tantrums and *God*, the need to escape my life—he's always been the one to guide me back from the ledge.

"Do you want to go back in?" he asks.

I take a deep breath, feeling more grounded than before.

"Do you love me?" I reply.

He eyes me like I'm crazy, yes, but also sparkling and magical. Like he's not quite sure how we got here. "I'm obsessed with you, sunshine."

Same thing.

I nod to him. "Then let's go back in."

———

Beth doesn't really skate. Hasn't in all the time I've known her, minus when we went out on the Frog Pond in Boston. And look how well that turned out, right? But she's a good sport about coming down to the arena and lacing into the pair of skates I hand her.

I put on my own, which have traveled with me from New York.

I send a quick text, then leave my phone on the bench in the locker room. I pick up a stick and point at the one she can take, and we head to the rink.

She didn't ask why I wanted her to come with me, when literally *anyone* would be more suited to getting out on the ice than her. She doesn't really ask many questions at all, just follows me to the ice.

The door opens inward. I suck in a deep breath of cool air and step out.

My first step, I wobble, much to my chagrin. Some hockey player I am. I right myself on the next step, slowly easing into it. Until I'm moving faster, suddenly racing across the glossy ice.

Clean, new ice was a luxury I only got once in a while. Especially when I was younger. When Dad made me wait until after the hockey players had warmed up and conditioned—arguably the most chaotic time on the ice—to join him. To skate after him in my pink helmet, my short stick in my grip.

I push that memory away.

"Aurora!" Beth calls. "I can't go as fast as you."

I ignore her, digging into the ice on the far side and sending a shower of snow into the boards. I drop a puck from my pocket, stolen from Knox's room, and adjust my grip on my stick. I cradle the puck, moving back toward the far goal, and twist my wrist in a smooth shot—that flies into the net with the slightest *whoosh* of air.

Worth it.

I fish out the puck and come back to Beth, dropping my stick and grabbing her hands. She's barely standing, but I get her out onto the ice. Drag her, really. She does nothing but keep her skates straight, and she's helpless to stop me.

My smile fades.

It didn't occur to me until I wrote more. Who in my life, who in *his*, would've been able to convince him I cheated?

Only someone who knew me well.

Only someone who *wanted* us to break up.

After the awkward lunch, Knox and Miles went to meet up with the guys, and I reread the last chapter I wrote. The one where I unwittingly chronicled Beth's envy and desire.

It was weird, reading it back. I hadn't noticed when I was writing it. Hadn't noticed how she took a front-and-center approach to Knox, putting herself in his line of sight again and again.

"Were you ever really my friend?" I release her hand and back out of her reach.

She blanches. "Don't leave me standing out here —Aurora!"

"Beth. You're fine. You're standing. No one's going to cross-check you." I raise my eyebrow. "Were you my friend? In high school?"

"What is this about? Of course we were friends."

I laugh and shake my head, gliding away from her. "Yeah, right. Up until you developed a crush on Knox."

"No—"

"Come on, Beth." I stop sharply in front of her, spraying her legs with snow. "Tell the truth."

She stares at me, and her face seems to morph from confused to angry in an instant. "You want the truth? I was crushing on Knox long before he showed you any interest."

It's a good thing I don't have my stick.

"So when the opportunity arose to drive a wedge between us, you took it."

She lifts her chin. "I only told him the truth, Aurora. You were getting close to Miles. Maybe too close, for someone who was *married*."

Unbelievable.

I gape at her, trying to comprehend it. "And then what? What was your plan, to go to Crown Point and make him fall in love with you?"

She waves her hand. "Please."

"I'm serious."

"It was one mistake, Aurora. One I've paid for heavily. I stuck by you—"

"That was your payment?" I shriek. "Staying friends with me?"

"No—"

My anger swells. And fuck it, I'm not going to hold back. She took years away from Knox and me. I'm not saying we'd still be together, but we could've worked things out while he was in school. I had been accepted to Crown Point University. I was prepared to follow him—*always following*. Instead, I got as far away from him as I could, just as he ordered.

He was so devastated. I can see his face, the way he believed the betrayal. And everything leading up to the moment I fucking proved him *wrong* weighs on me in this instance.

I just react, and I punch Beth in the face.

She goes down like a ton of bricks. Her skates slip out from under her, her limbs going everywhere. I inch closer, staring down at her and wondering if I could kick her in the stomach with skates on and somehow not slice her up.

Because I don't want to kill her, I just want to hurt her more.

"Sunny!" Knox runs out onto the ice. Slipping, more like, in his street shoes. He barrels into me, grabbing my arms. We barely manage to not go down, too. "What are you doing?"

Beth groans, rolling onto her side and spitting blood onto the ice. "She just attacked me out of nowhere!"

"You bitch—"

Knox grips my shoulders harder, shaking me a little. "Sunny, stop."

I look up at him. Funny how our height difference is

now. Me in skates, him in street shoes. He's still taller than me. Barely. It brings our faces closer, though.

"Get her off the ice," he calls behind him.

I glance up and spot Miles and Steele coming to retrieve my friend.

Former friend.

"You shouldn't be on the ice," Knox says, redirecting my attention. "And confronting her like this?"

I shrug. "You get to hit people on the ice. I missed it."

His expression flickers. Sadness enters his eyes, and he pulls me into him. He wraps me up in a hug, kissing my temple. "I know. Now let's make this a bit more civilized, hmm?"

I scoff. "Good luck with that."

Still, I'm curious what he means. I collect the stick and puck and meet Knox at the doorway. We go to the locker room, where Greyson, Steele, and Miles all stand around. Beth is sitting on one of the far benches, a wad of paper towels held to her mouth.

"Where's Jacob?"

"Running an errand," Miles answers. "That was a good punch, by the way."

I beam. "Thanks. Learned from the best."

"Me," Knox interjects. "When we were kids. Because I was the one getting into fights on the ice, not Miles."

"Because no one touches a goalie." Miles rolls his eyes. "Well, until I get dragged into a fight."

"Like you don't enjoy it," Steele mutters.

"Okay, let's focus." Greyson frowns. "Aurora, you have more to say to this one?"

I like that he doesn't name her. Because as of right this moment, she's never going to have a name in my head again.

I throw back my shoulders and walk to her. She has the good sense to cower, because I'm tempted to punch her again just to break her nose.

"Tell us everything." I sit across from her. "And maybe you can salvage the rest of your face."

Knox snickers.

She glares at him, then focuses on me. Her eyes are bloodshot and tear-filled, and when she lowers the paper towels, her split lip is revealed. Her teeth are stained pink from blood.

"I'm sorry, Aurora. My jealousy got the better of me. And then, it seemed to do more harm than good—"

"No shit." I undo my laces while I listen, replacing them with my street shoes.

"I was coming by your house to drop off homework. You were out because of those doctors' appointments, remember? And then I saw through the window you were hugging Miles, and he put his shirt back on. He came out, and I—" She sucks in a breath. "I asked you about it. About Miles. You said you were just friends, but then you smiled."

"You decided to ruin my life because I *smiled*?"

"He was shirtless in your living room, hugging you! What was I supposed to think? Knox was coming back for winter break, and I just figured you had moved on in the months he was away—"

"Asshole," Knox whispers to Miles.

"Shut up," Miles returns. "I spilled pasta sauce on my t-shirt and took it off to put my hoodie on instead."

"Because you regularly dined with the McGoverns?" She-who-shall-not-be-named asks, her voice cutting.

"I did when Knox was away. Because Aurora was lonely."

"Okay." I clap my hands to get their attention. "Right.

So. You saw something. And then you held on to it until the end of break to say something? Not to me, though. To Knox."

"Because he was flirting with you! And acting like nothing was wrong!" She bursts into tears. "And then you were crushed when he left, and I vowed to never talk about it. I thought you were over him, Aurora. And we stayed friends, even after going to different colleges, and then you met Joel, and got engaged and moved out here—"

"Jesus." I pinch the bridge of my nose.

I moved my entire life across the country because I wanted a change, and my fiancé living in the same city as my best friend seemed like fate. It was the change I so desperately wanted. And I *went*. I left everything I've known, I left my father with his new girlfriend, I left my doctors and job—well, okay, the job was ending anyway because of the book—and now I'm here.

"I'm sorry," she cries. She won't stop crying. "You slept with Miles and you got caught, Aurora, and I'm sorry I told, but you cheated on him."

"No, she didn't," Miles snaps.

"She really didn't," Knox repeats. "I'm not going to tell you how I discovered that. Because that's between us. But just know that no Titan will ever step foot in your bar again. And no Titan fan will either."

In this city, that's practically a death sentence.

My former friend crumples.

I stand. "Lose my number. Forget I exist."

It isn't until we're out of the locker room, leaving her there alone, that my throat closes. My eyes burn.

Knox hugs me to his side. "Hard part's over, sunshine."

Not really. Because we still have the Luke Abernathy problem. He hasn't reached out in a while, but after his latest move with my money, it feels like only a matter of time. And I can't deal with this on top of everything else. I'm emotionally strung out. It's all I can do to keep myself together long enough to make it home.

He's a guillotine hanging over our heads, and I have the worst feeling that the blade is about to drop.

43
KNOX

While Aurora was leading Beth to the arena to beat the shit out of her, the guys and I were scheming.

There's a very limited window of time when none of us have games. We've got forty-eight hours before Greyson and Steele have to be back to their respective teams, and another twenty-four until Miles will return to his.

Luke Abernathy has to go.

Jacob has been tasked with following the motherfucker, which is why he didn't join us for the fiasco at the rink. Although it was a hot fiasco. One I will be replaying in my mind over and over and over—

"Focus," Miles snaps, elbowing me in the gut.

"Right." I swallow, my chest tightening at the thought of something happening to Aurora. The whole reason we've been scheming is to try and protect her.

She will *not* be attacked again.

Part of our scheming involved upgrading the security in our building. It wasn't a particularly easy task, but Jacob and I pooled our sway with the building manager. If it helps keep strangers from getting access to the elevators, to our units, then I'm all for it.

"Okay. No, it's okay." I nod to myself. I just need to swing back to optimistic Knox. The one who will do anything for a laugh... except that feels hollow right now, too.

"It's not really okay," Aurora mutters beside me.

We leave the arena as a pack, all together. With her at the center, protected like she should be. She's sandwiched between Steele and me, with Miles taking up the front and Greyson behind us.

"Hey!"

I pause. Turn.

Camden Church comes jogging toward us from across the parking lot. He stops in front of me, silently regarding my friends, then Aurora. She still seems a little upset, if we're being honest. And then me.

"What's up?" I ask.

He narrows his eyes. "I was going to use the Titans' facility to work out. But now I'm curious what *you* were doing."

"Aurora rented the ice for an hour. We were collecting her."

"Uh-huh. You're a motley crew, aren't you?"

"Not really. We're all hockey players. These are my best friends. From college," I add.

"Crown Point University," he says. "Right. So you all showed up to escort her... Does this have anything to do with that hypothetical betting fraud you were talking about?"

Behind me, they all groan. All of them.

I spin around. "What? He said *hypothetical*!"

"For fuck's sake, Knox," Greyson snaps.

"We're *spies*!" What is with these people?

"We are not spies," Aurora says firmly. "We are not on a mission. We're not doing anything with betting fraud, hypothetical or not. Okay?"

He eyes us like he doesn't really believe a word she said. And that's fine, since, you know, we can ice him out anyway.

But then he says, "I want to help."

We all exchange glances. I shrug.

Aurora shrugs.

Greyson and Steele seem the most suspicious, and Miles only stares at me.

"What's to say you won't run back to—"

"Luke Abernathy?" Church tilts his head.

I hold up my hands. "I did *not* tell him that. Not even a little bit." How did he know? Is he a mind reader? Wait. *Did* I say it? No, I absolutely wouldn't have. "I didn't," I repeat.

"Okay." Miles shakes his head at me. "Whether you did or didn't is irrelevant. Why are you bringing his name into this, Church?"

"Because he's been doing this for years. But it's time he was stopped."

His expression is dark, and I think I like him even more than I did a few seconds ago. It reminds me of the look on Greyson's face when he told me he had a guy unconscious in the back of his truck.

"I want to put an end to it," he continues. "But I haven't been able to do it alone."

"Really." Steele crosses his arms. "And we're supposed to believe you're not working with him?"

Church shrugs. "I'll tell you anything you want to know. Believe me or not, it's up to you."

We all exchange glances.

I don't know. I feel too close to it.

"Meet us at Jacob and Knox's building in an hour," Greyson decides. "We'll talk it over."

Church meets my eyes, then nods slowly. He turns and heads back into the building, leaving the five of us standing in stunned silence.

"Do we believe him?" Aurora asks.

"I mean, he seemed serious," I say. "But we should vote."

Miles scoffs. "Since when do you care about a vote?"

"Since Aurora," I snap.

Silence.

"Okay." The woman in question claps. "Let's, uh, discuss this more in private. Yes?"

44
AURORA

"You know what's great?"

"No." I stare at the conglomerate of people in our kitchen, trying not to lose my edge. My nerve.

Knox runs his fingers down the back of my neck, brushing my hair to the side. He kisses my shoulder, then moves up. To the spot just behind my ear, which earns him a sigh.

"I don't feel guilty for touching you anymore."

I tip my head to the side. We're in the shadows of our bedroom.

Funny how everything became *ours*. Our home, our kitchen, our bedroom. Did the sex change that? Or was it something Knox and I did? Unlocking this new fever between us—I did that. I broke through to him.

"I hate that you felt guilty at all," I whisper.

I went to hide when they all started coming in. It was a lot of people all at once, too many voices, and I just needed quiet. So I scribbled in a notebook in the bedroom until Knox came to retrieve me, and he's been waiting for me to creep out into the open.

Because apparently it has to be my choice.

They debated for a long time about whether Camden Church should be trusted. And, after hearing both sides, we all voted that he should be allowed to sit in on our meeting. There's a chance he knows something we don't. At the very least, he could offer a new perspective.

He was the last to arrive just a little while ago.

Knox nips my neck. His hands are on my hips, then sliding across my stomach. One goes down to the edge of my jeans, and I grab his wrist.

"They can see us."

"No, they can't. And even if they can, they don't really give a shit." He turns my head to the side and kisses me. "How do you feel?"

He drags me out of the doorway and pushes my back to the wall. He goes to his knees, unbuttoning my jeans and shoving them down.

"Don't make a peep," he warns, looking up at me.

I bite my lip.

His black cap is on backward, smothering his curls. His eyes are devilish, and he smirks at me—then leans forward and kisses just above my pubic bone.

"Oh, fuck." I grab the top of his head as he moves one of my legs over his shoulder. Opening me up for him to—

Oh, fuck.

Fingers, tongue, lips. Sucking.

I think I black out.

He doesn't let me fall when I come, my hand over my mouth the only thing stopping a scream from ripping through me. Because I'm shattered, as easy as this. Most of my weight is on the wall, the door only inches away, and I shake my head when I finally come down to earth.

Knox's smirk is back in place, and he pushes up my

shirt, kissing my stomach. Then higher, straight up my sternum. He traces the old scar. My shirt is up to my throat now, and he seems content to linger there. Between my breasts, savoring my skin.

Until he bites me.

I jerk, and he immediately plunges two fingers back inside me. Coaxing more sensations out of me, knowing just how to touch me. Some pressure there, a little rubbing here. He figured me out faster than I've ever learned myself.

"Okay, enough," I manage.

"Adrenaline for courage," he says, righting my panties and jeans. Fixing me up while I just lean on the wall. "Don't want you to overdose on it, though."

"Fuck off." My gaze drops to his pants. "You're hard."

"For you, sunshine? Always."

"I mean—"

"I know what you mean, and it's fine. If we ignore it, he'll go away."

I snort. "He?"

"Knox Jr."

Oh my God. "You named your dick?"

He eyes me. "Yeah, obviously. It's not a very clever name, not like Bam Bam the Dinosaur, or—"

"Knox?"

"Yeah?"

"Stop while you're ahead." I eye him. "Speaking of head..."

Before he can stop me, I drop to my knees and return the favor.

———

Jacob Rhodes and Melody Cameron. Not yet married.

Greyson Devereux and Violet, formerly Reece, now Devereux. Married, obviously.

Steele O'Brien and Aspen. Married. Also, strangely, stepsiblings. They skate over that with a wave of their hands and sheepish smiles.

Miles Whiteshaw and Willow Reed, engaged.

And Camden Church. Single, as far as I know. Jacob's known Camden the longest, so his opinion slightly outweighed the rest of ours. Not that I was against it. I don't know him, and I didn't claim to. Knox had no objection either. So here he sits.

Then there's us. Knox and me.

Also married. How weird.

Camden spends a good deal of time telling us what he knows about Luke Abernathy. Luke's dad, Lucas Abernathy Senior, has owned the Titans for just under a decade. And apparently, it only took four years for his son to start crawling around in the shadows. Coming to practice, pulling random players aside.

This information isn't private. Camden gives us the names and phone numbers of a few former Titans, and a quick call to each of them confirms the story. That Luke Abernathy just had a weird way about him, that he seemed to be sticking his nose in places that he didn't belong.

It wasn't until after Camden was traded to the Titans a few years ago that things got... *weird*. In his words. Games they should've lost, in what their coach said was a rebuilding year, they won in hand. Games they should've easily won, against the lowest-ranked teams in the division, they walked out with a huge deficit in points.

But it wasn't all the time either. Just sporadically.

"Until another player approached me about the bribe."

We straighten.

Camden runs his fingers through his dark hair. "That player will remain anonymous. He trusted me, and I'm not going to drag him into this. He was conflicted, which is why he came to me in the first place."

"What was Luke bribing him with?"

"He offered to cut him in." Camden lifts one shoulder, then reaches for his beer. We broke those out not long after we all took our seats. "Help throw a game or two, do essentially whatever he needed—"

"Well, he's moved beyond bribes," I mumble.

The winnings from my hacked bet still sit in the account I can't access. Along with the rest of my money. I haven't mentioned it to anyone, because I've been waiting for a callback from the app's technical department. And I filed a fraudulent charge with my bank, too. But so far, it's at a standstill.

"He might not have, though," Camden points out. "He could've known that tactic wouldn't work for you. Or—"

"Or it was just a right time, right place."

"How did he get to you?" Greyson asks me.

"I accidentally walked into a meeting he was having in the back room of a club." I look away. "I don't know, I was with Beth, and I was drunk. She kind of pointed in the vague direction of the bathroom, and I got lost. Stumbled in after overhearing some stuff... It wasn't until I saw him again at a game that he realized I had connections."

"I stuffed that one up," Knox says. "Said you were my wife right to his face."

"And then he found out about Joel."

Willow holds up her hands. "Wait, time out. So, you were engaged to Joel Haverhill, the goalie. Which Abernathy finds out about after he sees you outside the locker rooms of a game—"

"Basically proving she wasn't just a random girl who wandered in," Miles says. "Shit."

"Yeah, shit," I echo. "So... what now?"

"Did you find anything out when you followed him?" Miles asks Jacob.

"Wait," Camden sputters. "You were following Abernathy?"

Jacob smiles. "Yeah. A little recon never hurt anyone, and my dad taught me how to tail someone without them knowing."

"Police chief dad for the win." Aspen laughs. "So is the goal to have him arrested? Or..."

"Please don't say dead," Steele says under his breath.

"I was going to go with *gone*," she replies. "Especially in mixed company."

Camden raises his hand. "I'm the mixed company."

"That you are," Greyson agrees. "Arrested should be the goal."

Violet eyes her husband. "And we're not just reporting him immediately because..."

"Because he's got my life savings tied up," I say. "And I have a feeling he's going to hold that over my head for a while."

"Okay, so, we go along with it. For now." Knox winces. "I say that with care, because you guys know it's killing me to be under his thumb. But if he got to me, then there might be someone else he's bribing. Who could fix games like that?"

"Besides a goalie?" Miles shrugs.

We all stop.

I do anyway. "Joel?"

Knox's hand on my knee tightens.

"What are you saying, Miles?"

"I'm saying it's easier for a goalie to make it look like he's having a good or bad night instead of trying to have one player throw off the whole team."

My head hurts. And more than that, my *heart* hurts.

I rise, dusting off my legs. "I'll be back."

Knox jumps up, too. "Where are you going?"

"Just to get some fresh air. I'll be back in twenty." I grab my coat and boots, ignoring the burning sensation of their gazes on my back.

There's hushed murmuring behind me, but I ignore it. It isn't until I'm at the bank of elevators that I realize I've been followed.

I glance over my shoulder, more expecting Knox than anyone else. Which is why I'm surprised by Violet Devereux. She offers me a small smile and steps into the elevator ahead of me.

I hadn't even heard it arrive.

Once we're in, the doors slide closed. We are both immobile for a moment, until she finally reaches forward and hits the *L* button. Lobby. Right.

"You okay?" she asks.

I sigh. "Just grappling with the knowledge that my fiancé might be in on this whole thing. I thought he was a good person. Deep down."

"Even good people can make bad choices."

There's a chime, and the elevator doors open. We head toward the exit, passing the doorman's station. At this time of night, they're not outside all the time.

"Mrs. Whiteshaw!"

Violet tugs on my sleeve. "I think he's talking to you."

The manager hurries across the lobby in our direction.

I make a face. Of course this guy is going along with the

freaking name change. Like I don't have anything attached to McGovern. *Asshole.*

Beside me, Violet snickers. "I don't suppose you're used to that level of domineering?"

"He used to be... I don't know. Maybe he was always like this and I just never noticed."

"Mrs. Whiteshaw," the building manager says when he reaches us.

"It's Ms. McGovern." I fold my arms over my chest.

He pauses. He kind of resembles a bullfrog—short, squat, and sweaty. His hands tremble, and he holds out a small box. "This came for you. I was going to have someone run it up to your unit, but since you're here..."

I raise my eyebrow and take it. I don't make a move to open it until he gives a quick nod and scurries away. Only then do I let out a slow breath. It's wrapped in brown paper, about the size of my palm. There's no note on it, no writing. Just carefully taped edges.

I meet Violet's gaze and shrug.

"I'm dying of curiosity," she murmurs.

"Okay, okay." I slide my nail under the edge of tape. The rest opens easily, until I'm left with a plain white box. The lid comes off, and I stare down at the piece of folded paper.

Thought you might appreciate the memories attached to this. – L

"Is the *L* for Luke?" Violet whispers, scanning the paper over my shoulder.

"I..."

In the box is the ring.

The engagement ring Joel gave me.

Violet frowns. "That's not good."

"I couldn't agree more."

45
KNOX

How do we take down Luke Abernathy without his father demanding we be traded to another team? How do we continue playing professional hockey when we're about to be caught throwing games?

It's like watching my career be thrown into the toilet and flushed in slow motion, and there's nothing I can do to stop it.

But I'm not mad at Aurora. I should be, but there's something else there. Something that wants to protect her. It's this urge I've never felt with anyone else, and I can barely contain it.

She and Violet return faster than I expect. They're only gone ten minutes when she unlocks our front door and comes hurrying inside with Violet on her tail. They shed their coats and kick off their shoes.

Aurora comes straight to me, her hand outstretched. She's holding something.

A glittering ring.

"Where did you get that?" I ask.

She hasn't had it. I was under the impression that Joel took it back...

She reveals the packaging. The folded paper that must've come with it. The note signed by *L*. Luke Abernathy?

"Why does he have this?"

She shakes her head. "I don't know. I can't—I have no idea."

My friends stand. It seems to be a unanimous decision between them all.

"We'll meet back up tomorrow," Jacob offers. "It's late. We're not being productive. Tomorrow, we can confront Joel—"

"If he tells the truth," Church interjects.

"He will." I ball my fists.

"Tomorrow," Aurora echoes.

They leave us alone. Alone with my thoughts, alone with my girl. The ring and note are a threat. Clear as day. I glance to where she's put it on the coffee table.

"Knox?"

I face her. She's wrapped her arms around her stomach. Her eyes are wide, her expression unsure.

She can't stay here. Luke Abernathy will take out anything we try to do on *her*. She's my biggest weakness. Removing her from the game board all together is in our best interest. Which means sending her away. Somewhere he can't reach her.

Home.

"I'm sorry," I manage.

She comes closer, taking my hands in her chilled ones. She inches into me, pressing her ear to my chest. She's hugging me, and I'm more frozen on the inside than she is icy on the outside.

"Why are you apologizing?"

I wrap my arms around her. She feels small, more fragile than I would've put on her in recent months. Lately, she's seemed so strong. I didn't think anything was wrong until she ended up in the hospital. But she said it was a fluke, didn't she? They said it was nothing urgent, just an ex-cardiac patient's past trauma coloring her perception.

That heightens my resolve. She shouldn't have to deal with this. I don't even know what we can do about it or how to extract ourselves from this situation. Short of turning ourselves in along with Abernathy or devastating our own careers...

"Because I'm sending you away," I say.

She flinches. "What? No, you're not."

"Yes, I am. Aurora. I'm sending you back home."

She extricates herself from me just as slowly as she approached. She stares at me like I'm something she doesn't recognize. Her witch eyes make her seem especially strange tonight—not in a bad way, in an ensnaring way.

I avoid her silent accusation.

"It's too dangerous."

"You need my help. What are you going to do without me?"

I step around her and go for her purse. I find the slim black phone he gave her and curl my fingers around it. "This is my problem now. And you're not stepping foot back in Denver until this is done."

She laughs. "Yeah? Who made you the gatekeeper of the city?"

I don't know—but she's not taking this seriously enough. "I am your *husband*."

"You haven't been my husband in six *fucking* years,"

she yells. "You are an asshole. You've denied me what I want at every turn. Even knowing what you know now—"

"This is different! I'm trying to save you!" I'm finally trying to *save* her, and I'm going to break before she does if she keeps pushing.

"You're trying to *smother* me!" she shrieks.

She picks up a forgotten beer bottle and chucks it at me. I duck, and the bottle crashes into the wall behind me. It cracks, then shatters when it hits the floor. I don't flinch, even when the spray of the remnant of liquid hits the backs of my ankles.

"Sunny." My words stop. My brain is fucking scrambled around her.

"You might think you're saving me, Knox," she swears, "but wrapping me in cotton won't save me. It didn't save me back then."

Back then.

"Or did you forget why we did this? You wanted to help set me free—"

I shake my head. The phone slips from my fingers, hitting the couch, and I turn away from her. I go to the windows and grip my head, suppressing the flood of emotions that threaten to steal my train of thought. And my resolve.

"It didn't save my parents the heartache, Knox," she whispers. "All of this was for nothing. You put us through hell for nothing."

I know it didn't work. I know my plan was a bad one.

I know that marrying her was the best and worst decision of my life.

She doesn't know that, though. How could she? Between sixteen and seventeen, then seventeen and eighteen, we were just teenagers. Kids. College didn't change me—but then I came back and...

I was going to tell her. And then I saw her with Miles, and I believed Beth, and the whole world got turned upside down and inside out.

It takes me too long to remember how to breathe normally. But when I regain control, I take her in. Her arms are wrapped around her stomach, her eyes wide. Her chest heaving.

She's too pretty.

She's too devastating.

I'm too obsessed with her to focus, to protect her, not when she's looking at me like that.

"You will get on the plane tomorrow morning." I grab my phone and search for flights.

There's an early one, that'll get her into New York at one o'clock. I book it, her gaze searing into me from across the room. She's not lunging at me or trying to toss my phone out the window again, at least.

"You'll get on the plane, and your dad is going to pick you up, and you'll spend a few weeks with family. And then I'll come back for you. Okay?"

If there's one thing I can control, it's this.

If there's one way to go back to *before*, it's erasing the danger from her path. And she can't be here while I try to figure out how to do that.

"Not okay. They know my dad, Knox. They called him up and insinuated that I had a gambling problem—What excuse do I give when I show up on his doorstep? That my fucking bookie took all my money and I'm on the run til you fix it?" She moves stiffly past me.

I follow her into the bedroom and pull a suitcase from the depths of the closet. I toss it on the bed and throw clothes into it. She rushes me, pushing at my hands and taking clothes out until I grab her. I practically carry her over to the headboard, where those damn handcuffs are still attached.

"Knox."

"Stop it," I growl. I lock it around her wrist and dodge her swinging arm. I go back to packing. I zip it all up while she glares, and then, when the suitcase is by the door, I unlock her.

"You packed my toothbrush, didn't you?"

I press my lips together.

She finds a spare toothbrush in the vanity and rips open the packaging. With a straight face, she brushes her teeth, washes her face. Strips out of her clothes until she's down to panties.

My chest tightens.

When she puts on one of my shirts, I almost cave.

Almost say, *never mind, I'll refund the ticket. Put your shit back. Let you stay here.*

But she's too fragile. Too vulnerable.

"You were just in the hospital," I say. "You were just in the hospital, Sunny. You can't—"

"You don't know what I can and can't do." She's not sad —she's furious. Practically vibrating with anger. "And you're sending me away? Benching me from this fight? How are you any better than my father?"

I stare at her. "Is this traumatic for you? Are you having flashbacks to being forced to quit hockey?" I laugh, but it's fucking forced. I know how much quitting hockey killed her. Now's not the time to throw it in her face, but I can't seem to stop talking. After all, this is *different*. "Jesus, Sunny, this is life or death, and you're equating it to a *game*?"

She gets into bed. "What time is the flight?"

There's this rift opening up between us. It's practically visible.

"Seven," I say slowly.

"Great." She points. "Get the light."

"Fuck off," I snap. I grab the covers and yank them off the bed. "I'm not someone to just order around, Aurora."

"And you think I am?" She stands again, poking me in the chest. "You think you can just buy me a plane ticket—"

I catch her wrist. "Do you want me to get on my knees and beg for you to get on that plane?"

"That might've gone over better—"

I kiss her.

To get her to shut up, yeah, but also because I don't know what to do with all the emotions I'm dealing with right now. Hate and fear and worry and lust and the craziest of all, fucking *love*. I can't love her and give her up at the same time. I can't—

I kiss her to get her to shut up and to get my brain to shut up.

She bites me.

I bite her back.

There's blood on our tongues, smearing across our open mouths. It unlocks something. We tear at each other's clothes, separating long enough to get our shirts over our heads. I tear her panties off with a delicious rip, my fingers cupping her pussy.

She's soaked for me.

I turn her around and force her to bend, to hold herself on the dresser, and kick her legs wide. She groans when I thrust into her hard. Her tits swing, her whole body moves with the force of it. I hammer into her over and over, reaching forward and fisting her hair. I yank her head back.

She rocks back, meeting my thrusts with a punctuation

of a gasp or cry. I dig my fingers into her hip. She's got bruises already from my rough handling, little finger-sized bruises on her ass and thighs.

A fading bite on her neck.

I pull her up by her hair, catching her around her middle to keep her back against my front. My angle changes, not able to go as deep, but it doesn't matter. I latch on to her shoulder, biting until she screams. Her pussy clenches around my dick, sending a wave of electricity up my spine.

The hand tangled in her hair moves to her throat. Her pulse is quick, her chest heaving.

"Touch yourself," I say in her ear.

She does. She runs her hand down her body, between her legs. Her fingers brush where we're connected, feeling me pumping in and out. Then back to her clit.

Immediately, her muscles tense. I groan, my breath harsh. I pull out of her, release her, and spin her around. I push her back on the bed and go on one knee.

"I want to watch," I tell her. I lift her legs, her calves on either side of my head, and slip back into her.

She's positively dripping.

"Did I say you could stop touching yourself?" I demand.

Her gaze is a delightful mix of lust and loathing. I wrap my arms around her thighs, keeping them together and raised. It makes a tighter fit, a new angle, and *fuck*, I'm not going to last long like this.

She strokes herself slowly at first, then faster. Her tits bounce with every thrust, and if I had a third hand I'd reach out and palm them. She reads my mind and does exactly that, pinching her nipple between her fingers.

So. Damn. Sexy.

"I'm close," she says, her breath hitching.

"Good," I growl.

I chase the high right along with her. There's still the taste of blood on my tongue. Blood and sex. Fitting for us.

She cries out, arching on the bed. Her eyes roll back, and her cunt squeezes me. I bury myself to the hilt inside her, my balls tightening. I come *hard*, seeing stars and nothing but white for a second.

"Hope your birth control is the good shit," I manage to say.

I release her legs slowly and pull out of her. My gaze drops to her core, and I follow suit, dropping to my knees. Her legs hang off the bed, and I hoist one over my shoulder.

She sits up on her elbows. "What are you doing?"

"Watching," I murmur.

"Watching—"

"My cum seep out of you." I lick my lips, then lean forward and taste both of us. I plug her back up with my tongue, my fingers going up to her clit. Drumming a familiar tune that has her shaking all over again. I switch, thrusting two fingers inside her and sucking on the nub. Drawing out the torture.

This is a goodbye fuck, after all.

May as well make it memorable.

When my dick hardens again, I scoot her back and crawl over her. Ready for another round. The orgasms seem to have lessened her anger. At least, I think so until she bites me again. On the shoulder, hard enough to draw blood.

Ow.

I look down at it, at the way she broke skin.

But it doesn't dull my appetite for her. Really, it just cements that we're soul mates.

46

AURORA

I'm exhausted. Weirdly satiated. And I really wanted to fall asleep next to Knox.

I practiced my deep breathing, even going so far as to leave my mouth open and drooling a little on my pillow to drive home that I was *sleeping*. He stroked my hair and looped his arm over me.

Once he falls asleep, though, and *stays* asleep, I slip out of bed.

It's just after one in the morning. He probably has an early alarm set to get me to the airport, but that's not going to happen. I'm not running from this fight. I should consider myself lucky he didn't leave me handcuffed beside him.

Luke Abernathy sent me the ring that Joel proposed with. So now... I need to see Joel and give it back. And to question him, because what the *fuck*?

Funny how things come full circle.

I pack a very different bag to the one Knox packed me. The last thing I add is the ring to my pocket on my way out the door.

First stop: the lobby bathroom. Not the best place to do what I have in mind, but I can't risk making a noise in the condo. I take the pliers from my bag and find the tooth that had been knocked out in the assault. The one Knox apparently paid to have a tracker implanted when the dentist put on the crown.

I dry the area, hold my breath, and open my mouth wide. I grip the tooth with the pliers and... three, two, one, *pull*.

The pain is almost worse than getting punched in the face. It's localized to that one spot, and I groan loudly as the crown comes loose. I examine it, confirming that it's a tracker, and wrap it in toilet paper. I drop it into the trash.

The broken piece of my tooth is still intact, at the very least.

Anyway.

I bite down on the gauze, pack the pliers away, and continue on.

On the way to Joel's, I examine the ring Abernathy returned to me. It feels strange now. Heavy, almost. A thousand pounds packed into one diamond. It didn't feel that way when I wore it every day.

There's no doorman at his place, just a key to get in through the front door that Joel never bothered to take back from me. And suddenly, I'm at his door.

I knock.

And knock some more.

The taste of blood is still on my tongue.

Finally, the door is yanked open, and a sleepy Joel stares at me.

How different we are now. How differently I see him. Before, I saw him as a means of escaping my old life and a way to get closer to Beth. After all, he lived in *Denver*, a shiny new city where my best friend lived.

It was kismet, in a way.

But what if it wasn't?

What if he was just another piece being slid across the chessboard?

"Rory," he says, his eyebrows lifting. "What are you doing here?"

I hold up the ring.

He tilts his head, eyeing it. Then me. Whatever he sees in my expression has him faltering. He steps aside and waves me in, and I take the invitation with no small amount of trepidation.

"Joel Haverhill. They call you Hammerhead, don't they?" I turn in a small circle in the center of his living room.

"It's the middle of the night, Aurora."

I'm Aurora now. Not Rory. Not a fiancée, or a girl he loved, or...

"I'm just wondering if you knew about Knox before I told you." I drag out a bar stool and sit, dropping my bag on the counter in front of me. "If you had some reason for our fast-tracked relationship outside of my stunning personality."

He comes closer. He's in boxers and a sweatshirt, undoubtedly thrown on when he woke up. I resist the urge to peek down the hall that leads to his bedroom, lest I see a girl sneaking into the bathroom.

I have no doubt he could have whatever girl he wanted.

"You convinced me to move to Denver," I say. "You collided with *me* that day."

"I'm a goalie," he says. "I don't skate much."

"Whose idea was it? Did they show you my photo? Suggest maybe..."

He laughs. "No, Aurora, no one bribed me to talk to you."

I narrow my eyes. "I didn't say anything about a bribe, Joel."

He goes quiet. The whole apartment is quiet, and my jaw aches, and I long for my bed. My body is sore, and I wish for the comfort of being wrapped up in something familiar. Which is ironic, since this apartment used to be that. How many nights did I crawl into bed alongside him, kissing his jaw, seeking solace in his arms? When I was homesick, when I was lonely. When he and Beth and me seemed like a thin slice of a vast world.

Knox is the opposite.

Knox makes me feel like we're the world.

"The truth will help." I reach for him and stop. Clear my throat. "Please."

He retrieves a bottle of tequila from the freezer. Two shot glasses. He leans on the counter across from me, his biceps flexing, and pours two. He slides one to me, and I pick it up. But I don't drink it until he's downed his, his throat bobbing with his swallow.

"The NHL has known about Knox's marriage since he was drafted to the New York Guardians."

Okay, yeah. Shot time. I pull the gauze from my mouth and toss back the alcohol. It burns going down. My broken tooth is a knife stabbing my jaw, reacting to the cold. I make a face.

Joel smiles a little, raising his eyebrow at the bloody gauze now on his counter.

"Continue," I say.

"It's also known that Knox Whiteshaw, while a great

player, can be a bit of a wild card. Which is how I ended up in Boston."

"To... find me?"

He inclines his chin. "To talk to you, at the very least. To get a read on him before he joined us. But then..."

"Don't say one thing led to another," I warn him.

He refills our glasses.

This time, I take it without hesitation, and he follows suit. After a minute, the warmth spreads through my belly and up into my chest.

"Did it start as a planned meeting? Yes." He meets my gaze. "Did I like you more than I thought? Yes, Aurora. But then... I was nudged to make it more serious. To get you to Denver."

And I went.

How happy I was, telling my father I was engaged and moving and *thriving*. The book was selling at that point. I could afford a high-rise condo, the down payment, all of it. It was like I snapped my fingers and I wasn't drowning anymore.

Overnight success on multiple fronts.

Too bad only one of them was real.

"You freaked out about Knox—"

He sighs. "I'm sorry. It was getting to be too much, knowing I was seeing my teammate's wife, putting his play at jeopardy, and he wasn't even being used—"

"Used? Just say it, Joel. Tell me who organized this." I exhale. "I already know, so you may as well just *say it*. Tell me Luke Abernathy has been pulling the strings in our lives for *months*."

He still hesitates. But then, he breaks.

"The Titans' owner's son has been messing in all our lives for years. Not months. *Years*. You think this is the first time he's done something like this?" Joel's laugh is like sandpaper. "You think someone that calculated, that money-driven, starts with rigging NHL games and bets? He owns the damn app, Aurora."

"The—"

"The gambling app," Joel confirms.

"I—"

"You put it on your phone. You got curious, you wanted to watch the odds and confirm your suspicions—I know you. Six months might not be as long as Knox had, but I still got to know you. The parts of you that love mystery and puzzles, especially."

My mouth opens and closes.

"How did I not know?" I whisper.

"Because he owns the company that created the gambling app. If you didn't look at the board of directors for that company, how else would you know?" He sighs. "Listen, they're more dangerous than you think—"

"They?"

Luke said he had a boss. So now, it's just a matter of figuring out who's on the board. Take them down that way, or something. I don't know. It's all illegal, right? Is everyone corrupt, or just a few?

"Why did Luke have this ring?" I hold it up again. It sparkles in the light, as pristine as the day Joel proposed with it.

"I gave it back to him to cover my debt."

He doesn't flinch away from that, so I do my best to extend the same courtesy.

"How much are you in debt, Joel?"

"A few hundred."

"Okay, that's not so bad—"

"Thousand."

"Shit."

"Yeah." He winces. "I was taking bribes. But then I got involved on the app, and the next thing I knew…"

"Joel. You can't gamble—there are rules against sports betting for NHL players."

"I know. Trust me, I know. And Abernathy made me very aware, as well. So unless he's silenced for good, I'm going down with him."

Shit.

I thought I was in love with him at one point. Obviously, I had a misguided view on love. And still do, if we're being honest. But at the *very* least, I cared for him. Care for him. Enough that I'm not going to let him be dragged down with Luke Abernathy.

"Did you know Luke has been using me to make Knox do certain things?"

"Yes. And, Aurora—"

"No, no, please don't give me an excuse. I just…" I exhale. "Did you know he had someone assault me? They attacked me in my own home."

He pales. He crosses around the island and takes my hands. "He—"

"Yeah," I whisper. "Bruised ribs, bruised face. Black eyes. Broke a tooth."

"Jesus." He hugs me. "I'm so fucking sorry."

"Knox wants me to leave the state," I say against his chest. "And I know I should, just for my safety, but I want to end this. Please help me end this."

Unfortunately, that's when his door crashes open. And the next thing I know, I'm ripped away from him.

47
MANUSCRIPT

CHAPTER 6

Knox shows up at my door with red-rimmed eyes. He takes my hands, both of them, and guides me out the door and all the way to his house, walking backward the whole time. Neither of us speak until we're in his kitchen, with his mom standing between us.

"Marriage," she says.

Knox's grip on me tightens. "Please, Mom."

"I'm sorry, Mrs. Whiteshaw—"

"Do not apologize to me, honey." Her features soften, and she cups my cheek. "My boy explained it to me. All of it. And I'm so sorry you've been shouldering this on your own. Your parents are doing their best."

"Something is going to happen. I can feel it." I gulp. "I just am worried I'm going to work my parents into the ground, and all these medical bills... I just think we're drowning, and another surgery is going to push us so deep we won't be able to resurface. I never wanted to ruin my parents' lives."

"Your parents love you," his mom says. She glances at him. "Knox, can I talk to Aurora for a moment alone?"

He reluctantly lets go of my hands, and we watch his back until he disappears out of sight.

"That boy will be listening at the doorway," she whispers, her tone conspiratorial. "Come with me."

I smile. He would eavesdrop.

We go outside, into the cool, fall sunshine. I tip my head back and let it warm my face, but all too soon I realize she's waiting for me to look at her. To ask me something she doesn't want her son to overhear.

"Go ahead," I whisper. "Ask."

"I know why it makes sense, honey. On paper. Knox made a logical argument. But then... something broke in him." She touches my chin. "I love you like a daughter. But I need to know... what about Knox? You're agreeing to marry him, and him you. That includes through sickness and health—"

"I don't know if I love him, if that's what you're asking." I frown. "I mean, I think I do. I've never been in love, but I just get this feeling in my chest when I look at him. And when I think about him. Even when I'm not trying to think about him, like during math class."

She chuckles. "Yeah?"

"My parents make love seem like... it's normal, I guess? It's just a way of life. They do what they have to do, they kiss and stuff, but is that more a reflection on their style of love, or how love actually is for everyone?" I shrug. "And then the movies make it confusing. Butterflies and heart palpitations—isn't that funny? The thing that sets my teeth on edge is supposed to tell me if I'm in love, too."

"I see your predicament." She gazes at me. "And have you told your parents about this plan?"

"I didn't want them trying to convince your family one way or another."

"Okay. Well. I'm going to talk to your mother when she gets home, okay?"

My attention drops to my shoes. They're worn out and dirty, covered in scuff marks. But they're still the best pair of shoes I own. "Mom's working late. She should be home by seven."

"All right. You hungry?"

I look up.

She smiles and hugs me into her side. "Yeah, thought so. Let's recruit Knox, you two can help me make dinner."

It's not that bad cooking with her. And she must text my mother, because she comes down to the Whiteshaws to collect me instead of going straight home. Knox's mom shoos us off to his room shortly after she arrives, and the two of them disappear into the kitchen.

Knox takes my hand. "You okay?"

"I'm surprised your mom took it so well."

He shifts. "Yeah, well, I can be pretty convincing."

"You seemed like you were crying earlier."

He reels me in and kisses my forehead. "Maybe I was."

"About what?"

"Regretting not helping you."

Oh. For some reason, I had hoped it would be more. I mean, she was asking about love. So I thought, maybe he loves me and that's why he's doing this. But wait. Did she actually ask about love? I jumped the gun. I blurted out my feelings.

I tip my face up and silently ask for him to kiss me *for real*.

And he obliges, making tingles shoot through my body until our moms call for us to come downstairs.

They're both eyeing us.

And then my mom gives me a slight nod, her eyes filling with tears.

Mine immediately flood, too. A tightness in my chest snaps, allowing me to finally shed some of the anxiety hounding me for weeks. I leap forward and throw my arms around her neck, and the sobs that come out of me are far too dramatic for something happy.

"Thank you," I whisper in her ear. "Thank you."

I don't have any other words. She strokes my hair and kisses my temple.

And no other words are necessary.

48
KNOX

My alarm goes off bright and early. Well, not bright. It's winter, and the sun decides when it's going to come up—but it's not the crack of dawn, which is what time it is now.

I stretch and reach back for Aurora.

My hand hits an empty space.

I groan, killing the alarm and rolling toward her. She must've shifted farther away in her sleep. She was angry. I thought we had sort of come to a resolution, but when I finally crack my eyes open more and find her spot empty, I let out a huff.

Moving to the couch is a bit of a low blow.

"Aurora," I sing, forcing myself out of the warmth and out the door. "Time to get—"

I'm talking to an empty room.

My brow furrows. I search the other room, the converted guest room-slash-office, which is similarly empty. Her pink typewriter sits untouched. I was going to pack it. I actually should've packed it, knowing her. She'd write a litany of profanity in my honor, maybe.

Hopefully.

It's clear she's not here. She's not in the bedroom, hiding in the closet or bathroom, she's not in the main living space or kitchen or the closet by the door. Which I check out of desperation, just in case.

My phone, plugged in on my nightstand, has a notification waiting for me.

Some glitch with the tracker.

I frown, opening the app, and stare at the blinking dot. It's not really helpful when it doesn't show how high up she is, because according to this, she's close to the center of the building. Where my condo is not.

Our condo.

Whatever.

I yank clothes on, stuff my pockets with my keys and wallet, and head to the elevator. I check her old condo first, but that doesn't line up. Then Jacob's floor—not that she'd be there in the middle of the night, even if she was super pissed at me. It's just after six, and she's been gone for at least an hour.

To be fair, though, she *was* super pissed when she went to bed.

Shit, and my mom warned me to never go to bed angry. Never mind that I've been angry for years straight without reprieve.

That doesn't match up either. Back on the elevator, down to the gym.

Nope.

Main floor?

I go down a hall and stop outside the women's restroom.

No...

But really, *yes*, because my phone's location is almost on

top of hers.

The restroom is empty. I check the stalls, and something makes me stop in front of the trash. It's mostly empty, but there are a few paper towels at the bottom. I drag the whole thing back out and overturn it on the counter.

There's a *plink* of something hard hitting the surface.

Fuck.

It takes me another minute to find it, brushing away the paper towels, and I pick up the artificial molar.

She took it out.

Damn, the girl is ballsy. Especially when she's angry.

I call for reinforcements and head back upstairs. The thing is, I have no idea where she'd go. Before, she would've run to Beth. Crossed that option off. And she would've run to Joel, but I screwed that up for her, too.

Going home would just be going along with what I planned, so, nope.

"Hey." Greyson pushes open my door. "Am I the first one here?"

"Yes. Yeah. Thank you. She was just—" I show him the tooth. "She pulled it out in the lobby bathroom. Who *does* that?"

He looks at it. "Did you tell her about it?"

"Well... yeah..."

"Why?"

I scoff. "Why? I don't know, it just came out."

He stares at me, then slowly shakes his head. "Listen. We've done our fair share of fucked-up shit together. This is just another time, right?"

"Right," I confirm. "Well, I don't know what we're doing besides finding Aurora."

"Uh-huh. Steele is getting us coffee."

"Good plan. Good plan." I rub my hands together and

go to the window. Such a great view, and I don't think I've truly enjoyed it since I got here. "Where would you go, Sunny?" I ask the cityscape.

This has to be my punishment for being an awful husband.

"Where the fuck did she go?" I repeat, this time to my friends. "Where would she go? Why did she leave? I mean —obviously it's because I tried to get her to leave Denver. She was upset. I handcuffed her to the bed while I packed. I—"

"Knox."

"What?" I snap.

"Shut up for two seconds."

I glare at Greyson. He lets in Miles and Jacob, and I stay quiet while Greyson gives them the short version of my blunder. He repeats it again when Steele enters with coffees balanced in his arms.

"So..." Jacob grabs Aurora's laptop from the office. "Any guesses on her password?"

"Knox-is-an-ass-sixty-nine?" I guess.

Steele snorts.

Jacob sighs and types something in. "Hey, it worked!"

My jaw drops. "She did *not*—"

"Nah, she didn't. Sucker." Jacob grins.

Great. "She's *missing*. This isn't the time to make jokes."

Steele flops on the couch. He makes a weird face and shifts to the side, pulling out the slim black phone.

I stare at it. "Wait. We know where she went."

I'm such an idiot.

"She's playing right into his hand."

"Whose?" Jacob demands. "Abernathy?"

I pocket the phone. "Of course, Abernathy. Why would

he give her the ring? So she'd leave here and go see Joel. I just didn't expect her to go in the middle of the night."

They nod. They're agreeing with me. It only makes sense, doesn't it?

Off we go.

49

AURORA

"Are you kidnapping me?" I demand, fighting Camden Church's grip on my upper arm. "Knox is going to kill you for this."

I mean, I *trusted* him. Not a lot, but enough. More than any of the other guys did. And when he burst into Joel's apartment and dragged me away from him, I didn't really have any words. Not when Camden just pointed at Joel and snarled something about owing him something.

Joel let us leave his apartment without a fight.

"He'll understand when you both realize Luke is on his way to Joel's apartment," Camden snaps. "Stop fighting me. I'm trying to *help* you."

We're in the stairwell of Joel's high-rise, going up instead of down.

I give in, and our steps come faster. He breathes out a small sigh of relief, then opens the door onto the fifteenth floor. My chest is pounding by the time we stop. I lean over, focusing on catching my breath, while he peeks around the corner.

"What the fuck?" I gasp. "Explain. Right now."

"I think Joel's been taking bribes for a long time. There are rumors that he's been gambling—"

I nod shortly.

"Right." His blue eyes bore into mine. "So where's his loyalty, Aurora?"

"Come on, you have to believe in him more than that—"

"Do I?" Camden shakes his head. "No. Why'd you go to Joel in the middle of the night anyway?"

"Knox wanted to ship me back home. This would've been my only chance to get some answers."

"You're becoming a problem to Luke. I have no doubt we've been making waves. Just by involving you with black-mail instead of bribery is a risk to him. Jacob has stayed off the radar, kept his head down, but you, Knox... hell, even me. Joel could be considered a loose end, but I think Aber-nathy considers him all tied up. In debt and other things."

He might have a point. But I'm more concerned with where we are.

"Why are we on the fifteenth floor?"

He lifts one shoulder. "Come on, I'll show you."

We go halfway down the hall, and he stops in front of one of the doors. He knocks twice and steps back, slipping his hands in his pockets. Like this, he looks rather unas-suming. Boy-next-door vibes. Ironic, since Knox *was* my boy next door.

The door cracks open after a long wait, and a girl's eye stares out at us.

"Camden."

"Grace. Can we come in?"

Her focus switches to me. "Who's she?"

"My teammate's girl. We just need to lie low..."

"And you come here?"

"We were downstairs, to be fair." Camden eyes her. "Are you going to let us in or what?"

She sighs. The door closes, and I glance at Camden. Then it opens fully, the chain swinging from the doorframe. She wears a Titans sweatshirt and dark-blue shorts. Bare feet.

It's winter, and she's wearing shorts—just like Knox.

Are people in this town insane?

She's familiar. Makeup-less, though, it takes me a minute to place her as Camden's sister. From the charity gala.

"Grace, this is Aurora McGovern. Aurora, Grace Church."

"We met at the gala," I offer. "I was with Knox Whiteshaw..."

"Right!" She smiles and steps back to allow us in. "I remember meeting you."

"Oh, good." Camden rubs the back of his neck, then seems to mentally say, *fuck it*. He walks farther in, toeing off his shoes and turning in a small circle. "You've cleaned up since I last saw the place."

"Right," Grace scoffs. "You last saw it when I moved in. Eight months ago."

Yikes.

"I feel like I'm intruding." I frown. "It's so early—"

"No, she's fine," Camden says. "She's a night owl. Were you even sleeping yet, Gracie?"

His sister flushes. "No. But... well, shit." She stares at me a beat, then turns and rushes down a hall. She comes back a moment holding a very familiar book in her hand.

My heart skips.

"I'm reading your book," she says sheepishly. "It's fucking addictive."

"Holy shit." Camden laughs.

"Shut up, Cam," Grace snaps. Back to me, her smile is more tentative. "Could you sign this?"

"Of course!" It's surreal, but I take the well-loved paperback from her and wait while she finds a pen. I flip through the pages, and it takes another moment to register that I actually haven't held a copy of my book in a while.

I bought myself copies when it first came out, gave them away, and then... moved.

I've been distracted, I guess. Go figure.

"So, the reason for lying low—is it dangerous?" She hands me a pen.

I scrawl my name on the title page, finishing with a little heart, and hand it back to her. Camden watches with a bemused smile, although he doesn't answer her question. And I can't, because I have no idea what the hell is happening.

"Well?" She faces her brother.

"I think someone was coming to take Aurora," he says. "Or at the very least, hurt her and frame it on Joel."

"Haverhill?" She squints. "Does he live in this building?"

"Yes." He waves her words away. "Don't go looking for trouble, Gracie. He nearly got Aurora killed."

"And you think Luke would have someone come for me *there*?" I question.

"Your husband upped the security at your building. It was to make it more difficult for someone to get up to your floor."

"How do you know that?"

He rolls his eyes. "Knox mentioned it during practice."

"Of course he did." I frown. "Okay, so, he didn't think he could get to me there undetected. But here?"

"Our elevators are shit," Grace interjects. "And as far as I know, there aren't any cameras."

Right. Even I got in with no problem—and Camden must've, too.

"You prevented a kidnapping in the middle of the night," Grace says, patting her brother on the head. "Good boy."

"Knock it off." He swats at her. "It was a lucky break."

"Lucky is right."

"And a little bit of eavesdropping," he admits. "I cloned Luke's phone last week."

That would've been good to know. I scowl at him, which he also ignores. He pulls the phone out—his or the clone, I have no idea—and scrolls through it. Then shoots off a text.

"What did you just do?"

"Texted your phone."

I pat my pockets, but my phone doesn't go off. I check it just in case, finding the screen empty of notifications.

"Your *other* phone."

"Why?"

"To freak out Knox." He shrugs. "That guy needs a good shove to do anything. Besides, if they come here guns blazing, it'll probably scare away the guy Luke hired. Then we can get you back to safety."

"That's a Band-Aid," I point out. "I mean, what's the point of any of this?"

"You'll live to see another day, Aurora McGovern. That's the important part."

Well... yeah. He's got a point. But then what? Let Knox

force me out of Denver until he deems it safe? Let him rule my life for even longer?

My mind twists this like one of my books. If I were a character, if I were the hero, what would I do?

The problem is—I built this new, budding career on writing an anti-hero as the love interest. And while Knox definitely has anti-hero qualities, he's also been my knight in shining armor.

Too bad I'm starting to crave the tarnished armor look.

What would Knox do to end this? If my life was actually on the line?

"If we want to end this... why drag it out?" My plan is taking shape. Not a good plan, but it'll do for now. "I trust you to point Knox in the right direction."

He shoots to his feet, but I'm faster. I beat him to the door, and his sister's voice behind him makes him slow. The elevator arrives before he can get to me. I raise my eyebrows as Camden slams to a halt, the doors closing in his face. I press the buttons for Joel's floor and the lobby.

It stops at his floor first.

And waiting for me is a bloody-knuckled Luke Abernathy. Not some hired dickbag.

Okay, so, maybe not the best plan. But I'm here, and he's here, and I'm definitely screwed.

So I smile at him and step back, giving him room to come on.

"Doing your own dirty work, then?" I ask with a tilt of my head.

He smiles. "Just the lady I was searching for."

He enters the elevator, and it's like the air gets sucked out with his presence. After a moment, the doors close behind him. A prickle of nervous energy slides down my spine, but I ignore it. I ignore everything except the way his hands tighten into fists.

"Bet you wish you were the one who beat me," I murmur. "For all the trouble I've caused you."

"The pictures didn't do it justice," he answers. "But I'll see you curled on the floor again soon enough."

I accept that. Because sometimes, the only way to get a monster put down is to force the hero into action.

50

KNOX

Camden: Aurora's walking into a trap. Joel's apartment.

The text to the burner phone clearly wasn't sent for Aurora—it was a message for me. It makes *no sense*. What game is he playing at?

I tighten my grip on the phone. Greyson and Miles stuck with me as I *ran* the three blocks to Joel's building. We caught someone on their way out, which solved the locked door issue, and went up to Joel's floor.

We stand outside his door now. It's open, which made me slam on the brakes.

"Why do they always put themselves in harm's way?" Miles mutters. "Running into danger without any plan."

Referring to Aurora. And probably every other damn girl in our group. This feels like an initiation of sorts.

I shake my head, trying to understand it. Aurora came *here*? At this hour? When I try to go through the door, Greyson stops me. He gives me a look that says, *Don't be an idiot.* Then he goes first.

I glower at Miles, but my younger brother shrugs me off. He goes in after Greyson, leaving me alone in the hall.

So naturally, I rush in after them—and stop short.

Haverhill is on the floor in the middle of the room. Unconscious? Dead? I have no fucking idea. I don't want to know. The thought of it kind of makes me sick, to be quite frank. Aurora was here. And when Greyson reappears from the bedroom, shaking his head, it confirms that she's not any longer.

"Is he—?"

"Alive," Miles confirms, rising from where he had crouched next to Joel. "Just passed out."

"Great. Let's wake him up, see what the fuck is happening—"

"About time you showed up."

We all whirl around.

Camden Church steps in, his hands in his pockets. Unassuming as always. Except right now, I want to beat his brains in.

"Before you start, Knox, Aurora was already here when I sent her burner phone that text. For you." He lifts one shoulder. "And she was safe from Luke Abernathy..."

I stare at him. "And why should we believe you?"

"My sister lives upstairs. I have Luke's phone cloned, as I explained to Aurora. I knew he was sending someone to come intercept her." Church eyes me just as hard as I'm eyeing him. "And to answer your question, she left in the middle of the night because she was afraid of not getting any more chances."

"How do you know this?" Greyson asks. "No offense, man, but you seem to be showing up at the most opportune times."

Church lifts one shoulder. "Knox mentioned some

things that helped put the pieces together. I went from there. As I said—I knew of Abernathy's involvement for a while now, with no way to stop it. Plus your added security—"

Miles shoots me a look.

Okay, so maybe I told Church about that, too.

"It meant he couldn't get to her in your building."

That's what we had concluded, too. But where is she?

"If you kept her safe—is she upstairs?" I start toward him.

"He said was," Greyson says quietly. "She *was* safe from Abernathy."

Church's expression turns to regret. "She said to point you in the right direction. That she trusted you to find her."

No.

No, no, *no*.

"You let her go?" I roar. I lunge forward without thinking.

Miles and Greyson catch my arms before I can take down the Titans' captain. And oh, I'd rip his bloody face off if they let me.

"What the fuck?" My voice bounces around in my ears.

They haul me back and toss me on the couch, but I'm on my feet in an instant.

Camden pulls a phone out of his pocket and tosses it to me. "The cloned phone. Track it, do whatever you want with it. But I'd start with the arena."

I stop. "What? Why?"

"Because he texted his father to meet him there in an hour. Check it if you don't believe me. And come on, Knox. He owns the rink, just like he thinks he owns us. Why wouldn't he go somewhere he thinks is safe?"

51

AURORA

"This is cliche," I groan. Everywhere hurts. It doesn't *feel* cliche, that's for sure. But even I can recognize the resemblance to any action movie ever. "And it doesn't even really make sense."

"It will." Luke leans against the wall.

And I'm strung up like a fish on a hook. Chains are wrapped around my wrists, and a hook holds me up. If I'm still, the balls of my feet can touch the cold floor.

I signed up for this.

I literally walked into this.

Because I've been puzzling over the best solution as much as I'm sure Knox and his friends have, and I've just reached the answer faster than them.

Luke Abernathy needs to die.

Now, murder isn't really my style. It wasn't, actually, until I met *him*. But for the last hour, while he's slowly covered me in bruises, I've been picturing the different ways he could die. In the most satisfying manner.

"You could've just taken me from your office last night." I shift my weight, and I slip in the blood. For a moment, I swing wildly around by my wrists, my shoulders and back screaming.

He watches me regain my footing. My chest heaves.

"I could've," he allows. "But it wasn't until after that I was notified of the plane ticket you purchased. That set this whole thing into motion, Aurora. You trying to leave. To renege on our deal."

I scoff.

Fucking Knox.

"You're saying I wouldn't be in *this* position if Knox hadn't tried to get me to leave Denver?" I laugh. I'm losing more vision in my left eye, although I can't tell if it's because blood is dripping into it or if the socket is swelling shut.

Everything hurts, but the vision feels more pressing. The loss of it kicks up a newfound panic, and I lose my balance again.

Suddenly he's right in front of me, gripping the collar of my shirt. Righting me, although I doubt that was his intention. My toes barely touch the floor.

"Listen to me, girl. I'm not in charge. I was never in charge. The only thing I did was orchestrate your movements."

I shiver.

"That's right," he murmurs. "That fear? Hold on to that. It's what's keeping you connected to reality. My boss will be here shortly. The one who's been running this deal for a decade."

"I'm not a problem for him," I say. "I didn't do anything—"

He releases me and laughs. Then his phone is in my face.

The little ring of us in the parking lot, just the other day.

Knox and me, all his friends sans Jacob, plus Camden
Church.

The door opens.

Luke doesn't look away from me. "Right on time, Dad.
We've got ourselves the key to—"

Bang.

I flinch.

"Honestly, Aurora."

I open my eyes, and Knox is right there. There's a gun in
his hand. Where did he get a gun? How did he find me?
Why is he here?

No. Wait.

His eyes aren't brown.

Why are his eyes brown?

Am I dreaming?

Cold water sloshes over me.

I gasp, jerking awake. The chains that hold me up rattle
with the sudden movement. The water soaks my hair and
clothes, and by the time it drips off my legs, it's tinged pink
with blood.

"Have a nice little nap?"

There's a flash.

I groan, trying to regain my footing. My limbs feel like
jelly, my muscles cramping.

"This is cliche," I say, the déjà vu of my words striking a
weird chord inside me. "Torture for torture's sake feels...
disingenuous."

"Are you worried about my sincerity, Ms. McGovern?"

"Maybe."

Luke Abernathy comes closer. "Here's the thing. My
investors have become... *spooked*, let's say, by recent events.
We're dissolving our operation, but not without one last

payday. Which means nothing can go wrong. It's going to be a team effort."

I cough. Blood comes up, spraying all over his crisp white shirt. I lick my split, swollen lips. "Oops."

His lips turn down, and he pulls at the ruined fabric. "Do you know how long you've been here?"

I readjust my grip on the chains. I can hold them and take some weight off my shoulders, which I do periodically. "Long enough to fall asleep like this, so..." I shake my head. "I don't know."

"It's been thirty-six hours since you got in the elevator with me. But you're not done, yet. You're going to hang out here as my insurance for this game to go *exactly* the way I want. If it does, you live."

"If it doesn't?"

"Then your husband will get you delivered back to him in pieces."

I shudder. Was any of that dream real?

"Where's your boss?" I ask.

He stares at me, seeming fascinated with my face. And then, with a small smile, he leaves me hanging.

Literally.

I shouldn't have pulled out that tooth. Out of all the things wrong, that spot in my mouth seems to pulse worse than the rest. Probably because, of all the things, I did it to myself. I cut off my nose to spite my face, in a way.

Tears burn my eyes. My dream seems to blend with the rest of the conversations I've had with Luke Abernathy since he took me.

I got into his car willingly. Maybe not a hundred percent *willingly*, but more with a sense of duty to just get this over with on my terms. Because running isn't going to get me anywhere. And if the dream conversation was real, it was Knox who triggered this.

If we don't get free of him, we'll be bound to the Abernathys forever.

My feet slide in the blood under me. He didn't beat me —he had someone else get their hands dirty. I think Joel was his exception. The one person he didn't expect to give him up ended up spilling all his secrets.

To me.

And now I hold them, although he hasn't asked me about any of it.

I know he owns the gambling app, and he has all my money tied up out of my reach, and there's the fate of Knox and his friends to consider.

Gosh, I wish I could go back to hating Knox. Not that I ever *hated* him. I nurtured that intense dislike to protect myself from him. From his loathing.

If seventeen-year-old me knew, when he yelled at me on my doorstep, that it was because he thought I'd slept with his brother... what would I have done?

The new problem that arises now, an interesting complication, is the water.

Every so often, a chilled breeze sweeps through the room. My hair is plastered to my head, the front of my shirt and pants are soaked. Goosebumps rise on my arms, down my back. And after a few minutes, the shivering starts.

It's December in Colorado. Needless to say, it's *cold*.

Thirty-six hours, he said.

So much for Church helping me out.

5²
KNOX

I leave a trail of bodies across Denver.

It sounds dramatic, but that's me. *Dramatic*. And furious.

My knuckles are split, and some of the guys I was taking my anger out on got in a punch or two before I put them down. But *damn it*, Abernathy has been keeping me on the move. We got to the arena only to find it empty, save the owner. Lucas Abernathy Senior.

And he didn't have a clue what we were talking about. Maybe we should've pressed him more, but the look he gave us when we brought up his son... He spit out something about his son always meddling in the team's affairs, an unwelcome endeavor, and we decided to leave him.

For now.

"We have a game." Jacob pulls me up from where I'm slumped against the wall. "Come on. Get up."

I never really understood the whole burn-the-world-down-for-her vibe he and the others exuded. It made me feel different. Something must've been wrong with me, right? Because they'd literally kill for their girls, and I felt *nothing* toward Willow.

The truth? I tried.

I tried to love her.

But I couldn't sleep next to her without thinking about all the ways she could betray me, and I couldn't open myself up.

Ironic, wasn't it? She struggled with the exact same thing. And still, she at least tried. I just shut her down and blamed the bet. It *was* for the bet. But there was a spark of fear that coursed through me at her confession, too. Like her getting close to me was suddenly very real and very, *very* terrifying.

Did I think of Aurora in that moment?

Did I think of the way she would judge me for laughing in Willow's face?

No.

Not until Miles punched me, and I realized that his reaction is exactly what I wanted to do to him after I found out about—well, after I thought they slept together.

"Let's go," Jacob urges.

I shrug him off.

The latest guy to get in my way also happened to be the first. Jerry the doorman.

I step over his body on the way out of the room, and I'm a bit like a zombie in the car on the way to the arena. The arena that we scoured, so fucking hopeful.

Thirty-six hours ago.

"Your phone." Jacob jostles my arm.

I shake my head. "My phone died hours ago."

"Well, something's buzzing."

I twist around, eyeing our hockey bags. The lightbulb goes off, and the buzzing stops. I lunge for the zipper, almost falling into the backseat. I manage to find the burner phone, and almost immediately, it starts up again.

"Shit." I answer it before Jacob can question it. "Hello?"

"Knox Whiteshaw, just the man I was hoping to speak with." Luke Abernathy's voice is ice-cold. "I've texted you a photo. Listen very closely…"

I put it on speakerphone, sinking back into my seat. Jacob glances down at it, then refocuses on the road. Abernathy details exactly how our game is going to go, in excruciating detail about points, goals, assists. Like he can orchestrate the whole thing.

Joel will play.

Church will play.

I will play.

And if none of us get on the ice, Aurora dies.

The effort it takes not to chuck the phone through the window at that is extreme.

He leaves out Jacob, though, which leads me to believe he doesn't know about my best friend's involvement.

We exchange another look when Abernathy ends the call, and I open the photo he sent. Aurora is in chains, hanging by her wrists. Her feet barely touch the floor.

My heart jumps into my throat.

"Okay." Jacob blows out a breath. "Plan B. Don't freak out."

"I think we're on Plan F—for *fucked*." I cover my face. "This is a disaster. I *am* freaking out. Where the fuck is she?"

"We follow his rules and everything will be fine," he assures me. "We've got nothing else to go on, Knox."

"*Or*, we follow his rules and he decides that we're actually good for something, and he has us do it again and again and again until we're dead or arrested." I glare at him. "Let me out."

He squints at me. "What? Why?"

"You have his directions—I don't know, make up something to Coach."

"You don't—"

"I have his cloned phone." I hold it up. "And I'm going to do something crazy. Okay? Okay."

He pulls over, and I hop out.

"Just show up to the arena and act like everything is fine," I tell him.

He grunts. I slam the door before he can tell me again that I'm an idiot. I *know* I'm an idiot. I let Aurora walk out while I fucking slept like a baby.

I didn't fight hard enough for her.

Goddamn it.

I open his phone and scroll through the settings. There's an app that teenagers use—which is kind of strange for a grown man to have it, honestly—but it tracks location. I don't know if *he* knows that, because he's at least thirty-five.

Shit, Melody is thirty-four.

Okay, he's at *least* forty-two. He's got gray hair coming in at the temples, after all.

Does Melody dye her hair? She might not be going gray yet. Aurora's definitely not, she's younger than me by a year. Which means I'll probably get wrinkles first. And I'm on my way to losing a tooth or two, but that's life. It's actually a sign of making it in the NHL, in a way.

I might've made that up. But she's already lost a tooth, so she's ahead of me. Damn it.

Focus.

His location loads, and it's not fucked up by me being in

the app. His ugly little character is across town from where I am now. Which means Aurora could be there, too.

I stuff my hands in my jacket pockets, and my fingers brush something cold.

When I pull it out, in my hand is Miles' trusty folding knife.

The one that already has someone else's life on it.

I don't know when he might've slipped it into my pocket, but I do know why. He's the smarter of the White-shaw brothers. And he already knows where my head and my heart are.

With Aurora.

So now it's time to find her and teach Abernathy that there's no one scarier than a Whiteshaw out for payback.

53
AURORA

My chest hurts. It's probably from dangling, from repeatedly losing my footing on the now-slick floor. I'm so cold, I can barely feel my fingers anymore.

But after a while, my resolve comes back.

I had it before. The will to live, the lack of fear that came with facing death. I wasn't afraid back then, but I'm scared now. I'm scared of not finishing this thing with Knox. I'm afraid of dying and leaving him to deal with his messy emotions on his own.

That wouldn't work out for anyone.

So instead, I plant my toes on the floor one more time, adjust my wrists, and I propel myself upward as hard as I can.

The chains slip and catch on the tip of the hook. I have even less of an angle now, and I swing wildly for a moment. As soon as I slow, I try again. Heaving myself up, my arms and shoulders screaming in pain.

There's a *pop* in my shoulder, and fire flashes down my arm.

But then I'm falling, free of the hook that's been tormenting me for thirty-six hours. They only let me down long enough to use the toilet twice, and even then it was a two-minute break. And by toilet, I mean bucket. With my hands still bound.

I hit the floor hard, and my vision goes dark.

"Get up, Sunny," Knox calls. "You've been knocked down harder than that."

I press my hands into the ice. Touch the helmet on my head, and the stick lying next to me. And the guy skating away like he didn't just check me into the boards.

Knox digs his blades into the ice, showering me with snow. He has his hand on his hip. He's young. Fifteen, maybe, with that goofy grin and floppy hair.

His eyes sparkle. "Get up, Sunny. No one's going to pick you up when you're facing Canada at the Olympics."

I grit my teeth. Catch my breath.

And force myself up.

My eyes open. I wheeze, rolling on my side and coughing up blood. But on my side is easier, pushing my bound hands to the floor and getting my knees under me. Then standing. Slowly, shakily.

I can't seem to get the trembling under control.

There are footsteps outside the room. I bolt for the far wall and press myself against it. I can't let fear choke me. Can't let it hold me hostage.

Only one of us can leave this room.

And it's going to be me.

I stay still, quiet, calm. My pulse is rioting, my heart pounding against my ribcage. The door opens, and I'm doused in shadow.

Luke comes in and stops dead. Before he can react further, I push the door shut. It slams, echoing in my ears. I dive at his back and get my arms over his head. The chains on my wrists pull tight across his throat, and I drop to the floor. He's tall, and I might not be as heavy as him, or as strong, but my dead weight is focused directly on his windpipe.

He makes a gurgling noise. He scrambles at the chain and falls backward over me. He does some rolling maneuver, dislodging me completely. I lose my position—but he grabs my wrists before I can get out of his way.

"Mistake." His voice hoarse. "You bitch."

I kick out. My heel catches his shoulder. I kick again, badgering him until he releases my wrist. The chain. I'm still at a disadvantage, still fucking bleeding, still bound. Every move hurts, every breath makes my chest ache more.

But I don't care.

This is life or death, isn't it?

He crawls over me. Pins my arms over my head. He stands, dragging me up by my hair. I hold his wrist and scramble to go with him and against him. The pain in my scalp is searing. He picks me up, ignoring the way my feet connect with his shins, his thighs. I scream and thrash, and he somehow gets my wrists back on the hook.

When he drops me, my legs don't work fast enough to catch myself.

Dislocated shoulder.

I scream again, gripping the chain with my other wrist. Trying to keep my weight on the one arm. I can't feel my fingers, or my legs, or anything.

Luke staggers in front of me. His eyes are wild, his throat red where the chains cut into his skin. If only I was stronger. If only I had moved faster, kept him upright—I don't know what would've worked. What would've killed him.

He grips my hair, yanking my head back.

"I felt a little bad, Aurora, knowing you were going to die." He rubs at his throat with his free hand. "But now, I don't feel a thing."

"You should," I choke out.

The door behind him swings open.

"And why is that?"

Knox moves quieter than I could've imagined. Or maybe Luke is just fascinated with the way I bleed. But it doesn't matter, because in the next moment, Knox jams the blade of the knife into his neck.

Luke's hold on me releases, his eyes widening as Knox steps around him.

Knox rips the blade forward, releasing a spray of blood. It spurts out, his artery cut, and soaks me in blood. More blood. He falls to his knees, then slumps over. He's clutching his neck, trying to stop the bleeding, but he can't. Just like in the dream.

Except this time, Knox has blue eyes. The right shade. He lifts me slightly and undoes the chains from the hook, setting me solidly on my feet. Solidly—*ha*. He has to hold me up. He tries to direct my attention away from my captor, but I can't stop staring. I feel like I owe Luke that much. To watch him die the slow, ugly way.

Not like my mom, whose death was peaceful in retrospect. I cataloged her death in my head, too. Seared it into my mind so I'd never forget what death looked like.

But now there's a new version. A darker version reserved for horrible men.

Every last gurgle documented, until he goes still and quiet and *dead*.

"I don't feel a thing either," I whisper.

And that's the end of it.

54
KNOX

I didn't mean for him to die so quickly.

I know that's morbid. I *know* it's bad. It's kind of sick, in a way, to have wanted him to suffer longer. But he was up in front of Sunny, and I just wanted it to be over. I wanted him to stop touching her, stop hurting her—

So I stabbed his throat and covered her with his blood in the process.

She's like that movie character, the girl who gets drenched in blood at prom or whatever. Minus the white dress. And the crowd of laughing teens—you know what, never mind.

We look down at him for what feels like an eon, just waiting. Part of me thinks he's going to burst back to life. But he doesn't. I scoop her up, holding her close. She buries her face in my neck, but she's not crying. She's not even shaking.

"My chest hurts," she whispers.

I look down at her, keeping her close. Her chest. Her heart?

"I'm getting you out of here," I promise. I carry her out,

my steps coming fast. Through the long, dark hallway. Up a flight of metal stairs.

My friends are just arriving when I burst out into the alleyway.

Greyson takes one look at us and goes running for something in the trunk of his rental car. He pulls out wipes and roughly swipes at my skin. My grip on Aurora tightens, but Greyson ignores us until the blood is gone from my face and neck.

He turns to her, and she flinches into me with every touch.

"Sorry, Aurora," he murmurs. "We need to get you guys in new clothes."

"She has to go to the hospital," I reply. "Right now."

Jacob stops beside me. "You cannot go like this. They'll ask too many questions. We either clean you up, or they'll call the police."

I nod slowly. Greyson gets us clothes—leggings and a zip-up sweatshirt for Aurora, a new shirt for me. When I set her down, she only clings tighter.

"Just a moment," I whisper to her, kissing her hair. The guys give us privacy. We're blocked by the car's open doors. I change out her clothes, dropping the wet, bloody fabric to the ground.

It's then that I notice her shoulder.

It looks… dislocated. Her expression is vacant.

"Guys?" My fucking voice trembles. I get the sweatshirt on, zipping it up so they don't see anything they shouldn't.

Steele appears.

"Her shoulder is dislocated. We need to get to a hospital *now*."

"I'll drive." He flashes keys at me.

I pick Aurora up again and follow him out. She buries

her face in my neck again. We get in the backseat of Jacob's truck and Steele takes off. Out of the alley, bumping out onto the main road.

Her wet hair soaks my shoulder. She's a mess. It physically hurts me to see her like this, and that rage that made me act so quickly, so *hastily*, comes rushing back.

Suddenly, she coughs. Blood comes out, on her lips and across my neck.

Shit.

"Drive faster," I order my best friend.

He calls ahead. It's a blur of quick, choppy conversation that I can't seem to hold onto. I tell him what's happening, her medical history, and he relays it. Otherwise, I just stare down at Aurora. Checking that her eyes are still open—they are, and she blinks slowly. She coughs again, a pink foamy spray on her lips.

That's a problem with her lungs, right?

We arrive at the hospital and are swarmed by medical workers. I'm barely out of the car with Aurora when they pull her from me. It's almost comical how fast they move. Like a movie. But she *screams*, even with her eyes shut, and I rush forward. I grip her hand, drawing her face to me. Even as they put her flat on the stretcher and wheel her in, I stay *right here*. I say it, too, over and over.

I'm right here.

I tell them her medical history. I tell them that she said her chest hurts. Of everything, why would she say that if she wasn't worried about her heart?

She thrashes.

A nurse sticks a needle in her upper arm, sedating her. It takes a minute for Aurora to stop, to take a slower, wheezing breath and relax on the stretcher.

I'm right here. Until I can't go any farther. Someone stops me from following through a set of double doors.

"I'm her husband," I say, my voice splintering. "I..."

I don't know what to do.

I run my fingers through my hair. My stomach turns, and I rush over to the closest waste bin. I throw up, coughing and choking, and then *I'm* swarmed. Nurses checking on me, taking the bin away, leading me to a chair in a quiet room.

Their voices are buzzing.

It's not like I was the one held for thirty-six hours.

Should I feel more guilt?

Did Miles feel guilty when he—?

I didn't sleep while Aurora was gone. I hurt people who may or may not have deserved it. I don't give a shit about them, though. I don't give a shit about anyone but Aurora. She's a beacon of light in the darkness.

Finally, I know.

When my brother steps into the room, I suddenly see him with an understanding that makes me wish for a knife across *my* throat.

"I'm so sorry," I choke out.

I don't know if I'd be able to exist in the same room as him if he was responsible for Aurora's capture. And yet, he still looks at me. Still talks to me.

Still considers me *family*.

He sighs and sits down beside me. "You're sorry?"

"For all of it. For everything I've done to you and Willow. I was angry and crushed and I didn't understand."

"You didn't want to understand." He leans back, watching me.

"I didn't want to understand," I agree.

"But now you do."

"I've loved her forever," I admit. "Even when I thought the worst of her, I still loved her. And I hate myself for being so weak-minded that I couldn't let her go."

Miles laughs. *Laughs*, at a time like this.

"You're not weak-minded. You're just as fucked in the head as the rest of us. Except you found your girl long before we did."

I close my eyes. I did find her. I found her, I lost her.

"I hate hospitals," I admit.

Almost as much as Aurora does.

Miles tips his head. Deciding something. He reaches into his bag and pulls out a sheaf of papers, and after a moment of consideration, he holds them out to me.

I take them.

It's Aurora's manuscript.

I flip through the pages slowly, carefully. Trying not to bend any of the corners as I do so. It's a marvel. "How did you get this?"

"She told Willow about it. Said if anything happened to her, to go into her office and get it for you."

"Nothing's happening to her," I bite out.

Miles looks at me.

Really looks.

No.

"No, dude, she's fine." I stand. "She's okay. She's a little beat up. Broken ribs, maybe, or..."

A lump forms in my throat.

"Stop staring at me like that." I shake out my limbs. My muscles ache, the strain from the last few days starting to catch up with me. "Stop thinking the worst."

"I called her dad," he says quietly. "I talked to the nurses when it was clear you were out of it."

"I'm not out of it." I whirl around. "I'm right here. I'm paying attention, Miles."

God, I hate him.

"You're not." He rises. "You're not *listening*."

I shove him. Not hard, just... just a little. Because I don't know what else to do. I push at him and ignore the truth in my face, and I want him to hit me like he did after I broke Willow's heart. Because that was cruel of me, but *this* is cruel of life.

Her heart is failing.

Do I deserve this?

Does she?

I think I'm crying.

Still, he takes it. He barely moves, and I hit him harder. Both hands on his chest. Until he returns it. Until he slams me against the wall next to the door, getting in my space.

"You have to face this, Knox. You cannot bury your head in the sand. It never works. Trust me." He meets my gaze.

We used to be alike. Competitors, but also *brothers*. Best friends. And then I ruined our relationship. Band-Aids don't fix things that are cut this deep, and one truth I don't want to face is that we're never going to get back to where things were.

He wants me to trust him, and I do. But he doesn't trust me.

And I deserve it.

He releases me and steps back.

I stay where I am, eyeing him warily. The pages he gave me are sitting on one of the chairs, and my attention goes to them.

"She might die," I whisper.

"Yes," my brother agrees. "She might."

A lump forms in my throat. "Can you do me a favor?"

He regards me.

"If she dies... can you kill me, too?" My voice is hoarse, broken. I mean it with every fiber of my being. If she's lying dead in the morgue, I want to be right next to her.

He sighs. Pats my shoulder. And he leaves me alone with Aurora's words.

55
MANUSCRIPT

CHAPTER 7

Our wedding is not perfect. It's not the fairy tale I thought I'd get. But then again, I thought I'd get married at twenty-six, maybe on the beach or something. It would be glamorous, but everyone would be barefoot. Because, you know, *sand*.

Instead, there's just us and both of our mothers in an upstairs room of the local courthouse.

I wear a white dress. Something my mom surprised me with. There are tears in her eyes now, and I fight to keep my composure. It's weird how emotional I am, too. I didn't think I would be, leading up to this.

There's a lot of different thoughts that go into marriage. I mean, for one: I'm promising my life to someone. My life that may or may not be short. It's not guaranteed any more than a long and happy one is.

Whether or not this is a strategic move on Knox's part, as a way to save my family, there are still emotions between us. Something that seems to be inching toward love. But as

I told his mom, I don't know if I love him. I don't know what love *is*.

There's a surge of emotion when I see him. He wears a suit for me. It's dark gray, with a white shirt and a gold tie. "Because you're my sunshine," he whispers.

I don't roll my eyes.

I don't find it cheesy—instead, it's sweet.

"Ready?" he asks.

Am I?

I take a deep breath.

Outside, thunder booms. There's one window in here, this room dedicated to courthouse weddings. Which, seeing as how it's a room where people are tying their lives together, is rather plain.

"I'm ready," I say to him, smiling a little.

My breathing doesn't come easy these days. It took some time to organize this, to get the proper forms and signatures and approvals. And now we're here, marriage license signed, for a judge to proclaim us husband and wife.

How strange.

"Sunny—"

The judge strides in. "Mr. Whiteshaw and Ms. McGovern?"

"That's us," I say.

I eye Knox and ponder what he might've been about to say. But his face is unusually pale, and he doesn't try to finish his sentence. He does take my hand and lead me up to the judge, and it's a little surreal.

We confirm our commitment. There's a ring exchange —his mom hands him a slender, silver ring for my left hand, and my mom passes me the dark metal ring we found last week. I slip it on his finger, and he does the same.

"You may kiss the bride," the judge says.

Knox and I lock eyes. My cheeks flush. Our kisses have been reserved for quiet spaces. For private moments that always seemed to be stolen or protected.

But he cups my jaw and tips my head up, and when he kisses me, I truly feel pretty. In a white dress, with a ring on my finger and flowers in my hair. Even if our fathers and his brother and my best friend aren't here to witness it. Even if lightning flashes outside just as his lips touch mine.

Well, that last one makes it feel like it could be perfect.

Our moms clap and cry, and they both smother us with love.

"You're beautiful, Aurora," Knox's mother says, her hand on my shoulder.

Knox hasn't let go of my hand. He touches the ring on my finger, spinning it slightly. I didn't even get a good look at it, but I bring up our joined hands and examine the ring.

"Did you pick this out?" I ask him.

He flushes. "Yeah. Do you like it?"

I nod, suddenly shy.

"I have a surprise for you," he says. "Okay?"

I glance at my mom, but she only smiles and nods. Encouraging me to go with him. So I go down the hall into the elevator, which we ride alone. And as soon as the doors close us in, he kisses me for real.

His lips taste like sugar and hope.

We exit into the parking garage and get in his car. He drives us across town to the hockey team's practice rink, and I sit up straighter.

"I'm in a dress," I remind him.

He shrugs.

We park and go into the locker room. There, sitting on the bench, is all my old hockey gear.

"Stop it," I whisper.

"It's okay. We're going to take it easy. Just a few laps around the ice, see if you can get a shot off against my excellent defending."

I roll my eyes. "You're a terrible d-man."

"Well, then you'll have an easy time of it."

Dad kept this stuff tucked away in the attic after my surgery. One day, I was playing hockey. The next, it was off the table. Or off the ice, I guess.

It's only been a few months, and but it seems more like years.

Pads, skates, helmet. I grab my stick and take my time taping it exactly the way I like, running a puck along the blade's edge after I'm done. Then the top.

Knox watches me with a small smile. "Ready?"

"Yep."

When I step out onto the ice, I can't fight the grin that takes over my lips. I skate in a wide circle and pick up speed, until the wind whips the ends of my hair, not caught under my helmet, back behind me.

"Easy," Knox yells. "I said to take it *easy*!"

"I'm fine!" I coast toward him and dig my blades into the ice, showering his legs with snow. "You're going to turn into a snowman if you stand there any longer."

He shakes his head. "You're something else."

"From a white dress and flowers in my hair to *this*, you mean?"

"Yes."

"Well, let's see what you've got." I knock a stack of pucks off the wall and cradle one, taking it away from him.

He follows me, shadowing my movements. When I shift toward the net, he blocks me. His reach is longer, and he knocks the puck away.

I frown and retrieve it, then come at him again. This

time, I'm ready for him. I slip the puck between his feet and dart around him, taking a wrist shot at the net.

Top shelf.

I grin at him. "Take *that*."

"That was your one allowance."

I shake my head. "You're a concrete cupcake, babe. A five-year-old could've got by you."

"Doesn't say much about your skill then, huh, Sunny?"

We go again. And again. And again.

While I ignore how easily I'm getting winded, the net fills with pucks. Eventually, Knox waves me off and heads to clear them.

I hop up onto the boards and swing one leg over on the bench side, then unhook my helmet. I lie backward and stare at the rafters. A not-so-perfect, cookie-cutter wedding... but it's okay. I got to do my favorite thing, perhaps for the last time. Judging by the way my heart pounds, I'd say it's an accurate guess.

"Sunny?" Knox's face fills my vision. "What're you doing?"

"Just breathing," I murmur.

"Keep doing that," he advises.

"Okay." My eyes close.

"Sunny?"

I groan. "Shh."

"What are you doing now?"

I crack my eye open. "Usually it's the younger brother who's the annoying one."

He shrugs. "Miles took the quiet solemn route, so I had to pick up the slack. Thought you knew that about me, sunshine."

Well, yeah.

"Okay," I finally sigh, swinging my leg back over and

sitting up. The rink tips. I lurch and grab his shoulder. "Whoa."

He grips my wrist. "What?"

"Just dizzy. Sat up too fast." I force a smile. "It's fine. Let's go."

He gives me his back. "Up ya go."

"Knox."

"Get on my back, Sunny."

I groan. But then I do, inching forward and wrapping my arms around his shoulders. He grabs my knees and hoists me up higher. Once I'm secure, my skates safely out of the way and his grip on my thighs solid, he pushes off.

Instead of going for the door, though, he takes a lap.

Without the helmet, my hair picks up and blows out behind me. The rush of going fast—he's quicker than me, with longer legs, I'll give him that much—is an adrenaline rush. But not so much that my chest might explode. And definitely better than trying to attempt this myself.

"Put your arms out," Knox calls.

"What?" I've got a death grip on his shoulders.

"Do it," he urges.

I press my chest to his back and do it. I let go and hold my arms out.

It's a whole different level of flying.

56
KNOX

There's no news. No updates beyond her going to surgery.

She's breaking my heart with this story because I know what's coming.

But I keep reading.

57

MANUSCRIPT

CHAPTER 8

My sixteenth year started with a stay in the hospital. Seems only right I should send it off the same way.

The last day of my sixteenth year, one day before my seventeenth birthday, my parents call an ambulance for me. It's bad enough that they don't try to drive me on their own, I guess. I only remember the sirens, the lights in my eyes. The groggy way I keep trying to resurface, but something is holding me under the water.

Everything fades out after that.

It's kind of scary to think about. Like being here one minute and gone the next. And it's not like snapping my fingers and waking up hours or days later—I *felt* gone. Drifting, unable to catch something to pull me back up.

It didn't hurt, though.

Maybe I should be grateful for that. For the lack of pain.

When I wake up in the intensive care unit, the pain I was so glad to have escaped waits for me. I'm almost blinded by it, and doctors respond to my crying by upping the pain medication. Flooding my body with morphine, until my muscles unclench and I'm able to breathe again.

Time moves funnily after that. From awake, upright, understanding... to not. To being unable to string together a sentence. My parents blame the medication, the agony in my chest that the doctors are trying to control.

I catch vague words.

Infection.

Sepsis.

I turn seventeen.

"I'm here," a deep, dark voice whispers. "I'm right here, sunshine."

Eventually, I wake up for real.

There's a weight on my shoulder, and it takes me a long moment to look down. Knox's head rests there, his mouth open slightly. Sound asleep. His body is curled alongside mine, our fingers laced together. My other hand has an IV taped to the back of it.

Tears prick at my eyes.

In the cot beside my bed is my dad, also asleep. A peaceful feeling settles over me at them both being here. It washes away some of the immediate fear, the need to know exactly what happened. I watch them both and try not to move.

Sometime later, a nurse enters the room.

She sees that I'm awake and smiles. "There you are," she whispers. "Welcome back."

She gives me water and asks me questions. My name, where I am, my birthday. I answer all of it in a hoarse voice.

"Your throat will be sore," she says. "You had open-heart surgery. The catheter that was placed to help your heart dislodged, and it was blocking the blood flow. You developed an infection in your chest and became septic. The doctors put you on a ventilator for about a week while we got it under control."

Oh.

"It was removed this morning. You were breathing on your own under light sedation, which worked its way out of your system gradually. Then it became a waiting game for you to wake up."

"Thank you. And they've been..."

Her lips quirk. "We had a hard time getting him to leave your side. Although he wasn't allowed on the bed when you were ventilated. Your mom's been here, too. We finally sent her home to sleep in her own bed and shower. I'm sure she'll be back first thing in the morning."

"Thank you," I repeat.

"Hit the call button if you need anything." She writes something on the whiteboard near the door and slips out.

"I dreamt I heard your voice." Knox shifts, lifting his head to look me in the eye. "And then I realized it wasn't a dream, after all."

"I'm..." I clear my throat. "Thank you for staying."

He kisses my temple. "No need for thanks, sunshine. Just stick around a little longer, okay?"

The next few days pass in a blur of card games, tests, and boredom.

It isn't until after I'm discharged that I realize the date.

Knox gives me a *look*. One that says this day has been coming barreling toward us, and no amount of ignoring it would stop it.

The day Knox leaves for college.

"The hockey team is getting there early," he says, his lips pressed to the top of my head.

Standing in my kitchen in fuzzy socks, pajamas that

now feel a size too big, staring at his Crown Point Hockey sweatshirt, I latched on to him and haven't been able to let go.

"I'm sorry, sunshine, there's no other choice. Today's the day." He doesn't seem to want to let me go either. "You'll visit me, yeah? Come to some games. Meet my new teammates."

"Of course." I clear my throat. "Yeah, no, I'll come see you."

There's a jagged scar down the center of my chest.

Okay, it's not jagged. It's only in my mind that it's jagged, ripped edges splitting me open to reveal the ugliness inside me.

The ugliness that wants Knox to stay. To wait for me.

To put his future on hold.

There's no way I'll do that.

"You're going to kick ass, Knox Whiteshaw," I tell him.

"I know. And you're going to have a killer senior year. Then you'll come to Crown Point, and we'll be together again." He lifts my left hand and brushes the ring on my finger.

They had it in a plastic bag with the rest of my belongings at the hospital, and I was eager to slip it on. It's kind of loose now, apparently even my fingers getting slimmer with the coma-related weight loss.

"Promise?" I tip my head back.

He kisses me easily. Without hesitation. "Every time I step on the ice, I'm thinking of you. Even in Crown Point."

That will have to do.

And it does, for a while. Until everything changed.

58
CAMDEN

I didn't really make a conscious decision to go with them. One minute I was trying to help Jacob's friends locate Aurora and Luke Abernathy. The next, Knox had found her and we were piling in two vehicles. A rental and Jacob's truck.

Both of which, it seemed, were equipped for the kind of *mission* this turned out to be.

Now, in plastic fucking booties around my shoes and gloves on my hands, I can't quite believe I'm staring down at a dead body.

"You guys have done this before?" I question.

Because Steele and Greyson brought in plastic, which they're rolling out beside the body, and Jacob has some sort of giant spray bottle filled with bleach. He mopped up Aurora's blood, and now he's removing any trace of it.

I glance up at the hook and the discarded chains off to the side.

The guy took her and beat her. Tortured her, if we can be so crass to say.

And it's my fault.

"We've got some experience," Steele murmurs.

Miles went to pick up their women and be with his brother, so it's just the four of us.

"Ready?" Greyson asks.

I nod and step up, taking another look at the awful gash in Luke's neck. It's nothing less than what the bastard deserves, and I find myself not squeamish, or shying away from it.

It's hard to know how you'll react to your first dead body. But so far, I don't think I'm doing so poorly.

I squat down to help Greyson and Steele roll the body onto the plastic. "This is not what I thought I'd be doing on a Sunday night."

That gets a chuckle out of them.

"Well, Church, now you know how we'd handle your body if you ever spoke of this." Greyson's voice is pitched low, and he looks up at me. He fucking smiles.

I roll my eyes. "Noted."

"Well?"

I glance over at Jacob, who's still spraying and scrubbing behind us.

"Well, what?" I ask.

"What's the worst thing you've ever done, Church?" Jacob pauses and meets my gaze. "If we're in the trenches together, we should know something about you."

I consider that.

My present, my future.

And my past, which I effectively buried the moment I moved to Denver.

We finish wrapping the body, and I rise. We're going to haul it out of here, drive it who-knows-where, and hopefully never speak of it again.

Still, in the face of all of that, my stomach churns at the idea of giving up my secrets.

I force a smile at the three of them. "I'm here, aren't I? Just as complicit in this cover up as the lot of you. That'll have to do for now."

CHAPTER 9

I'm sad.

My scar is neatly healed, my heart working as it should. By all accounts, I should be able to return to normal activity levels.

Except my father won't let me play hockey. That was the firmest *no* I've ever heard, and one that shook me so completely, I didn't have the wherewithal to formulate an argument. Besides *wanting* it, which I did. But, you know. That counts for nothing when there are other things to consider.

Miles has been keeping me company lately. Beth got weird after the surgery. She keeps eyeing the ring on my finger and shaking her head, seeming to not understand the *why*. I told her the why, which might've been a blanket lie about caring about him. Mainly because I'm not sure if this qualifies as insurance fraud, and I don't want to find out.

I see Beth in class, and sometimes we hang out after school. But once Miles gets home from hockey practice, we go for walks through the neighborhood. Sometimes he humors me and we'll jog a block or two, until my muscles scream at me to slow down.

We both miss Knox.

It's weird, being the oldest in our high school. Top dogs, kind of, although the lowerclassmen are terrible. Maybe all senior classes think that about the younger teens, watching with disdain as they make the same mistakes we did.

Miles doesn't really fill the void of Knox, but we relate to the experience of being hollow. For him, though, I think it's a relief. Like stretching. Painful but necessary.

For me... I don't know. It's not like stretching. It's like ripping.

He teaches me how to play stupid racing video games. Dad gets our living room television all hooked up with a new game system, trying to keep me up here instead of at the Whiteshaws. There's some unspoken agreement about it being our turn to keep Miles busy, lest he turn to more destructive habits in his brother's absence.

Not that I think he'd do that.

So anyway. My parents have cut down on their hours, Mom quit her second job. They're home more often, and there's a relief as they get financially caught up. They're not being chased by the bills anymore, or picking and choosing what to pay and what to stave off.

The weeks turn into months. Knox doesn't come home for Thanksgiving, but then it's only two and a half more weeks until winter break.

We wait with breathless excitement.

Okay, Miles isn't breathless. He's happy to see his brother, though. I've learned to read him, and I know that he missed him. Even if he'd never admit it.

Knox comes over two days after he gets home. While I

am restless with the urge to knock down his door, my parents urge patience. He has family to see, things to do.

The moment I see him walking across the lawn between our houses, my heart goes to my throat. It used to worry me when I'd feel that sensation, but I'm chalking it up to nervous excitement. I burst out of the door and meet him halfway.

He catches me and swings me around, my feet coming off the ground.

"Aurora," he says. "Wow, you look good."

We talked while he was gone, of course. Texted and stuff. Even talked on the phone. But it's really not the same as seeing him in person. I don't even notice that he calls me Aurora instead of Sunny.

"I am good," I tell him. "Especially now that you're back."

Good is how winter break goes. *Good* is how I would describe our attitudes.

But *good* is not how things end.

I could describe every moment of that winter break. Having Knox back. Sneaking out of the house to kiss him in the snow, drinking hot chocolate in front of the fire. Celebrating the holidays with an ugly sweater party at Beth's house, and counting down to New Year's in the driveway with our other neighbors. Blowing kazoos and wearing party hats, and sharing a kiss that should've been toe-tingling but instead seemed *off*. Or maybe it was only hindsight that gave me that impression.

Little did I know it would be our last kiss.

———

I want to tell him I love him. Like, actually. Fully.

I don't tell anyone this, but I've been nurturing it like a seed in my chest, willing it to grow. It's taken root, and I can't shake it. I'm glad we're married, I'm glad he's tied to me. Because surely he feels the same.

Surely.

He's going back to school tomorrow, and my heart is rioting. I woke up crying, dreading the separation. I was struck with the wild thought of sneaking into his house and crawling into his bed.

Doesn't fortune favor the bold?

But alas—I'm not bold. So I stay in my bed until my mother knocks on my door and tells me that Knox is downstairs. We're going to spend the day together, I think. We're going to make it good until he comes home in a few months for spring break, or until my parents can take some time off and we can make the trip to Crown Point.

But what I'm faced with is not a sad Knox. It's not like the last time he left, his blue eyes staring into mine like he was trying to give me strength. The day suddenly doesn't seem to be stretching ahead of us. There's a big *stop* sign, red lights flashing.

His expression is like nothing I've seen—

No, wait.

It reminds me of the first time we met. When I reached for his hockey stick, desperate to play and fit in with my new neighbors, and he pushed me into the mud.

A chill sweeps down my spine.

I step onto the porch and close the door behind me. "What's wrong?"

He shakes his head slowly. "I've tried to wrap my mind around you, Aurora McGovern."

"I don't know what that means."

"I've tried to understand you. Your motives." He lets out a harsh laugh. "It's pointless, by the way. You're complicated in all the wrong ways. You make decisions that don't make *sense*."

"I—"

"Do not talk."

My lips press together. I've never heard him speak so sternly, not to me. Maybe the kids at the hockey intensives, but that's different. They're not *me*. They don't have his ring on their finger.

"I can't do this with you. We're done."

He looks away, his jaw muscle ticking. When he lasers back in on me, my breath catches. He's somehow sad and angry at the same time, the emotions warring in his expression.

His words take another second to register.

"What do you mean, done?"

"I mean, we were never meant for this. There was no way you and I were ever going to be happy or live out some fairy-tale dream. Those don't exist for people like you." He steps forward, crowding me.

And God, if this was any other moment, I would welcome his closeness.

But right now, I don't know.

I stare up at him, my eyes beginning to burn from how long I've gone without blinking. And his words. They're knives to my chest, but I just don't understand. I don't know what I did, if I did anything.

"I swear to you, Aurora McGovern, this is the last time you're going to see me in person." He touches my lower lip. "I'll be famous one day. You'll see me on your screen playing in the NHL, you'll see me winning the Stanley Cup. You'll *see me*, and you'll think of me, and you'll know in your heart that this is the moment I stopped giving a shit about you."

"Divorce me, then," I blurt out.

My heart is literally breaking.

"Divorce me and cut ties—"

He laughs.

Laughs.

"No. So you can move on? I want you to remember me. I want you to suffer." He shakes his head and drops his hand from my mouth. "Suffer for me, sunshine. It's the least you can do."

I can't move.

He bounds down the steps off the porch and crosses the yard between our houses in long strides. In a matter of moments, he's gone.

My legs give out.

He's right about one thing. I did suffer.

And I will remember.

60

KNOX

Suffer for me, sunshine.

Did I really say that to her?

There are no more chapters, but I can fill in some of the blanks. She went to a college that wasn't in or near Crown Point. She stayed friends with Miles up until she left. Her mother died. She got a degree in something or other, graduated, wrote a book. Met Joel. Got engaged. Moved to Denver.

And for the first time in six years, we were in the same space.

Her mom is all over these pages. She worked hard for her daughter, to keep their family afloat. She was with us when we got married. She was always *there*, and while Aurora didn't write it, I know she was there to pick up the pieces of her daughter that I smashed.

But the thing that haunts me the most is that Aurora had no idea why I turned on her like that. She and Beth, as far as I could tell, carried on their friendship like the latter didn't do anything wrong.

She got what was coming to her, at least.

I don't know what to do. I rush to the restroom, passing all my friends in the waiting room along the way, and my heart squeezes.

My brother and Willow, Jacob, Melody, Greyson, Violet, Steele, Aspen. Camden Church. He stuck around, after all.

There's still flakes of blood under my nails. The closer I examine myself, the more I see the cracks in the façade Greyson tried to help me create. I take my time scrubbing myself clean, although part of me wants to rush to get it *off*.

I dunk my head in the sink and let the cold water wash over me.

She was wet. Her shirt was soaked. There was a puddle under her that wasn't just blood.

What kind of sick *fuck* does that to a girl? Over *money*?

I'm glad he's dead. I would do it again. Easily. For her? No question.

Once I shake my head like a dog, getting water droplets everywhere, I pull out my phone and scroll through my contacts.

My finger hovers over my mom's name.

Mom, Aurora's, is right beneath it.

I click her name. It's been four years, but I hold my breath as the call rings through. I just want to hear her voice on the answering message, even if she's just saying her name. Which is silly, because—

"Hello?"

My mouth dries up.

"Hello?" the woman repeats.

It takes me a moment to realize that it's not her. That they let go of the number. It belongs to someone else now. And it makes me realize that I can still picture her mom's voice. That piece of her hasn't left me.

Does Aurora still remember it? Things fade from

memory, it's only normal. But... I don't know. I haven't asked, and I'm afraid of what her answer would be if I did.

"Wrong number," I manage.

I hang up, my face burning from foolishness, and call my mom.

"Hey, honey," she answers immediately. "Are you okay?"

"Am I—" My voice breaks. "No. I'm so far from okay."

Shit. I'm about two seconds from losing it. A lump forms in my throat.

"I'm here." Her voice is warm, and she *feels* here. Next to me. "Miles told me Aurora is in the hospital. Her father left this afternoon."

I don't even know what time it is.

But thinking about her dad coming across country at the drop of a hat makes it seem worse. I've been strong for a really long time. Or maybe not strong, but... sure of myself. Confident, even in the face of stupid choices. I never looked back, never second-guessed myself.

Even when I should've.

"I don't know what to do."

I sink to my knees, my eyes filling with tears. They spill over, and suddenly I'm uncontrollably sobbing. Everything hurts. It's an exorcism of grief pouring out all at once. I fucked up so much time with Aurora. Six years' worth of festering *anger* coming off me, keeping her at bay. Yet, keeping her tied to me.

And I'm so glad to still have her—

But now I might lose her.

"Knox," my mom says. "My dear boy. It'll be okay."

"It's bad, Mom. It's so bad, and I've been a terrible person to her." I rub at my eyes, but I can't seem to pull myself together. "What if she dies?"

"She's not going to die," Mom says firmly.

But she might.

"Why didn't you tell me about her mom?"

She's quiet for a long moment. I focus on her breathing, the steadiness of it. There's one thing I could always count on, and that's my mother being a rock. My dad, too, but he's not as nurturing. He was the one taking us to hockey, but she's the one who would bandage us up if we got hurt while roughhousing.

"I was protecting Aurora," she says. "We saw how you broke her heart, honey, and none of us understood it. I thought you coming back when she was at a low point—it would've only made things harder for her."

She said she wanted me there.

But I wouldn't have been nice. I wouldn't have understood her innocence, and I wouldn't have been supportive.

Which means my mother did the right thing by keeping me away.

I swallow around the fucking meteor-sized lump in my throat. "I really fucked up. I believed a lie about her, I blew up everything. I loved her, Mom. I loved her when I was sixteen, seventeen, eighteen. And one lie clouded my judgment."

"And now?"

"I love her now, too."

The bathroom door opens. Miles sticks his head in, then fully enters when he spots me on the floor.

"Miles is here," I tell her.

He takes the phone from my hand and hoists me up. "Everything is cleaned up, and the doctor has news. You need to talk to him."

I tense.

"Go," he urges, pushing at my shoulder. "He's waiting for you."

I wipe at my eyes again, and I take the phone back. "I love you. Thank you."

"Love you too, honey," Mom answers. "Be brave for her."

Be brave for her.

I can do that.

61

AURORA

The first people in the room after I wake up are two police officers. They have a list of my injuries from the doctor, and although I don't know what Knox's *plan* is, if he has any at all, I figure it's better to lie.

I tell them that I was showering when my heart felt funny. I collapsed, and that must've been when my shoulder dislocated. No, I don't remember being brought to the hospital. No, I don't remember anything else.

When they leave, a nurse helps me raise the bed a little more.

My chest hurts. There's a good amount of pain medication flowing through me, as well as something to help hopefully prevent infection and sepsis like last time.

And then Knox is here.

My eyes fill with tears—and so do his. His eyes are already red, and he doesn't seem to be bothered when they spill down his cheeks. I haven't seen so much emotion from him in years. And yet he's giving it all to me now. All his worry, heartache—no irony intended—and his relief. He climbs on the bed, ignoring the nurse's quiet gasp, but he doesn't so much as graze my chest. He kisses my forehead and leans to the side, curling around me in a way that's heartbreakingly familiar. His arm comes down across my abdomen, a secure weight that grounds me.

I was in heart failure.

They cracked open my chest again and cleared out scar tissue and replaced the valve, which should hopefully give me more of a fighting chance to stay away from more open-heart surgery.

"Be easy with her," the nurse orders.

"Yes, ma'am," Knox replies.

She slips out, I think. The door clicks shut a moment later.

I raise my hand, and Knox takes it.

He meets my gaze. "I should've told you I loved you that day on your doorstep instead of telling you to suffer. You didn't deserve that from me."

"I didn't," I agree. But... "Did you just say love?"

"I did. I do." He clears his throat. "I mean, I've been in love with you forever, Sunny. Obviously."

I laugh. It aches, but it also feels good. "Obviously, Knox? *Obviously?*"

He smiles. "Maybe not so obvious, then. I mean, why else would I not divorce you?"

"Because you're insane."

"Well, yeah." He sighs. "Your dad's on his way."

I suck in a breath. "What?"

"He should be landing soon. I thought you should know. And I'm taking the rest of the season off—"

"Absolutely not."

"I am." He glares at me. "Don't argue, sunshine."

"You're going to drive me nuts if you don't have hockey." I roll my eyes. "The bad guy is gone. I'll heal. You have to keep playing hockey. Seriously."

Because I can just picture it now. Him hovering over me, asking a million questions, talking about literally anything and everything with boundless energy...

I mean, there's a time and place for boundless energy.

My cheeks heat. And, unfortunately, the heart monitor's beeping speeds up.

He eyes me. "Are you thinking dirty thoughts?"

"What?" I squeak. "Why would you ask that?"

The freaking beeping goes faster.

He stretches out. "You dirty girl. I'll get you off between rounds tonight."

Oh, jeez.

But also... not a bad way to spend a hospital stay.

62

KNOX

"Easy," I mutter, helping her out of the car. Her dad and his girlfriend are not far behind me. "You know what? Just—"

I reach in and loop my arm around her back and my other under her knees. I pick her up before she can protest, avoiding hitting her head on the car, and straighten.

It's snowing. It's fucking cold out.

All I want to do is curl up in front of the fireplace with her.

Her dad and Ashley have been staying in her condo. The movers couldn't take her bed and other larger furniture. Besides her office supplies, the desk and all her books, there wasn't space for the other stuff.

Which comes in handy.

"I can walk," Sunny murmurs.

"Yeah, but you don't have to." I kiss the top of her head. "Just let me carry you."

She sighs.

The new doorman opens it for us, and her dad and girlfriend trail us in. They're sticking around, at least for the time being. Until Aurora is back on her feet—in a literal sense, and also mentally.

She had nightmares in the hospital. I'd wake to her building wail, the thrash of her body against mine. It took every trick in the book to get her to wake up and calm down, to come back to me. To climb out of the darkness she lived through.

But how do I help with that?

Luke Abernathy is, as far as anyone is concerned, *on the run*. The police have promised to look more into this betting ring, and in the meantime, the whole app has been shut down. The company that owned it abruptly declared bankruptcy. And that took out old Lucas Abernathy Senior, as well.

Aurora's money that was held hostage was returned to her account.

Another piece of shocking news? The Titans have a new owner.

I guess the whole scandal the Abernathys are facing forced Abernathy Senior to sell. That, and from the media reports, all his money dried up with the company he funded and ran with his son.

The day before Aurora is discharged, the new owner calls a meeting. Coaches, trainers, players, *everyone* arrives at the arena, and we meet the club's new boss...

Theodore Alistair.

The name sounds vaguely familiar, until Jacob elbows me and mutters something about him being Melody's best friend's husband.

He's in his thirties. Well-fucking-dressed. He doesn't say much, just a quick word about leaving us in our coach's good hands, then goes around and introduces himself personally to everyone. He gives Jacob and I an extra eyebrow raise, which should make me suspicious but instead just brings a smile to my face.

When Jacob and I told Melody, she snorted and told us she knew already.

"Did you redecorate?"

I focus on Aurora. "What?"

She motions around vaguely. The couch is in a new spot, yes. Because I wanted to be able to lie on it and see the front door. For no other reason than insane paranoia. Which meant I had to move the television. And that required some rewiring, so I had an electrician out. Then the walls needed to be patched, and if they're patching, it may as well get a new coat of paint...

"Yeah, it just needed a change."

She rolls her eyes. "Okay, we're inside. Put me down."

I do. Carefully. Her face scrunches up, and her dad frowns. But she ignores us and shuffles to the couch, slowly lowering herself down with her hand on her ribs.

"I'm really okay," she says.

"Your face is black and blue," I mumble.

If that asshole wasn't already dead, I'd kill him again.

I get us all drinks. Water and painkillers for Aurora, whiskey for me and her father. One of those seltzer things for Ashley. We join Aurora, and Ashley finds something to watch.

The thing I realized in the last week, waiting for the doctors to clear her for discharge, is that quality time beats every other type of love. I would rather sit with her and talk about anything and everything—and I do mean *everything* —than, say, have her tell me how good I am in bed.

Wait.

No, actually, I think I'd like that, too.

"Knox."

I focus on Aurora.

"You have a game tomorrow."

I frown. "Yeah. I already told you that I'm sitting out—"

"Dad, Ashley, and I are going to it. So you may as well play," she says. "It's a home game. Jacob talked to your coach, you're fine to return as long as you go to morning practice."

She shifts forward, and I jump up. I help her to her feet.

"I could," I hedge. "But I think I'd better just stay here—"

"We won't be here," she argues. "Stay here. Sit."

I let out a sigh. She returns with my freaking hockey bag in one hand, dragging it a bit, and my two sticks in her other hand.

"Aurora—"

"Stop," she hisses. She sits back down and finds the tape, wincing until she's leaned back. "You tape it wrong anyway."

I scoff. "I tape it like you."

"No, you're trying to tape it like me." She proceeds to tape my sticks for me.

While I just gape at her. What love language is this? Acts of service?

I don't think I've ever been more in love with Aurora Whiteshaw than right this moment. Well, that's a lie—I've definitely been *this* in love with her for a while. But right now it's swelling in my chest, reminding me that there's a definitive reason for my love.

"Mr. McGovern," I say without taking my eyes off Aurora. "Maybe we'll catch up with you later..."

He laughs.

Aurora looks up, her cheeks turning pink.

Her dad comes over and kisses her temple, one of the

non-bruised spots, and Ashley pats her shoulder gently. They leave us, and Aurora slowly finishes up on the tape job. Blade and grip.

"There," she says.

"Good." I kiss her, careful to mind her injuries. And her ribs. But my hand has a mind of its own, slipping under the waistband of her leggings to cup her core. I don't really give a shit about my own pleasure. I can jack off and let her watch, if she wants. But hers—

I don't want her to go a day without feeling this.

"You're going to be the death of me," she breathes.

"You've already killed me a few times," I counter. I steal another kiss. "By the way, the paperwork came back."

She eyes me, gasping when I hit *just* the right pressure. "Paperwork?" Her voice is high.

"The name change, Aurora Whiteshaw."

"Oh, fuck," she groans. Her eyes close, and she shudders as she orgasms. It must hurt, because she winces and touches her ribs. When she comes down, she blinks sleepily and murmurs, "I think I like the sound of that."

"Good. Because it's not reversible."

Her laugh is the best sound. "You think?"

I scoff. "I know. It's like superglue. Never coming off, sunshine."

AURORA

FIVE MONTHS LATER

I skate onto the ice, grinning at Knox. The doctors cleared me of all activity restrictions last month. This surgery, unlike the catheter from when I was sixteen, is meant to last longer and be more stable. Which means things like ice skating aren't out of the question.

Professional hockey is, at this rate, but that doesn't mean I can't play with my friends.

And by *my* friends, I mean Knox's friends.

We're visiting Crown Point for a week. Jacob and Melody have a house here, and Knox actually surprised me when he said he had a house, too. He used to rent it out to the hockey players, but during the summer is when all their upgrades and clean-up happens.

So, right now, it's completely empty. And it's where we're staying. Although with no furniture, it's been an adventure of blow-up mattresses, paper plates, and plastic cutlery.

But being on the ice is a thrill I knew I was missing, I just forgot how much joy it brought me. My whole body feels lighter—even though it should be the opposite. I'm covered in pads, a helmet, a mouth guard. Gloved up, stick in hand.

We're on the rink where Knox played college hockey.

It's kind of surreal being here.

"Ready?" Greyson yells. "What was the bet again, Aurora?"

"I think I just said I could outskate you, Devereux," I reply. "Although we could make it a bet if you want to up the stakes."

"Kind of a sore subject, don't you think?" Miles has his goaltender helmet under his arm, and he skates in a wide circle around us. "Betting on a game?"

"A friendly game," Knox corrects. "Between friends."

His brother rolls his eyes.

"How are we playing this?" I ask, eyeing them.

The only ones who couldn't make it out were Jacob and Melody. She's preparing for an art show that we'll all be attending next week. Willow and Violet are spending the day at the ballet studio, leaving the five of us here.

"Two on two," Knox says. "Obviously. If you bring the puck into the zone, you're on offensive. If defense gets possession, you have to take it out and bring it back in. Fair?"

We all nod and break off to warm up. Nothing serious—or maybe it is. I suddenly have butterflies in my stomach. Knox comes up next to me and taps my skate with the blade of his stick.

"Like riding a bike," he offers.

"Uh-huh."

We've been on the ice a few times in the last month while we planned this trip. So as much as he's offering support, he's really just blowing smoke up my ass.

Finally, the five of us meet in the center of the rink.

"Pair up," Miles says, sliding his helmet on his head.

"I've got Sunny," Knox immediately says.

Greyson and Steele exchange a look and shrug at each other.

I bite back my smile.

Since there's no one to drop the puck, Knox and Greyson face off for a classic rock-paper-scissors game. Greyson wins, so Knox and I move back toward Miles.

"Just like old times." I beam at both of them.

They mirror my expression.

I adjust my helmet and stick, slip my mouthguard in, and wait. Steele brings the puck down. Knox drifts up to meet him, while Greyson moves down my side. Steele passes to Greyson, who takes a fast slap shot at Miles.

Luckily our goalie is nothing to sneeze at. He bats it away, and after a quick scuffle, Knox reclaims the puck.

We skate out of the zone, regrouping, and he passes it to me.

"Take it down."

I cradle the puck and push it out ahead of me, charging down the line. Greyson is ready, and I sneak a pass to Knox. I dodge around Greyson, getting in close to Miles. Knox whips it back to me, and I deflect it at the goal. The quick hit reverberates up my stick, the angle changing too fast for Miles to catch.

It goes in.

"Yeah!" Knox cheers. He skates for me. He picks me up and spins me around, patting my helmet. "Just like that."

"Oh, game fucking *on*," Greyson calls.

I grin.

Defense. I spent a lot of time watching guys play hockey. Maybe not Greyson or Steele, but most have a tell. And it only takes another play—in which they score on Miles and knock Knox into the boards—to figure out Greyson's.

When he angles toward the net, I lunge forward and somehow intercept that shit. I take it fast out of the zone. Knox follows, just barely getting over the paint before we're diving back in. No rest for the wicked, right?

Out of sheer annoyance, I take it down and almost collide with Greyson, spinning and sending the puck dancing between his legs. Knox lets out a whoop, and I fake a shot at Miles. It lures him out, and I tip the puck toward Knox, whose slap shot is fucking wide.

"Wider!" I yell.

He shakes his head at me.

I race Steele to the puck and shove him into the glass. He lets out an *oof*, and I skate up to the top of the zone with the stolen puck.

"She's a filthy player." Steele laughs. "What the fuck?"

We're currently tied. One to one.

Knox and I play keep-away for a little while, and I look down the lane at Miles. My wrist shot has always been dirty as hell, and now is no different. Knox delivers the puck perfectly, and I twist my wrist and send the puck sailing.

It fucking floats. Miles reaches for it, but it hits the top bar and shoots down.

Going in.

Knox rushes me. "We won! We're the winners! You did it!"

I laugh and tear my helmet off, hugging him tightly. I know it's just a game, but it feels good to be *good* at something again. Not that I was ever bad at writing—minus the whole writer's block thing—but there was the whole existing thing for a bit. My heart was bad at working.

Oh my God, Knox's rambling is infectious.

"Sunshine." Knox plants me back on my feet.

He immediately goes down, so fast that I reach for him thinking he fell. But then he looks up at me, and the pose…

"What are you doing?" My voice is wary.

"I want to give you the big wedding." His eyes are glassy.

Or maybe it's just my imagination?

He blinks rapidly, squeezing my hands. "I know you didn't get that. The dream wedding with the perfect white dress and your dad walking you down the aisle and everything. The party. You know I love you. That I'd do anything for you." His voice wavers. "Let me give you the wedding you missed out on. Let's start our life over again—the right way."

I've got a lump in my throat.

This time, when my heart skips a beat, I know it's because I'm absolutely, a hundred percent in love with Knox Whiteshaw.

And that I have been since the beginning. As he said to me: *obviously*.

So the answer is simple. "Yes, please."

THE END

Get ready for more of the Colorado Titans in an all new series by S. Massery.
Pre-order Camden Church's book here:
https://mybook.to/ht1

ACKNOWLEDGMENTS

It's over. The Hockey Gods series, that is. Which is such a weird thing to say, because they've been with me since January of 2022 (when I first started writing Brutal Obsession).

All I can say is thank you.

Thank you for loving these characters, for picking your favorites, for your seemingly never-ending excitement and kindness. This series changed my life in the best way possible.

I'm so excited for the future, but first, I want to highlight some absolute gems who kept me grounded and sane (and encouraged me to lean into my dark side) through this series.

My core team: Emmy Ellis with Studio ENP and Paige Sayer Proofreader for your editing talents. Najla Qamber and her team for their transformative model and hardcover covers. Cat with TRC Designs for the gorgeous alternate covers. Ari (Chaotic Creatives) for honestly keeping me on track in a lot of ways, for your dedication and always being there. Rebecca, my OG cheerleader, early reader, best friend, super human. I don't think I'd be here without you, bestie.

To my early readers who have read every dark and twisty word, who shared their tears and yelling moments with me: Erica, Caitlen, Stephanie, Thalia. And you all are also motivators to keep writing better books, and cheer-leaders when things go right. Thank you doesn't quite seem to cover it.

And last: to Knox. You motherfucker. I love you.

ABOUT THE AUTHOR

S. Massery is a dark romance author who loves injecting a good dose of suspense into her stories. She lives in Western Massachusetts with her dog, Alice.

Before adventuring into the world of writing, she went to college in Boston and held a wide variety of jobs—including working on a dude ranch in Wyoming (a personal highlight). She has a love affair with coffee and chocolate. When S. Massery isn't writing, she can be found devouring books, playing outside with her dog, or trying to make people smile.

Join her newsletter to stay up to date on new releases: http://smassery.com/newsletter

WHERE TO FIND S. MASSERY

Thank you so much for coming along on these crazy boys' journeys with me.

If you like my stories, I'd highly encourage you to come join my Facebook group, S. Massery Squad. There's a lot of fun stuff happening in there, and they're who I go to for polls about future books (fun fact: some key details in this series is decided by their votes!), where I share teasers, etc!

My Patreon is also an awesome place to connect and get exclusive content! On release months, I do signed paperbacks. Plus, get ARCs, audiobooks, and artwork before the rest of the world. Find me here: http://patreon.com/smassery

And last but not least, here are some social media links for ya:

Facebook: Author S Massery
Instagram: @authorsmassery
Tiktok: @smassery
Goodreads: S. Massery
Bookbub: S. Massery

ALSO BY S. MASSERY

Standalones

Sticks and Stones (co-write with S.J. Sylvis)

The Pucking Coach's Daughter

Hockey Gods

Brutal Obsession

Devious Obsession

Secret Obsession

Twisted Obsession

Fierce Obsession

Sterling Falls

#0 THRILL

#1 THIEF

#2 FIGHTER

#3 REBEL

#4 QUEEN

Fallen Royals

#1 Wicked Dreams

#2 Wicked Games

#3 Wicked Promises

#4 Cruel Abandon

#5 Wild Fury

DeSantis Mafia

#1 Ruthless Saint

#2 Savage Prince

#3 Stolen Crown

Broken Mercenaries

#1 Blood Sky

#2 Angel of Death

#3 Morning Star

More at http://smassery.com/ebooks

Made in the USA
Middletown, DE
15 February 2024

49815661R00298